# OUTERMEN

# OUTERMEN

## BY BP GREGORY

### 3RD EDITION

# Copyright © 2023 BP Gregory

## All Rights Reserved

This is a work of fiction. Places and place names are either fictional or used fictitiously. Any resemblance to persons either living or dead is purely co-incidental.

This is the third edition, published 2023.
ISBN-13: 978-0-6457319-0-3

First edition was published 2014.

# ACKNOWLEDGMENTS

Thank you to my wonderful friends Erin, Tristan and especially Rosie for sitting up with me through those long university nights, mug in hand, telling ghost stories. I've never stopped being disturbed by the horrors we conjured.

Also thank you once again to my dedicated proof readers Ahren, Diane and Martin. Jason, I miss your mad grammar skills, but am pretty confident your beautiful new baby daughter Emma gets first dibs on your time.

Outermen cover images by Sergey Kamshylin courtesy of Shutterstock. Visit the House image by Peter Dedeurwaerder, Automatons cover image by NinaM, The Town cover images by Pavelr and Tim Bird, and Orotund cover image by Alex Malikov all courtesy of Shutterstock.

For more information, more stories, or to stay in touch visit bpgregory.com.

# CONTENT ADVISORY

This story features adult themes including agoraphobia, kidnapping, loss of a loved one, mental health issues, misogyny, and suicide. It may not be suitable for all readers.

# CHAPTERS

# OUTERMEN

## ONE (PROLOGUE ONE)

## WORK OUT WHAT THEY WANT, FAST AS YOU CAN

I STOOD BESIDE my sister the day the Capsule launched, front and centre.

But only under dire threat of never hearing the end of forsaking her to wade alone, knee deep in the idealists and freaks.

Perhaps that's how everyone finds themselves washed up on the shores of historic events, bedraggled and spitting out seaweed. The solemn witnesses elected by a mash of obligation, familial guilt and simple rote chance. It wouldn't blow my tiny mind one bit.

Although that said, there *were* an awful lot of people that day. Around Angela and I a huge crowd had assembled out in the warm morning light. Recklessly grouped into an identifiable public package, might as well slap a ribbon on it. You wouldn't catch the like of it these days!

All of us to a man squinting hopefully up at the coral dawn, as it blushed its slow way across the Shell overhead. All of us looking like jerks. Threshold Station was, of course, far too high up to see with the naked eye. Clamped firmly to the surface of the Shell itself.

We were there because the Capsule, that tiny engineered bubble of safety, would be the first manned vehicle to ever venture Outside the Shell that encircled our world. Who wouldn't want to say they'd waved it on its way?

For the first time as a scrabbling, bickering species we stood united. Every sodding person on the planet looked up today and whispered the same question, whether it be in awe, greed, or terror. *What's Out there?* Answers were sure to be forthcoming, ready or not.

The mixed crowd made an odd enough collective, from all walks of life; but social humanity delights in kicking down, so we counted our fortune that the *real* crazies stayed a long way off. It would only take one to really arse-up the mood. But you wouldn't catch sight of them within bare kilometres of the dirt beneath Threshold. Couldn't drag 'em near with chains.

Only last year, a show went belly-up on a concept I'm sure they thought was pure shiny awesome at the time. They went ferreting out nutters and tempting them with such basic human rights as, say, housing. Food.

Top of the line healthcare, let's fix those rotting teeth of yours. And all they had to do to earn these wonders was spend a single night on camera, cowering in Threshold's ominous shadow.

Other than a presenter needing stitches to patch his pretty face, as you can imagine the debacle went nowhere. Funny how miserable fear was like that. I'm sure the phobics wouldn't be rooting through garbage and stewing in their own piss if they could stand to do anything about it.

So at least the weird unease of knowing Threshold lurked overhead kept the neighbourhood neat. An improvement you didn't appreciate unless you flipped on the news to flinch from what anti-Capsule chaos and placard waving engulfed the rest of the world.

*I* appreciated the ever-loving crap out of it. A peace and quiet girl from way back. It was the only good reason to live here.

I hadn't planned on attending, which Angela sodding well knew when she phoned me out of the blue. Not a peep on it, but with the ease of practice I'd been able to hear my dear sister's brains bubbling so hot the accusation scorched down the line. *Just whose side are you on, anyhow, Cathy?*

Ha. Like that warranted an answer. There was only one side. And if there's no merciless pressuring of your own flesh and blood to back your stupendously worst call, well, then there weren't any sodding sides left at all, were there? Just a great mass of cold, lonely folk. All bumping around together in the dark.

Besides, pending the Capsule's return and my sister's hasty nuptials, Angela and I would remain the entirety of each others' worlds. So little time. Over our lifetime I'd never imagined there'd suddenly be so little of it. But it could have been worse, I suppose.

Imagine my breathless relief when every reputable officiator, *and* all the less dubious ones had been apologetically booked solid right up to the launch.

Angela's, it seemed, was far from the only ill-considered union spurred to fruition by the prospect of the future.

Married or not, circulating awkwardly amongst the crowd's rabid enthusiasts like a leavening effect were a handful of folk just like Angela and I. The half-proud, half-embarrassed significant others of those thirty on board the Capsule. Those at the heart of all the fuss.

Some of these other odd ducks had dressed to the nines, but with our nondescript clothes and expressive smirks we identified like a secret society: *Hey, it's ok, we're legit too. But look at these groupies! Can you believe all this?* It was by far the warmest simpatico I'd ever embraced.

Somebody's kid impacted my knees, bumping my thoughts loose. Shrieking preschoolers flocked about the gathering's lower strata, in funny little home-concocted helmets that'd clearly started life as cereal boxes. Without peripheral vision they knocked awkwardly into strangers and each other.

I sure hoped their parents could tell which from which, when it came time to haul them off home. The driveway was far too late to exasperatedly yank the helmet off and discover you'd got it horribly wrong.

The costumes were a sweet way to laud the thirty … Well, I guess you could say those strapped into the Capsule were a type of explorer. Just like in the good old days of undiscovered shorelines. Idealists in pantaloons, casting off rashly in their dinky little tubs, with no worldly idea of what to be ready for. Imagine their sour disappointment; setting foot to a new frontier's soil, only to discover the same stultifying minds everywhere. Stuffing every corner of the globe: folk who no more wished their horizons broadened than those left back home.

Although sometimes with a more brusque way of showing it. Injury to insult.

The most frequent accolade those early entrepreneurs garnered was to be lashed to a stake and char-grilled. The agonising flame set with their own incriminating, lovingly inked maps. Their last vision being of that incandescent line creeping through cerulean seas, the ochre contours of deserts and high flinty mountains, leaving the world nothing but ash. Problem solved.

Setting off in an arguably more hopeful clime, our modern conquistadors had been dubbed "The Outermen." So far as I could see, it was mainly to give this celebratory crowd something to print on their t-shirts.

But they needed a name. After all, Outermen stood way above boring, snoring grunts such as you or I. Outermen were *heroes*. Thirty bright, shining heroes that the media beamed relentlessly into every second of our day until folk lost their bearings in the sea of celebration and plum forgot to go to work, tricked into thinking life a holiday.

There were the interviews, a slew of endorsements (and what were sneakers to do with Outside, anyhow? Did you even *need* shoes beyond the Shell?). Even the time-honoured medium of an Outerman jingle, popular in the crippling tedium of the school band circuit.

I wondered when "Outerman" was likely to pop up on the income tax form's immense scrolling list of occupations. It was an annual treat, that list. Trolling through, and realising anew just how hideously boring one's life was. Up until recently there'd been no such word as Outerman. It certainly didn't exist when I was born.

But now they; "they" being the public en mass, which tended to blunt any pricks of intellect, were marching about trumpeting how mankind stood poised to become a brave new name. To rule a bold new era.

In short, it was nigh-impossible for the most disinterested or even overwhelmed party to block the glittering spectacle out.

Or a fearful one.

And while Outside used to be merely another country, humanity's fearful paranoia had never really grown up. It was something you could particularly feel in big groups. The urge to burn the evidence and make it all go away had merely thickened and deepened.

Until under this new pressure of the Capsule program bursting onto the scene, some poor sods'd snapped so badly they could no longer keep pace with life. Sometimes they scrabbled for purchase for a while but always, eventually, they fled. Accumulating miserably where the dregs of society have always washed up, a sort of scum around the drain.

Our world was poised for change. Ready to bloom Outward. Those who couldn't manage would have to content themselves with being left behind. The hard truth was, nobody cared two short cuts for anyone unable to hack it. Those lacking sympathetic support from family or friends slipped gently through the cracks. They were going off the grid, where you were rarely troubled to look at them.

The Screws were the only ones who stood resolutely by those who didn't feel so brave. They'd pegged this whole venture as foolish, right from the beginning. They shook their collected heads sorrowfully at such dangerous romanticism. But in all honesty nobody wanted the Screws on their side.

Oh, people feared Outside, they had that right. Deeply, viscerally so. Part of the Outermen's mystique was the way they had been rigidly fortified against such terror. When the time came, when they actually *arrived Outside* they'd need to accomplish better than simple hysterical screaming. They'd need to buck up and prove what humanity could do.

The Screws maintained this was all folly. Mankind would never be ready for Outside because it wasn't a natural thing to strive to overcome normal, healthy fear. Fear was what made us who we are.

In fact, while they were at it why should humanity long to "overcome" anything? What was wrong with being human? Humanity was marvellous—something we'd realise with a foolish grin, once we got over worrying what we should and shouldn't be.

So, the Screws' argument was that we ought to aim to be as human as possible. And then, with that on board, why would you even bother with Outside? After all, there ain't nothing beyond the Shell. We don't have to impress anyone. Trying to be better than we were could only lead to failure, despair, and neurosis.

The Screws' pessimism aside everybody (and in this context, "everybody" stood on par with "they") knew that the clever, almost autonomous Capsule reeled Out there on its thick cable was only the first.

In a few years we'd see thousands of such habitats played Out into the dark like lures, far beyond the Shell's embrace. Lines of them exploding from our world like  puffballs. If there was anything to be found Out there, we'd find it. And if not, well, then we'd fill it, wouldn't we?

Faces in the crowd grinned goofily at one another, or to nobody in particular, proud and patriotic almost despite themselves. There was something intoxicating about being swept up in the moment. A part of something greater and sure.

Perhaps *this* was why people felt drawn to historic events. This chance to feel *more* than what life allowed. It likely also explained why irresistible forces of nature like my sister were so adored. She stood beside me like a bright figurehead, shading her eyes. The gleam in her long, extraordinary strawberry blond hair transformed her into a pale icon of dazzling light.

When it came to any attention, let alone such rabid public adoration, Angela's fiancé Michael was the man to come scrambling shamelessly to lap it up. Like a big dumb retriever knocking clumsily through the room, overturning furniture, and all for a pat on the head.

No modest bowing to the whimsies of fate for *him*, which was how all twenty-nine of the other sodding Outermen graciously handled it.

Oh no. *Michael Formir* fully expected other diners to be bundled from the restaurant still clutching their forks, to furnish him with an instant table. *And* the cheque gratis to boot! He'd explode with outrage if they dared ask payment—I nearly died of shame to witness it. In the swollen cocksure world-according-to-Michael, all this hysteria was no more than his due, finally coming home to roost.

Angela stubbornly propped up his case through a stinging haze of oxytocin. *Well why not? Surely those brave enough to shoulder the risk for everybody deserve a little fucking kudos.* The warm biochemical deluge made her clutch at any straw to justify her fiancé's outlandish ego, which could fill a stadium on its own. *Anything* to avoid toppling the idol. The larger-than-life effigy she'd erected inside her head.

Which was pretty much how my sister dealt with everyone. Either you were like the rest of the herd, a snore to be dismissed out of hand, or she built you into something bigger and brighter than anyone had business being. And if you knew what was good for you, you'd perform. Michael sure took to it like a pig in shit. For myself, I couldn't help feeling there was a lot to be said for the safe anonymity of snoredom.

Among the blizzard of flags I made it my business to clap and wave along with the rest. Even when Angela shot me a scathing look like I was a big fat dork, and she was sorry she'd ever brought me. *I* was more worried about the chance of

Screws scattered throughout the crowd. I tried to keep an eye out for anyone scribbling notes.

Keen whiskered weasels, on the sniff for anybody not throwing themselves wildly into the moment. For people *suppressing* things. They'd want to have a very serious chat to you about that.

Someplace private and searingly bright. Where every layer could be stripped free.

But then again, perhaps not. I've been paranoid from way back, and the shade of fear often distorts simple memory into something monstrous. Screws weren't such a big thing back in the day. If they *did* pounce on someone in the crowd, the worst you'd face was a lecture and a pamphlet.

Still, to my credit, following the Disaster I was the only one not wearing my shocked face when the Screws came out on top. It couldn't have been better orchestrated for their rise. And once entrenched in power, they could do as they liked, couldn't they? It's only low status that corrals one within the bounds of decency.

With a stifled bellow the Capsule shuddered. As one we all flinched back, and then coherency broke apart in nervous titters and whispers. The mighty engines needed to reach the Shell were raring to throw off the constraints that protected the frail Outermen inside. Keen, in the way of combustion, to throw off all bounds of functionality, to become a glorious freed explosion.

Far more could have been achieved in half the time, of course, using automated probes and the like. But sitting on the sidelines watching a screen would never satisfy humanity. Sod our drive to get in there and stir the guts with our own hands before we'd concede that anything might dare be real.

Beautiful in the dawn, Angela only had eyes for the roaring Capsule. But I watched her. There were tears welling, which was getting to be quite the tradition where her relationship was concerned. They broke and spilled down her cheeks, emphasising the purity of her face to such a degree that people either side gazed at her in awe.

I really couldn't blame anyone for coveting my sister. She was Angela, anyone would love her. Fierce. Bold. Sharp enough to slice a straight razor in two.

But I recognised Michael's sort, and would've vastly preferred he'd kept his sodding urges to himself. At least to the extent the useless git was *capable* of feelings, beyond making kissy-face to himself in a mirror. Wishful thinking, I know. Such jerks could never keep *anything* to themselves. They had to spread it around, foul up the water for everyone.

Respecting my sister's adult decisions was one thing. But how on earth could I wish *Michael* on anyone?

Unfortunately, the one time I sat Angela down and tried to lay it all out over lunch wasn't one of my prouder moments. In slow motion things rapidly degenerated into a farce of the grandest scale, I couldn't have done worse if I'd tried.

Angela merely waited, silent and stony-faced, so I could appreciate the melodic sound of hanging myself. All the incriminating fragments that'd meshed so seamlessly in my brain tumbled out piecemeal. What did I hear? Neurotic chunks of baseless resentment. *Whining.* And we got together so seldom these days. Why was I ruining a perfectly good meal?

Eventually I gave up and meandered to a pointless halt, defeated, and dreadfully sorry I'd ever started. Ignored, our soup was cooling on the table between us, with a big plate of crusty bread neither of us had touched. But after spending all morning painstakingly roasting the sting out of garlic and sweating chunks of sweet potato into buttery melting goodness, I found dread left no room for appetite.

Angela made sure I was good and done. Which I was, shamefacedly. *Well fatguts, you brought this on yourself.*

Then she took a deep, measured breath and raked me with one of her matter-of-fact looks. With her jaded eyes that knew how the world was wired.

Those eyes sneered: *I've got your number, Cathy. You'd better fucking believe it. Better than anyone, I know what you're about.* Which made my face burn, which I hated.

She only brought it out when she was right on the sodding money and about to tell you *all* about it.

'Cathy, hon, I get that you have this "thing" against lying. And I'm sure it sounds all noble and pure within that thick skull of yours, but it shouldn't automatically translate into blurting out everything *you* see as the truth.

'Just for a second, try entertaining the idea that *your* truth isn't the be-all for the entire world. Otherwise you'll just keep making yourself look as foolish as you did then.'

Despite my best efforts my face was tightening into offended immobility. And Angela *did* know me better than anyone, no fibbing there. She softened a bit, reconfigured her approach.

'Look, seeing as you never have anything nice to say anyhow, I'm not implying you should make shit up or anything. But it wouldn't kill you to keep things a bit closer to your chest. You know. Just on the vague *off chance* someday you might be wrong.'

Her expressive lips quirked, daring me to join her in a smile. Ends of her long hair in her soup. It was a difficult invite to resist; by then, I just wanted out of the whole miserable topic.

'I guess I could give that a go,' I mumbled.

'*Especially* seeing as the only thing you fancy less than lying is *arguing*,' she added archly. 'Best keep yourself well clear of both. I won't always be around to do it for you, now, will I?'

Ah. So that's what this pep talk was really all about. I was getting my due warning that following her joyous nuptials, keeping me out of trouble would no longer be Angela's sisterly duty.

*That's it, time to be a grownup, fatguts. Cough up those ideals you can't really afford.*

Angela nodded briskly as though I'd come to agreement merely by sitting and staring sullenly at the table.

Such conflict had never bothered *her*, she throve on it. Anything to keep the excitement flowing. Even now it pinkened her cheeks.

'Now hurry up and eat your lunch. It's getting cold.'

Out of options, I choked it down meekly like a good girl.


Slowly, a column of grade-A pollution pushed the Capsule on its way up to the Shell. To Threshold Station, where they had dared to cut a hole in our sky.

It was all so far above our heads that the naked eye couldn't pick anything out. Not even a speck on the beautiful morning that unfurled across the Shell's inner curve. Yet stop to ask anyone on the street, and they'd turn and point confidently to Threshold. Invariably incorrectly, but that didn't prevent every human being on earth being convinced of their native ability to just *feel* where the Shell had been violated.

I ought to have been swept up in the excitement, all of these people hollering and waving their arms in the air, dancing around, embracing strangers. Instead I couldn't help wondering if we'd all be stuck breathing the Capsule's filthy launch-exhaust forever, endlessly recycled around.

Or if, when Threshold opened its trapdoor to outside, the stink was likely to rise and leak away through the hole.

Memory being a traitorous beast, I was thrust for a moment

back amongst the vivid fears that'd piled on when they first began cutting through the Shell. Doubtless I wasn't the only one to have endured bad dreams. But to awaken sweat-soaked and trembling is a special sort of nightmare when you live alone. You have to push it from your mind as fast as possible. Brighten up the place with clatter and noise.

You absolutely can't afford your home to become infested by a creeping dread of the dark—you'd never be able to live there anymore.

I didn't dream of strange whispering voices, not like Angela. Things that get inside your skull and start gnawing. I recall when we were little she was particularly prone to vivid dreams and sleepwalking: the voices, always with the voices. At first they only exasperated her with their refusal to shut up, although fear followed quickly after. That would all be Michael's problem now.

I dreamt of suffocation.

During those exhausting months while they worked away at Threshold, my nights were all stifling nightmares. Dreams where they broke through the Shell, and all our air promptly leaked away. The whole world.

Like a low-flying aeroplane my dream eye would zoom everywhere and it was always the same thing. I saw everyone forced choking to their knees in a scrabbling panic. Clawing at their blue faces. And then face-down in the dust. A few managed to run, to seal themselves in buildings but their deaths only came slower. And all because of no greater malice than the curiosity and hubris of a few careless people.

The most horrible part was how for all their desperation, nobody was able to help or comfort a single person they loved. Not their partners, writhing beside them on the ground. Nor children convulsing and weeping just beyond arm's reach. Everybody died alone, within the closed-off ramparts of self.

I remember holding my breath and trying with what was left of my hoarded air to phone Angela. The very best I could manage was to collapse flat in the kitchen, like a flan dropped on tile. The sound of the dial tone went away with the air. My poor sister would be so scared, and I couldn't even tell her I loved her.

When I woke each morning I almost picked up the phone, before remembering that *Angela* wasn't waking alone.

Eventually the construction up at Threshold stopped, and so did my dreams. I'd forgotten about them until now.

Suddenly I felt short of breath, and dizzy enough to miss my balance. I stared up, along with everyone else, through a forest of waving arms that seemed to stutter and strobe against the bright sky. Up, up the inside of the Shell. So terrifyingly huge and far away. What right did humanity have, to be messing with something so immense? So incredibly beyond us?

Was I having a panic attack? My fears certainly weren't rational. Everybody already *knew* there was air Outside. But then, why did the Outermen wear helmets? Why would the Shell exist at all unless we needed it?

A scientist would doubtless know, an expert. Me, I was merely a scared, ignorant person. Staring wide-eyed up at the sky with sweat rolling down my face while the crowd crashed and surged around me. Exactly the credulous everyday breed that politicians love, and the science-folk hate with a passion.

In her impatient way, Angela used to comfort me over shit like this when we were very small. *Oh for goodness' sake, be brave Cathy!* I was often too timid to try this or do that, to go on the adventures she craved. Now she stood right beside me and I couldn't even open my mouth.

My chest hurt. I pushed on it with both hands, trying to remind my lungs they had a sodding job to do. In my current state of dreamy panic, boobs came as an odd surprise. I'd recalled being a cowardly kid so vividly, it felt like only yesterday. The good old days, when my chest'd been flat as a pancake and I'd been free to toddle around wearing whatever I pleased. Fairy wings to dinner. A superhero cape. Even a cereal box on my head?

That brought a smile, and thankfully the band of constriction eased.

Once the Capsule had lifted beyond sight, there wasn't much left to celebrate.

Talk about a comedown. A last few hurrahs shivered through the mass, before petering out awkwardly. There was no longer enough group identity to hold it all together. Even those most enthused to keep the rush going gradually dropped their waving hands, and reluctantly returned to being individuals.

A fresh breeze began sweeping away the launch's stink, stirring Angela's bright hair about her thin shoulders. This was why inspiring films always roll credits at the summit of triumph. Once the ordinary folk have enjoyed their three cheers, everyday life must come creeping back to fill the void. Nobody wants to find themselves watching that.

People glanced uncertainly to the milling strangers either side, restless for a cue as to what to do next. And finally, my sister looked away from the sky, wiping her eyes. The very last to do so. Angela hurried for nobody, and was never at a loss—in the unlikely event she ever might be, I'm sure she'd fake it so brilliantly nobody could claim to tell the difference.

When she turned to face me sadness was tucked away in whatever pocket she stashed it, and her game-face was cranked to maximum. All flawless confidence and smiles. 'So, what do you reckon, Cathy? Coffee next?'

'And bacon!' Neither of us had stopped for breakfast, the key difference being my sister could ill afford further weight loss. She'd eat, if I had to sit there and pipe it down her neck like a frail baby bird.

Women stack *on* weight when happy and confident in their relationship. They metamorphose into a sort of walking advertisement of content, all cuddly and curvy and smiley. What they *don't* do is whittle helplessly down to pallid skin and quick, angular movements. A grin so thin you can see through to the other side.

Angela, so brilliant in other matters, had quite simply picked the wrong man. And she was the only one who couldn't stand to admit it, which was a cruel shame.

Even should you turn a wilfully blind eye to it, the truth remains true. It's stubborn like that.

Truth was, in fact, everything.

Your ability to accept what was true in the world dictated whether you grappled with reality on its own terms, or retreated to fanciful dreams like a child with hands over its face. Huddled on the floor with blocking, negating palms pressed against your ears, *la la la, I can't hear you.* A fist crammed down your throat.

I was dead right, and as impossible as it would have been, I ought to have insisted on it somehow. But instead, I kept my big trap shut on the matter, exactly as dear Angela commanded. She strode off in search of breakfast, and I trailed obediently along in her wake.

# OUTERMEN

## Two (Prologue Two)

### Don't Let Them See What You Feel

THE SEVEN O'CLOCK PRESENTER was everything a newsreader should be. She segued effortlessly between reports: brightly smiling one moment, grave the next.

Stunningly beautiful, of course. To stun anyone out of ever questioning her words.

Aloof, yet still warmly human. Somebody the average workaday, recumbent and numb in his lounger, could idolise without feeling threatened. A woman of dulcet tone and perfect skin.

Really, all that distinguished her studied grace from some digitally created avatar was the prohibitive cost of lifelike graphics. The infinitely cycling labour pool of cheap, fleshy humanity was forever gagging for such jobs.

'… So, we say a fond farewell and good luck to our weatherman today …'

Espousing sanity and order, her voice radiated like safe comfort from glowing televisions everywhere. And in the soothing ambience of a late afternoon the world briefly made calm, comfortable sense.

She spoke in that pocket of time when you get to lever your shoes off, stretch your cramping toes, and dial your mind away. Knowing you deserve it. Still knowing you'll have to drag yourself back and do it all again tomorrow.

'… today completes an outstanding twenty years with our station. Dave, we'll miss you.'

That smug curve of painted lip betrayed no apprehension *her* job might be next. I supposed it should, though. An on-screen career had a far briefer half-life for women than what hoary, professorial chaps like Weatherman Dave got away with.

Following the condescending farewell piece I wondered how she'd feel driving home in the rain tonight. Rain always made things seem worse. It weighed you down inside. The windscreen wipers thumping away. Inevitability rushing over you like a wave. Perhaps she'd scrub off all her precise makeup with a rough flannel, and spend the wee hours staring morosely into her small bathroom mirror. Willing time to stop.

As though the unkind force of my envy had given her a jab, the newsreader faltered. I felt instantly, hideously guilty.

How often does a presenter miss a beat on air? Once in a lifetime? You certainly had to assume it'd be once in a career.

After all, the news services were all about *pacifying* the public, not stampeding us in a panic. The reader on duty was supposed to manage us with her own calm. Encompassing what turbulent emotions and skittering helplessness we couldn't master alone. She provided the structure and sanity the natural world so sorely lacked, asking little more in return than we listen and concur, and that was what kept us coming back.

But now. One elegantly manicured hand raised to her pink shell ear. To the tiny speaker concealed there, and what came pouring hysterically through it. Took a lot of investment to maintain nails like that, on the off-chance they might be glimpsed on screen someday. A decent chunk of salary blown on merely holding appearance. And that investment in baseline maintenance could only skyrocket as time nibbled about the edges.

Her smooth brow furrowed between two lovely arched brows. *Oh, don't do that honey! The wrinkles'll slice your career in half!* So, joking around while she listened, I still wasn't taking this seriously. Not until her smile, that ticket to the viewer's heart, bled right off her face. Along with all the colour out of her freshly powdered complexion. Then I started feeling sodding serious, all right.

It was likely that across the world, millions slowly turned their heads on the same queasy realisation that something had gone wrong. Drawn in dread silence by the horrible magnetism of the newsreader's stricken face. Even children must have stopped pinching and biting at one another long enough to cower on the carpet, sensing thick dread if not comprehending it.

Humanity shivered together in the presenter's unspeakable silence, and clenched its teeth for what was coming.

A multitude of lovingly prepared dinners lay forgotten on laps, just as with Angela and I, as we sat side by side on the couch.

I'd sort of forced her to come live with me. Classic intervention. Since the launch people had been getting *better*. All except for Angela, who was gradually wasting away. Transplanted, for the whole first week she'd benefited in numb silence from all my lavish cooking and housework. Barely leaving the apartment. She was, embarrassingly enough, *pining*. What other word was there? And what else was I supposed to do?

I certainly couldn't have left her sitting alone in the echoing spaces of "their" cavernous house—although so far as I'm concerned if one party shoulders all the mortgage with no kids as an excuse that makes it theirs, which made it *Angela's* house. Isolated, no idea who the neighbours were. Getting so bony and pale. Likely sniffing his pillow in the night to perpetuate the agony, and weeping agonisingly to the sappy romance flicks I'd ruefully shaken my head over.

Removal to my place had been by way of an abrupt sea change. Even while at work I rested easy knowing my viewing collection only offered up monsters, explosions, or exploding monsters. Difficult for even the most determined sad-sack to beat her breast to. Although she'd started having the nightmares again. That put the wind up me.

Those terrifying sodding nightmares were a symptom of hers. Probably co-incidence but we even got sick in tandem from it, just like when we were kids, with streaming noses and prickly burning eyes. The moment I heard her crying out in the night for awful voices to just go away, leave her alone, the shivering fever came on and instantly stuck my sheets down to my skin like hot plastic.

It was so horribly creepy; I lost a whole bunch of my good-girl points in considering packing her back off home.

Until I reminded myself with quite a firm shake that this wasn't playtime. I was no longer some snivelling brat, refusing to share her sister's bedroom 'cause of fears of the dark.

Angela wasn't well. It was my job to look after her.

Eventually, stubborn perseverance began to pay off. My lunchtime calls to check on her kindled a spark of weary humour. *I'm not some child, Cathy. Promise I'm not sticking forks in the sockets while you're gone.*

I'd never felt so relieved in all my life. I'd *almost* sunk to wishing Michael would hurry his useless arse back home and marry her already. Almost. All but for that tiny space inside where I kept my trust in humanity, tucked away like some dirty little secret. It was somewhere I retreated to, to hope against all evidence Angela might wise up someday.

The newsreader still visibly fought for her composure. With the camera rolling she'd no choice but to face it, pinned there in her seat. Likely from watching too many cop shows I was poised to hear her briskly rap out "News just in!" But instead she lurched painfully into speech, like some out of control learner at the stick.

'An ... an explosion! There's been an explosion!' Her voice had dropped entirely from schooled calm into ragged reality, which was a disaster in itself. Nobody wanted reality right now. They cowered in the face of it. Her wild eyes stared straight into mine. Beseeching aid, as though I alone could rescue her. '... some kind of disaster, and ... and it's gone! The Capsule, it's just ... gone!'

The lapse shocked even her, and she stiffened in her seat as though slapped. Two cherry red dots glowed in her ashen cheeks. As her eyes started to dart about frantically it became obvious nobody in the studio was doing a sodding thing to help.

The autocue fed her nothing. Only gibberish poured in through the hidden earpiece, derailing her thoughts.

Chaos and hysteria wanting to sweep her away, taking the

rest of the world with it.

It was here and now, faced with the Disaster, that the newsreader stopped herself. She took a deep, trembling breath, and came into her own.

Only the luckiest people ever recognise such a moment when it's upon them: to be the right person, in the right place, at the right time. And if you seized it: three cherries, coins pouring into the tray! Your one opportunity. Succeed or fail. Either way, it was a rare chance to be brooded over the rest of your days.

*This* newsreader had been hiding an innate, well-honed ability to find the *right* words. Unwanted in her rigidly scripted job. And so tucked carefully away like a rare jewel, kept only for best. It'd landed her that seat in the first place, ahead of scads of applicants, equally pretty. Pert looks came a dime a dozen and some had been willing to perform *unspeakable* acts for that foot in the door. In the scrabbling rush she might've stooped to such low tactics herself, were it not for the happy fact of not needing to.

Now she leaned infinitesimally toward the camera. Toward the viewer, as though offering comfort. And the *right* words spilled out like the break of a golden dawn.

'In this time of deep tragedy we must find it in ourselves to set aside our own terror, and think only of the family and friends left behind. For it is they who most keenly bear the loss of our thirty brave Outermen.

'Our heroes, who gave up their hopes, their dreams, and ultimately their lives, that mankind might someday conquer our fear of Outside.'

"Set aside our own terror" indeed! And for *compassion*? It was the cant of an idealist, and I couldn't see how it could be done. Already I was sweating. Shaking, the cutlery rattled. And the television screen floated about my field of vision like an untethered balloon.

A phobic reaction can't truly be appreciated until you've had the pleasure yourself. How utterly beyond control you become. Panic swept aside any heed to fancy words, and paralysis was all that kept me from blundering mindlessly down the hall, fleeing nowhere. But of course, if the Shell was damaged it wouldn't matter. Nothing would matter. There'd be nowhere to go.

I swallowed hard, against the leading edge of bile's own bid to escape. Middle of the bell curve, that's me. All those personality tests in school had me buried smack bang in the spare tyre of distribution. Which meant that something far worse was happening to a whole bunch of other people out there right now. Those poor outliers. As if on cue there was a desperate scream from somewhere in the building. It modulated into a raw, bereaved wail that just went on and on. Surely they had to breathe sometime?

Despite the newsreader's sincere efforts, there were some who wouldn't survive to the end of the broadcast. I didn't even like to think about it. Life was all we had.

Finally the autocue had something official to spit out and the newsreader's eyes flew across it, albeit resentfully. After all, she'd been *handling* this. Soaring free for the first time. As a naïve young applicant, this was how she'd envisaged the job would always be. Perhaps a career change might finally be in order. Before the station shelved her aging ass, and trotted out the next dupe.

'It appears from early reports that the remaining fragments of the Capsule were propelled *away* from us by the blast. I'll repeat that for you viewers at home: as the information stands, the Shell is *not* in any danger.'

I knew she was managing her best, but now she sodding well tells us. They must be struggling to salvage what they could of the public psyche. To so openly discuss the Shell, let alone hint at the horrible void of Outside, was as simply not done as mentioning toilets in the 1970s.

'... Attempts to contact the director of the Capsule program, Dr Ashley Cormac, have so far failed ...'

Oh, I'll just bet they had. If anyone was having a bad day ... who'd have a press release prepared for something like this?

Apparently this was no time for me to wallow in rank cowardice like everyone else. From the lofty upper reaches of the bell curve Angela was already on her feet. I, in return, got the shock I needed to get moving, in finally seeing her so galvanised. I'd grown reluctantly used to this new, lethargic sibling who cried all the time.

Ricardo, Angela's miserable excuse for a cat, came rushing from beneath the couch with his thin worm of a tail waving. Keen to take advantage of the dinner spilled heedlessly from her lap to the floor. Sod forbid she should visit without bringing the ammonia-gagging pleasure of Ricardo's litter tray tucked beside the toilet. The bathroom's where I like to go in order to *clean* up, not *throw* up. It was unusual for the sullen creature to venture forth, but who wasn't willing to chance an occasional risk for enough reward? Even a cat.

Through sheer lack of options, I sternly set aside roiling panic and nausea. And more materially set my plate down, where Ricardo would no doubt avail himself in early course. Good. Stuff your fat head with pie, until you're too bloated to cram yourself back under the couch. See where that gets you.

I'd laboured over that pie. Shepherd's pie, with real shepherds; because when Angela's feeling down everything has to be her favourite. Flustered and overwhelmed, in my hurry I managed to plant my bare foot in Angela's abandoned dinner. To Ricardo's disgust, as much as my own. Rich cumin gravy filled the air. You might think that hot, buttery mashed potato squeezing up between bare toes and down into the rug might feel nice, but you'd be wrong.

'Angela …'

I already had a read on the turmoil inside that perfect strawberry-blond head.

Angela wouldn't accept that Michael was gone. She never credited *anything* without digging through the facts herself. At the very least, she'd need to stare the bearer of bad tidings grimly in the eye. To hear it in person.

She was already striding determinedly for the door, not quite running. I had to hurry, skidding on my slippery mashed potato foot. But I had no chance of ever keeping up with Angela.

# OUTERMEN

## THREE (PROLOGUE THREE)

### ONLY EVER BY YOUR HAND

GRIMLY INDIFFERENT to the passing world, Dr Cormac sat alone on a worn, faded couch, staring in turn at each of the brittle sheafs of paper in his hands.

Just staring, in silence. Until it seemed his intense gaze must burn its way through and crumble the whole lot into ash.

For most, life has this way of accelerating mercilessly. Until you barely have any hours for accomplishment, all manner of grand designs sacrificed to the mere necessity of keeping up. If you're one of the lucky ones with family to arrange such things, you get dumped out the other end of the chute into a nursing home. To sit dazedly with a scratchy throw-rug across your knee, wondering what happened.

Following the devastation of the Disaster, Cormac had somehow dropped out of the flow. Duties gradually wound down and left him locked in this backwater. A bubble of fractured time bounded by his airless apartment, where each day, and yesterday, and tomorrow remained *now*. There was only now.

Which suited Cormac to a T. He wasn't wasting time on despair, although nobody would have blamed him for hurling himself in head-first. No, he was there to *work*.

The furnishings, along with the rest of Dr Cormac's life, had once been rather fancy. But regardless of outlay, enough neglect reduces the entire world to shabby beige. Even the stultified air smelled yellow. It made you want to sneeze, and scrape it out your nose with your fingers.

Cormac's surrounds sighed eloquently of a place where you just *knew* the fridge would be barren, without needing to tug the door open. Bereft of any of those little comforts that take the edge off distress. Clearly this was a man nobody was bothering to care for, not even himself. It was a bad sign to lose the basics of maintaining a bearable life, even in crisis. Fellows like him perished all the time, sealed up in their homes, and weren't discovered for months.

At least there was no discomfort or shame for him in any of it. Ashley Cormac never let things slide through simple ennui. Rather, it was because the intense beam of his self-imposed goals focussed elsewhere.

Before him sat a smoked glass coffee table of a sharp-edged, woefully outdated masculine aesthetic. Branded with the rings of generations of indifferently rinsed mugs, over which yellowed manila folders had dropped like leaves. The edges of these once crisp documents had gone as soft and fluffy as down, as though they trailed the Capsule program in blurring their way out of reality. You could count the suspended years there. Eleven years measured out since the loss of the Outermen and resulting downfall of Cormac's ambition. Eleven long years gone from his set, finite lifespan.

And he'd count them well spent, if only he could find what he was searching for. Dr Cormac was an old-fashioned guy that way. Ironically, as it was his labour that'd mistakenly birthed this new era. A world he resisted with all his might and diminished influence.

Those wads of paper he kept to hand might explain matters, although none of it was new. Nothing you'd call news anymore. Schematics, reports, interviews, contracts, sub-contracts; *lists*, lists of everything: names, addresses, arcane formulae, suppliers, once-keen sponsors … He'd compiled with his own hand the interminable roll call of antagonists and outright enemies, not trusting anyone else to the task and ignoring his eye rolling secretary.

The telling documentation, spilling across the table and onto the floor, plotted a great network of humanity. A collective that, pulling together, could make a daring endeavour take flight. Or scuttle it, in the worst possible way.

But perhaps there'd been no deliberate act of malice after all. A whole submarine had once been doomed by a single misplaced drop of solder. The answer was here somewhere. It had to be.

Lacking wreckage to examine, witnesses to interrogate, the papers were all he had. Dr Cormac could not do anything else, not until he was sure. And he couldn't be sure of anything.

Notably missing from his rats-nest of clutter were the thirty personnel profiles, with their clipped and curling passport photos of heroes. The Outermen. The program's weakest link of all, for their humanity. Those files had pride of place beside Cormac's bed, for fondling obsession to gnaw at deep into the night.

There'd been no anniversary specials or fundraisers for the bereft families. Such picking over the bones was endemic to lesser disasters, in the effort to wring every last drop of public sentiment dry. Instead by some silent consensus, the world had hunkered down and tried to forget that the Capsule had ever existed.

Well. Not the *entire* world.

During the early days, when everyone was still flailing about in panic, anarchist broadcasts would randomly break in on legitimate television. They flashed up stock footage of the lost, trying to trigger seizures in unsuspecting viewers. Sometimes the images were upside-down, or eerie inside-out looking negatives. The transmissions never lasted long: somewhere between pests or a health menace, depending on how hard it hit you.

Sensing an ally, Cormac had run himself to exhaustion trying to trace the source. All to no effect, even those few times he'd arrived breathlessly in advance of the outraged authorities. Whoever was responsible had always cleared out, quicker than a jackrabbit, leaving Dr Cormac standing foolishly to take the heat. At the officer's exasperated shout of "Not *you* again!" Cormac had smiled faintly as though finally getting the joke, and folded up on the floor as his legs gave out. He did wake to enjoy *most* of an undignified overnighter in lockup—the cops weren't serious about holding him, just pissed off.

When Cormac emerged, it was like heavy clouds had cleared away from his mind. Although he couldn't stop watching for footage, the broadcaster was an illusion. There were no allies for him, no help. And there never would be.

Urban legends festered, that to see the broadcasts foreshadowed some personal calamity. It was the same brand of credulous rubbish catered to by poorly spelled spam, that threatened "*U or soMe1 close 2 u will suffr a TERRIBLE ACCIDNT, unless …*" While nobody quite subscribed, they swayed in an undercurrent of very real superstitious fear.

Free to air TV rapidly fell out of favour with all but the poor, or the desperately lonely who just wanted a voice in the house. Once the audience dried up, the phenomenon eventually ceased. The last transmission Cormac caught stopped him in his tracks as he was crossing the midnight lounge for a glass of water. It was a blurred reversal of his own face. A black and white, inside-out distortion beneath which the late movie special still fizzed and scrolled. Cropped from some long-defunct interview his lips moved, but for the life of him Cormac couldn't work out what he was saying. Something inspired and full of promise, no doubt. Something from the lost past. Before his disbelieving eyes, it all died away.

When the phone shrilled Cormac flinched, papers stuttering from his fingers. So many of the utilities presented so much dead weight that he'd stopped bothering with the bills, which had obligingly descended through the spectrum from reminder to ultimatum. Apparently though they couldn't stand to let go of a customer, even a rotten one.

Without bothering to say hello, he cradled the receiver to his ear. Anyone with the audacity to phone would already know his habits.

The caller of course couldn't see him, but while listening his eyes flashed rapidly about, itemising his surroundings. Logging what they might betray to the casual observer.

His interlocutor finally ran out of steam, and switched from gabbling to waiting impatiently for some exclamation, a reaction to this incredible news. And as the awkward silence dragged on, the caller was keenly reminded what a massive sigh of relief everyone had enjoyed when Ashley Cormac withdrew his abrasive presence from the corporate offices.

Quite frankly, when he put his mind to it, Dr Cormac could be a real dick.

The doctor conceded only two parsimonious words before hanging up. 'I see.' At the other end, his caller goggled at their handset in disbelief.

Dr Ashley Cormac staggered upright, pins and needles sparking sharply down both legs. Life was rushing back into the man. A sudden, dizzying flood following a long somnambulistic drought but, true to form, he refused to be swept off his feet.

Selecting this and that as he cruised the apartment he creased paper into wads, hastily stuffing it into the deep pockets of a jacket, which he threw over his sparse shoulders. From the bedside table he carefully plucked one folder only, carrying this one like it was made of gold. He grabbed his keys, forgetting that his car had been repossessed last year, and the door to Cormac's frayed, neglected apartment shuddered in its frame with his exit.

So, how do I know all this? I certainly hadn't been lurking there, after all, wrapped in his faded curtains like the world's most uninspired pervert. In fact, the moment Dr Cormac received his oh-so critical call, I'd been carrying on with my day, with no earthly idea what terrible things were happening. Otherwise I'd have instantly packed everything worth taking, which would've made a sodding small bag, and gone on the run.

Actually, that's vain fancy speaking. It's easy to claim bravery and daring in hindsight. A sight near impossible to actually accomplish any of it. It's likely that even forewarned of all that stood poised to crash down, inertia would still have pressed me numbly about my routine. I'd just go on wearing the same dull track in the world, until I was snapped up.

What I *did* know about Ashley Cormac without needing to watch him or shake his long pale hand was that people, even coolly intellectual people, invariably carry out short predictable patterns of behaviour. They perform how they think they're supposed to, even when nobody's looking. So what else could he have done, really?

# OUTERMEN

## FOUR

## TRUST ISN'T CURRENCY

**THE MORNING EMERGED,** cold and colourless as a wet gob of oyster. It took a greater feat of mind over unwilling matter than usual to peel myself from the bed. An ominously slow count to three did the trick.

The rule is that the day I fail to rise by three, I might as well give up on leaving the bed at all. Become one of those women they have to cut out of their room, and hoist from the bed with a crane. Which just wouldn't work. My bond wouldn't even *start* to cover the hole in the wall.

Successfully up, I hadn't the heart to glance out my tiny bedroom window. What did it have to show, anyhow? Other ugly grey panes, stacked right up into the clouds. With faces just as pallid as my own peering back hesitantly from each one, the insane replication of population density. All layered like some hideous gateau in bands of motionless sooty grey mist.

And to think, Angela and I had once found the urban decay *charming*. A pair of hopelessly naïve girls who wore mass produced op-shop leather with the silk lining crumbling away to nothing, and thought themselves quite the cosmopolitan ladies. Went to show how budding youth was only good for cringe-inducement. Assuming you finally made it to an age where you knew better.

I may have ducked the slippery slope to becoming a housebound recluse for another day, but joining the world brought its own hazards. Today it was my back; oh sodding crap, my back! It stung, ached, burned, right where my spine grounded in my hips. Leaving me standing straight as a ruler, waiting dumbly for the spasm to pass. Whoever claimed exercise was good for you obviously never ground their flexibility and ambition away against a desk job.

Ricardo miaowed at me querulously. Arguably smarter, he'd stayed burrowed in our night-nest of doona and shed fur. Smarter or no, he was a bad cat. Tolerating him was like co-habiting with a cranky, weird, deeply selfish little old man, who constantly harangued me in a foreign language. No matter how fastidiously I vacuumed, even breaking out a comb to scrape the upholstery, a dismaying eau de cat lady hung about the rooms.

My hands shook so much I could scarcely crank up the thermostat. The glamorous second step of my studiously observed routine was to huddle pathetically over a vent until the heating kicked in with a gush of odd-smelling air. Shivering like one of those hyper little bug-eyed dogs. It were as though the building's kilometres of clanky old ductwork connected up to an asthmatic giant with poor oral hygiene, hidden away somewhere in the basement. Probably not out of the question, if it stood to save the landlord a few measly bucks.

Still, that first whiff of warmth was a pleasure I willed myself to enjoy without envisaging the power bill. My nose dripped constantly all winter, and mysterious red lumps cropped up on my sore toes. Out on the street I'd often pause in the hot billows of exhaust streaming behind idling trucks and buses. It was a dumb invitation to be smashed flat. If I didn't poison my idiot self into a stupor first.

Shuffling awkwardly in broken down slippers I headed for the fridge. Step three was always, and urgently, to shut Ricardo up. Silence his fat head before the urge to fling him through the window swelled too great to ignore. Yelling back at him never worked. Besides, it stirred up the neighbours. The world according to Ricardo was food, or get the fuck out.

It was Angela who taught me the trick of peeping 'round the refrigerator door, sheltering behind to avoid the cold blast. Hers were all the brilliant little cheats for getting through life. Aaaaand, skim milk it was. It'd have to do. Pay wasn't due until Thursday, a distant horizon. And these tight patches would only get squeakier until I faced facts. My earnings couldn't cover this place.

I'd hoped to stretch things just a little longer, though. This had been *our* flat. Mine and Angela's. And necessity had already prised my grip off all the other "our" things. Ultimately, the feast of memory wasn't filling any bellies.

A quick mouthful for me, no glass meant I needn't bother washing one, and the rest of the milk I dumped to mingle with the water residue in the cat's bowl, which rang on the tile.

Ricardo came charging in a direct urgent line from bed to bowl. Tail straight up and pink butt-hole waggling, which I didn't need to be seeing first of a morning. Or *any* time. When stuffing his greedy face was at stake I had to hand it to him, that was one determined animal. Had a brick wall stood in his way, I doubt it would have even slowed him down.

At least I was the only one worse off for nostalgic folly. Lack of civilisation being a virtue, Ricardo could always pop out and supplement his diet with a few less successful pigeons, the lucky sod. Just let one of my neighbours catch *me* going up the fire escape with a net and a stick, and the Screws would be hammering down the door before I'd finished plucking.

I was halfway to the toilet, not relishing the prospect of a cold porcelain kiss to the nethers, when the phone shrilled. Markedly *not* part of my regular dawn schedule, or much of any schedule for that matter.

It was a mad scramble to regain the kitchen before the line rang out, during which one slipper sailed off for lands unknown. Luckily for its recovery, the ranges didn't roam exactly wild and free in here. Snatching up the handset impatiently, I nearly belted myself in the head with it.

'Yes? Hello?' Sure I'd missed it.

'Ms Hanberry?'

'Speaking.'

'Ms Angela Hanberry?'

The quick stab of rage caught me unawares. I pinched my nose, feeling queasy with it. Eight sodding miserable *years* since my own personal disaster, a horror to rival the Disaster that'd cowed the world another three years prior. So, gee, one might *hope* the Screws'd grow tired of their incessant "checking in."

This was where wishful thinking got you. Gagging to scream and dash the phone against the wall, and completely unable to do either.

If usual patterns of benign harassment held they'd be popping up on my lunchbreak next. Just here to visit, in front of everyone, and I'd have to *smile* as they asked for a quick chat. So carefully unseen. Not a single curious head popping over cubicle walls, where you usually couldn't fart without getting noticed.

I couldn't let myself get mad. I used *calm blue ocean*, a soothing internal litany. Although the seaside I recalled from childhood was desolate, grey and seething, and I'd always wanted to go home. Still, there were oceans blue as postcards out there somewhere. Probably hoarded up for the rich folk. Beaches of uncluttered white sand. And my pallid office-shrivelled toes curling fearlessly in the surf. A fantasy that came with no threat of stepping in junkie spoor, not like on a real beach. Everyone dreams of somewhere.

Normally I was pretty slick at keeping my temper. But the Screws'd surprised me, popping into the day like that. I bottled it up, and stored it away carefully. Lashing out would mean they'd finally succeeded in screwing some real emotion outta me, and that wouldn't do. It was the kind of thing they fed on and fed on, leaving you with nothing. And with the way shit panned out, to *not* grieve was about the only tribute I could manage for my Angela.

'Uh …' I let my voice peter weakly, and faked a trembling sniff, hoping the ham wasn't too chewy. 'I'm afraid not. This is Cathy. Angela … was my sister.'

'Ah, my apologies. Do you have a number where we could reach her?'

These little games of theirs. Pressing on the dark and rotten bruise. My remaining smiley-face slipper beamed up from beside my bare foot, like a reminder to hold it all together.

And, both suddenly and weirdly, I recalled the slippery feel of that one time I stepped in shepherd's pie (with real shepherds). The hot gravy that had burned a bit, leaving a patter of tiny blisters that were agony against socks for days afterward. The hallucination was so vivid I actually flapped my foot frantically in the air, trying to dislodge it.

This was how badly things could slide off the rails, once my routines got interrupted.

'Angela … she passed away. Quite some time ago.' As if you didn't know. Sodding arseholes. Outright sobbing would be overdoing it. I settled on a small strangled noise that held just the right measure of pathetic. 'I'm not really … I can't.'

I dropped the handset briskly back in its cradle.

Cutting the Screws off was petty, and potentially dangerous. But if you failed to help yourself to the small pleasures where you could, it wasn't like the world was going to come doling them out. The phone shrilled again. They were nothing if not tenacious, always digging. Digging at your skin, trying to get under it. I let it ring out. They could assume I was occupied with being a useless wailing mess on the floor.

Humming, I put the kettle on and began the hunt for my escaped slipper. Blithely enough, on the face of it. But the damage was done, the numbing familiarity collapsed. And my thoughts, so carefully soothed, pricked up their ears and began asking questions.

Whenever I came in view of the phone it seemed to glare accusingly. But I couldn't sneak around avoiding my own appliance! *Go on, fatguts*, my treacherous brain urged with dark glee. *That Screw will still be there, asking questions, sanding back the scab. Asking, asking.* When times were bad, for some reason my inner voice often picked up a sinister echo.

I caught myself listening intently for the line ringing. Even to the point of leaving the bathroom door ajar, in case my paranoia missed it beneath the shower's rattle.

Ricardo sauntered in and sat on the toilet seat, with his runty tail curled neatly about his paws, because there's nothing the creepy little sod loves more than to leer intently while I'm naked.

Under the hot, but never hot enough—all my foulest curses reserved for economic shortcuts—water, I hacked horribly. Lungs spitting up something yellow that swirled down the drain before it could be identified, my bare feet dancing frantically to avoid it. But the glorious transition, cold to heat, was loosening my seizing back. Humidity prised open my airways. I bestowed on my carcass all the improvements cheap beige soap and a scrubbing brush could manage.

With visions of water bills dancing in my head, by the time I steeled myself to step out I was even vaguely proud. Steam erupted everywhere air met pinkened skin. Sure, I was a wreck. But see me keep that wreck reporting for duty, day in and out! On little more than spit and goodwill.

Despite my apprehension, the sinister phone failed to ring again; although my heart jumped when the kettle screamed its little lungs out and I mistook one for the other. Watery milo swirled rather miserably around in my mug. The malty steam was the first thing I'd managed to smell all morning, besides the stinging cold. Perhaps I ought to have saved a little milk.

It didn't help, of course. I never got over missing coffee. No matter how many years went by. It felt like I hadn't taken one of those epic morning dumps in forever. The kind that leave you all unstoppered, free to face the day.

The heavy black stuff was one of the first things the Screws cracked down on with their new authority. They'd been biding patiently for any excuse; even an idiot could see that, in the wondrous glow of hindsight.

The Disaster happened, everyone was shocked, and the world rubbed the sleep from its eyes one morning to find the

Screws firmly entrenched at the top. Flush with vindication and fresh power.

It didn't end with coffee. Once most of the key offenders had been cleared from the shelves, excepting grog which served *their* purpose by loosening your nuts and bolts, the Screws turned their merciless attention to feelings. Specifically, anyone who might be bottling them: an unhealthy symptom of an unbalanced mind.

Eventually, any degree of calm acceptance or pensiveness got you shipped off to the Screws' intensive "emote and release" seminars. Programs run from huge cinderblock edifices with blacked-out windows. Buildings that got acquired and outfitted disturbingly quickly, ready to roll almost overnight, it seemed.

Then there were the poor saps who actually *reported* for therapy. Great long snaking queues of them, in the early days. It was a daily spectacle on my way to the office, one I'd sped up to pass. Anxious hands clamped to suitcases stuffed with whatever they thought they'd need. And a driver's license clenched ready in the other fist for processing. Sunken, sleepless eyes. They camped right there on the pavement, sometimes whole families, as though once-in-a-lifetime tickets were on sale.

While the past was doubtless fascinating, all this added up to too sodding long spent brooding this morning. The loss of momentum'd see me late for work.

I managed to upgrade my efforts finally, from fluffing about to actual departure. Still in the usual three-ring juggling act of bag, coat, and a fistful of scavenged train fare. I've spent my whole life rather wistfully envying organised folk. Sadly, there comes a time when you have to just accept what you've got and do your best anyhow.

No sooner were the locks engaged than Ricardo began to wail demandingly from inside the flat. I sagged against the door. Double-nuts.

As it only takes waking once with your hair frozen to the pillow to encourage good habits, I'd been cranking the windows closed overnight. And sidetracked by all the morning's excitement, I'd forgotten to chisel Ricardo's window back open again.

I was already late. I considered just leaving it. Typically though, if the wilful beast was shut in all day he'd spurn the litter tray in favour of befouling all I've ever loved. Out of sheer feline spite. He was a *bad* cat. A curse. With no concept of patience, personal space, or my growing predilection for defenestration.

Not to mention his fire escape escapades being the only light in Ricardo's rather narrow life. Who was I to deny a cat his few pleasures? Guilt. It always did me in the end. Felt like I was lugging the conscience of two people—somewhere, somebody must wander the streets pillaging with impunity.

In the interests of exasperation I dropped my keys trying to yank them from my pocket. Then dropped the change too, as I bent for the keys. Weirdly, instead of sniggering—or an even more obvious offer to help—the two suit wearing fellows who'd been strolling the dim hallway quickened their pace. No longer so casual.

In a belated flash of brilliance I realised two things. Never claimed to be quick off the mark here.

One was that of all the flats in all the buildings of the world, they'd been intending to walk into mine. And the other: when I'd turned back to the door, they thought I'd spotted them and was trying to run. Assuming I'd reason to flee likely meant that I did. Screws!

Along with the organised, I've reason to envy quick thinkers, the happy improvisers of the world. The suits had already crossed half the distance before my lagging brain puffed across logic's finish line. By then it was too late.

But of course, it was already far too late this morning. For all my petty satisfaction, slamming down the phone had been a mistake, I saw that now.

Painfully obvious in the way of all bad calls long after the fact, and future-you wants to shriek back at the past, *No, you idiot!* It was the sort of fuzzy-headed slip I'd have never made back in the coffee heyday. And I'll bet no bugger felt even a twinge for denying *me* what brief pleasures made life bearable.

On impulse, and a wave of stinging resentment, I made a poor choice. Which was pretty much par for the day so far. I lunged for the doorhandle. Stabbing foolishly at the lock in a panic with the handful of coins instead of the keys.

Moving to a better choreography, the suits stepped neatly to either side of me. They took possession of a bicep each. My frazzled nerves were drawn to how limp and doughy my upper arms were; not that guns of steel would have helped much.

'Ms Catherine Hanberry. Would you kindly come with us.' Not a request. Although nothing as unmannerly as a demand, either. Delivered in a tone as dry as their getup: must be something they teach at suit academy. Both their heads swivelled as another aggravated plaint wailed from inside the flat. How *dare* I delay letting him out *this instant!*

'Ricardo!' I lunged against my captors, more on principle than hope. Even though there was quite a bit of me to lunge, they stood firm. No, one better. They began towing me away. Escalating yowls followed the three of us down the hall.

'Just come along, Ms Hanberry. I'm sure your cat will be fine.'

'He's not my sodding cat!' Genius, Cathy. But I couldn't help myself. Establishing that one solid fact had become one of the touchstones of my life.

Nary a neighbour poked their head into the corridor to investigate the fuss. Conspicuously shut doors whirled by in my confusion.

But then again, why should they open? This was the city. Its brutal density crushing down on us.

Walls on all sides barely muffled the maddening music, the coarse shouts and occasional raw screams of despair. All top volume, you know, as though proximity lifted the usual bounds of decency. All those needs and demands. *Surely somebody was listening? Somebody must care!* The unmanageable cacophony worked against itself: people merely shut their ears tighter. Not from malice. Out of self-preservation, lest they burn out in an instant.

And that was *before* the Screws. Nowadays, not even a beloved relative was worth getting *involved*. Folk used to put themselves out there all the time for kids, though, and not always their own which was nice. There was even this guy who started a real stink over getting his *dog* confiscated, wrote to all the papers. He'd been an old bugger, old enough not to fear anybody. A widower who'd lost his wife early on in some kind of wreck, all the family and friends who might have shushed him long gone. The curse of long life'd practically stranded him in his home. That dog had been all he had. Of course, it ended just how you'd expect.

So, I could hardly condemn the other residents. The twit who held the lobby door as I was frogmarched out, however, was a special kind of turd. Were I the sort of psycho to treasure a hit-list, write it in lipstick on the mirror, he'd be headlining.

A long silver car waited at the kerb. Sleek like a dolphin out of water, mysterious with its tinted windows, and so far beyond my pay grade as to appear like a fairytale coach. You could get married in a car like that. If you were the marrying sort, that is.

The suits bundled me onto the bouncy upholstery in the back, which was sprung like a jumping castle, a gentle hand on my forehead to forestall any mad death-by-doorframe attempt. The contact felt weird.

Sort of indecent, and I realised I couldn't even remember the last time somebody touched my skin. There just wasn't a lot of call for it.

Nobody on the street crooked an eyebrow at brazen daylight abduction. A jogger even came right by the open car door, without glancing in at me, trainers slapping the pavement. But of course, crossing the street to avoid the drama outright would've carried its own risk of getting noticed. And once the titillated Screws started monitoring you 'round the clock, eventual fuckup was inevitable.

I wondered what he'd do if I cried out for help. Not that I *would*, mind. That'd be a horrible thing to do. He looked like a nice, ordinary guy. Maybe someone's dad trying to stay in shape. This, here, was grand old reality. You can't ever be seen to turn squeamishly aside. For the love of your dear life, don't flinch.

Silly details registered. Irreverent things that could hardly save me now. Such as, trapped in the back, I couldn't peer out through any of the car's glass. Not even the panel cutting me off from the suits up front. I'd assumed the heavy tint was to stop the curious nosing in, but rather, I was sealed in here like some sort of contagion. No door handles guaranteed my death in a blazing inferno should we crash.

'Don't forget to do up your belt,' one suit advised solemnly before shutting me in. I almost laughed in his face. Was he scared of getting a fine?

We started into motion, and I sat and fidgeted uncontrollably. Tells, too many tells. Were this poker I'd be sunk. The harsh upholstery stink and unpredictable rocking were already making me dreadfully carsick. On top of the loaded hand of fright and confusion I'd already drawn.

I tried holding my breath, but the retch-inducing smell still crept in. Even tried counting backward, but that made me weirdly drowsy, the widdershins of my trick for waking. Stupid behavioural conditioning. And the urge to sleep didn't assuage my scrabbling fear any.

Deep down I think I always understood the Screws were bound to sink me eventually.

*Screwed if you do, screwed if you don't*, Angela used to sing out after a few tots of champagne, screaming with laughter. But really only screaming. My sister's fate had proven that faking your way while laughing up your sleeve couldn't pass muster forever. And if *anyone* slipped the Screws' net, it ought to have been her. The queen of the perfect lie.

Skills she'd introduced as silly childhood games—and how like her to have recognised the threat, back when Screws were a joke. Deception was an infant skill, honed obsessively to shield the adult. I once saw my sister foam at the mouth, and claw out a chunk of her beautiful hair. Later she chuckled wryly while I circled with blunt kitchen scissors, struggling to fashion a style around her new bald spot. While little strands gleamed red and gold, drifting about our feet. While I bit my tongue and lip until they bled, as she boasted and boasted.

Finally I flew off the handle. Ended with me slamming the door and going on a long angry power-walk, brushing cuttings of her glorious hair from my sleeves. To this moment, I wish I hadn't yelled. I was just so angry, and *embarrassed* to have been taken in. Hook, line and sinker. Knowing what she was like. Genuinely believing she'd flipped her wig in a frenzy of Michael-related guilt and sorrow. Well, when we got home and she gave her usual smirk, the cat that got the cream, I could've killed her.

The joke being all on me, of course.

Nothing I understood until the Screws got their hooks into Angela. Then wasn't I shocked to discover she really *had* been boiling black with remorse all along. So far as I'd known, we'd never used our tricks on each other, which went to show how amazing she was at it. Buggered if I knew how they'd managed to see through her in the end. Not unless the Screws flat-out had superpowers like I'd always feared.

My own brand of sneaky hadn't fared much better: got me this far, and no further. Although I'd always conserved information, hiding it like a miser, the few words I released were always, always truthful. The more they wanted me to feel, the less genuine feelings I allowed. The more power the Screws gathered, the more resentful I became and the even less I could show.

Doubtless they'd love to crawl inside my brainpan and fix all this right up. Just as they'd done with my sister. Make me as loud and carefree as anyone. Worst was my niggling suspicion that the Screws' world might actually *be* better for us. How would I know? I no longer woke from suffocating nightmares of the sky draining away; I'd exchanged them for paranoid days.

Not to mention the non-stop assault of everyone's showy, grovelling emotion. We lived in a world of howling, unappeasable children. Venting instantly, thoughtlessly, "healthily," just the way the Screws liked it. Only last week at the supermarket I saw some big truck driver fellow stub his toe and immediately burst into tears. Just plonked himself down next to his trolley of steak dinners, started bawling and rocking away. Nobody could squeeze past to reach the frozen goodies, and soon a little heap of shoppers piled up. All wailing their ridiculous frustrated distress at being denied icecream. No insidious repression *there*.

I abandoned my basket and went straight home to nurse a migraine. To merely play along with a sympathetic grimace wore down nerves and energy like a red-hot cheesegrater. Knowing my luck I was likely seeding a little crop of stress tumours, that'd erupt forth for harvest one day. I suppose it was too much to hope they might take me down before the sleek dolphin-car reached its destination.

Angrily I imprisoned both fidgeting hands beneath my thighs. *You settle right the sod down, Cathy, right now.* The best I could manage was as I'd always done: hunker down and wait them out.

But … what if they shipped me to an emote and release? Would I end up like Angela? There was nobody in the world to look after me. A grotesque spot of justice, considering the bang-up job I'd done with her.

*No!* I shook my head fiercely. *Quit thinking like a loser.* It was my business to ensure things never went that far. I had to stop chewing the memory of the shivering thing the Screws had returned to my doorstep. And the serene faced young twerp who said, "You'll need to keep an eye on her for a bit." Just keep an eye on her, like pale sobbing Angela were merely drowsy following an examination. The sort of state a nap and a cup of hot tea would set right.

*Watch her*, they said. If I failed to get a grip, I'd end up like Angela. And there'd be no-one to watch me.

Well, if I intended to escape today's total arse-up, my first impression was to be made with the two suits who'd surely report on me higher up the food chain. They'd at least been genteel thugs, but how well were they disposed?

My face was probably swamp-green but I composed my scattered nerves as best I could. Smoothed my hair and clothes. By the time the engine stopped, we'd either reached our destination or run out of petrol, I'd even managed to string up a pinched and brittle smile. No mirror to check how genuine it looked. Have you ever heard that homily on how many muscles it takes to smile as opposed to frown? Either way, it's a lot of twitches to be monitoring. Fortunately folk generally only skim the outlines of what you give them, anyhow.

When the door opened, I was ready.

Ready to laugh my guts out in relief! They needn't have bothered with all the suit-and-dagger, not with the huge scarlet and gold GATE Corporation logo that flared up in my face. Emblazoned huge on the building's brick wall, as though to offset the structure's inherent squat ugliness.

The logo looked familiar in that jarring way of coming upon a brand from your youth. Only then realising it wasn't around anymore. You wanted to say, *Where did you go?* GATE was the clout behind Threshold Station and the ill fated Capsule program. The brains trust who'd shot Angela's fiancé off into the void and failed so miserably to bring him home. An organisation which, to the greater extent of my knowledge, had absolutely no authority to go abducting people and making them late for work.

The happy realisation these suits *weren't* working for the Screws buoyed me so much that I shoved imperiously out past the offered hand, tottering a bit on crunchy gravel. The benison of brisk cold air drove back nausea and restored my reason. Such as it was.

The last time I'd seen the GATE logo had been an awful moment for the world. Printed on the pathetic remnant of the Capsule's cable. The weeping anchorman had shown it retrieved uncomprehendingly slack and empty, coiled on the floor of Threshold's hanger like a loop of dead snake. A final, slow zoom on the blackened end, as the violins swelled … The soundtrack had been a crass, theatrical touch resulting in fines for the network. But the anchorman's tears had been real. Even made me wish I could weep along.

Every bit as melancholy as the building I faced now. GATE were once a powerful entity. Now crumbling in this stained industrial wasteland, with its cheap chemical reek. The long progression of corners cut showed everywhere, especially in once lavish gardens now poured with gravel, dead leaves and cigarette butts. Even the looming logo could do with a lick of paint. Likely, nobody wanted to advertise they were proud of it anymore. This was the place despair came to die.

The acrid wind was rapidly stripping away the last of my warmth. I shivered, and crunched my way briskly up the refuse-strewn path. Best get this over with.

Sharing an alarmed glance the suits lengthened their stride, but couldn't catch my indignation until the locked door halted me. There I waited, with arms crossed. Tapping one foot impatiently as they got out their little cards and swiped me through. Overconfident, perhaps, following my scare, but I wasn't about to play the gracious victim. Not under those precious few circumstances I *wasn't* required to grovel.

Another suit manned the front desk. We made a regular convention. She came tricked out in ID swipes and even a pistol, all the trappings of Security Guard Suzie. I guess GATE would've found a sudden need for protection following the Disaster. The traumatised public weren't likely the worst of it; there'd been a lot of severely pissed off sponsors, determined to see their names weren't dragged through the mud alone.

The guard stood, startled, as I marched myself straight over. Apparently she didn't get too many visitors. But my escort slipped in before I could speak. Likely for the best. Too drunk and reckless on indignation, I'd no idea what might burst out of my mouth.

'We've brought in Ms Hanberry. Dr Cormac requested to meet her.'

Inwardly, without dropping my stiff little smile, I boiled over. *Requested?* Last time I whipped out a dictionary, forced kidnapping did *not* fall under a request!

The desk-suit grimaced. *Just more of the bullshit you get 'round here, hey?* She buzzed through, speaking with a hand over the mouthpiece so I couldn't hear. My smile became just that bit glassier.

Then we all stood around the reception area like jerks. Awaiting the pleasure of this Dr Cormac. Looking off awkwardly in different directions. Through the tinted window, I watched dead weeds wave in the chill breeze outside, and thought about nothing in particular. I'd had a lot of practice.

Eventually, a door clicked open and a rail-thin man approached my menagerie.

Somewhere about late middle aged-ish, or at least his grey hair and expanding brow thought so.

Up close I wasn't encouraged to find his face harsh and sarcastic. As people age the more firmly habitual expressions stamp themselves: vacuity, discontent, sourness. Until, just like that warning when you were a kid, the wind changes and you're stuck with it.

I don't set too much store in eyes, but his looked sharp. And they were that weird hazel colour, that isn't really any colour at all. I didn't want to know what they tallied up as he looked me over.

'Ms Catherine Hanberry?' No hand was offered.

'I certainly hope so. If not, your lackeys have abducted the wrong woman.' My tone was pleasant enough, but he raised a single critical eyebrow. I instantly hated him. *Years* of scrunching my forehead before a mirror before finally admitting defeat. There are those who can arch a single elegant brow to express volumes, and the rest of us can't.

'Ms Hanberry … May I call you Catherine?'

'No you may not.' *Don't buddy up with me, chum!*

I inspired another eyebrow to join its fellow. Luckily there was plenty of forehead for everyone. Dr-Cormac-I-presume then smiled. The faint "we are not amused" quirk, the inheritance of suits everywhere. In my own office it made me want to scream.

'Ms Hanberry, your presence is a regrettable necessity. My office phoned this morning searching for your sibling. However, circumstances being as they are we find we must resort to the next best that can be managed.'

So, I'd no monopoly on rudeness. Besides, he was largely correct: stood beside Angela, how could I be anything but a make-do? Nobody here was a Screw, though, so I refused to don the hair shirt over my sister. Instead I glared coldly right back into his eerie eyes, my fake confident smile planted firmly in place.

He appeared to examine me again, more carefully. Was he looking for something?

Then abruptly he offered his hand. Whatever he saw, he'd decided to work with it. 'Dr Ashley Cormac. In a rather broad sense, you could say I'm in charge here.'

Disparate bits clicked together. That's why he seemed so familiar, beyond my prejudices and stereotypes. GATE was his company. We were standing in his whole sodding building. *Threshold* was his. Once upon a time, hopeful kids had worn his logo.

I must've even met Dr Cormac once or twice, when tagging along with Angela to all the cocktail parties and galas. She went through this phase of wanting me to snag a celebrity of my own. Lessen the guilt of the new yawing rift between us. Fat sodding chance. Given dying alone as a crazy old cat lady, or being saddled with a glitzy A-hole like Michael, I'd gladly be Ms Kitty Litterhaus any day.

As immaculately clipped and disinfected as he appeared before me, Ashley Cormac sure had altered since those days. The slick media star, grand conductor of the masses, was nowhere to be seen. He'd shed weight, where there wasn't much in the first place, and a once-expensive tan had faded to a look as commonplace as mine. The unhealthy hue of forever indoors. No matter your ethnicity, it was a sallowness that spelled *office*.

Only that sneering curl running up one corner of his mouth remained the same. A vinegar charm all his, as though he could never quite believe his ears. What kind of doctorate did he hold, anyhow? Obviously not something that'd kept its value in this changed world.

I accepted his hand because, you know, it's just the done thing. 'It's interesting meeting you again, Dr Cormac; but would you mind explaining why I'm here?'

He'd no recollection of meeting me before. But he also wasn't racking those big brains trying to find it.

'Of course.' Dr Cormac keyed a lock and held open the door to GATE's inner sanctum. 'If you please.'

In passing, I caught his stern undertone to the suits I'd abandoned.

'Return to your duties. Filching her from the street was *not* part of your instruction.'

My turn to grimace. I felt bad for the poor suits, who merely stared expressionlessly back at him. I'd no doubt they'd been under orders to drag me howling from one end of town to the other if necessary. If Cormac hoped to score points by upbraiding his underlings now, he'd another thing coming. *Or*, another suspicion popped up. Perhaps they weren't allowed to pick me up where any idiot might see. I shivered, wondering if I'd brought calamity down on that hapless jogger. Somebody who merely wanted to mind his own beeswax.

Dr Cormac chatted in what I'm sure he imagined was a pleasant manner as he escorted me along a corridor. I kept to my sister's advice and held my tongue, peering about. Like most nine-to-five workplaces, which were really seven-to-nine, the décor held all the vivre of congealed gruel. The flat, lifeless, easy to wipe grey walls were broken at intervals by beige doors, each fastened by a glowing green keypad. Endless bland hallways. I seemed fated to end up in such places.

'Ms Hanberry, during your stay I am to serve as your … well, let's say "liaison." This being a critically sensitive issue, it necessitates your contact remaining limited to as few faces as possible.'

I really must learn to pay attention. The situation was rapidly deteriorating.

'My "stay?"' Dr Cormac, I'm not going to be *staying*. I'm already late for work.'

'I assure you, at this juncture I require your assistance far more than your employer. Your assistance, and discretion.'

'I don't think you're hearing me, I have to get to *work*. I'm never late.'

Nothing so hard to break as habit, even loathed. No, *especially* loathed habit, if one took perverse pride in sticking with it. Not that the office'd fall apart without me; one secretary's as good as another in their eyes, but the work would be piling up. I felt sick just thinking about it.

'This is an issue regarding the Capsule. I feel confident that you …'

'The Capsule's gone!' I burst out, as astonished now as impatient. 'It's been gone *eleven years*, Dr Cormac. I fail to see how it's even relevant anymore!'

The thin man changed tack. I don't think he liked my take on modern times very much. Well, suck it up, princess. That's merely the way things are.

'Ms Hanberry, I realise the tragic loss of Mr Formir must have shaken both your sister and yourself deeply. I quite understand you wishing to move on with your life, gloss over that time …'

I shook my head. '*Michael*? I don't know what you imagine, but nobody could ever have called Michael and I buddies.'

Now Cormac seemed perturbed. I could see those thoughts behind his eyes whirring, whirring. What on earth are you figuring now, Dr Cormac?

'You had some issue with Mr Formir?'

In that tone as well ask, or he with you?

'You want to know about Michael? Michael was a massive unrelenting jerk, twenty four seven with no days off. He was the sort of revolting meathead to pull up at the lights and beep disabled people to cross the road faster.'

'How well would you claim to be acquainted with him?'

'Well, he and Angela lived right the way across the country. She only came to stay with me again following the Disaster.'

Cormac stiffened, which was incredible. He was already rigid as a girder. 'We refer to the loss as "the Accident" around here. If you don't mind.'

Right-o. By any other name, you still crushed the world and left it to grow back all wrong.

'So, I mainly knew Michael via talking to her. And mainly through what *didn't* get said, if you catch my drift. About as close to him as I ever wanted to get. Besides,' I quipped lightly, 'How well can anybody know anyone?' It was kind of fun to be so unhelpful. It'd certainly been quite a while since I'd bantered with anybody. Life was a lot flatter *sans* Angela.

'Pardon me for saying so Ms Hanberry, but I find you speak a sight more freely than most allow themselves these days.'

He was clever, I'll give him that. I wasn't. I froze mid-step, like a dumb bunny in headlights waiting to get flattened. Dr

Cormac's thin mouth quirked and I was furious. He knew he had a handle on me now. Never let *anybody* get their hooks in, not even your nearest and dearest. Nobody can resist using it.

'I was about to say,' he breezed on, 'I find it quite refreshing. A freedom of conversation all the more enjoyable for its scarcity. Our, uh, political situation discourages most from thinking before opening their mouths, leaving you with twice as much at half the value.'

Maybe he really did love a good chat. But I was sure he valued leverage more. There was nothing safe in standing out.

'Tell me why I'm here, then,' I snapped irritably, striving to regain my game-face.

Cormac took a deep breath, running one long fingered hand over his head. A few cobweb strands of hair refused to surrender to his encroaching forehead, and poked straight out like antenna. I could tell he was arranging the facts within his skull like some fancy cake display. How much shall we feed her? Not a lot, from the size of me.

'Just tell me straight.'

'Ah, well. Two and a half weeks back, the remains of the Capsule impacted against the Shell.'

Well, I asked for it. I could have done with a little sugar-coating after all. My overstretched smile snapped back all wobbly, but Cormac wasn't done.

'From our investigation, we discovered that two survivors of the Accident were on board at the time. One unfortunately perished on impact. The other, we recovered and brought here. I believe you must suspect who it is.'

Of course. Some cockroaches wouldn't be crushed, no matter how hard life stepped on them. Cormac's stiff solicitude told me I must not be taking the news well, but I shrugged him off. 'It's Michael, isn't it? Why else would I be here. You've got Michael.'

'We have recovered Mr Formir. He has finally come home.'

I ruminated on that for a moment. Literally stood grinding my teeth like a cow in a field, waiting for inspiration. How was I supposed to feel? Dr Cormac studied my developing expression so intently that I kept my eyes on the dreary carpet. He gave the long wait more patience than I'd have credited. Me, I found myself trending toward irritation. And anger.

'So,' I managed eventually. 'What do you expect me to do about it?'

I don't think that pleased Dr Cormac at all. His lids dipped and hooded his cold eyes. 'This in no way revolves around what *I* wish from you, Ms Hanberry.' The hauteur was tangible. You could scrape it out the air with a knife and spread it on your toast. 'It is what you *must* do. Mr Formir has to date refused to speak. All that has passed his lips has been a croaked demand for your sister, and then he clammed up like a toddler holding its breath. We understand he's not catatonic, although he may appear so at times. Given the appropriate ... stimulus, Mr Formir is quite capable of snapping out of it.'

Dr Cormac drew down his crisp shirt collar with two fingers, diffidently drawing my regard to the dirty looking bruise that bloomed across his shoulder and collarbone, the skin stretched so tightly. It looked for all the world like the pale flesh had putrefied, through lack of adequate care.

'He attacked me. In fact, he attempted his level best to remove my head before security piled in. Mr Formir has no intention of speaking with just anybody, Ms Hanberry, and with your sibling gone that makes you the last surviving emotive link he has.'

By link he meant leverage, of course. Something that could be used.

'You are going to be the one to talk with Mr Formir, and find out what went wrong aboard the Capsule. What caused the

Accident? There is so much we have yet to understand. Where did the rest of the crew go, are they dead? Thirty people. Why were there only two left?'

Cormac leaned in close to me, his pale eyes all lit up like predawn light. Horribly cold light. On the sort of morning you only find yourself up because the frost gnawed your numb extremities all night, too cruelly to sleep. A precise, unforgiving illumination that exposes every year you've lived, clear on your face. All the poor choices called home to roost. I leaned instinctively away, and that was noted too. You didn't get a lot of leeway with Ashley Cormac.

'Ms Hanberry, you are to find out what awaits us Out there.'

I gaped at him. 'You mean you don't *know*?'

'All that's known for sure is that an explosion blew the Capsule off its cable, in lots of fragments which flew off in all directions at great speed. Nobody can even explain how *this* piece made its way back. Which begs the question: did something Out there send it?'

For a moment I feared I couldn't breathe. I didn't need to ask why the world didn't know yet.

No telling what the average Joe would do with this kind of newsflash; likely keel over. Most folk still glanced up anxiously when stepping from buildings and cars.

Probably didn't even know they were doing it. Or else, they considered it a mere sensible precaution, like looking both ways while you cross the road.

'This is crazy! You don't need some woman off the street; you need experts, specialists.' Me, I'm nobody. Why don't you leave me alone?

'The experts went first. And in all their wisdom produced a grand total of nothing. We are now running out of time, and are totally out of serious options. Quite frankly, things look desperate. I personally have both the authority and intention to try every possibility, no matter how far fetched, until I get my answers. And you are the absolute last of them.' I think he smiled. 'Bottom of the barrel.'

'Surely Michael had family.' It was one of those things you're often sensitive to when going it alone: the abnormality of your situation. Everyone has family.

'None surviving. The last of his line.'

'Friends?' There had to be *someone* to take this off my plate.

'Mr Formir was more into colleagues than friends. People who stood to better his situation. And all his close workmates were with him aboard the Capsule, that's where the glory was. Well, unless you choose to also count the exotic dancers we were able to track off his corporate credit card. I have already been in contact, and of those who recalled him none did so fondly.'

Colour me unsurprised. On a palette, it'd be a sort of blasé puce.

'But *I* hardly knew Michael at all, either.' Which was just how I liked it. 'I'm telling you, I'm not your girl.'

'You aren't, no. But I am taking a gamble that you knew her best.'

Between them, my two raised eyebrows had to convey everything he managed in one. 'Well sure, Angela and I *got* each other. On everything but her taste in men, that is.'

'And it is your sibling alone that Mr Formir desires so desperately.'

Lose my temper, you say? Yes. I believe I shall.

'Yeah, well, it's funny how screw-up asswipes like Michael always target great women. Go out of their way to mess up their lives. Why can't the jerks just fixate on other jerks, and leave the rest of us alone?'

'You may not savour this, Ms Hanberry, but it is becoming quite notable to me just how much you and Mr Formir appear to have in common.'

'In common?' I bristled.

'Only one profound human connection in the entire world. And an unusually intense, possessive link, at that. To Ms Angela Hanberry.'

'So my sister was amazing. What do you want me to say?'

'I have been wondering if perhaps she enjoyed being the crux of other people's worlds. If she sought out those who were on their own. Perhaps even arranged to keep things that way.'

I was shocked, because his theory *sounded* right. Dismayed too, because nobody ought to think of anyone like that. Even if it were true.

Dr Cormac paused and unlocked another door. I entertained a brief fantasy of wrestling that card off him and making a break for freedom, which made me snort. Yeah. Right. What was I going to do, sit on him?

I lingered. 'What's your big plan if Michael decides to leap across the room and throttle me, huh?'

Cormac turned and his nostrils compressed fastidiously, for no reason that I could see. Maybe the unsavoury mental image of anybody laying hands on me.

'Highly unlikely, at this stage. Just endeavour not to get too close. And don't let your feelings get the better of you.'

Oh, hey, thanks for the wisdom, there. How about I teach your grandmother to suck eggs?

I glanced up and down the corridor, but all the doors were numbingly identical.

There was no way of even telling how far we'd walked. I cursed my lack of attention.

'Ms Hanberry, I must caution you not to be startled. Mr Formir's appearance is drastically altered from how you must remember him.'

'Oh, I don't know. All I do is picture a giant asshole stuffed into a polo shirt, and I'm there.'

I meekly followed him in. A small antechamber, with the obligatory guard. They sure were into keeping folk employed around here. A large screen showed us the next room. And its occupant. What I recalled of Michael was a big, black haired man, boomingly loud to ensure no-one missed him. A cruising zeppelin of bombast.

I shook my head.

'It isn't him. You've made a mistake; that isn't Michael.'

'Of course it is.' Not for the first time, Cormac's tone took on nuances of humouring the lady. Surely not for the last, I manfully resisted the urge to smack him one. 'We cross-checked his dentistry, DNA, retina, every test you can imagine right down to the moles. So there's another good question. What happened Out there to turn a healthy man into *this*?'

'Will he get better?' Even as I asked, I doubted the autumn leaf thing in the next room could do anything but curl up and blow away. Every small, mean maliciousness I'd ever wished on Michael now seemed amateurish compared to what'd actually befallen him. And by his own actions, too. The next time some sour old biddy held forth that whatever goes around, comes around, I'll remember not to roll my eyes.

'Mr Formir ought to be improving under the care he's been administered. However, something about returning home appears to be making him worse. When we brought him back inside the Shell we inadvertently commenced the process of unravelling him completely.

'The best we have managed is to stabilise his decline to some degree, but as you can see ...' A helpless gesture. '... With such enormous damage, it's difficult to know where to begin.'

'What's ..?' My throat was so dry, I had to try again. 'What's wrong with him?'

'You fancy the tally? Mr Formir's musculature has atrophied. Bones like cheap chalk. Add to that the late stages of starvation, some kind of toxin build-up from recycling consumables too intensively. Physical injuries sustained in the crash. Other old injuries from who knows what. Somebody rattling his gourd for him. Odd damage at the cellular level. And we have little measure of psychological trauma until somebody gets him talking, although my personal dollar is on *lots*.'

Dr Cormac crossed his arms. 'The abridged version of all this is that Mr Michael Formir is dying. The best we can hope for is to string it out, hopefully long enough for what he knows to do some good.'

Somebody was dying. I supposed I ought to feel sad, but it was a man I'd disliked, and who wasn't very nice. Honestly, I didn't feel anything. Michael had survived, somehow. Endured Outside, and then travelled all the way back home, only to die sealed away in this ugly building.

'Why isn't he in a hospital?'

Cormac glanced at the guard, and then guided me to the far side of the room, which I guess was a close enough stab at out of earshot. The guard didn't seem to mind. And by mind, I mean care. It was similar in every workplace: being planted at your desk narrowed the world to your own worries, the next mountain of paperwork waiting to be choked down.

'The world is far from ready to face all this,' the doctor provided gravely. 'Not by a long shot. Not until we uncover precisely what we're dealing with, and the safest way to release the news.'

'But surely some people deserve to know *right now*? Family of the other Outermen, the government—this changes everything, doesn't it? I mean, everyone's been so *terrified* that going beyond the Shell's a death sentence. That we're all shut in here with each other forever and ever, and ... and maybe Outside might sodding well get *in*, someday, and that'd be the end of all of us. Everything we've built. But now, somebody *survived* Out there!' Even if it was only Michael.

Cormac looked exhausted, suddenly. As though a huge weight were crushing him. 'The Capsule program was intended to inspire the populace, Ms Hanberry. Together we were to overcome our fears. Regrettably the Accident made matters so much worse. We don't have *anything* yet, no answers. Telling the public the wrong thing is bound to inflict more harm than good. I refuse to walk that path again.'

I wanted to claim he was underestimating humanity, our capacity to be better. But it was more rote statement than belief. I'd never seen a shred of supporting evidence with my own eyes.

Insinuating his matchstick body between myself and the guard, Dr Cormac dropped his voice further. 'Certain … groups could potentially manipulate any careless announcement. To make the population *more* afraid. To garner even more power and control than they already wield. I take it you comprehend my meaning, Ms Hanberry?'

I sucked in a very careful breath, stalling. And to think, by my lights *I'd* been rabbiting on incautiously, the one taking risks! Since losing Angela, this had to be the first time I'd heard the Screws spoken of in anything but grateful positive. But that didn't necessarily make this Dr Cormac an ally.

As I've said, it never, ever pays to let anyone get a handle on you. Even those of the purest intent will use it to jerk you around. And I very much doubted this cold man with his hard eyes had my welfare at heart.

'In light of all this, are you willing to attempt speaking with Mr Formir? It's not so much to ask.'

Cunningly worded. Perhaps Cormac's doctorate lay in twisting things about, to lead people into doing as he pleased. I spoke quickly, eager to get this farce over with, and be away from here as fast as possible.

'Dr Cormac, I've a funny feeling you won't be letting me out of here 'til I do.'

At least he had the good grace not to demur.

Then they sodding went and closed the door on me! That was *not* part of the deal!

Although I knew in the next room a whopping great screen broadcast my every sniffle, I had the illusion of being alone with what was left of Michael. Only, the illusion bothered me. Angela had been full of rules, but one of her more useful was to always perform as though you moved beneath unfriendly eyes. Being observed wasn't too far a stretch from habitual life.

The door behind me, I hesitantly approached a glaringly bright, floodlit bed in the middle of a dark space. And the more I moved into the light, the further the rest of the world receded. Even the boundaries of the room crouched hidden beyond the curtain of dark.

The thing that lay prone on the bed never so much as blinked at my arrival, and I immediately felt every centimetre as stupid and awkward as I looked. What was I supposed to say, that wouldn't sound trivial and pointless? What on earth did Cormac expect of me?

Well, I was here, regardless. Might as well kick off with the obvious.

'Hello?'

Nothing. Not a sausage. Perhaps he'd done us all a favour and slipped into oblivion in his sleep, while next door Cormac'd been spinning conspiracy theories in my ear. Although if that were true, I'm sure all sorts of alarms would be trumpeting. Bringing scores of doctors and hopeful dissectionists sprinting down the hall.

Shrink-wrapped in pristine sheets, Michael's wasted figure was both dwarfed and dirtied in the huge white circle of light. Not a single hair left on him anywhere, so far as I could see. Stripped bare like a worm. And the closer I stepped, the more thickly a sweetish fermenting apple smell pervaded the air.

I tried again, venturing into the banal.

'Michael?'

The apple smell gusted over me, solid enough to taste, to bite into. Earth cellars, old and forgotten, threatening to cave in. The rotting bottom of wicker baskets left to sit through the season. A scuzz of mould on the tongue. What turned listlessly to face me was not a face.

No more than a scrunch of parchment hung off the front of a shrunken skull. All withered skin and frantically fluttering arteries, that looked like moths in a bag beating to escape. His sunken eyes were a hectic grey.

So now I had his attention. It made me want to run wailing from the room.

'Michael, do you remember me?' Still feeling a big fat goose for even being here. Sure, I'd be right up on his priority list. 'Do you remember my sister? You were going to marry her.'

I couldn't shake the feeling this was some gross mistake. No way could that be Michael. Angela had always fancied the bulked-up lads, you could see their brains swinging around between their knees. Michael had been such a tall, broad-shouldered fellow. As bursting with arrogant life as an overripe fruit.

Not this tiny stunted figure, with all the juice pulped from it. I thought rather uncharitably of preserved tribal heads behind dusty museum glass. Things no-one goes to see. Or desiccated peat bodies, carelessly chopped in half and turned up by a farmer's shovel with a curse. And my skin crawled. Not because Michael was ill, although severe sickness can be confronting.

Something about him was just plain *wrong*. Something dormant, but there. Something that stank of an old harvest gone bad.

Still Michael had nothing to say to me. Glittery, wet grey eyes, staring. He might not even be breathing, and I sodding well wasn't touching him to find out.

I'd become a little turned about in the space, unsure where Cormac's hidden camera may be lurking. 'Dr Cormac?' I called to the room at large. Also a tad sarcastically, as there's nothing the human animal loves so much as being right. 'You'd better just let me out. He doesn't remember me. Or *her*. This has all been a mistake.'

I'd put my back to the bed. A faint rustling movement alerted me and I froze, then turned around slowly. Michael had coiled up, as much as his sparse ruined body would allow. A centipede about to strike.

'You reckon I'd dare forget *her*?' His voice, rusted shut like a trap. '*Angie*?'

It were as though all Michael's faded internal processes had suddenly ramped up. Everything racing feverishly. It accelerated him instantly from being a relic to a threat. All my instincts screamed that I was daring something poisonous, about to bite, and I couldn't help myself. I backed up hastily, terrified this withered scarecrow might be about to fling itself off the bed at me.

Michael's rumpled features twisted in a sneer. I was seeing a lot of that lately. Perhaps not undeservedly.

'Of course *you'd* think so, wouldn't you. Well you can tell that shitheel Ash I'm not fucking around. He can't keep me from Angie. She's coming for me.'

There's a point in every conversation that goes on long enough, when you realise your opposite might as well be speaking another language, that's how far off their track veered.

I switched the things Michael had croaked at me around, even stood them on their head, but could make no sense of it.

'What?'

'You think I don't know why *you're* here, you sour bitch? Oh, my Angie used t' go right on about *you*. No shit of a topic I could be more sick of hearing. Do you want t' hear for yourself what she said?'

'Not really.' My heart was hammering, *trapped, trapped!* So much for recalcitrant Michael. What I wouldn't give for him to shut up. It was just like the old days.

The hateful lisp continued, little curls of lip barely moving. 'Angie knew you were never meant t' survive on your own. She'd always be fretting away that you couldn't cope with this, couldn't fucking well take that, like you were some baby. Couldn't be brought t' parties, 'cause shit forbid you might have fun. Couldn't make friends on your own. Without *her*, you weren't anything! Left t' your own devices, you might as well dissolve away completely.'

All that bile. I wanted to screech indignantly, "Angela'd *never* go saying that about me—especially to *you*!" but that would be mere candy coating for my pride. My sister was perfectly capable of coming right out with any edged truth that needed to be said. Probably hundreds of times a day without breaking a sweat.

*Dissolve away?* My solidity mocked the prospect. But where had my life gone without her? Trapped in a hopeless maelstrom, I'd circled my sister's absence for years. Only to crash here, in this room, in the twisted remnants of what would have been her marriage.

Us rag-tag ends, who somehow miss jumping on the bright merry-go-round of engagements, weddings, bouncing babies.

Left out in the cold, we rarely appreciate having the fact brought to our attention. I let him have it. 'You never deserved my sister in the first place, you pig! She ought to have been thrilled when the Disaster swallowed you up!'

'GET OUT!' Michael heaved with the furious violence of it and I cowered, like a dog beneath a raised stick.

Either those spindly arms were about to break, or he intended to break me. '*Out* you fat false bitch! OUT!'

I fled to the door, jarring my knee against the bedframe hard enough to shoot pain down my leg, and send the whole assembly swinging around. Michael's contorted face tracked me the whole way, swivelling unnaturally on his neck like an owl's, far too smoothly and way beyond the breaking point. I gagged helplessly at the sight.

The portal opened, and I fell through onto the startled guard. Behind me Michael was howling, '*You can't keep me from her!*' like some gore-maddened beast thrashing in its own entrails. It wasn't until the door clapped shut on him that I was able to halt my frantic retreat. Pressed right against the far wall, a barrier I'd been about to claw my way through.

*Safe*, I chanted silently, as though that could make it true. *Stop it, dumbass, just stop. You're safe.*

Dr Cormac leaned and watched, his face as still as glass. My cheeks began to burn, awareness of the spectacle I'd provided arriving readily enough.

*See?* I thought at him furiously. *This is what you get for sending the wrong idiot in. A debacle.* If Angela were here, I wouldn't be going through this. Yet another mess she'd left me mired in. Would I ever quit stumbling across them?

'Ms Hanberry, as I'm sure you've surmised from the screen, everything that goes on in Mr Formir's room is recorded,' he stated flatly. No, *Are you alright?* or *Would you like to sit down?* He could've been letting me know my shoelace was untied.

I shook my head, not getting it, and he sighed and continued.

'There are a certain number of … specialists, as guests here, who review the footage hourly. They are going to want to speak with you.'

Now would be the perfect time to start trembling, but my nerves were already shot. 'You *said* you didn't want them involved!' I growled in a low, furious voice, and sod the eavesdropping guard.

'I do not.' Cormac replied stiffly, uncowed by my outrage. 'As even they are quite well aware. However, like everybody, I tolerate them when I must. As you yourself have said, the world is no longer all it was. Rare is the luxury of being an island, when we reluctantly subsist in one another's pockets.'

I knew what was coming next. Being afraid of it wouldn't change anything. So, no point in being scared, right?

If only it worked like that.

A quiet room, with no windows. A place meant to seem away from it all. Being out of context sometimes loosens the tongue on secrets you'd otherwise keep locked down tight. I was sat down, with a soothing cup of tea that tasted like dogwater.

And in came the Screw.

That term, "Screw," I now remembered, came like all good things from Angela. The mere thought of my sister laughing at this fellow made me steadier.

He was a prime example. Everything so calculatedly inoffensive, he made my skin crawl. If they judged Screws competitively, he'd win best in show. Take home the blue ribbon. Physically pretty unremarkable, of course. With a smooth non-confrontational manner. Deep chest, tall at the hocks … I smothered a smirk. *Now isn't the time, Cathy!*

Urban legend held that Screws were supposed to remind you of your parents. Fast track that tiresome earning of trust.

Fat lot of good it'd do with me: Angela and I were orphaned so early, we'd run wild like ferals.

A social worker had braved our door with groceries and vitamins twice a week, but she was anything but motherly. Never hesitant to administer a good clip 'round the earhole should we deserve it, either.

My only paternal memory was a sort of tweedy, oily smell. I think it'd puffed out of my father's green jacket when squeezed in a hug, all green wool and comfort. The Screw was unlikely to manage nostalgic smells, except by request I suppose.

Still, the moment he entered I felt my shoulders tighten, and forced them down. *No handle. You're doing his sodding job for him. Don't feed him cues.* He'd be well trained to spot them. And scrupleless about grabbing hold.

Setting it all aside I assumed the mandatory relieved smile as he sat down opposite. *Oh, thank goodness you're finally here, Mr Screw*, my inner voice expounded in squeaky falsetto. *Please, please take away responsibility for my feelings. They're oh-so heavy for me to lift and I don't want to be a grownup.*

*Stop it, Cathy!* I scolded sharply. *Don't be resentful.* I had a terrible track record with resentful. I took another gagging sip of dogwater to forestall conversation, but such minor gambits were nothing to the Screw.

'Good afternoon, Ms Hanberry!' He couldn't have sounded happier to see me if we were dating. 'I hope you wouldn't find it intrusive if I call you Catherine?'

As a matter of fact, I'd quite the chip on my shoulder over strangers tossing my name around. Especially before I'd told it to them. But demurring gives the impression you've something concealed, guaranteed to get a Screw's fingers itching.

By that stage you might as well be trussed up in a van. On your way to have the privacy within your skull blasted loose like a blocked toilet.

'My name is Charles. I'm the head counsellor of our little delegation here, and incredibly pleased to meet you.

'Now, I'm sure you've been hearing a lot of chat about how dire and important these current happenings are. Being an astute lady, you'll have already seen how intently certain individuals are focussed on that. To the exclusion of every other decent thing, it seems.

'Well, amongst all these odd ducks and their agendas, there's only one thing *I'd* like you to keep in mind. I, at least, am here for something entirely different. Catherine, I'm here to help *you*.'

Charlie gazed so earnestly into my face, all dewy-eyed, that I worried we might actually be dating and nobody'd told me. This was the sort of fellow who went about forcing folk from their day, headfirst into emote and release. Unfortunates later handed back to society with a flippant, "You'll need to watch them." Who flinched when you touched them to guide them to the couch, speckled with strange tender scabs they tried to conceal under baggy clothing. Eggshell wrecks glued imperfectly back in place.

Just how they'd like us all to be, and thank statistics they didn't have the resources to reprogram everybody. Perhaps one day. It made things all the worse to see how Charlie-boy *really cared*. He seemed to genuinely want to look out for me. Was determined to *save* me, even, if it lay within the power of his two hands.

'I have just watched the footage of your confrontation with Mr Formir. But I'd quite like hearing you describe it in your own words—if you feel you can manage.'

I tried to will the blood from my face. The Screw took my hand sympathetically, and I even managed a slight quiver to my lip.

That last wasn't entirely fake: I found Charlie's fingers

disturbingly warm and moist. Possibly overwrought at the prospect of rescuing another lost, wandering mind.

'He ... Michael *yelled* at me. Told me to get out.'

'Uh huh.' Charles leaned further, really craning in. Perhaps it'd be easier if he just sat on my lap.

'Please try to understand, Catherine, this certainly isn't a failure. It's significant that Mr Formir—*Michael*—engaged with you at all. I've yet to be permitted direct contact myself, but doubt even I might've made the impact you just managed.

'You see, Michael Formir is clearly a man driven only by strong emotional triggers. All of his feelings and desires are drawn in and bound irremovably to himself. And to your sister, Angie.'

*Yet to be permitted* contact? Who had the authority to deny a Screw anything? It seemed Dr Cormac had been modestly hiding his light under a bushel. Holed up here in his crumbling fort, he could still wave his sceptre.

'It is important to discover, if we can, what happened to Michael and the rest of the Capsule's crew. What failed, what went wrong.' Charlie squeezed my hands, and it was like wearing hot sponge gloves. I couldn't afford to shudder. 'But not, in my opinion, at the expense of your wellbeing.'

'Thankyou Charles.' Not overly heartfelt, but he seemed to expect something.

'Now, you told me Michael yelled at you. How did that make you feel?'

We were back to regular Screw stuff, questions I could answer by rote. *Oh, ever so afraid, good sir! Weak, powerless*; which was true enough, although I got plenty of the same merely strolling down the street. I also implied a kittenish undercroft. Of being ripe to fall into some big strong arms. Stroke his ego a bit. Everyone likes to feel needed.

Gradually, the tingling sensation of walking a tightrope

receded.

If I were honest, and I preferred to be, what I most felt now was embarrassed. Ashamed of having stampeded from Michael's room like that. Doubly-disgusted to now have to sit and pick the bones with Charming Charlie.

The confidence of being marginally ahead of the situation came creeping tentatively in, for the first time today. Until I looked up, and saw Ashley Cormac leaning in the doorway. *Nope!* Security tucked its tail and fled.

A sardonic smile twisted Cormac's lips as he listened. As though he believed himself far better at reading me than any Screw could ever be. Charlie-boy finally twisted in his seat to see what could be more engrossing than himself. Although not made for anger, his mild face scored points by trying its utmost.

'Dr Cormac! I really must ask you to leave!'

Cormac shrugged lazily. 'It's my building.'

'Quite. A forum in which you've lavishly demonstrated your failure to care for anyone or thing else en route to your grandiose goals. Humanity has already endured much of what *you* can bring to the table. Does the world really need a repeat performance from Dr Ashley Cormac?'

If sparks struck, they didn't show, and Charlie continued on. 'Michael Formir, every bit as much as Catherine here, needs the treatment and care only we can provide.'

'You already have my response, no doubt in some little file somewhere. At any rate, what do you imagine you'd accomplish? It appears Ms Hanberry has well outshone us both on every front.'

Setting a laptop on the table, Cormac flipped up the screen and addressed me like spluttering Charlie wasn't even there. 'I have brought something for you to witness. Somewhat of a short film. I promise it won't take up much of your time.'

'You intend to show her …' Charles snorted. 'Like *that* will help Catherine get *anything* straight in her head! Oh, no reflection on you at all, my dear. What Dr Cormac's putting on display like some carnival gimmick is not only profoundly distressing, but has obviously failed to teach *him* a single thing. So now he parades it for you like you're magic or something.'

Cormac dimmed the lights. He seemed secretly gleeful, like a small lad showing his butterfly collection. I already had a grim feeling about this.

What came up on the laptop screen was old, almost historic-looking footage. With a poor grainy resolution you could practically strain through your teeth. Going through life you seldom notice how far technology's come, not until somebody pulls out something like this and you go, Oh *look!* It's so *dated!*

Not even any sound. And not exactly shot by a professional. Whoever held the camera waved it about wildly, conducting with the other hand. Grinning faces popped in and out of frame against an unlit background so dense that each appearance, no matter how friendly, seemed a malignant jack-in-the-box darting at me.

'I don't understand what I'm seeing,' I said in frustration. Modern audiences are so conditioned to want something *now, now, now!*

'Just watch.'

The clowning figures in their dark murky world wore puffy Outerman suits. They were in the process of settling big cumbersome domed helmets on their heads. Gradually, it dawned on me what manner of footage I was watching. I squirmed in my seat.

Illicit, this viewing. Like a snuff film. Threaded through with a sense of calamity about to befall. The camerawoman bounced the shot around to capture her own face: sparkling, overwrought fever-eyes. Pupils big and black like a cat ready to attack, so huge they seemed ready to obliterate heavyset features not too dissimilar to my own. Her mouth moving silently as she cheered something we couldn't see, something they were all swept up in.

In desperate fear I wanted to lunge through the screen and shake her: *Stop! Just stop!* It was flat-out horrible to sit silent witness to this. Even after all these years, watching that happy excited woman felt like she could somehow still be saved.

I clenched my fists around the need to do *something*, containing it. Because of course these people, all these Outermen were gone.

Dr Cormac seemed to sense how easily I identified with the woman on screen; he had a keen and whiskery nose. 'This is Samantha Rohner. Sam to her friends. Somewhat of a home movie enthusiast, as you can tell.'

Sam swung the camera back around: *well, enough about me, there's happenings afoot!* Next she took to zooming rapidly in and out on somebody's name patch as though she thought it hilarious. So rapidly that in league with the poor image quality I could scarcely read it.

'Lizard?'

'Isabelle. "Izzy-Lizard." Couldn't be kept away from rock climbing. Almost flunked out of the program for ducking meetings. What you are seeing is Isabelle White, and her partner in crime Grant Heng suiting up in an airlock to venture Outside. These are the last moments of the Capsule. Ms Rohner unwittingly filmed them, broadcasting to a wireless hard drive, and we picked up the signal at Threshold.'

As though trailing Cormac's dry narration, the screen flickered, and then picked up the image again. A black screen. At first I thought the camera must be broken, or we'd run to the end and I wouldn't have to see it. Then I saw the pale, puffy figures. So far away and seemingly *floating* against a backdrop of absence. And I was literally breathless.

'They're … they're …' Not enough air.

'Outside,' Cormac confirmed with satisfaction, and Charlie shot him a sour look.

'You don't have to watch this, Catherine.'

But I was already watching. Too, too late.

The Outermen, I now saw, were reeled out on some kind of cable. Bobbing around like pendulums that couldn't decide which way was down.

They both milled their arms comically in revolving circles, and although in a crazed fashion, moved with a purpose. Approaching something.

The void was not absolute. Any moment I felt I might be sucked forward into it, empty chair clattering to the floor.

By dint of wiggling, the dual figures were edging closer to some kind of light. And it was nothing mankind had dragged Outside, that was for sure. A ball of brightness, floating Out there all alone. Even with the gritty imagery you could see within their helmets, the angle being just right. How it lit the wonder on their faces, like a child's birthday candles in a darkened room.

Sam did something to the focus, and suddenly Outside wasn't blank and empty like I'd always imagined. It was sprinkled here and there with these tiny lights, like a handful of glittering sand tossed into the air to spin there forever. So far away, and safe on the ground, I felt my own face light up with the same innocent species of wonder. Nothing was how I'd thought.

On reaching their glowing target Izzy-Lizard waved a triumphant arm to Sam, and the camera juddered as she waved back. With them practically on top of it I finally got a sense of scale for the mysterious light. No larger than a basketball, but so bright. Sam's camera flared and dimmed, the light balance fighting to cope with being pointed dead-on at the thing.

Helmets together, Izzy and Heng seemed to confer excitedly. It was Heng who put his hand out toward the light. Izzy clung to him anxiously and seemed to want to reconsider the plan. My fingernails were digging into my palms, my mind one long howl of, *nononononono …*

Grant Heng's hand passed straight through the light, upsetting his balance into a bit of a whirl, stopped against his partner. There wasn't anything solid to the glow.

He and Izzy faced each other in mirrored postures of surprise. He pointed at the bodiless light, and she pointed at him, questioningly. What were they saying? Was Grant somehow different? A difference that could be detected immediately, she seemed to be edging back from him.

Suddenly the camera started to quake. Our perspective jumped about sickeningly as Sam tried to work out what was going on. I could well imagine the confusion, the screaming, who needed sound? There was a shear of light across the picture, from the bottom-left corner. A distortion of colour.

The last thing I saw was a frozen, glitched image of Sam's face filling the frame. The distortion gaped Sam's terrified mouth impossibly wide, torn beyond the boundaries of her head. She looked ready to bite, rabidly. To swallow the camera whole. In the little slice of void just behind her ear were two white smears on long threads of cotton, zooming away from each other, incredibly fast. No longer figures, that had been taken from them. Gone from being discrete shapes to long blurred streaks. You could imagine the screaming. Oh, the screaming.

Then it really was the end. Darkness. The everyday radiance of the laptop screen.

Dr Cormac switched the overheads back on, and we three were sitting in an ordinary corporate room. Now I could see myself, and I was shaking so hard it interfered with my ability to draw breath, allowing only hitching jerky gasps.

'Catherine?'

I wanted to leave. I tried to get up, but neither leg co-operated, spilling out from under me and running away like water.

Only Charlie's timely intervention kept me off the carpet; he leaped to the rescue so nimbly his chair went clattering away.

'Oh! Poor Catherine here *must* have some quiet time to rest, and privacy. I insist, Dr Cormac. She's really experienced the most terrible shock.'

With Cormac cajoling in one ringing ear, and the Screw snivelling in the other, I felt pulled between them like a dog's rope toy. *What Cathy wants*, I thought dismally, *is to crawl home and into her own bed. Pull the covers up and wait for oblivion.* No-one seemed much interested in asking me, though.

'Just one more shot afterwards,' Dr Cormac bargained. 'If Mr Formir declines to speak any further, then I promise you can go home.'

I somehow ended up in a little white room of my own. Sparking a desperate curiosity as to what lay behind all those rows and rows of GATE's locked, glowing keypads. But my imagination was being melodramatic: each didn't hold a quivering, shellshocked prisoner. More likely this was a nap station, for employees too plugged in to consider going home. It's dead-easy to get trapped in the overtime cycle. Especially if you've no-one nagging you to be at the table for dinner—corporations love that. Click, snap, you're in their trap.

So far as I could tell, there was no all-seeing camera like in Michael's room. So far as I could tell. No windows, either. It was like staying at a hotel, only without the fun. I creakily arranged my shuddering bones on the bed (single!), but unsurprisingly it was a sodding long time before sleep.

My guts hurt, for one. I'd rushed to use the facilities with relief, but being all emptied out like a saggy deflated balloon was a reminder of the bugger-all I'd had to eat today. One of the few pleasures in life, and I'd missed a whole day of it.

It was only then I realised they'd taken my handbag.

I sat bolt upright in alarm. When ..? When I got out of the car, perhaps? Stupid!—I'd no idea!

Humans rose to planetary dominance as a tool using species, yet in my time of need all I had at my disposal were the contents of my coat pockets.

Amounting to a raggedy tissue, a ticket stub (a dark cinema being one of the few places folk don't surreptitiously monitor you for being alone), and the tail end of a packet of mints.

I sorted through the stash. Strangely, I found being thrown into extremity with sod-all to my name wasn't terribly worrying. Or at least, not appreciably *more* so than everyday life. Not a whole lot of point, I supposed, wasting perfectly good anxiety on circumstances I couldn't change. Save it for all the crap I'd be expected to *do* something about.

Any resources were going to have to come from within me. And they'd just have to do. I ate the mints.

Trying to nap, to dull my brain and not think of anything, all I could see against my eyelids were my sister's shining eyes on the day of the launch, as she followed the Capsule's ascent. Up, up beyond sight. Up the gentle curve of the Shell. A gleaming waterfall of rose-gold hair shimmering down her back. And in the beginnings of the dream I tried to warn her, *Terrible things are going to happen, Angela! You ought to be afraid!*

But she merely smiled, her glowing hair drifting about her face. Things would only and forever go as Angela planned. She wouldn't allow anything else.

# OUTERMEN

## FIVE

## WHATEVER YOU DO, DON'T LET THEM

**NOBODY ENJOYS WAKING** up. *Nobody*. Anyone who goes about claiming to is a straight-up filthy liar, pants on fire.

Blowing the Screw's sage opinion from the water, as I ticked them off I found a nice refreshing nap had cured exactly zero of my ills. I was still *illegally* sequestered away in the bowels of GATE headquarters. Not that anybody who noticed me missing was likely to raise a stink. All crazy eyes were still fixed on me, to somehow yank Michael's reluctant tongue outta a magic hat. Oh, and I was probably fired by now.

You had to wonder if this situation cropped up often. How many stepped from their ordinary lives to the call of something grand, only to discover too late that the good of mankind never vanquished any bills. Just how many noble heroes ended up as destitute bums, when they tried to come home to reality?

I was pretty much screwed, in anyone's parlance.

In addition to these first world woes my empty gut was now raging, although clearly not wasting away, more was the pity. And the cut-price mattress had left my poor beleaguered spine with a sclerotic pizzazz. Perhaps the GATE staff who normally bunked here worked themselves into such a pitiable state first that they failed to notice. Yeah, that sounded about right. Burnt-out corporate shells would be grateful to crash anywhere.

*And* the idiots had never turned the light out in my room! I'd've settled for a little ambient dimming, but no. What did the pervs expect me to get up to alone in the dark, anyhow? Despite my inability to locate hidden cameras, deep paranoia must be the GATE watchword. Too ingrained for them to let up surveillance, even for a second. Well. If they were silly enough to pay some sap to watch me snore and dribble into the lumpy pillow, so be it. Plenty more ridiculous ways to scratch together a living.

Oh yay. There was even a wonky little mirror tacked up, to show the nap's damage in glorious technicolour. I couldn't look more unprepared if my pants were on my head. The hair in particular grieved me.

Unknown to anyone but Angela ... well, I guess unknown to *anyone*, now; I've spent years shivering over the sink with a dye packet, blotting out my own feathery blond crown with inky blue-black. A hangover from girlhood aspirations to be a slick superhero.

Like all kids, my sister and I zipped around with tea towels pinned to our shoulders, collected bamboo staves for epic battles. Only I never grew out of it. Although not even youth's boundless imagination reconciled ideal with the spiteful looking glass, the woman I had grown into. My grand swell of belly and cartoonish, drooping breasts better suited some fertility idol dug out of ancient Africa. At least I could have the hair.

Just to grind the point home, I'd taken a few humiliating adult stabs at living the dream. Bought a motorbike once. No, really. Me. Laid out a pauper's fortune on all the trimmings. Postured timidly before the mirror in my gear, and for a moment felt that I really had it.

Of course, I promptly tumbled myself all over the stinging asphalt. To the great hilarity of onlookers, including Angela, and the bunch of *real* bikers she'd invited around to watch the show. A hero. Huh. With a super ego *almost* as tender as my generous hams. The little 250cc went to languish in a rusty storage cube, along with all the other failures I couldn't admit to by tossing them away. If there were ever a champion of banality, I'd be your girl.

When I opened the door into the hall, Dr Cormac was *right there*! That was off-putting. In the building's confines I'd no way to gauge the passage of time, how long his precious investigation had been stalled by my miserable human frailty. For all I knew, he'd been camped in the corridor the whole time, bouncing off the walls with frustration.

Did the good doctor never sleep? Probably cradled in something obsessive and weird, like a scale model of Threshold crafted entirely from toothpicks.

I certainly wasn't panning out to be the lucky break he'd been dreaming of. In fact, as they thrust at me out of the hall, it occurred that Cormac's bitter features must be the result of the buckets of disappointment life poured over him.

Now, he clearly felt he'd been patient long enough. Dr Cormac unapologetically yanked me from the room and bustled me straight down the corridor to the antechamber of Michael's quarters. If I hadn't been such a dire, bend at the knees lift, there was a good chance of him flinging me across his narrow shoulder and sprinting there.

On the privacy-nullifying screen (again I commiserated some poor sod, condemned to watching folk sleep. Probably mourning, *I went to university for this?*), the stranded Outerman looked like nothing from Earth. Those washed-grey, canted eyes glimmered out of a face so bitterly angular he scarcely seemed human. His lower jaw advanced from the ruin, like the muzzle of some cunning animal.

The weirdest part was how you could squint, and still make out how the natural bone contour had once run. How it had been, before the years lost Outside had grasped the whole taffy assemblage and *pulled*.

Perhaps Michael, shrivelled on his bed, represented the misbirth of what would have been a whole new race of humanity. The Outermen. If our fate had been to bloom rather than collapsing fearfully in. The future that might've been, had the Disaster not descended.

If so, it was a sad token.

The pathetic nest of skin, bone and dry wasted tendon stirred restlessly in place beneath pristine sheets. Hospital-corners snugged tight as though to bind him securely down. Only Michael's bald head remained free, and it rocked ceaselessly from side to side in endless futile negation. Lost flesh and fat had pulled that mouth into a jolly rictus grin I'm sure he wasn't feeling, exposing abnormally white teeth.

Newsreader-grade teeth, without a blemish on them. Almost glowing blue in the hospital-like light.

'What's he doing?' I whispered, and immediately felt a right goose for whispering. It wasn't like Michael could hear me through the wall. It was just all a bit too creepy, like stumbling across the setup for some late night horror flick.

'Mr Formir moves like that every few hours,' Cormac supplied, failing to leer or in any other way conform to my fancy of theatrical monster-maker. 'Ever since we brought him in. I suppose it may be a self-comforting gesture, or nerve damage, or … well, anything, really. Until you prise open the lines of communication, it's rather difficult to make any assessment of how to assist him.'

Oh, so that was on me too, was it?

I stared at Michael. He couldn't look further from home if he tried. 'And all he wants to talk about is Angela. Michael doesn't know she's gone, does he? How could he not know?'

I'd meant it to sound more accusing than plaintive, but Cormac got the point.

'Let me share a theory with you, Ms Hanberry. I have come to suspect that regardless of its veracity, this grand ideal Mr Formir treasures of your sibling is what kept him staggering on all this time. A belief so encompassing, it is literally the reason he survived. Just him. One man, out of thirty equally trained and qualified crew, all of whom wished to live just as badly. If I am correct, were we to strip that support from him now …'

'What, you reckon he'd keel over dead? Well, *good*,' I responded savagely, which made him blink. 'Angela's death is the truth *I've* had to deal with every sodding day! If Michael can't manage the same, what good is he?'

'A great deal to me at present.'

Sure. At least, until you plumb his brain dry. 'Dr Cormac, I don't *want* these answers you're assuming he's brought back. I don't want any of it!'

'And yet, Mr Formir will speak with you.'

'He'll flap his gums, but we haven't seen a great deal of sodding sense out of him so far. What makes you so sure he'll spill what you want?'

A different approach occurred, and a sinking feeling. I ought to have guessed Ashley Cormac would never accept meek disappointment. 'Dr Cormac, what have you done?'

'While you were resting, I merely employed what Mr Formir has given us. Played to his neurosis. At any rate, we were already nothing but bit-players in his odyssey back to her. I have taken the opportunity to build you up in his mythos as a final gatekeeper, after a fashion. A test, to prove that following all he's endured, he remains worthy of returning to your sister.'

I gaped. Not an iota of shame in him. 'You prepped him to think I'm some kind of bouncer on his way to my sister? My *dead* sister?'

'Mr Formir is rapidly nearing his own end. What do his beliefs matter, so long as we get our result? Besides, the anticipation of reunion brings him comfort.'

'Comfort,' I scoffed.

'And then, there's that.' Dr Cormac had a quiet way of speaking, that compelled you closer to hear. 'Ms Hanberry, you've made your dislike of Mr Formir plain. The opportunity has finally arisen to preside over him, as judge. The chance to flay back the lies, to expose what he truly is. Don't tell me that is something you wouldn't relish. Even after so many years, and your sister no longer with us to appreciate it.'

The chance to rub proof of what I'd known, all along, in Angela's dead face. I guess the first step in achieving shameful, secret desires must lie in bringing yourself to own them.

As Cormac admitted me into the inner sanctum, I had to go nervously reminding myself that Michael was just a man. And not even much of *that*.

The way fixations were revolving around him, it was easy to lose your grip on it. Even his Spartan room was figuratively the beating heart of GATE. Everything leaned in with hushed breath, waiting to hear what he'd have to say.

Only a man. Hold on to that. *Not* a hero, or some unimaginable corruption from Outside, poised to tear down all humanity'd managed to salvage since the Disaster … I reigned in my hysteric imagination firmly.

Best not wander down that path. Especially seeing as once upon a time, Michael sodding Formir *had* done all in his power to destroy everything good in my life. Might as well've yanked down his strides and taken a big solid dump over all of it. At least with Angela gone, he couldn't hurt me anymore. Sour consolation at best. Not to be dwelt on, lest I stuff one of those pillows over his twisted little face.

I hadn't even decided yet if I intended to play the odd cameo Cormac had written for me. Hoping not to have to commit either way.

'Michael?'

Well, this wasn't going so great. I already sounded jack of him. My nose reported in. *Apples fermenting in neglected vats. Feathery with scum. Down in the dark, forgotten …* I flinched in revulsion.

The hairless back of Michael's head and neck wore the vivid, spongy texture of a strawberry's flesh. Grated raw from continual rubbing against the stiff pillows as he shook his head. Frail transparent eyelids clenched, in a futile effort to shut the whole world out. Stop it all happening. Only bestial whines spurted through the gaps in those so-white teeth.

Ah.

'Dr Cormac,' I called to the room at large. 'I really think you ought to turn the light out. Looks like it's hurting his eyes.'

Of course, they would have drawn that conclusion days ago. Along with dozens more beyond my paltry reach, these oh-so clever science types.

They hardly needed some jerk yanked in off the street to point out which end of the patient to wipe.

Which led on to the likelihood, however far-fetched, that Cormac had orchestrated this whole vignette. To force a connection between Michael and I. *Shudder to think it!* The long bow did seem to be the doctor's raison d'etre—he'd even served up the experience of my own fitful snooze in an overbright room, just in case I was too thick to connect the dots unaided.

So much effort. Merely to gift me a little efficacy in the Outerman's eyes. And probably in my own as well, were I being perfectly honest. Priming me to get all puffed up and intolerable with righteousness, get me assuming folk actually *needed* my opinion. Somewhat along the lines of, *Lawkes, couldn't these awful science-y types see what they was doin' to the widdle old Outerman?*

Dr Cormac was that willing to put Michael through further misery, merely to get a foot in the door. *My* foot. I'd harboured sensible little doubt that he wasn't a nice person. Now my suspicion progressed to peering nervously off the lip into the horrific abyss of how far Dr Cormac'd be willing to go.

If they gave enough of a hoot, folk never ought to hesitate laying their coin on the table, but Cormac here was another breed altogether. Eager and willing to spend us all, empty everyone's pockets. He'd fling the whole world down the hole of his ambition, if it promised some answers. Beneath the man's stiff suit and sober tie burned a raging fanatic, and if I wanted to find my way out of this trap then Dr Cormac would have to be bargained with very, very carefully.

There was a long thinking pause, while I stood waiting, and Michael whined behind his teeth like a sick dog. No doubt both looking every bit as stupid as I felt; I could stand around like an idiot on my own time.

The wait was so long I began to wonder: perhaps they weren't going to "listen to me" after all. Had my suspicion spun too tall a tale?

Then we were plunged into vindicating, depressing darkness.

I hate being right all the time.

I rather fancied sitting down. On the floor, it'd have to be, due to the scarcity of chairs, so I remained on my feet. I didn't want to settle in and belong here, not to any part of it. Instead I stood and waited some more, and could feel Michael staring. His wet eyes gleamed in the dark. And that choking fermentation odour welled to fill the room. *Apples and metallic water. Horrible secret mould, in the dark. And apples. Andapplesandapplesandapplesand.* The air curdling with it, until it became nigh unbreathable, and I shuddered trying to take it in.

There's good reason why folk don't fancy the dark … unless it be those activities where they'd prefer to close their eyes to the truth of one another. Of course Michael preferred the absence of light, to hide and sprout in, like some loathsome fungus. It was dark Outside, wasn't it? And Outside was all his existence'd been about for … oh, how many years?

I couldn't even come up with the number. My head spun too giddily, from the bout of groggy unsatisfying sleep. I'd never been good with dates, anyhow. The days were too alike. Got into the habit of counting forward or back from Angela's funeral as a valid workaround.

I waited. Eventually out of the ominous dark and suffocating stench Michael spoke. Just as Cormac'd set him up to do.

'You're here with that prick, Ash.' He coughed dryly. 'Why am I not surprised?'

'I certainly didn't volunteer.'

'Here with Ash. Angie's sister, Angie's sister.'

As nauseating as it sounded, Michael seemed to be tasting the words. Slipping them out staccato, between gasping breaths, like an obscene phone call.

'Angie's sister, huh? I'd barely remembered you existed.'

*Told you so*, I beamed furiously at Cormac through the wall, who'd squandered so much of my time on top of his own. But Michael wasn't finished. It appeared his old compulsion to rule every stage was a long way from being humbled.

'I don't recall a lot of things, though,' he continued dreamily. 'Not so well. But I sure remember Ash. Shit help us if we're in his clutches.'

"Ash" again. Dr Cormac really didn't strike me as your nickname kind of guy. I'd've had him pegged toward a compulsive "Mister." With eternal regrets for missing out on the military "Sir."

'He's got ears in the room,' I felt compelled to caution. Fair play, and all that.

'Oh, I'll just fucking bet. That's because good ol' Ash is such a bastard of a driven, sociopathic shit that he just can't help himself. Hey, I'll bet he still harps on about all those historical crazies, like they make a shit of a difference. And now … now he's desperate t' know if they were right all along, t' be so afraid. Huh? Have I got it? He wants that from me?'

Still every bit the same smug, opinionated asshat, then. Michael had always lauded himself as a maestro of humanity. Just another gimmick he peddled in the mystique of the cult of Michael. And anyone who dared raise dissent was just, "too blind to get it," the perfect argument.

He was an embarrassment.

'I really don't know Dr Cormac that well, to tell you the truth.' Nor wish to. 'He wants me to ask you what went wrong with the Capsule.'

'So he sends Angie's sister in t' petition for it. You're the one who's going t' make the final call, huh? I guess so. Before she takes the final step back int' my arms, Angie wants certainty. Of course she does. She was always testing me, you see. Always digging at things. Checking t' see if I was still "on track."'

A sob, quickly stifled. 'The hoops I've leaped through for that woman! Well, I'm more on Angie's track now than I've ever been. I can see exactly where it goes. Huh. You reckon you're going t' convince her otherwise. *You*. How much better would our lives been without *you*, if Angie was an only child, too? It would've been a dream. Both of us cast adrift as adults, with only each other t' rely on.'

Michael grimaced. 'You don't know it, but I've been real forbearing. If our situations were reversed, I reckon my fierce Angie would've offed you, and sunk the evidence in the backyard. Basked happily ever after, the undisputed queen of the heap. But you're her sister, and she always listened t' you. Shit knows why!'

'Because *I* always told her the truth!'

'Ah, yes. The hopeless sister, and your precious "truth". How we used t' chuckle over that one. This thing you call truth has never been more than the sourness of your own curdled jealousy. *You*, who always put Angie in such a state. "What am I going t' do with her?" she'd cry. You who've always gone through life with a shitting *fist* instead of a heart, now *you're* here t' keep me from Angie?'

A contemptuous laugh, scratchy and low, while I reeled and cast about desperately for anything to hit him back with.

'Angie's heart burns so bright I could feel it calling me home, even from Outside. So good shitting luck keeping me from her. Have your little trial.'

'I don't want your pathetic story,' I snarled. 'Just like I never needed to find out about … what was it you called those women? Your "side projects." I just want to leave you here to rot in this bed, and go back to my life!'

'Your life, ha! You, and all you know about *living*. This, here, is your ordinary, painfully nothing existence, Angie's sister. These, cowering in the corners of the room are your dreams, without wings, that crawl along blindly in the muck.'

Did I hear something slithering behind me in the dark? Suddenly I was pebbled in gooseflesh and wanted out, just out. 'You're crazy, Michael, you know that? You've actually gone off the deep end.'

'Don't you go telling my Angie anything of the sort!' Agitated, he struggled, and the dry linen rustled, but the mysterious tucker-in of sheets had done too firm a job. Restraint without apparent restraints, really clever.

Somehow the childish indignity of it calmed me right down. I didn't need to waste effort lashing out at this pompous git. And I *certainly* hadn't forgotten who else was listening in: Charlie the Screw, here to save everyone's day. Weighing my words against his own standard.

Michael was still carrying on, becoming increasingly distressed as though he could sense my warming humour. '… I can prove, I can *prove* I'm not crazy! Angie just needs t' understand how it happened! Whatever stirs around inside your brainpan doesn't matter, it doesn't matter at all, madness is denoted by *action*!'

Ah. Another Michael-ism. These ridiculously pat catchphrases he cooked up to justify himself, put his own spin on things. The first time I'd heard Angela brightly parroting one, I'd had to choke back the vomit.

'On the Capsule we did as best we could, under a shit set of circumstances! One moment all was dandy, and the next: all flashing red lights and alarms screaming everywhere. I'll bet just as many shorts filled at Threshold as on board—the great fucking Outside wasn't so great anymore, was it?'

I tried to get a word in edgeways. 'After the Disaster …'

'Hah, "Disaster," is it? I'll bet it made the world sit up and take notice, too. Nothing the social animal loves more than a good tragedy.'

You stupid creep, I wanted to hiss venomously. *The sodding world fell apart! And then the Screws crowned themselves arsewipe commanders of piecing it all back together, any way they saw fit!* But I had to stay mindful of Charles, and his anxious urge to help. If I didn't cherry-pick my words, he'd be liable to help me right out of my own skin.

As Michael rambled on, I almost wished Cormac would let Charlie in here. See how much the Outerman enjoyed the new world.

'Nobody'd ever forget the launch. That was an awesome day. Everything'd been going so well at first, went off like a dream.' Michael's wizened face creased fondly. I was beginning to make out more of the room around us, although I resolutely refused to glance into the darkest corners, where I couldn't have heard that rustling sound. Just in case.

'It was one butt-ugly bitch, our Capsule. Turning on its long axis like a pig on a spit. And when I slept in those early days, *if* I slept, I always dreamed of the great vast shadow the Capsule cast on the Outside of the Shell.

'I dreamed it sprouted these long, trembling sticklike arms, too many joints, joints bending and crunching everywhere. And it reached out t' embrace me. Around and around and around, wrapped in those too-long arms, the cracking joints popping and snapping all over me.

'Which was odd, because in reality it didn't *have* a shadow. I often glanced nervously out the window t' check, and double-check, because I thought I saw one quivering from the corner of my eye. But nope, no dice. Not nearly enough light Outside for shadows.

'Nothing t' be spooked by on board. Everything gleaming new, as much as dull grey *could* be made t' gleam. And we took turns beaming our proud smiles back t' the world.

'We'd done it! Achieved *everything* that sour shit Ash made us out t' be: pioneers of the future. We felt it, we really did. We were the elite! Out there, taking this huge step forward so that others could follow.'

What was he trying to do, win me over with awe? Was this the sort of crap that worked its spell on Angela? Well, sorry laddie but mere proximity to something wondrous does not make you wonderful, not by a long shot. And Michael could field sodding little merit of his own.

'What was it like Out there?'

'Oh.' His mood shifted again. Flighty bastard. 'Oh, no. You don't want t' go Outside. Don't you know *they're* Out there?'

'They? The crew?'

He became urgent. 'You have t' explain it t' Angie, it's … it's *different* Out there! Not like she imagined at all! Outside there's no … no *normality*. No morality. All that's left are the original realities, just like when you were a kid and they filled up the whole world. Fear. Suspicion. Rage.'

Sweat rolled off him, soaking yellowish through the sheet and outlining what was tucked in below so clearly I had to avert my eyes. I could smell it, like too-sweet juice left out in the heat, pouring from his pores to slicken the room.

'Michael, what are you frightened of?'

'Something horrible,' he moaned. 'Who knows what they really are?'

He peered up at me, and sweat wasn't the only thing streaking his collapsed cheeks. 'Tell Angie I'm sorry. I'm so sorry; I was *scared*. I just wanted t' come home t' her, but … but the others would've let them *in*! *They couldn't come in!* I had t' do something, *anything*!

'But ah, shit, that sound, the sound of them *screaming* so hard …'

He would have covered his face if he could, hid despair's indecent nakedness. Instead, Michael's twig fingers twisted beneath the sheet like he wanted to tear it off.

I didn't know what to do. I didn't want to hear *this*. But there was no getting around it: I was standing there for Cormac's purposes, not my own.

'Tell me, Michael. Tell me what happened.'

He sniffled. 'I'd been hearing them in my sleep at first, and that was easy t' dismiss. Thankfully not voices, not like Angie said I would; that would've been the fucking end of me. No, what *I* heard was knocking. A tapping, that reverberated right through the Capsule's hull and int' my metal bunk. Every second or third night for a while. Soon enough it progressed t' every shitting time I dared put head t' pillow, even for a second. Tap, tap, tappity-tap. Jaunty, you know? Like a drunk friend at the door. But then growing impatient, the mood turning foul. The sort of drunk you'd call the police, rather than let them in.

'There wasn't any fucking rest for me. Wasn't even anyone I could tell. We mostly all avoided each other. I hoped it might be my imagination: too wound up, not enough sleep. But then I started hearing them in the shitting *walls*, and I sure as fuck wasn't asleep! So I did what I had t'.'

'What did you do?'

'I only wanted t' stop them getting in,' he whined, ducking his head. 'If I stopped it, maybe the others might get t' live, too.'

'Everybody thought … We were *told* you'd all died in the Disaster.'

'We did die. That's what John said.'

Now my gooseflesh was back, and the hair lifted into prickles at the back of my neck. In the dark, the ludicrous could suddenly sound plausible and threatening.

'If he was right, we sure didn't know it at first. Trouble was, we were hobbled by humanity's one great failing, even as the Capsule exploded around us. One thing, t' push suffering beyond all that's endurable. We could still hope.'

**'FORMIR!' THE CAPTAIN** snapped, sick of his hysteria. 'Of all times, now is the one to start acting like a fucking professional.'

Then the lights went out.

The small control section had stopped shaking once liberated from the Capsule's main structure. It gave no vestibular indication that they were hurtling outward, fatally untethered, because Outside was a fuck like that. But the alarms screamed in fear. Different pitches of alarm, all wailing their panic like tortured cats. The dark space was filling with smoke.

'Circuitry fire!' Sal sang out over the racket. Even as she reported, her hands were shooting out across the control panel. Sal was motherfucking *on* it. She'd drilled exhaustively for disasters, even run the board blindfolded in the middle of a firing range. She'd trained at taming emergencies with the whip of her will for her entire *life*.

But so many of the myriad switches were dead in her hands.

No real information was rolling in yet, fire and all. Nobody knew how bad it was. But you could feel the building panic crackle in the air.

'Status!' the Captain demanded, her voice a foghorn booming across it all. Even if it could be ignored, you did so at your own peril. 'Fuck the lot of you fucking amateurs if you can't even give me our status!'

'The fire's contained!' Sal barked back, working feverishly to produce something fresher than this first wonder.

'There's been a major explosion …' John Porliet, never a big shouter at the best of times and in poor company here, became audible as, one by one, Sal gagged the alarms. 'Our section is sealed, but I'm seeing minor breaches. This is a disaster. We've got to get positive pressure!'

The last alarm wailed itself away. Their ears rang hollowly in the silence.

'What happened?' He sounded bewildered.

'This is Captain Sarah Orchid!' Her beacon of a voice rang out, stirring the smoke. The Captain wasn't about to entertain a single second of frightened speculation. Not until they established the hard and fast, such as where the fuck they were at. 'Who's here? Names!'

'Sal Shepparton.' Always the quickest off the mark. The star pupil.

'Paul Jonas.'

'You're shitting me. Who dragged your ass up here?'

'Children! If you don't mind, I'd like to move on with the day while I still have my fucking youth.'

'Michael Formir.' He coughed wretchedly in the rancid smoke.

'Jeshu Miller.'

'Beth Hanrekson.'

'Batheba Schult.'

'John Porliet.'

Silence. And the control watch was missing one.

'Jen?' Jeshu called anxiously, already fearing the worst. He was numbly, and rather forlornly wondering, *Who'll play secret snap with me now?* Even though the Captain had banned the ridiculous card game, 'cause they got sauced and went at it violently for hours, until their hands were too swollen for work. 'Jenny, answer me!'

The others could hear him stumble across the darkened space to her station.

'Jen!'

There was a sharp crack, like lightening.

A painful flash of blue-white light stabbed everyone's dark adapting eyes. In that quick instant both Jenny and Jeshu were etched in a brilliance so intense, it was like a stark hole cut out of reality. You couldn't look away. Even if you wanted to.

Jenny was already dead, slumped over her console. Jeshu gripping her shoulders where he'd intended to shake and scold her for frightening him so badly.

The man's slight body curved back from that point of contact, gripped by an intense shock that stretched his rapidly cooking muscles against their inclination to contract.

Michael found his smarting eyes focussing, not on the burning tableau, but on the shattered fragments of Jen's favourite mug still rocking to and fro on the floor at the couple's feet. She'd bring the fucking roof down if she caught you drinking from it—sometimes they'd hide it out of boredom, take hostage pictures. Always got her going. The chunky pink ceramic was bled of its colour by the unnatural light, and you could still make out the bold black lettering that asked ARE WE HAVING FUN YET? Amazing, how the brain could do that. Put the story together from pieces. The sweet-bitter smell thickened like a blanket.

Then it was dark again, everyone blinded anew by the intensity of the flash. Clamour erupted.

'Stay back!' the Captain bellowed, striving to wrest control of six terrified people, turn them back into useful units. 'They're caught in a current, don't touch them!'

'Jeshu ..!'

'If you put your hands on him, the only thing you'll do is fucking fry! Stay where you are!'

'She must've been zapped by her own equipment during the explosion,' Sal proposed quietly, the only one to sound unruffled. When technology turns on you, what can you do, right? Like she was a fucking robot or something, but that was just Sal being Sal. 'So does anyone know what happened? Did we hit something?'

Contemptuous snorts shared by all.

'"Hit something." Ain't supposed to be *dick* out here. Not so far as anyone with half a brain in their head knows.'

Michael turned away so none caught his appalled face. Nothing lurked Outside, so far as anyone *rational* thought. Or wondered, or schemed to find out.

If there were warnings to be had, now was the time to spread them around. But, *don't tell anyone*. What an idea for his sweet bride-to-be to have lodged in his cranium, before packing his shit and marching him Out here.

Never to tell. Safer that way. Credulous legend had it that *they* knew when you spoke about them. Or even when you thought it that bit too hard, while desperately trying not to. Drawn to you slavering irresistibly. Whoever the fuck "they" were.

*So, what, your voices, they can hear me? Like, right now?* he'd joked, severely unnerved by her recital and trying not to let on. Angie only fancied the big strong lads; she'd that hard unforgiving spark in her eye. The ballbusters, the alphas. Only to be transfixed by her stern gaze, shrivelling within his skin like a chastised boy. Nope, none of this was at all a shitting well laughing matter. What she'd said next had put the horrors up him right good. Following their date, he'd gone straight home to throw up and wish he'd never been born.

*Exactly like now. If you want to stay safe from them, keep your nice normal life, be sure to do as I say, honey. 'Cause they can hear you right now, and always if they choose to. Never, ever forget. But never tell, either.*

Most likely it was an intended demonstration of control. Angie never loved him better than when she set him a real fucking curly one, and he exceeded all expectation.

Besides, if it were so incredibly dangerous to spread the warning, then why would she have spilled the beans to *him* about it in the first place?

*Oh, because you're so very brave, my sweet Michael. Better than the others, any of those people. Because you can find out for sure, honey. Out there. Don't you dare disappoint me.*

Because she needed someone.

Times like now, when he was terrified enough to piss his shorts, Michael could practically *hear* Angie whispering her sweet nothings in his ear.

Nothings, that sounded awfully like scratchings and tapping against his skull. Her secret song. Tugging his hair for emphasis, until the roots were bloody.

Michael kept his fucking mouth shut. Never let you down, Angie. You'll see.


'Michael?' I asked quietly, because he'd stopped talking and was just reclining weakly against the pillows. Looking down at the twisted bumps his spider-hands made beneath the sheets.

His shoulders shuddered, and I realised he was weeping.

But years of watching others cry, mostly at the drop of a hat to garner sympathy, had hardened me into an awkward impatience to have to see the Outerman doing it now.

'Keep talking, Michael.'

'Captain Orchid was dead set on keeping things together.' He laughed hollowly through the pathetic sniffles. 'One functioning unit. That's how she harped on, we had t' work together as a unit, and not seven dickheads all trying t' save our own skins.'

He was quiet again, engrossed with his misery. It struck me how strange it was, to be loitering here in the dark, listening to this dickhead whom I hardly knew, and barely tolerated.

'Just talk. Tell me what she had you doing.'

'We checked the supplies, of course. The Captain had a bee up her ass about food.

'So many of the compressed caloric cubes, we weren't looking t' starve anytime soon. But right after she slapped Jen and Jeshu's corpses in the freezer, she came back with seven plastic containers. The type you stick leftovers in, so they can sit forgotten in the fridge for months and stink the place out.

'Right from the start, we were all t' feed our wastes back int' the food cycle, and that was an *order*. The Captain was all about how we had some *duty* t' stay ticking, as long as possible. Keep trying.'

My initial cynicism drawled *sodding why?*, but was instantly put down by the shuddering counter-reaction. Everyone knew why, of course they did. Everybody wants to live. The alternative was nothing, gone forever. Almost like you'd never been. Faced with that yawing emptiness, giving up was practically unheard of. Why sprint to annihilation? Every man, woman and child dawdled, and dragged their feet for each bare second to be gained.

I was turning to leave, but Michael wasn't quite done. An unsettling fey gleam lit his eyes. His croak was so low, I didn't know if the microphones'd pick it up.

'Tell Angie, you hear? Tell her she was wrong about them. They weren't like anything she thought. I heard them! At night … Only there was no day, so it was always night, wasn't it. Always dim, and hard t' think clearly, with no promise of dawn.'

A high frustrated whine, like a mongrel pushed back from its food while the owners laughed. Human beings shouldn't be reduced to this. I felt we were going in pointless circles, Michael getting himself more worked up each time.

'Tapping,' he muttered. 'Always tapping on the hull.' Something behind his staring eyes quickened. Like the scuttling shadows of thoughts I could almost see. 'They were smart about it, too. Only tapped when I was there; and not even I picked them up unless I put an ear t' the wall. Couldn't be caught doing that. Cunning shits. They *knew* if even one other person heard them ...'

'Who?' Abandoning caution, I knelt right down by his face. His roving, burnt-out eyes. '*Who are they, Michael?*'

The scream had already begun way down in his chest with that reedy whine.

And now it came boiling out. Michael screamed his horror straight into my face, and I recoiled as though scalded, tripping and falling on my tailbone. And still that scream came on and on. His mouth a yawing cavern, fringed by jutting teeth.

'Michael, for crapssake!'

Before I could get off my big ass, the guard burst in, syringe in hand. So he wasn't just there for looks after all. Light entered the room with him, sweeping away the illusion of a private audience.

Surely huge sodding needles fell in the same category as not running with scissors? Luckily, the guard didn't slip. Merely hastened to pump the shrieking Outerman full of sweet dreams. After a bit, the racket tailed off. You had to ask yourself how many drugs they were packing into that shrivelled little form like preservative through lunchmeat. Wasn't like he was ever going to walk free, anyhow: might be more efficient to plumb him straight into a machine. They could have one button for talk, and another for when they wanted him to shut up.

The guard then made it his business to come over and help me to my feet, which was so kind I blushed. I'd already fallen into the lazy trap of dismissing those around me as cardboard cut-outs; although to be fair, all the suits and uniforms made them look quite similar. I wondered what he thought of all this, and wished I wasn't too shy to ask. Perhaps life here at GATE was already so weird, this fell into the camp of ordinary, and he looked on my shock and confusion with the contempt of an old hand.

Cormac, of course, stood waiting in the anteroom.

Despite all this cutting edge at his disposal I couldn't shake the suspicion he'd been listening eagerly at the door. What would the doctor stoop to next: peeping through the keyhole? At least gussying his fixation up in technology made the practice seem less deviant.

Sadly, Charlie-boy was hanging out right there with him. All my pleading eyes at Cormac to be spared won me absolutely bubkus.

'Catherine, I really must speak with you urgently.' Charles commandeered my elbow, which seemed the world's favoured method of steering me about these days. 'It's a topic we can chew over breakfast. I'm sure you're every bit as famished as I am.'

My heart leaped with joy. I'm pretty sure I caught both men cracking a smile, which immediately set me back to scowling. That's right, boys. Fatguts here likes her grub, shouldn't come as a shock.

Wait—breakfast?

I'd been here all day *and* all night?

This was the moment I seriously entertained the prospect of being locked up forever and a day. Dr Cormac might *never* let me go. I almost clutched at Charlie as he drew me from the room—that was, until I recalled *who* my companion was. Talk about a rock and a hard place! Enemies on all sides. And my only leverage, to serve as Cormac's mouthpiece, wasn't a real power at all.

Although, to put it like that, *eew*.

Our destination brought old, long-interred memories tumbling back. Of my school cafeteria. My classes had been packed with deadbeats and faux-hippies, rather than these bustling crowds in suits; but the smells, the jostling atmosphere, and most likely the hygiene were one and the same. I boggled around, wide-eyed. This was about as far from Cormac's "contact with as few as possible" as you could get.

My gut groaned forlornly at the festive scent of raisin toast. It was only once we stood halfway along the line that I recalled my de-accessorised state in a panic.

So used to lugging my handbag everywhere, I'd been fooled by its fossilised imprint beneath my arm, the elbow crooked out permanently like a wing.

Red with humiliation, I began a stumbling explanation that if we could track down who'd taken my bag, I'd a couple of twenties in my wallet. Charles waved off my offer, with the pointed contempt that's modern man's rebuttal to feminism.

A tray each, and then he took off. Skilfully weaving through the tumult to a newly cleared table with the assurance of a birddog. There, he waited courteously for me to bump and grind my way through the crowd, in the sort of manoeuvre rarely seen outside the clubs Michael'd roasted his card in, thoroughly enough to follow the credit-stench many years later.

Charlie even held the chair out for me. Definitely anti new-woman all the way. I complied awkwardly with the outdated ritual, leery of having him so close behind me. The Screw assumed his own seat.

'There's no need to remain so wound up around me all the time, Catherine. I'm unlikely to bite.'

Buggered if he was getting in first. 'If there were ever someone to get tense about, I'd say Michael would be it. I was very much hoping you might tell me all you know about what happened to him.'

'Your toast is getting cold,' Charlie rebuked mildly over his styrofoam cup. I refused to be called on small talk and social niceties by a man who cross-wired brains for a living. As badly as I wanted it, it was only once he started talking that I picked up my toast and bit into it. Immediately my tastebuds had the mother of all orgasms.

'I'll share what I know. The piece of the Capsule Michael returned to us in was part of the control segment, which is likely why he survived. According to my sources it was intended to be somewhat independent from the main structure, and could be sealed at need.'

'Why would it need to be sealed?'

Charlie sipped his tea. Some acid-green concoction, that'd no doubt scour your insides clean as a whistle.

'I apologise. With all that's happening, I've a tendency to lose sight of how little detail was released to the public back then. How little *anyone* understands, really. Even now.'

He peered at me narrowly, as though I'd missed some secret cue to plunge into hysterics. 'Are you quite positive this is something you want inside your head?'

Better it than you, mate. 'Not even slightly. But I seem stuck in this situation for now. Under the circumstances, it might be a sodding good idea to find out everything I can.'

'You're a very pragmatic woman,' he noted approvingly. Ooh, good, pragmatism! That'd bring the men hammering down my door! 'Alright, but I'd like you to red-flag me should you become too uncomfortable to continue.'

I nearly suggested we should establish a safe word, too, like blancmange, and then bit my tongue.

Charlie settled himself. 'Outside the Shell, it is very dark – obviously, with no Shell to give us its glow. There are some little points of scattered gleaming. A very chilly light, though, very disheartening, and they appear way off in the distance regardless of how close you get. They don't shed much illumination to speak of. Theories, as you can imagine, have ranged through every nutbaggery; from holes in reality, to entire other Shells with their own worlds tucked inside.'

'That's what we were watching in the video!'

'Correct. And you saw the result for yourself, the fellow's hand passed right through it. They aren't really there at all. Saddening, but perhaps not surprising to find there's nothing to them.'

I chewed and listened, entranced. I think I'd forgotten to breathe.

'The air is strange. That's the main reason for the seal on the Capsule. It's neither warm, nor cold. Perfect skin temperature, which I find highly suspicious to say the least.

'In fact, the air seems to *adjust* to individual body temperature variations, like it's actively trying to nullify your ability to feel anything. A person with a raging fever would get no more sensation than one with a chill.'

'You sound like you've been there.'

Charlie smiled. 'Hardly. Not one of our specialists, whatever their qualification, ever managed to secure a place in Dr Cormac's grandiose exercise in ego. I don't exactly mourn that, now. Everything humanity will ever need is here, while Outside, Outside is *empty*. Telescopes and cameras and radio probes have turned up nothing. It's no place for us.

'Although ... I suppose I shouldn't say we've gained "nothing." The Capsule program *did* supply the final, ultimate motivator to turn away from the unwelcoming void. Our first ever exquisite images of the Shell from without. More lovely than you could ever imagine.'

I jumped superstitiously, to my own surprise, spilling my hot chocolate. I could only watch in horrified slow motion as the warm brown tide slid over the polished tabletop and straight into Charlie's lap.

Lunging instinctively at the mess with wads of serviette, I was bemused to find my fingers trembling uncontrollably. Shedding scraps of crumbling napkin everywhere. The Shell from Outside. Who could conceive of such a thing?

Had there been a shadow cast against it, all of jittering, crackling arms?

And now I became belatedly aware of shivering, and sweating. My body'd been trying to raise the alarm, *pushing some limits here, girl*, but old fat-head had been too enraptured to listen. Now I wanted to hide. Pull the comfort of the cafeteria's thick walls and enclosing ceiling around myself like a blanket.

Also, there were no two ways about it. With that big chocolaty stain, Charlie-boy looked like he'd loaded his pantaloons.

A dizzy, queasy feeling was doing its best to squirm up my oesophagus, and I clapped an aghast hand over my mouth, uncertain if we were about to hear a giggle or a big gassy burp spurt forth. What was wrong with me?

Charlie wisely moved the remainder of the drink beyond my reach. 'I *do* apologise, Catherine. It was quite ridiculous of me to have spoken so frankly. After all, Threshold Station tied up an entire *year* shuffling personnel to get a full deck who could stand even the *idea* of Outside. And the Capsule's crew … well, let's just say that the Outermen possessed a quality humanity's not likely to see again. Which, should you ask *me*, is all for the better.'

I could well believe some tasks took a special type of person. Ol' Charlie sat there composedly, with a huge humiliating stain soaking through his expensive slacks, like it wasn't anything.

'I am so *incredibly* sorry …' I started in.

'Don't be silly. I consider this entirely my own doing, lesson learned. Are you feeling steadier?'

And he was worried about me!

Probably concerned I might flip my wig, and start firing the condiments at him next. Not trusting ye olde voicebox I merely nodded, a trifle frightened my nerves had let things down so badly. You never appreciate what peace of mind you have, until things go disturbingly skewiff.

'Let's leave Outside for the present. I'll talk about the Capsule instead. Unless you think it best we stop?'

I shook my head emphatically.

'Are you sure? There's nothing to be gained by pushing yourself.'

He wouldn't be satisfied 'til I found my voice, so I scraped some together. 'Keep going.'

Charles rolled his shoulders, not quite a shrug. 'As I mentioned, the control section could be largely isolated from the Capsule's other segments.

'I believe the idea being that in event of emergency, the "brain" could survive and in due course bring the problem under control.'

I had a sudden, terrible thought while surreptitiously tipping my toast back and forth to let the coronary-strength yellow butter skim about its surface. My hands had to do something with the cup confiscated. 'That was the only section that could be sealed, right? There aren't any others Out there, are there? Floating off alone?'

I found it hard to meet Charlie's eye after anointing him, even on something so serious. Staring at his discoloured crotch was no better. The least awkward fascination I could manage was with my toast.

'No,' he answered decisively, working his fingers methodically over his skull to massage the data loose. 'With the way the Disaster took the Capsule apart, the chances of even the control section surviving were considered unlikely.

*Two* such flukes are out of the question.'

'But it *did* happen, once. Against all the odds.' The argument, I supposed, of a yutz who didn't really get how statistics worked.

Charles sighed as though he'd turned up the same criticism. Well, sucks to you, chumly. *Nobody* could pick at my faults like I could.

'The other sections … It was certainly never planned for the Capsule to break up like it did. Even if crew survived the blast in some other secured area, they'd have no access to fluid, food or air recycling. No way to put out fires, or re-route power.'

He'd no need to elaborate further. Such unfortunates would merely be screaming, suffocating bodies, spinning away through Outside. Waiting hopelessly for an end. Any end. As unnatural as it sounded, death in the explosion would've been something of a mercy by comparison.

'So how did the equipment in the control section keep Michael alive so long? Surely it can't have been designed for that?'

'Actually, it almost was. The Capsule was intended to go at least a decade on minimal maintenance and resupply, while the crew rotated, to see if it could manage. A test bed for habitats of the future. Of course, no-one knew the absolute parameters, that's what testing is all about. And I suppose with it reeled all the way out on that bloody long cable, they didn't want to go hauling it back in more times than was needful.'

'So you're saying it was well built.'

'Some aspects of the Capsule were exceptionally well engineered. As much as I frown on the rather naïve aim of the program, when it came to construction they weren't messing around, Michael Formir's return is evidence of that. There were … signs of further survivors of the Disaster, which gels with his wandering narrative. But we have no real evidence, no way of being sure what happened to them.'

Charlie leaned forward intently. 'Catherine, when you're alone in that room with Michael, has it occurred to you there's a very real chance he murdered his companions? He is obviously extremely lost in his own mind.'

Mentally ill might well equate to normality in light of what Michael'd been through.

'If everyone's going to discount what he says, why go to all this trouble of making him say it?' I burst out, exasperated. 'Michael seems to really believe he heard something Out there. Something worth being scared of.'

'Auditory hallucinations have never been uncommon in association with thoughts of Outside. They're the documented by-product of years of repression: a chronic, neurotic fear. History is positively squirming with famous examples of this illness.

'People who believed obsessively in the Outside beyond the Shell, and who claimed to hear voices. All of whom came to sticky ends, I'm afraid.

'Even in this day and age, those afflicted with voices give up everything: family, friends, work. Eventually even themselves. We've seen a dreadful increase in resulting homelessness since the Disaster; people simply unable to cope. Misaligned from reality. And it's all dictated by fear.'

He smiled. 'Of course, *we* have the luxury of seeing things logically, a recourse the terrified mind knows little of. Rationally we *know* people can't possibly hear anything from Outside. It's just too far away. It's physics, and you can't argue with physics, can you?'

'But Michael was Out there! He's not speaking about being thousands of kilometres from danger, snug on the ground—we put him Outside! Right in the face of it. *Humanity* hung him Out there, and for what, to *find out*! And now nobody wants to listen!'

Did I really just yell at a Screw?

This was worse, far worse than any scenario my overheated imagination could crank out. A few nearby tables glanced over and shrugged; my tone was riled, but I'd been largely lost in the general chatter.

Instead of shooting my voluminous arse full of sedative, to be dragged off to an unmarked van, Charlie was grinning broadly with a satisfaction only dream-logic could explain.

'Finally, you're showing a little natural concern. And for someone you dearly dislike. Bravo Catherine! I was beginning to grow concerned. You seemed so profoundly disassociated from all those around you, with so *little* empathy. Anybody ought to find room for a few scratchings of pity, seeing what Michael has endured.'

'Endured?' A faint, strengthless echo was about the scope my brain could manage.

'Living conditions, if you can call them that, in the control segment were downright filthy and getting worse all the time. To be lost, like that, Out there with no hope of home ..'

Charlie finished off his gruesome tea with a final, decisive slurp. he'd yet to touch his food. It was that kind of story. 'Well, I've rattled on for a bit, here. I guess now it's time for you to share something.'

I made a helpless gesture. 'You've listened in on my "conversations" with him. What else is there?'

'Catherine, let me be honest with you. Dr Cormac dragging you in was the sort of desperate long shot you only read about in gaudy magazines. Once all sane official methods had failed, Dr Cormac found himself faced with either allowing us our access to the Outerman, or trying something this ridiculous and desperate. Right now, he is behaving much like a terminal patient. One who would rather fly all over the globe chasing charlatan treatments than make his peace with the inevitable.'

Screws were the inevitable, all right.

'Michael needs people properly trained in this sort of thing. He needs us.'

I was tellingly still. To call Screws "properly trained" was a gross insult to the profession whose mantle they'd assumed. Once upon a time shrinks had been thoroughly educated, rigorously monitored. They'd devoted themselves ethically to their charges. What we had now with the Screws was a bunch of ham fisted yokels, barging around with a lot of power and blinkered good intent.

'Dr Cormac is going to have to let us in eventually. His need to know is just too strong, and he's running out of time. I fear his last-dash hope that you'll secure him what he wants is grossly, grossly mistaken—and that's by no failing of yours.'

I glanced around the warm, noisy cafeteria. 'Nobody will be wearing their shocked face when I arse this up.'

'Catherine, this is a rather dangerous time. For you, for Michael. Even for the desperate doctor. I believe he is going to make an offer to take you somewhere, soon.

'I highly recommend you decline. This place is somewhere I won't be able to assist you. You'll be totally within his power.

'In fact, I cannot iterate this enough. Do not at any point imagine that Ashley Cormac, the GATE Corporation, or any of his people have your welfare in mind. If you forget to look out for yourself, nobody is going to do it for you. I'm afraid that life in general doesn't owe anyone anything, regardless of how well behaved you are. Whether you abide by the rules. And that's where I come in. It's my task to furnish people with the tools to look out for themselves, in any situation.'

Charlie stood, absently brushing at the chocolate stain, before dismissing it as utterly unimportant to his goals. 'In fact, I'm expecting the doctor along to make his underhand offer any moment. The choice is of course entirely yours. I won't, uh, "loom over you" or anything to influence your decision. And as I've made my opinion on the matter plain to that gentleman already, there's really no need for me to stay.'

My plate was bare, even of crumbs, reminiscent of the fridge back home. Despite pushing his own around, Charles hadn't eaten a thing.

'You sit yourself back down and eat your breakfast first!'

He looked a little taken aback, which was how I felt. It'd burst from me like a reflex. Such a painfully long time since I'd stood over Angela with arms crossed and forced her to finish her meal, but apparently some bikes you can just hop back on. Smirking a little, Charlie fished up his toast and bit the corner off.

Just in time for Dr Cormac to slide into his vacated seat. No chairs held out politely *there*.

Cormac fired a snide eyebrow at Charlie's departing back, clearly wondering with displeasure what in the name of arse *he* had to smile about.

I was beginning to tremble, which I'd always done following a bout of fight-or-flight.

A great, quivering jelly. I hadn't felt threatened while chatting with the Screw; oh no, he was far too good at his job for that. Only afterward, when it was all too late, and the repercussions of my blabbing mouth came home to roost.

I breathed measuredly, trying to bring panic to heel. Concentrated hard on my therapeutic rich person's beach. For a concept I'd cobbled together out of holiday brochures, that sweep of imaginary platinum sand could be amazingly soothing.

'Ms Hanberry, your presence here need not be by way of an endurance trial.'

I cleared my throat, not wanting to come across all wobbly. 'And here I understood I was to prise his saga out of Michael, or die trying. Don't tell me I had you all wrong.'

'Not quite the aspect I was referring to.'

'No?' Innocent as a babe, giving nothing away.

Cormac leaned close in classic conspirator's pose, mocking my caution. 'No. You need not be so guarded with me, Ms Hanberry. Credit it or not, but I hold those inept brain-squeezers in every molecule the same contempt as you do.'

My eyes flew to meet his amused gaze, and then dropped in utter confusion. I was in disarray, and didn't dare answer. *Nobody* was powerful enough to shoot their yap off like that. Not openly, in public, where anyone could catch wind of it!

As usual, it was as though Dr Cormac could hear my scurrying thoughts. 'The difference that yaws between us is that *I* am currently at my leisure to say so. I would like you to know such circumstances can alter. I could bring you beneath my wing, so to speak.'

The nurturing image of sheltering my bulk beneath Dr Cormac's scrawny limb was laughable, to say the least. What an odd bird he'd make.

'And the catch is ..?' I queried.

His thin lip curled upward in a not-smile, and I elaborated. 'Well, I doubt you'd make the offer unless there was some pretty big catch involved. Otherwise you'd have just off and done it already without needing *my* consent.'

'How little and low you think of me, Ms Hanberry.'

I waited. I had a warm, full stomach. I could wait forever.

'However, in this particular instance you'd be correct.' So urbane. I wanted to throttle him.

Instead I picked under my fingernails and glanced up coyly through my eyelashes, tilting my chin a little. According to the literature this creates a kind of big-eyed, infantile aspect; one that men were likely to respond to. A brave effort. In my case, I suspect overnighting had destroyed any illusion of charm I may once have had.

Dr Cormac was polite enough not to notice the attempt. Likely the first lesson taught at Snotty Gentleman's Academy. 'At the earliest possible juncture, I propose to relocate both Mr Formir and yourself to Threshold Station.'

Ah. I felt pale. Do you get fair warning prior to a faint, or does it simply drop like a hammer from the sky?

'I anticipate, by the attempt, to extend Mr Formir's remaining life. Also, it is the best method for placing you both entirely above Charles' jurisdiction. His ideology takes no root up there. Ms Hanberry, Threshold is the last remaining place where one may still think and act freely. Speak as you please. Might you by any chance harbour a craving for some manner of contraband? Up there, I can supply it, with nobody the wiser for your enjoyment.'

Just like that the craving hit me so hard I wobbled in my chair. It *had* to be psychosomatic.

Any physical dependency would've filtered from my poor watery bloodstream years ago. Nothing but devastation in its wake.

'Ah. There *is* something. I never mistake that gleam to an eye, the regret of what's been lost. Do tell.'

I cupped a hand around my mouth, terrified one of the jolly employees either side might hear. 'Coffee.'

'Pardon?'

'*Coffee.*' Scarcely louder. I cleared my throat.

Genuine humour lit Cormac's face, with a startlingly humanising effect. 'I see. When was the last time you indulged?'

I didn't even need to think.

'Well … the hardest job to get after the ban was as a waitress. Rich business folk and the like could still get coffee in the right cafes – I guess money's such a fast river, it'll swish right around any obstruction.

'Waiting tables at *those* joints was a real shitty job, of course. You had to give up sleep, in case they called you in anytime. The pay barely existed. And of course, fiscal immunity didn't apply to *staff*, so every now and then there'd be a raid, and somebody'd get hung out to dry. You spent every moment in terror of being next. While the rich clients treated it as a bit of fun.

'But. Sometimes a customer'd get up and leave a little spill in the saucer, or at the bottom of the cup. The ultimate gesture of lavish wealth, you know, to not even finish. En route to the kitchen if you were quick, you could nip 'round the corner and slurp it up without getting busted. The most successful staff had brown teeth, their own kind of status symbol. Had to fair drown themselves in perfume to mask the smell.'

'And that was the last time you enjoyed coffee? Another's leavings?'

'Oh, my no! I'd have given my left foot to be brave enough to work in a café!' I smiled. 'Angela did. She came home with the aroma in her hair, and would throw herself on the couch and describe how good it was. Listening to her was almost like the real thing.'

'Almost,' Cormac said dryly.

'You wouldn't even be *having* these problems if she were here instead of me. She'd sort Michael out, and Charlie. Angela … she always went on how she was dying to know more about Outside. Didn't care who heard it. I used to think that if you hadn't developed the Capsule program already, she was exactly the sort to do it herself.'

'It would be inaccurate to suppose myself the only one to reach for Outside,' he agreed. 'Should you desire anything so profoundly, you find that you *must* do something about it. I was unspeakably fortunate in having been born into the first era advanced enough to make it happen. History is littered with the impotent madmen who couldn't keep from wondering.

'In fact, Outside preys on many an ordinary mind, as well. Were you aware that during Threshold's construction, occupancy rates plummeted for the entire city below?' He shook his head in amazement. 'The *entire city*. Eventually the buildings filled back up again with a braver sort, but that is precisely the breed of self-limiting fear I'd like to see drummed out of mankind.'

'Only there isn't much that can be done about it, is there? It's a way of life now. You'd have an easier time uprooting humanity entirely.'

'Do you truly believe so? I'm not nearly so sure.' Cormac stroked his chin, appeared to come to a decision. Do or die. 'Ms Hanberry, I have spent these past years submerged in the belief that the Accident was no accident. I strongly suspect the Capsule may have been sabotaged. And who, I ask you, who did not wish humanity to inherit our destiny? Who would it have displeased to watch us progress and expand? I desire your assistance to confirm these suspicions.'

'Let's imagine I *do* go up to Threshold.' I seriously couldn't believe I was saying this. It was like my mouth was being run by an entirely different person. But *coffee*. My tastebuds had no inhibitions about that. 'I'd like to go home first, get some things. Oh, and call my boss.'

'I'm afraid I can allow neither. You must come as you stand, no conditions. I cannot possibly risk any leak of information before we're adequately prepared, however inadvertent on your part.'

Dr Cormac's hazel eyes had changed, somehow. A green element I'd not noticed before now blazed and I mentally flinched, repulsed. It was like he was *willing* me to submit. Which made stubborn resistance my knee-jerk reaction.

Freedom from the Screws was a powerful lure. Wasn't it all I'd ever wanted?

Yesss … only, I'd wanted to win it for myself, somehow. Not have it wrapped and handed to me with a ribbon. As a lasting victory, not a holiday. Whether it be on a beach or not, I'd very much dreamed of someday carving out my own little pocket of peace.

But seriously, how likely was *that* to happen? I'd no plan, no strategy. Only a vague, undifferentiated need to be out from under the eye. Someplace peaceful. Somewhere private. Surely any drone in my place ought to quickly snatch at whatever unlikely chance came within reach?

*Nope*, my rational, logical self asserted grimly. *Screw Cormac (haha). You're no hero, fatguts. You just trudge your double-barrelled behind back to your stoic little life cycle of work, home, work. Dodging the Screws' tender mercies. Leave Michael sodding Formir and his living nightmare to be carved and served up to them.*

But Dr Ashley Cormac already knew what my answer would be. He smiled his aloof, superior smile. And there was no point even opening my mouth.

# OUTERMEN

## Six

### They Can Take That From You

I GOT MY CHANCE to blow chunks in their big fancy car after all.

I certainly couldn't be permitted to traipse alone and shivering down the crackling gravel of the front drive, with its dusting of frost.

What if my nerve broke, and I bolted for the hills? Someone'd definitely be fired. As it turned out, my escort was the very same brace of suits who'd levered me from my nice, safe life in the first place. Tricky to tell in the low light, but we all still seemed to be in exactly the same rumpled clothes. It'd been a rough week all around.

It wasn't until I stepped out of GATE's drear lobby and my heart sank, breath clouding in the crisp nighttime air, that I realised how desperately I craved the day. Warm light, raining down from the Shell. So bright you can close your eyes and turn your face up and feel yourself dissolving away. The need was like a bad itch that got under your skin. Even during the drudgery of my job a little natural illumination managed to bounce through the cubicle farm and find me.

GATE's sealed, secretive building was a nightmare. No wonder Cormac was such a butthead, spending his days encysted in such bland corporate surrounds.

I sucked in fresh cold air to contrast both stifling GATE, and the threatening confines of the car where it waited at the end of the drive. My personal trial, thrumming engine sending up plumes of exhaust. The dome light beckoning me in from the night. I suppose this was the sort of neighbourhood where you could leave your car running. Nobody about to steal it.

Lucky me, I got to travel up to Threshold in the dark and sodding cold to minimise any chance of the curious public noticing. Dr Cormac wasn't about to risk them sparking up with dangerous questions, but I thought he was exaggerating. More likely, they'd pack their bags with a whimper and scurry off to safer pastures, leave the house and everything to the bank.

'I don't envy you,' Shorty piped up at my elbow, somewhat unexpectedly.

Mentally I'd progressed to dubbing the pair Tall Suit and Shorty. Not that one was particularly short, nor his companion especially tall; but I felt I'd missed the social point where I could just ask for their names.

Tall Suit gave Shorty a glance of pure poison. It wasn't done to fraternise with the captive, weren't they in enough strife? Shorty just rolled his eyes humorously. A fellow without much to lose. I wasn't sure if I admired that, or found it the silliest thing I'd ever seen.

Scratch that. On second thought, I'd witnessed way too much stupidity for mere fearlessness to top the charts.

'What do you mean?' A current of healthy paranoia coursed through me. Had they seen my life? Really, in terms of the unenviable you could take your pick.

'Going up to Threshold. And saddled with that last Outerman, too; not a thing to envy there. That guy's an ass no amount of wiping'll save.'

'Tell me about it. My sister almost married him.'

Shorty grimaced. 'No accounting for taste, that's for sure. But … are you positive you want to go up there?'

I looked ahead to the car. 'It's a bit sodding late for second thoughts,' I said bitterly.

Shorty scratched thoughtfully behind one ear. 'It's never too late, though. Not really. Circumstance is something we invent moment to moment.'

A surprisingly philosophical bent. I blamed the late hour: nighttime feels more private, it brings out the bad poet in everyone.

'What about once you're dead?' I challenged.

He squinted at me critically. On my other side, staring off into space, Tall Suit seemed to be pretending none of this was happening. 'Are you?'

I wrinkled my nose. 'I'm starting to smell it, without a shower for so long.'

'There you go, you wouldn't be able to complain. Just forget the dead. Concentrate on things not being too late for *you*.'

It was all so convenient for him, handing out good advice like candy. As well ask me to chop my own arm off and mail it to the Screws.

I lowered my eyes to the gravel and switched topics. 'Have either of you guys been up there before? To Threshold?'

'I have,' Tall Suit supplied. It seemed our exchange was too aggravating to be blanked out any longer. 'Back in the day. And I don't envy you none, either.'

'You wouldn't care to venture an opinion as to why Dr Cormac didn't just shunt Michael and I straight there, if that was where he wanted us?'

Tall Suit rubbed thoughtfully behind an ear. It seemed to be a shared tic for these two. 'Well, Threshold Station's a big old derelict. Nobody's occupied her since the, uh …' he shared a glance with Shorty, '… the *Accident*. I wouldn't go putting any serious dosh on how safe she is anymore.'

'Jake, quit being a dick,' Shorty cut in. 'Can't you see she's already tense enough to jump outta her skin?'

Oh, good. Jake. Now I had one name out of two.

'It's nothing but the truth. Ms Catherine here looks like a lady who'd rather the truth. Was some government chat a while back about dismantling the station and having the old girl junked before bits started raining from the sky, but so far as I know no-one got 'round to it. Likely didn't want a song and dance in the papers reminding Sally-Joe public she's still up there.

'So, yeah. I can't in my wildest dreams imagine anyone voluntarily making that trek. With all that's happened, it's downright ghoulish Dr Cormac'd want to go back now.'

Shorty crossed his arms, really getting into this. 'See, Jake, there you go again. You always fall for the assumption that folk make considered, rational decisions. *I* reckon the good doctor's just reacting emotionally, same as any of us. Retreating with his prize to somewhere he used to feel safe.'

'Of all the shitholes to feel safe in,' Jake mumbled.

'Besides, since all this started, work's been going on up there. 'Round the clock, or as close to while keeping it secret.

'Last of the welders only came down yesterday and they looked shagged. So, I'm sure Ms Catherine wouldn't be going if it weren't safe enough.'

See, it was his use of the qualifier "enough" that made my guts roil. And this was before I even set foot in their sodding car.

Tall Jake held the rear door open for me with that kidnappery old world charm, but I hesitated. Squirming a little.

'Uh … say, guys. What are my chances of getting a window open on this ride? Cars make me kind of motion sick.'

'I'm afraid the windows in the back don't open. They've all been sealed.'

For the second time that night my heart sank, more than enough to be broadcast pathetically on my sleeve.

'I'll do my best to drive gingerly, how's that? The sooner we start, the sooner we can get this over with.'

And to his credit, he did try. He really did. I tried my level best as well. I was however, simply doomed from the outset, like so many of my endeavours.

I breathed deeply, kept my gaze fixed as far distant as possible, in this confined space with its stupid tinted windows. But the car's suspension bounced the chassis around corners in long, soft loops. Swinging like a cradle between acceleration and braking. That, and the suffocating upholstery reek were too much for me in the end.

And I hated chucking my guts. Not at all one of those pert misses who sticks a finger down after a big night, and bounces out of bed fresh as a daisy the next day. My throat convulsed, blatantly ignoring my brain's pained cry of *stop! stop!*

It was worse than horrid. I spat out runny strings, before the acid taste could make me upchuck again.

The mess I'd produced sort of slid back and forth across the slick upholstery as the car bounced, spreading itself around.

I'd a hard time keeping out of its way.

A big puke always brings back that time as a kid when I lost it in an elevator; much to the dismay of Angela, the other passengers, and especially the poor janitor lady who had to come deal with it. Again, the same horrendous, enclosed smell. The creeping shame. Luckily it was tricky for even the most revolted party, even Angela, to be cruel to a small child grizzling chunks of vomit and tears down her t-shirt. Her new birthday t-shirt, no less.

Angela and the janitor ended up having to scrub me in the building's restrooms. My sister boosting me with a grunt, to rinse my whole head in the sink. They took my top, while I stood shivering in the unfriendly lighting. Body-image sets in early, and I'd been vaguely ashamed of the janitor witnessing my pudgy pale torso. Even though she seemed a nice enough lady, telling me to dry my eyes now, what good did tears ever do anyone?

The t-shirt came up good as new and mostly dried under the hand dryer. Only a bit clinging and clammy when they tugged it over my head, a team now, working in concert. Angela had whispered something to the lady, a conspiracy I missed entirely under the roar of the dryer.

Finally, after the unscheduled detour, the janitor saw to it that we made it all the way to the skyscraper's observation deck. My fist clamped timidly to her unfamiliar hand.

The view was what Angela had brought me to see on my birthday. She'd secretly hoarded up our admission through months of sneaky fare-evasion—and now got to keep it, as the janitor with the woolly hair and vague, smiling blue eyes led us straight through the gate. Blue by default, as they had no other particular colour to be but you couldn't mistake the kindness.

This was where tourists once came to admire the city from above. Now all the telescopes were pointed, not down, but up.

Up there was the first ever man made instrument to be clamped to the Shell. The forerunner of Threshold, although of course nobody knew it yet. Both Angela and I had had to stand on boxes to see. Open mouthed, all my copious embarrassment washed away by awe, I'd pressed against the eyepiece hard enough to bruise. I looked like a raccoon the next day, and our social worker shrieked in dismay.

It didn't matter. Suddenly, it seemed, nothing mattered anymore. The people who put that *thing* in the sky could do anything.

The car finally, finally stopped. Here we go.

I'd warmed up out of the wind. As the door clunked open, the cold night air hit like a punch. Tall Jake stuck his head in. Unaccountably cheerful, like a dog that just loves going for rides, he got as far as, 'Did we all survive ..?' before the laden air rushing *out* hit him.

Blanching white to the gills, he stumbled a few steps back. Shorty now filled the portal, looking puzzled at his partner's horror. *What, did she explode in there?*

Kind of, actually. I shoved my way past. Sod manners. All I wanted, the only thing in the world, was to be out of that sodding car.

Jake was crumpled against the boot, lit cavernously by the crimson taillights like some horrorshow special. And *he* was throwing up. A neat steaming little puddle between his shoes.

I staggered some steps like a wobbly new fawn, then sat heavily on the car park asphalt with my head in my hands. Waiting for my traitorous gorge to get with the program now we'd stopped moving. Heart-stopping chill flowed up into me from the ground, like I sat in an invisible river of ice. But even with its exhaust flavour, I savoured shallow, careful breaths of the wonderfully crisp air.

'The smell of puke makes me puke,' Jake groaned.

*Yes, we got that, thank you.*

On rubbery legs he crept away from the puddle, before its stink could trigger a perpetual cycle.

'I am so sorry.' I ventured in a small voice. 'Look, when I eventually get my stuff back, I'm happy to pay toward getting the car cleaned.'

Shorty's expression couldn't decide to be revolted, amused or angry. As he vacillated between the three states, every time he hit *angry* I flinched. It was like playing the pokies in reverse. Surprisingly, when he settled it was on an old buddy of mine. *Resignation.*

'You know, Ms, I've got three toddlers at home. Count 'em, *three.* So I guess in the scheme of things, having to scrape up a little puke ain't so bad.'

'You think?' Tall Jake groaned.

'Man, once you've had a baby drop a big runny custard pie in your lap, things just don't disgust like they used to.'

'Can you *not!*'

I guess Tall Jake had bowed out of the joy of offspring, then.

Shorty's wry pragmatism didn't put a cork in my agonised apologies. I kept it up all the way across the massive car park, and was beginning to repeat myself by the time we reached our goal. We moved by romantic penlight, but pretty confidently with no fear of stumbling into any car other than our own. Nobody came here. This was where the Capsule had launched from. It was a wasteland chained off and forgotten.

Shivering, rubbing our arms, we stood inspecting the little gondola that would hoist me up the cable to Threshold. With the speck of light playing over it, it looked very much like an amusement park ride. All stained glass and candy-frosted metal. I wasn't feeling amused, though. You couldn't help but notice how all that pretty paintwork had been slapped back over weeping rust quite recently. The ground beneath it was stained indelibly brown.

And standing there in the dark, in the weed filled derelict lot, I couldn't resist mulling over the last thing I should have been considering. How nobody had used this equipment in years.

It'd been abandoned on the spot, like everything to do with Cormac's program. Almost the very moment the Disaster struck. Items released from appalled hands to fall to the ground; a perfect, frozen snapshot of an old, old moment everyone now wanted to forget.

It had been intended to rot away, the lot of it, the sundered dream. Perhaps a fresh coat of paint wouldn't be enough to hold it all together.

'I'm sorry you can't have the light on during the ascent. We've taken out the bulb.' Jake was graciously speaking to me again. Which made him a bigger man than I'd be, given the circumstances. 'A glimmer in the sky would probably ruin this whole covert thing we've got going, give rise to some nasty rumours.'

I couldn't argue with that. No matter how I wanted to.

He gave me a considering once-over, bit his lip, and then fished something out of his pocket. 'Here. I highly recommend taking one of these before you get in.'

Shorty crowded in and angled his penlight to see what Jake'd handed me. It was a ratting blister pack of little white capsules. Far too dark to make out the brand name. Well, this was quite a step up from taking sweets from strangers.

'What is it?' Although, really, could I be any worse off?

'A nice little taste of tranquillity. Lots of people used them going up to Threshold. I spent my time half-bent myself. Luckily I'd never gotten around to chucking the stuff out. It occurred to me this morning you might appreciate it.'

I blinked away sudden surprise, knowing my nose'd be deepening to a telling crimson nonetheless. Somebody had thought about me!

Tall Jake's thoughtfulness, and to a total stranger, was so incredibly kind I couldn't think what to say. Even the obvious "thank you" escaped me.

Of course, I also had that nice little titbit bouncing around my mind about the Threshold personnel stumbling about half off their tits on sedatives. Just what kind of operation was I getting myself into?

Fortunately, Jake didn't seem to expect thanks. The sort of guy who did things for their own sake.

'As Sammy said, *nothing* to envy 'bout going up there. I've been thinking about her a lot, lately. Threshold. Always dreaded going when my roster came up: they'd call out my name and I'd just sort of wince inside. A little clench, every time, my stomach going *oh no, not again*. Had rotten dreams about her, sometimes. About jumping off her into Outside.'

He scuffed his foot a little, embarrassed. 'P'raps that's why Outside's so feared. Not because of it, but us. Some destructive urge we all carry around to just fling ourselves Out there.'

Sodding midnight confessions. This was right up there with maudlin literature bums, drooling out their philosophies around a campfire.

Short—no, *Sammy* clapped me on the shoulder, which was a bit of an odd gesture to use on a lady. It felt rather bloke-ish, but I had to admit warmly inclusive at the same time. 'Now your gut's void, better stick with just one pill for the time being. Otherwise, once you make it to Threshold they'll be pouring you out.'

You know what else I hate? And yes, I know, it's a long tiresome litany. I hate dry swallowing chalky tablets. But with Tall Jake and Sammy watching I managed to choke one down.

'Take care,' was the last missive from my suits as the gondola's heavy iron door groaned closed. A hiss of air, sealing me in. And it wasn't so bad at first. Warm. I'd begun to shiver anew in the night air, and only partly from nerves.

Old cogs groaned against inertia, against time. I felt them slip, and then bite in and shoulder the load. There was a sense of hidden power; gargantuan clockwork and pistons, papered over by the thin pretty veneer.

With a sudden alarming jerk that had me clutching the seat and nearly peeing my pants, the gondola left the ground and began its ascent.

Through the cracked vinyl padding beneath me I could feel how we jerked and bobbed our way up the cable. My already mournful stomach could certainly attest the motion. And now, well too late in the day, I wondered what to do if anything broke; there was no safety gear I could see. Did the gondola have emergency brakes like an elevator? Or would I go sliding helplessly down the cable, picking up speed, destined to reclaim the ground in a big way?

This, however, was a thousand times better than the car because I could see. Once we reached a certain height the lights of the city began to spread out in the dark below me. Painted through the candy-colours of my ride's stained glass windows. Folk down there being characteristically wasteful with power, or night-owls, or just so *amour fou* for advertising they had to keep the shopfronts lit, even with nobody about to see.

Crap, but it was pretty. Beautiful, with the sort of romance Angela and I had been helplessly seduced by when we first moved to the city. A bright promise we circled and beat our powdery wings against.

It was only once you crawled along at ground level that the streets gleefully spread the cracks in their façade. Garbage and cigarette butts choking every drain so badly the pavement never truly dried out. The pervasive stench of urine, and not just down the dark alleys where you'd expect, it was right out in the open. Wafting through thoroughfares. The splattered vomit outside eateries where you were expected to sit. And the constant threat of *others*, pressing in from all sides.

The city deceptively resembled a place of hope from such a distance. Somewhere your actions might mean something. On the day of the launch Michael would have looked down on a view quite like this, to the very spot where Angela and I had stood. One tiny little bit of ground made special by her presence.

I wasn't there the night Angela and Michael met. You can bet your bottom dollar I'd have done something about it. Instead I received a classic warning sign when she came floating home from their impromptu date, her eyes all bright and shiny.

But I was sour and grumpy, laid up with a flu that swelled ready to split my head right open. So I mostly felt relieved to see her fervour directed elsewhere for a change. To listen, it seemed my sister had finally met somebody as crazy, impulsive, and just plain larger-than-life as herself. Except, as I quickly discovered, this Michael fellow was all mouth no pants. Any idiot with ears could pick that out of her tales in no time.

When I'd stomached enough of the blow-by-blow to choke a horse, I'd weakly levered myself far enough off my sickbed to implore, *Please, please do not take up with some guy who encourages you on the "voices" thing. Please, Angela. If you never do anything else I ask, please trust me on this one.*

Looking back, I have to wonder if that was the exact moment she resolved to marry him.

At the time, crabby at being lectured, Angela had merely tossed her long hair in an irritatingly snitty manner. 'You don't buy into that superstitious crap, do you Cathy? That hearing the voices is a mental illness—that merely *talking* about them spreads the disease? If so, surely you ought to waste all that concern on him instead of me.'

Trying to regain the sisterly mood she playfully slapped my shoulder, right where I'd endured an expensive and so far ineffectual flu shot. 'I thought you were braver than that!'

Crap knows where she got *that* idea.

Ah. Of course my attention span wandered all over the road like lost livestock. Tall Jake's sedative was making itself known. There was no way he got his mitts on *this* across any counter! While intellectually I knew that Threshold loomed overhead, a warm morass of fuzzy-headedness kept panic at bay.

Thoughts that had been racing in circles became slow and thick wading through it.

The ceiling prevented me peering anxiously into the sky, as my brave little painted gondola creaked and swayed its way up the cable. In fact, given the angle, it was all but impossible to catch forewarning of Threshold Station until practically docked. She came up so suddenly I flinched, and actually squeaked at the rude shock of those baroque curling lines reaching, seemingly from nowhere, to snatch my frail tin-toy ride into her embrace.

The GATE Corporation building had been prosaic, solid, understandable. Nowadays few craved the reputation of having built something wonderful, not with all the obligation and deadlines crowding close. Durable concrete blocks were plonked down, retrofitted again and again long past their use-by in easy to scrub beige. Hose out the old residents, cram in the new.

Nothing like this! Only faintly made out in the dark, Threshold was all grandiose detailing and sinuous curves. She seemed almost *organic* in her elegance. A form belonging to the deep mysteries of the ocean floor, not suspended up here so far above the world.

There was a clang that reverberated through the gondola like a bell, and all progress halted. I had arrived.

Cormac had certainly gone all-out with my rooms. Everything a girl could need … bar a touch of humanity, of course, but I'd been proving my ability to live without it on a daily basis.

There was even an adjoining section, although I'd yet to venture beyond the connecting door. My own quarters were fascinating enough.

From Threshold's exterior and the corridors I'd been led through, I had rather optimistically been expecting to live in opulence. It even *smelled* good in here. Rich smells. Dark wood panelling, polish, wax.

That indescribable scent of comfort that thick warm carpet gives off, something like gingerbread. I was probably getting a whiff of how it felt to not have to give a toss about anything.

In the discreet, muted lighting I experienced the odd disorientation of having stepped back in time. Nothing here belonged to the cheap disposable present, the *now now now* that catered to the masses. And it was a dangerous proposition. Threshold Station represented an outdated, frivolous mode of thought I could ill afford to fall into.

In that sense my rooms were a relief, only venturing so far as Spartan and clean. Servants' quarters? I chuckled at that, it was a Threshold thought. Nobody kept servants. We had the service industry instead, which was sometimes worse.

I'd a double bed, with simple linen. New and clean, which was a pleasure in itself. You become resigned to milo stains and cat hair. I bounced on a mattress that hadn't yet succumbed to years of exhaustion. A frilly little bedside lamp seemed to serve no better function than announcing someone'd stood here looking at the room, and then taken a stab at making things "homely."

I hated frilly. It's for girls half my mass. I unplugged the offending fitting and stashed it beneath the bed, only then realising I was already in the process of making this space my own.

A tiny bathroom with shower, sink and toilet all lined up for inspection, but no bath, which made calling it a bathroom an odd misnomer. A toothbrush and paste still sealed in their original packaging.

Along with the other condiments of female grooming, a small rainbow of cosmetics clogged a whole drawer—it was obviously easier to buy one of everything than make choices. Nothing that'd get me up there reading the seven o'clock news, but it was nice to be able to make the effort.

The real shock came when I opened the cupboard.

Clothes!

Ok. So that wasn't shocking in itself. But the disturbing impulse to giggle when it was not at all funny shivered through me, as I flipped through the offerings. Shirts from various flash designers. A selection of pinstripe on hangers. Both long and short skirts, to suit cycles of prudishness, in a quality of fabric I'd fingered enviously in the past. With such slippery luxury, my skin wouldn't know what to do with itself.

Basically I was being kitted out according to how a classy, self-possessed dame ought to look. Never straying too far from the safe harbour of smart-casual. Never out of style. It was shocking a martini cabinet hadn't been included with the room. To my further, now slightly hysterical amusement I unearthed underthings, all in classic peach or classic ivory and if copious lace didn't spin my fancy I was shit out of luck. How had they even known my size?

Perhaps Dr Cormac hoped to squeeze me like plasticine into the shape of the creature he wished he'd snagged. Brave, and self-possessed enough to take this bold venture all the way. A woman, in short, like Angela.

This florid prison high in the sky would have suited my sister to a T. She would've already been plotting how to turn the situation to her advantage. That was the world she lived in, populated entirely by heroes to raise a glass with and villains to be smacked down. Spinning grand elaborations by the hour, to make everyone so much more vivid. More glamorous than boring old reality.

Who in my position *wouldn't* be tempted by a little wiggle on the fancy side?

And while part of me itched to blame Cormac for this whole ridiculous ensemble, the way we heap all the world's indignity at the foot of our chosen antagonist, the culprit was more likely some tragically lonely lackey.

Someone more like Tall Jake, who didn't have kids, who'd missed that train. A desk-jockey jerked from their keyboard and sent on an inexplicable shopping expedition with the corporate card.

Laying out their sad princess in a tower dream, for me to cackle over. What did they even intend for all this crap once I toddled off home? Would they gift it to me? Burn it?

While all this ponderous chin-stroking was nice, more practical considerations could never be shucked for long. Quite frankly, I stank. With a unique stewed aroma, that came of wearing my clothes too long, and then despoiling somebody's pricey vehicle.

Although tiny enough to bang my elbows against the sides, the shower rated a warm soapy ten above mine back home. No enterprising mould colony creeping across the ceiling, cunningly entrenched where bleach couldn't reach. I was spared jiggling naked foot to foot, waiting for things to heat up: the water burst out ready to scald the minute I spun the tap, and ran rust-free. A shadow of momentary joy flickered over me and I sighed, half-ruefully. It really was beginning to seem I'd happily sell myself for the right amenities.

What was this? Moisturising soap? Truly, I'd been dropped in the lap of luxury. The waves of giggles just kept on coming, I might be becoming hysterical. Where was a good hard slap when you needed one? Nonetheless I emerged looking forward to being dressed as a new woman. Correction: *Cormac's* new woman.

I was towelling myself with brisk industry, wobbles flying everywhere, when I heard them bringing Michael in next door. Or, more accurately, I overhead the right stink he was raising. Such shrieks spouted through the wall as would make you think they were peeling him alive.

Hurriedly tucking the towel about myself, and it went right the way around, another luxury, I threw open the connecting door. The room beyond was a darkened world. The light from my side slicing into it to expose two women and an equally beefy man manhandling Michael's twisting, howling performance off a trolley onto a bed. A huge syringe was still embedded like a hungry proboscis in his thin buttock.

'What's going on?' I asked stupidly; but what else could I open with? These three were strangers. Suddenly I missed *my* suits: Tall Jake, and Sammy Short-Stuff.

'Hope you can stand such a mouthy neighbour for a bit. We're moving him in, 'til his "special" room is ready.' Said with a knowing glance I didn't find reassuring, because I knew nothing. Were they seriously going to dump Michael here in the dark, yelling his head off, while they made up the sheets somewhere else?

'So what's in the needle?'

'A nice big dose of chillax the fuck out. Otherwise we *might* end up crunching one of these skinny little drumsticks just tryin' to keep 'im still.' Despite her buddy-buddy tone the woman's eyes flashed a more genuine resentment at having to explain herself, to *me* of all people. To her credit, professionalism remained in place, front and centre.

I could certainly sympathise with being rubbed up the wrong way, especially given Michael's melodramatic bullshit.

Michael himself quit yelling, and rolled his marbled eyes until he could see me. It was like his ego could hear you thinking about him. 'You! I know you, don't I?'

He grabbed the sour woman's bicep, and she did *not* take kindly to being grabbed. 'Look, if you lot are going t' try marching the naked sluts in here, at least have the decency t' shell out for it!' He waved a hand at me. 'This, *this*, this is classic get what you paid for.'

While she was rolling her eyes, get a load of this worm, Michael flicked his head abruptly forward in a whipcrack that should have broken his neck. He sank his too-white teeth into the meaty part of sullen suit lady's forearm. She yelped, more in outrage than pain. The butt-needle clattered to the floor.

There wasn't a sodding lot of help I could be, but her companions immediately leaped to the rescue, working their blunt fingers into Michael's jaw to prise him off. He snapped at the digits and hissed like a pissed off cat, stringy saliva flying.

My cowardly retreat back to my room brought dark glances of contempt all around, but at least I could shut the door on them. It was a delightful ability. Whether the door be physical or a barrier in your mind, nothing beat that solid negating "thunk" as it swung shut.

I sure wasn't venturing back until all was quiet. I used the time to dress and attend to the grooming that'd dropped by the wayside. Sadly, the wardrobe's glamour had faded. A nice set of duds no longer seemed sufficient to gird me for all this.

I also figured with a panicky gulp that Jake's pill must be draining away, like soap scum down the plughole. It was such a tiny packet. As tempting as it might be, I couldn't afford to back-to-back doses. Best strike while the iron was groggy.

A final paranoid listen through the wall, to be absolutely sure the three suits had skedaddled. Then I slid next door.

Once again I stood vulnerable in the dark, while Michael lay secure in his element. And it only now occurred that I might be wasting my time: he might be under the dream of the needle.

'Hello?'

'I'm here.' Awake, if not entirely aware. Weren't we poster kids for the Just Say No generation. 'Who are you?'

'Michael, you know sodding well who I am, *and* why I'm here. Are we going to dance this little jig *every* time I come in?'

No reply. Melodramatic git.

'Michael?' I kept repeating his name as though by invocation, a shortcut into his head. *Flies with honey, flies with honey.*

Of course, I could always go fetch that frilly lamp and crack it over his fat noggin. 'Who am I, Michael?'

'You? You're Angie's sister. That's all you are.'

Good enough, especially for the here and now. 'Speak to me, then. You promised to tell me things. For *her.*'

A hideous cackle erupted. Michael's laugh had once been booming, but the sustaining lungs had eroded away. Humour as warped as his body. 'Tell you things? Perhaps you'd fancy the sort of things you can't scrub from your head, once they take root.'

'If those are all you've got.'

'You want t' hear how there's no law Outside? No … no decency? Out there, there are only the old companions, the ones who've walked alongside humanity every step of the way. Who can't be escaped, no matter how fast we run. They've always been waiting. Fear. And lust. Hunger, domination. Oh, and *shame*. Always plenty of that t' go around.'

'Why would you say that?'

Michael whimpered.

'Because Paul went Out.'


**DESPITE THE LINGERING** weakness and lethargy they'd all been dragged down by, Paul Jonas had been cucumber calm. Right up to the moment he entered the airlock.

Suiting up for the jaunt had been familiar and soothing in the face of all the craziness they'd gone through. Humans do so love their routines.

Especially Paul's busy hands, which with little to do had taken to picking at things lately, when he wasn't watching. Picking and picking, until he feared he'd pick himself into a million threads and disperse across the floor.

Suddenly idle hands knew their place again and briskly followed orders. He now understood, a little mournfully, that he'd never take that sort of purposeful certainty for granted again.

But once Paul hit the airlock the illusion of happy control began to flake apart.

Everything *almost* looked right. *Almost* identical to the interminable dry-runs, when the voice of this or that trainer had hectored mercilessly no matter how well he did. Just not quite enough to let him fool himself. The firm pristine thunk of the inner door shutting at his back didn't bother Paul. No, oh no. It was the charred, discoloured outer door that he feared.

Following all his mongering and wheedling that this *had* to be done, they *had* to get positive pressure back, he shamefacedly found that he desperately didn't want to go.

Safe in the control room, the others gaggled about the central console like a mother's meeting when the cork comes out. Crowding Sal as she worked irritably to coax responses from what was left of the Capsule. *Breathing* on her. She was going to deck someone in a minute.

Even in such close quarters none of them seemed to yet mind how richly they'd begun to stink. Accumulated grime, accumulating time. Thick with the body's oils. Soon, to measure how long they'd been stuck Out here, they'd be able to slice through the filth and count the rings, like trees.

Sal frowned into the mike. 'Paul, are you sure your suit camera's on?'

'Yes, mommy. I wiped the white mounds before yanking my shorts up today, too.'

He could see the little green light in his helmet, way off in the peripheral where it couldn't distract from more pressing alarms. Something else to no longer take for granted; green was a soft, natural colour they didn't get much of anymore. Green was for grass, green for trees. Green for safety.

It sure wasn't easy.

Most of the control room's state of the art speakers had been blown to a crackling, spitting mess by braying alarms during the explosion. The Capsule had literally screamed itself bloody. So much for the glories of surround sound. When his voice filtered through, Paul sounded eerily like he was standing in a far corner of the room. Facing the wall, no less. *The naughty corner*, Beth'd flippantly dubbed it with chuckles all around … but it was black humour that quickly died.

Gradually, a crawling unease began setting in.

Little by little, each of them had subtly adjusted his or her stance to exclude it. Nobody wanted to put their vulnerable, twitching back to the nervousness in Paul's disembodied voice. But they couldn't bring themselves to out and face the naughty corner either. No way.

It wasn't precisely a *smell* that wafted from it. More a paranoia, the suspicion of smell. Like when you swing the car around, rush back to the stove, convinced in a panic that it's been left on. So convinced that your nostrils shriek smoke, your eyes well up, even as your hands report in, all's cold. All's cold.

Nobody was game to confront what they childishly dreaded. And dreaded so brutally that even brushing by the idea was like feeling all your warmth drain out through the floor. It was a wonder that they kept their feet, stayed in their huddle, faced with the possibility there really *was* someone crouching there. Whether presentiment, and it wasn't the first time for some; or a hallucination they'd raised together, merely by thinking about it too hard.

A burned figure.

Trembling in the corner.

In the *naughty* corner.

It was the sort of thing you could almost catch from the corner of your eye, attracted by its faint motion before hurriedly looking away.

Attracted by the cooking steam rising off it. John's glasses fogged up and he wiped them skittishly; he was sweating, nervous and tense.

Nobody would look. Nobody wished to recognise Paul's devastated, blackened features pressed into the corner. Because here came his voice over the radio, trying to sound so cheerful and brave. Because Paul was going Out there, for everybody. And he'd no idea what their fears had managed to conjure in here with them.

Sal frowned and tried more buttons, more switches, for the fat lot of good they'd do. 'I'm not getting any kind of image from you.' Her tone was harshly accusatory. *Someone* was obviously doing all this just to piss on her chips, and when she found the culprit out, fuck help them.

She resisted the urge to just sling a primitive karate chop through the console and tried technical prowess instead, which yielded a predictable fuck-all. At least breaking her hand would've been satisfying.

Paul waited frozen in the airlock, while Sal bollocked around. The inset glass panel was blackened, and he couldn't make out anything beyond the outer door. And to think he'd laughed like an idiot at the insane proliferation of airlocks throughout the Capsule. *Couldn't the cash've gone toward something useful, like a karaoke bar?* Here was mud in his eye.

Paul cleared his throat nervously, not on hand to see those in the control room flinch. 'It's not an issue with my suit, is it Sal? You're always on about how one issue just leads to another ...'

'No, I'm pretty sure the fault's here. Somewhere.'

Sal glared directly into the naughty corner, the only one unfazed by what imagination stirred up. Imagination ought to be leery of *her*.

Let Paul sweat, this was all his fucking bright idea. And each new thing these assholes cajoled her to, "Just try, Sal. See how you manage," merely unearthed more life and death glitches for her to agonise over.

'I could run a diagnostic,' she ventured. 'Oh, wait. No. Those routines got fried, didn't they, along with *every fucking thing else.'*

Including Jenny and Jeshu.

Sal closed her eyes, restoring her outer shell to calm. Out of all they'd lost, practically everything once you got right down to it, she felt so fucking guilty over how deeply she'd disliked Jeshu. It really were as though she'd hated his dumb flabby ass to death or something. Of course, he'd been exactly the sort of numpty to rush in and forget the first principle of first aid: *check for danger*. Don't make yourself yet another problem in a disaster. Sal loathed those who failed to think, which was pretty much everybody.

'I don't recall anyone calling for sarcasm, Sal. But while we're on it, you reckon you're "pretty sure" my suit isn't a death trap?' Paul's nervousness slurred the words, the poor speakers worsening his gibberish. He could feel sweat soaking into the itchy cloth band at his forehead. 'Because, you know, I really do not fancy breathing that shit Out there, we've no idea what it does. My life is in your patty-paws, here.'

'What life?' Beth muttered sullenly, but the Captain snapped around to glare blue murder at her. She quickly followed the Captain's golden standing rule, for everybody to shut right the fuck up 'til spoken to.

'Just trust Sal,' the Captain soothed, bending close to the microphone. 'She's the best. She knows what she's up to.'

Michael's palms were damp and he swiped them surreptitiously against his legs, not enjoying the sensation of his fingernails all wobbly in their beds. And those thighs, so very thin and bowed through his pants. So frail they made his knees look abnormally wide. Cumbersome, thick wooden blocks stuck in his legs.

Sure, he conceded, Sal was the best—they all were. Likely every teacher needed a pet, though.

And this was where shining excellence had landed the lot of them, oh bravo. The taste was so bitter, he wanted to physically spit it on the floor.

It was hardly worth hoping fear alone might prevent Paul venturing Outside. He'd raised the issue himself: they needed more power, simple as that. And in all the time they'd worked together, Michael had never seen the placid little fellow back down from a single one of those jobs that fell into the "just get it the fuck done" category. No matter the scale of absurdity ladled on his plate, he'd just smile and choke it down.

Perversely, at the same time as Michael quivered to scream "STOP!" he also *wanted* Paul's suit camera to work. Let the dread image spring up crystal clear on the monitor, undeniable. They all deserved to see what they were in for. Why shouldn't Paul be the one to risk his fool neck for a bold look around?

And maybe … maybe standing safe here in the group Michael'd catch a glimpse of what made those faint tappings and scratchings when he was all alone. He couldn't stand the idea they might be private sounds, intended just for him.

Antenna for trouble, Batheba shot Michael the occasional disquieted glance. The only one with an idea of his keen building anxiety, she didn't at all like what she saw. Michael's handsome features looked drawn and shiny in the room's faint glow. Muscles working against each other rather than together.

She panned around for a reading on the group. Everyone looked nervous, of course. There were plenty of chewed lips and clenched, knotting hands. But Michael Formir had ramped the term *scared to death* up to a whole new level. His overreaction was an aberration, the outlier, and that rang all of Batheba's alarm bells.

Perhaps nobody else pegged him because they'd resolved to look nowhere.

Determined never to so much as glance into the squirming fright of the naughty corner. Some even closed their eyes in slack, unfocussed faces as they zoned in entirely on Paul's broadcast voice, like *not* seeing was ever any less frightening. Huddled about the flickering campfire glow of the console as it held back the darkness.

'Paul.' The Captain's voice was an impeccably trained tool for getting what she wanted. Sometimes, like now, it could fill you right to the brim with reassurance and understanding. Although she far preferred punching subordinates into motion with it, like some brutal sledge. 'It's alright if you've changed your mind. Somebody else can go.'

Hysterically white eyes all around, although none of them dared protest. Realising in the same instant, there'd be no way Paul would *ever* send another into danger in his place, not in a million years, not while he had his strength. And the Captain knew that as well as anybody.

Which was precisely why the cunning, manipulative bitch was in charge.

Paul gave a high, nervous giggle. It had a lack of manliness he instantly lamented. 'Oh, that would be sweet, wouldn't it. Me, all dressed up with no place to go; and after campaigning to get my ass out here in the first place. No, thank you Captain. I made this bed. I'm on it.'

'Ok, Paul. We're going to negate the airlock's gravity now.'

Not real artificial gravity, of course. Nobody'd cracked that nut. Just a clever mishmash of soundwaves outside the audible spectrum that amounted to *close enough*.

Flipping the switch put Paul within Outside's influence, and what passed for its funhouse-crazy gravity. Scarcely enough to keep you on the "ground," and a confused sense of *down* that had a tendency to switch about randomly.

Even with all the stiff cajones training could stuff you with, spend too long bobbing around Out there and even the most intrepid Outerman'd be filling their helmet with vertiginous guts.

'Right, I'm about to cycle our air out and their air in. Check your seals.'

The Captain looked to Sal sharply. 'Their?'

'Did I say that?' Sal shook her head as though dispersing cotton-candy clouds, nonsense. Why were these numbskulls bothering her with this, when she'd so much to keep track of? 'Never mind.'

Michael pawed at Sal's hand and she looked up, startled. Into a pair of red-raw eyes. She hadn't even heard him creeping around the group. 'What did you say?' he whispered.

'Jam a cork in it, Formir!' the Captain barked without deigning to glance his way. 'You can stick your diaper on and play at being the centre of fucking attention later.'

Sal brusquely whipped her fingers out from beneath Michael's. Of all the jerks to be trapped in a bloody tin can with! From merely starting out a weirdo, of the sort you'd cross the bar to avoid, Michael seemed to be undertaking intense study on making himself truly creepy.

'Opening the outer airlock … now. Alright Paul, you're free to go.'

From within the dense claustrophobia of his helmet Paul missed the soft click as the door eased open, but he could sure imagine it. In fact his imagination seemed inspired, cranking 'em out overtime, because what he *thought* he felt was an intense burning sensation. As though waves of near-unbearable heat were flooding in the broached portal to crash through him. It was a weird, unclean sensation, that made him want to instantly tear the bulky white suit open and scrub it from his skin with his nails.

He didn't, of course.

Giving in to overwhelming impulse was the very reason most folk never made it off the ground, couldn't go to the sorts of places he was at today.

Yay for him.

'Sal, um. Are your sensors showing any radiation? Anything like that?'

Her sharp eyes knew exactly where to glance, and what it'd tell her. Hardly worth bothering. 'Nope.'

'Well are they *working*?'

'Seem to be.'

'I'm sure there's something odd that's not getting picked up,' Paul mumbled unhappily, his rapid breath rattling and scratching across the mike.

'Just the farm-fresh aroma of chickenshit.'

'Oh, nice. Do you want to come Out here and do this?'

'Knock it off,' the Captain intervened, with characteristic "what the fuck now" weariness. 'I'm not in the mood to be putting you kids over my fucking knee today. But that ain't going to stop me if you keep pushing.'

Having gradually edged in beside him, Batheba caught Michael's trembling arm 'It's ok,' she murmured in his ear, too softly for the others to catch. Guaranteed, he wouldn't appreciate losing face. 'It'll be alright, Mike. Just relax.' The muscles beneath her touch were as rigid as a steel bar. Appalled, she tried to calm him with random patting motions.

At the same time, a dull excitement woke in Batheba's belly. All this fearful urgency dropped on them, following the long dull smear of inactivity and hopelessness they'd endured since the explosion.

'Now or never, Paul.' Sal's lip twisted. 'Do or die.'

'I'm ready.' He wasn't, but what the fuck, hey?

At Captain Orchid's command, Paul moved out of the airlock into what felt like a drowsy slow-motion world.

Outside was in a languorous mood today; he weighed very little, with occasional invisible currents tugging him this way and that. This was a place where bad things happened very sluggishly. Were drawn-out, and seemed to go on forever.

This was a part of the Capsule that'd been automatically shut off during the explosion, all partitions snapping closed with the insectile speed of computer reflex. No more than a dead limb, now. Paul's helmet flashlight only revealed his surroundings a fragment at a time, and they seemed to loom out of the dark. He lit up a melted globule of wires, all tangled and bulging from the ceiling above like a hernia. Then an aluminium chair, somehow embedded in a wall panel like it'd been flung across the room.

When picked apart this way, in bits and flashes, the jumbled space resembled a nonsensical metal junkyard waiting to fall to bits. A sprawling cluster of the loosest cohesion. Any surface Paul brushed against, and he was trying like buggery not to touch *anything*, left a thin black residue on his suit. The legacy of a burning long passed.

Paul swung to his right, and looked down.

And,

D

O

W

N.

Every direction was down.

He made a garbled sound, not quite sure what he meant to say.

'Paul?'

'I'm alright.' Inwardly he chanted the mantra, *I'm alright, I'm alright*. At least his audience were keen to be fooled. 'There's a breach in the hull here. A big one.'

His little spot of light wavered back and forth, picking out details. 'Actually it's, uh, rather more breach than hull.'

Paul's brave helmet light lanced out, into the darkness. Peering out through the hull like a blinking vole from its safe burrow, Paul was suddenly seized by the disorienting, and no doubt crazed certainty that each of those mysterious glittering points of light Out there was actually a heavily suited man. Looking out from the shattered wreck of the vessel he'd though would protect him. And each of them in their gaping dread and wonder recognised the faint glimmer of Paul's flashlight as one of their own, staring back.

'They're all *me*,' he murmured, enthralled and appalled.

'Huh?' The voice down the mike was all pragmatism and

business. Just what he needed to plant a steady anchor in reality. 'Could you repeat that, Paul? We think Michael just shit his fucking shorts in here.'

'I … I'm not sure where I am.' Paul took a deep breath, tasting plastics. But beneath that, it was good old bottled air from home. 'Everything's so scrambled …'

'Slowly,' the Captain advised down the comlink, projecting steadiness straight into his brain. Nothing ever fazed the Captain. Not even the things that really should. You couldn't go wrong with a guiding light like her. 'Tell us what you see.'

'*Nothing*. I'm looking Outside, and it's just … there's nothing. Not a thing. Like those little spit blobs of light aren't anything, not when you get up close.'

Oh yeah. He ought to have been a poet. Paul breathed out roughly. 'It's so empty. It's like being dead.'

'So we are,' somebody whispered back, but too softly for him to identify the unhelpful culprit. Eerily, the voice didn't even seem to be coming down the mike. It sounded right inside his helmet.

Paul waited to hear the Captain explode at whoever dared speak out of turn. But when it came, her voice was dead calm. She must've done it all with her eyes, then. He winced sympathetically.

Nothing cut you down to tiny size worse than those iron glares Orchid could fling your way, reduced until you felt so pathetically small. Such a scrap of worthless shit. So shape up, shit, and do better! Before you get flushed.

'Paul, the wiring you're after ought to be along the left hand wall. Get moving.' Hard and practical, that was their Captain. Not an ounce of flowery romance in her.

Almost without his command, Paul's eyes rolled up and drifted closed. He found the jarring contrast between the neat steps of ordered routine in his head and the ruined, jumbled reality all about too overwhelming. Everything illuminated by the light threw him deeper into darkness. Thus paralysed, he couldn't act. So Paul discounted reality, and reached out without sight. Trusting blindly in the procedure.

Even as his quick fingers unpinned the brittle, crumbling remains of wall panels, through flickering eyelids he watched himself opening a series of perfect metal rectangles. As polished and proud as the day the Capsule was launched. Freed from his grasp, the panels distained the floor. They drifted off through the ragged hole in the hull as though obeying some pull, with such purpose he knew without looking that his hands had given them their new destiny.

Now Outside was no longer so empty, even if only by the tiniest fraction. They were seeding it with their junk. Not terribly noble, but anything was better than *nothing*.

The wires within the wall matched the nice clean image in Paul's mind so well, that even through the cumbersome suit he could feel it. 'The connections are live!' he crowed.

The Captain's brute fists relaxed on the back of Sal's chair. Sal herself reached out and touched the console with an almost tender gesture, loving what remained of the Capsule for not disappointing, for hanging in there. Beth Hanrekson's thin mouth quirked despite her natural pessimism, and even John "Whining is the way of the future" Porliet, who'd so far remained uncharacteristically stoic, ducked his head to hide tears in the ridiculously foppish fringe, that ought to've been razored off in his teens.

You'd think the bloody circus was in town. A little extra power wouldn't brighten the fundamentals of their situation one whit. What on earth were they all so excited about? Other than, you had to get excited about *something*. Instead of capering about with dumb canine joy, Batheba looked to Michael.

His reaction was the most extreme of the little group. Knotting up, as though his body tried to grind in on itself. But whether it be by the power of what he suffered, or his effort to contain it, she'd no idea.

Noticing Batheba's regard, Michael's hand shot out panicky-quick and grasped hers. He was known for being a tad grabby with the ladies, and it'd earn him a right smack one of these days. But now, it seemed that something truly extreme gripped him. The only emotion Batheba knew of such intensity was fear.

The state of the wires had renewed Paul's tottering confidence. He opened his eyes, pulling himself along the wall and divesting it of panels as he went. Every centimetre of wiring had to be eyeballed carefully to find the break, a species of finickyness that guaranteed automation'd never fully replace cheap human labour. There really was, it seemed, no substitute.

It was as he clambered down the corridor that a flicker of white caught Paul's eye. Something moving. Just around the next bend, the Capsule's corridors all looping and spiralling about themselves like curly fries. He stopped cold. 'Captain, uh. There's something Out here with me.'

He heard a wretched moan over the link, and this time the Captain snapped, 'Formir, if I have to remind you *one more time* to shut your miserable piss-hole …'

Even in the sweating depths of anxiety, Paul couldn't help a smile. 'Captain?'

'It's fine, Paul,' she soothed back, switching states with the consummate skill of the bipolar.

He was lucky somebody else was copping the rough today, and no-one could claim Michael didn't dig his own holes. Paul resolved to enjoy it while it lasted. The smooth could be so nice, helping you slide through life. 'Trust me. There's nothing Out there with you, because there's nothing Out there at all.'

'There *is* something,' he insisted. 'Something pale.'

'It's likely one of the panels you've sprung loose.' The Captain was implacable. Try resisting a glacier. 'Proceed along the wires, Paul. Let's get this done.'

Paul obediently crawled on around the bend, in the opposite direction he wanted to go. The piss-poor gravity was especially broken here, and his legs drifted aimlessly. Probably missing home and earth where they had a proper job to do.

And then his thin, high scream filled his helmet.

Paul jerked and scrabbled frantically away from what reached for him with mournful arms. An identical suit plumping the figure up: himself, but different. All wrong. In the flailing panic to escape his helmet light strobed wildly, lighting up his dance partner in spatters like an insane rave.

'Oh shit, it's someone, it's *someone!*'

'What?' The Captain was unable to see for herself, couldn't target an enemy, and her voice snapped with frustration. 'Tell me what's happening Paul!'

'Somebody … in a suit.'

Paul steadied himself, steadied the other. He needed to get a grip, before the Captain came blazing out here herself.

'Are they alive?' Being in charge, she could voice hopes that none of the rest of them could bear. But of course, this bandaid had to be ripped free as quickly as possible. Nail the hard facts immediately. Don't let florid imaginations wander, lest they never be reigned in again.

Paul braced against a wall and positioned himself so that his light shone into the other helmet.

These faceplates reflected most of the time, like perfect mirrors, unless you hit just the right angle and pinged light directly in. Finding that sweet spot played merry ass when the bigwigs were trying to take publicity snaps. When all else failed, wardrobe had ended up knocking together some fake non-reflective helmets, all carefully labelled so you couldn't mix them with the real thing.

Paul found himself shrieking again, only this time in revulsion. The sort of instant, gagging aversion that makes your skin want to crawl off to be burned. The other's eyes bulged at him. That jaw dangled lax, as though they wanted to scream, too, at the end they'd come to.

Bacteria had been trapped within the suit. At the death of their host, all the little organisms that normally act in concert had rioted. What Paul could see of the other's flesh was all puffed up. *Twisted*, as though the face had been brutally battered, over and over, into a mass of gnarled tissue. A pale straw fluid splattered the inside of the faceplate from a swelling, an awful bursting that Paul thanked his fortune he'd not been here to see.

Those eyes would never see Paul staring in at them. But not even the damage done could disguise the pitiful expression they'd slipped from existence with.

At once, Paul's trembling changed. Instinct had had its flighty irrational day, charging all about the place. Now reason took over. All the disgust and terror were quickly overwhelmed in a tidal wave of sorrow, that crashed over him so unexpectedly he lost control. 'There's a dead body Out here with me!' it became keening, empty, a pitched loss.

'Get a fucking grip!' Captain Orchid sprayed the microphone with her vehemence; everyone else leaned covertly back. 'Of course there'd be crew trapped in that section when everything went to shit!'

'But they've got a suit on,' Paul whimpered. 'They died waiting to be let in.' Imagining the panic.

Seeing suited hands hammering at the outer airlock door with soft cushioned thumps, while inside they'd gone about their business, unheeding. The cries for help, deafening within the helmet. Impotently silent without.

Paul felt something important inside himself just pull up and die, because eventually it would've been the suit's gauges crying out too, crying warning, crying for air. Then, when voice finally gave out, only the gauges. They'd suffocated despairingly in their suit rather than let Outside in, and who could blame them?

'They tried to save themselves, and if we'd opened the door sooner ...'

'We'd have another flapping mouth to feed on what little rations we have,' the Captain finished for him bluntly.

'What's she on about?' Beth mumbled to John, ducking her head to stay under Orchid's unforgiving radar. 'We've got heaps; far more than we're ever likely to need.'

'Just how fucking long does she expect us to hang on Out here?' he returned in a mutter.

'Fuck. I'm amazed we made it *this* far.'

Paul still clasped the dead figure by the shoulders. Still gazed into that terrible face, like he no longer had it in him to look away. Surely there'd not been time for such awful degradation to set in, it didn't make any sense. Just how fucking long had they been Out here already?

To get so up close was convincing his gut to eject its contents across his faceplate, but Paul suppressed it ruthlessly, searching those withered features for any familiarity. No name patch, but they were cosmetic, a prop for ego, known for flaking off. The fingers of one hand hooked as though they'd clenched some object or tool, also long gone.

If it'd been him, and it probably should have been if not for dumb luck, he'd want to be known.

Acknowledged and remembered as something more than putrid death, and a suit that would have to be burned. Something more than a horrorshow. There had to be some small, warm human memory; perhaps some stupid joke the two of them had laughed about. A favourite film?

But if Paul had ever shared good times with this person, their corpse was unrecognisable. And the thought of dying Out here, without even your name, was too sad to bear. People were never meant to venture Outside. Not ever. It meant dying into true nothing, without leaving any memory. Without leaving anything.

'We shouldn't cart this poor sap along in the dead section like this,' Paul declared, mainly to himself. 'I'm going to set them loose.'

'No, Jonas.' Coaxing had left the building, along with the friendliness of first names. 'You are going to bring the body back here to be stored with Jenny and Jeshu.'

'What for, Captain?' Paul pulled his new buddy the corpse over to the rift in the hull, careful not to get it caught on any jagged bits of metal. 'Why not just out and tell us all what you're planning to do with them?'

'We are going to survive, Jonas. *All* of us, if I have to drag you kicking and screaming over the line myself. And that means utilizing every resource at our disposal.'

'Resource, Captain?' He shook his head sadly. 'Do euphemisms really help?'

'Paul Jonas, you bring that body to me right fucking now, mister! That's an order!'

Now Paul smiled. And it was well nobody could witness its sweetness. A lovely, almost heartbreaking expression, something you'd only ever expect to see from a young child. From an innocent heart, before the world's had a chance to dig in.

'Is now a bad time to mention how many years I've been waiting to hear you say that, Captain? I mean, it's for fucking sure I wouldn't have been nosing about the control room when things went tits-up, otherwise.

'Or landed my ass on the Capsule at all, for that matter. Chasing you from project to project.'

He gave a watery laugh. 'In fact, only this morning I thought to myself, *Paul old bean, you may have to guzzle down your piss, count out turds and nit-pick the milliseconds, but at least you get to do it with her.*'

Of course, Paul knew and regretted the harm done by refusing an order. What it meant to all of them, their cohesion and chances at survival. Command was a system of universal consent, and oh so very fragile. He was unlikely to see any hugs and kisses for this.

But releasing the body felt the *right* thing to do.

This was a dark secret Paul Jonas had always kept carefully tucked away from any employer's scrutiny, even from most of his friends. So long as none of his ideals were at stake, he found himself quite happy to plod along with the rest of the herd; but Paul was only ever truly moved by what felt right. And should that gut feeling ever cross purpose with the law, the rules, or whatever else society saw fit to throw up, then fuck 'em.

It'd driven his folks to distraction, his poor mother convinced he'd end up in jail before he reached ten. Even he had to admit that without a sound moral compass, it made an excellent recipe for a sociopath. He supposed he must be some kind of idealist, but what could you do? Merely hope that his best would continue to carry the day.

With a shove, the unknown body tumbled off into the void. Somewhat grotesque in his sympathy, Paul waved it off. 'Bon voyage. I sure hope somebody remembers you.'

Sarah Orchid abruptly spun and barged through the little crowd, disappearing down the hallway.

Staring after her John surreptitiously rubbed his shoulder: that woman was a force! He'd be black and blue in an hour or so; they'd all begun to bruise too easily, and healed slowly.

But she returned almost immediately and bashed by on his other side for a matching set. The Captain couldn't storm from the bridge, however sorely provoked. It was unprofessional.

There was a long, brutally uncomfortable quiet while Paul sheepishly returned to checking on the wires. Those about Captain Orchid worked very carefully to avoid looking her in the face.

Finally the speakers crackled into life. 'It looks like the entire length of wall cabling's good as gold.'

Sal risked a quick glance at the Captain and decided staying businesslike was safe enough. Tempting as a little mayhem may be, it sure wouldn't do to stir the pot right now.

'Paul, that means you'll have to climb out onto the hull and check the batteries. The disconnect must've happened there.'

'Oh, no problem.' Airily, like he pulled these outlandish stunts all the time. More likely, he was too chickenshit to drag his sorry ass back in to face the music.

Instead of going through the rigmarole of opening any more airlocks, Paul simply climbed out the gaping hole where the rest of the Capsule used to be. Outside was practically inside now, anyhow.

Michael was obviously having trouble getting back into his story. He wiped his perspiring forehead, and for a moment I saw the vague shifting restlessness behind his eyes clear. The smeared lenses of madness and trauma temporarily aligned to allow clear vision. They must be some potent drugs. Briefly I saw the stark misery of the real Michael peering out.

'They were going t' get him. I knew it. Oh, they were waiting. Shooting along with us through the dark. Always the dead of night, so far as we were concerned, slept whenever we liked. Lost track of things.

'John's watch was the last t' stop, he was a real magpie for the fancy stuff. Not entirely sure he always paid for it, either. You, you're reporting all this back t' Angie, right? That I did as she wanted?'

Such pathetic need. Angela's calling card, the hallmark of all those she left in her wake. 'What did she want you to do?'

There it was. The same arrogance that'd nearly made me puke as he kissed my weeping sister goodbye. 'Ah, so the ugly duckling *wasn't* privy t' all the crown secrets. How does that feel? Does it sting, t' know Angie didn't tell you all?'

'She never had to, Michael. I knew my sister.'

'But there *was* something you couldn't do for her, couldn't be for her. And Angie wanted it more than anything in the world. This one thing, that only *I* could accomplish. Ah, wait now.' He leered at me with insufferable slyness. 'Better make that *two* things, eh?'

Taking the time to splutter "You repulse me!" would have been profoundly redundant. I chose instead to wait him out. Waited for sanity to blow away like clouds from the sky, not wanting to squander my precious patience.

'I didn't want t' go Out there,' Michael whined piteously. 'That night I met Angie, I was all set t' pull out of the program altogether. Go back t' sales or something.'

'So why didn't you?'

'I can't tell you. Can't tell anyone. It's not safe.' He glanced about furtively. 'If you talk about *them*, they can hear, you know. And they notice who you're talking t', too. *Nobody's* safe!'

Ah, this was familiar. I'd bet Michael was just the credulous sort to go forwarding those emails that threatened bad luck, too.

Better to spread it around, than risk misfortune landing in his lap. Like it hadn't already done so with both feet. 'In that case, I suspect it's a little late for me.

'Besides, I'm not scared of shabby urban legends.'

'I was plenty afraid,' he confessed in a low, quavering tone. 'So scared of hearing Angie's voices, I couldn't *breathe*. But Angie, she turned me right around. Said it's no use being scared of something that might not even be there; no good if we didn't *know*. If I were the one t' find out for sure, come back with proof … I'd be a hero!'

I felt a familiar, sinking feeling. No matter the disaster that over swept my life, if you tracked it upstream it always turned out one way or another that Angela had smashed the dam.

Left to himself, Michael would have sunk back into obscurity. Become the nothing he was always intended to be. But Angela just had to seize the golden opportunity to find out about her precious voices. She couldn't just be practical, and ignore nightmares like a grownup, oh no. Her dreams had to be *special*.

And, no doubt, she'd wished to flaunt a famous boyfriend. Preferably one to match her shoes. Whichever way you sliced it Michael was of no good to her whatsoever if he jumped ship from the program.

So, sure, I didn't need everything about my sister spelled out. I *knew* Angela. And understanding now that she'd had her reasons for choosing a crotchstain like Michael, I couldn't sort out whether that made me feel better or worse.

'I always did as she asked.' His nose wrinkled a little. 'I'll bet you did, too. But once I was Outside, Angie wasn't there. We were all becoming a bit … strange. Paul, that asswipe, got himself a taste for Outside. Seemed he couldn't get enough all of a sudden. Kept wanting t' put that suit back on and "check" the hull again. Like he was afraid it was going t' be different.

'Beth, who was right in Paul's ear-hole, spent all *her* time sifting through the big fat zippo Out there with what was left of the antenna array.

'Every meal we had t' drag her out, physically haul her kicking and screaming between us, and plunk her down all sullen faced at the table. It was like living with a shit of a teenager.

'No choice, though. We were all t' eat together. It was one of the Captain's cherished rules t' live by. Orchid *said* it was t' keep us bound together as a team, but everyone knew it was really about stopping anyone scraping more than their share outta the poop chute.'

And thus I met the novel experience of feeling amazed and disgusted at the same time. 'The *what*?'

'We'd plenty of names like that for the food synthesizer—if you can't laugh, you might weep, right? Every fucking thing we ate was cut with our own waste. Now, anyone who went t' school ought t' know that's a weak idea. But there were we, paragons of mankind, grubbing through our shit for trace vitamins and minerals t' be recycled.'

Oddly, Michael seemed to almost savour airing the humiliation. Perhaps it was worth it to see his teammates brought down. 'In front of everybody you'd tip a big, stinking, embarrassing bucket load in the front, while their eyes measured and assessed what you'd made. I'll never wonder what it's like in a battery farm again! A torturous cage-farm, where the product was becoming increasingly difficult t' pass. So then you'd fill all the bowls at the spout, for the crew t' sit about and choke down. Just like some awful parody of a family dinner.'

His laughter rattled. 'Then out the back of the chute would tinkle this little hardened crystal of toxins, and all the other crap the machinery found no use for. Kicking them about underfoot. Those snowdrifts of waste crystals we were collecting represented the failure of our neat, closed little loop.

'Sooner or later there'd be no compressed cubes of nutritional goodness left t' feed in, and not a drop of piss or shit t' stretch it out. What were we going t' fucking well do then?

'We'd be left a bunch of withered corpses, drier than jerky. Sprawled amidst piles of the useless crystals as they sparkled away, with all our sins and poisons locked away inside.

'The disquieting bit was, we started out with stacks of the good cubes. Surely such a disgusting fucking dinnertime ritual wasn't necessary, not right from the start. But that was the sort of crazy bitch we had in Captain Orchid. She wasn't silly enough t' bank on us finding our way home; wasn't enough of a downer t' hope for some other explosion t' finish us off. I guess her logical middle was t' cling on grimly, and survive as long as possible, whatever the price.'

That sounded so similar to my threadbare everyday that I squirmed. And to hear that the logical extreme of that track came down to chowing on your own crap … didn't exactly fill me with burgeoning pride.

'Please, listen … You *have* t' tell Angie I love her. Just whisper it, if you have t', even if she doesn't seem t' hear. Like a secret note out of prison. Tell her I'm co-operating. You tell her I'll do whatever it takes t' be with her again.'

What would it take to be with Angela again? The cruel impossibility of it, for him or me, stung me so badly that my first words to Cormac were, 'Just what the sod is wrong with you people?'

There was no stirring the thick soup of the man's demeanour. He paused in the act of inviting himself in, and then held the door wide. 'Come for a walk, if you please. I've something to show you.'

'Me?' I had to crowd past him in the doorway. Even while wanting to smack the smug off his mug, I was suddenly reminded that dressing nice is rarely done for its own sake.

Still, clothes and all, I didn't feel quite fortified for Dr

Cormac's latest jaunt. It was reassuring to feel the sedative packet bulging my pocket.

'Mr Formir's latest recounting makes for quite the intriguing listen, don't you find? Quite riddled with the sort of cracks I'm sure *certain parties* would love to worm their fingers into.'

I lashed out. 'Don't you dare give him up to them!'

Wait – what? Why should I give a dead rat's dingle all of a sudden? Good, go; hand Michael off to whatever he had coming! Except ... that he remembered Angela. Almost as vividly as I did. We were the last, we two. In a way, it'd be like passively surrendering her to the Screws all over again, and that I could not abide. How many times in a life could one person's failure rise up to strangle them?

'And I was under the impression that I just wouldn't do. Ms Hanberry, as you must be keenly aware, Mr Formir's breadth of options consist entirely of myself or them.' As we walked Cormac flashed his special sneer, the one that said he was laying it out for the slow kids.

Thick carpet ruffled so noticeably beneath our feet that we left a trial of darker colour, one I could gratefully follow back to my room if needs be. There was that scent again, that teased my nose with slightly failing wealth and comfort, heaving itself up for one last stand against a world that only valued convenience. Lights glimmered in glass shades shaped like giant seashells. And the walls, even the walls were papered in that old-fashioned green my failing memory suggested had been discontinued because of poisons in the pigment.

'Now, you may not agree with my methodology but, really, what else can you possibly suggest? That, seeing as Mr Formir is clearly unfit to decide his own future, and having stuck my proverbial neck so far out to relocate him here, I ought to now turn his fortunes over to *you*?'

'Michael can't make his own choices because he has no earthly concept of what falling into their hands would mean. He's never seen what they do, he's been gone the entire sodding time!'

'Quite the irony, wouldn't you say? Seeing as he was part of the catalyst for their rise to supremacy. I can't imagine how one might explain today's world to Mr Formir: nobody truly comprehends how Charles' secretive kin choose to operate when the gloves come off. None are left in any state to relate their lurid tale rationally. To explain what falling into their hands truly means.' It took me a while to realise Dr Cormac's use of first names was not familiarity, but contempt.

'Well, *I* know,' I snarled grimly, slicing through his overweening satisfaction for once.

I'd been so caught up in trying to argue my way around a conversationally superior partner, our surroundings had been flashing by like a lifetime missed, when they begged to be enjoyed. Hallways, hallways. Plumbline straight, unnaturally perfect, as though a machine had drawn them with a laser. Yet very old fashioned. Like strolling through a health club's spa. And the soft, muting dove-grey carpet that seemed to stretch on forever. My only assurance that we weren't moving in circles was the trail we left.

But what Cormac halted us smack bang in front of was a huge door, one that refused to be ignored. I checked my latent memory for those we strode past while arguing. Yep, this portal was bigger and more ornate than anything else I'd seen on the station. Quite the aberration. The door exuded more than a touch of rich ol' boy, square calfskin panels fastened by brass studs. It sighed a breath of exquisite leather, established wealth, into the corridor. The expense of shipping such frivolous bulk up to Threshold spoke maniacal volumes of ego and power, as I'm sure was the intent.

This was where Dr Cormac would have escorted his bank representatives, sponsors, and other fatcat moneymen before the Disaster startled them all away, like pheasant from the brush. And now here stood I, itching a little in my new clothes. How far the mighty could plummet.

Cormac paused with one hand splayed on the door. He glanced back at me, then chuckled to himself a bit and ditched the theatrical pose. Sure, he'd hauled me up here to try and sell me on something. My expression was making it just as clear that a blatant pitch'd accomplish little better than pissing me off.

'Welcome to the boardroom, Ms Hanberry. There is something rather special within that I'd like you to witness. I feel it may illustrate what I require from Mr Formir, and why it's so important.' He smiled, and was trying to make it a nice smile. 'Afterward, I've arranged for a meal to be served in your room.'

Ah yes. The never-failing lure of attending to my monstrous gut. It was surprising I'd tipped so easily into Cormac's world of patchy meals and irregular sleep. Food when it became insistently necessary. Pity it hadn't turned out the same physical result; Cormac was built like one of those neurotic bony dogs they race around and around tracks. Should we experience a crisis I could picture him flickering off down the corridor on those long shanks at eye-watering speed while I huffed and lumbered at the rear, doomed by my inability to keep up.

Still Cormac lingered in place. Waiting to dramatically throw open his big man-door in appropriately grandiose fashion. 'You may wish to bolster yourself. One time, an attendee from the State Treasury lost his cookies on my shoes and then fainted dead away in the doorway. He was rather the hefty specimen; took four men to haul him out by stretcher.'

It was obvious he immediately regretted the indelicacy, and any aspersions. I waved a hand dismissively.

'Already had ample time to clear things out of my system today, thanks.' Thinking of the poor suits currently seeing in the morning by scrubbing my wretched stink from their upholstery.

Either Dr Cormac was already all over the sordid episode, or he didn't care to know.

'Well. In the end he did double all the standing contributions to keep his little mishap hush. I've never laughed so heartily in all my days as I did perusing his inventive press release, on the wonders he'd entirely missed.'

That solved it. As he pushed open the door I palmed another sedative and gulped it down. Better safe than sorry. Future me would just have to take care of herself.

Then I followed him. And it wasn't to my credit that I failed to upchuck or faint like Cormac's illustrious financier; I might well have done either.

Instead, some failsafe tripped in my head and I just went … blank.

I'm sure the intervention protected me from blowing out what few candles I had left. Later, when I had time to think, it also made me woefully disturbed as to how much went on without the lamps needing to be lit at all. It's a little scary discovering what your brain can happily do on its own; you at least expect to be consulted.

In my case it firmly decided, "Sorry, no more consciousness for *you*, missy! Now, you just stand there quietly and think about what you've done."

Coming back gradually I became aware of a heartbeat first, and was pleased to identify it as my own. Slow and steady, wins the race, which in my disassociated fugue was a comforting assurance things must be ok. Were there danger, I'm sure it'd be fit to fly right out of my chest. Then the warmth and fleshiness of my body returned. Often a curse, but right now a reassuring weight. Sometimes it helps knowing you're unlikely to be whisked away by the first breeze.

Sight was last. My surroundings came back slowly, resolving out of a grainy white static.

When I finally woke all the way up, I'd no idea how long I'd been standing there.

Dr Cormac was monitoring me blandly, with crossed arms, offering no assistance.

He'd obviously seen worse, and was prepared to let me muddle through for myself. But right now I didn't have time to bother with the man's posturing vanities.

The boardroom glowed richly before me, every inch as its heavy bombastic door had advertised. I'd seen rich old bugger clubs like this before, though. They sparked little interest and certainly not the intended awe, being primarily calculated to keep riffraff like me out. Or at least safely confined to the kitchen, out of mind. Perhaps slurping cold dregs from a saucer, while the chef turned a disdainful eye.

The staggering blow that'd cut my mind down came, not via the grand room, but from the *boggling* sight through the far grander window. It was a huge wall-to-wall custom job, the sort an architect only troubles with when there's one sod of a view.

And there'd never been a view like this before.

Entering as we did, at the top end of the long plush boardroom, left you gaping wide-eyed out the window at Earth. I'd seen old photos of this vista before, without fully realising they were taken here. You used to be able to buy them as postcards, now only sent as hate mail to terrorised victims.

Nothing corrects your priorities like the experience of standing there in person. Staring down at the vivid green and blue of our heartbreakingly lovely world.

By all rights I ought to have been terrified, useless and whimpering for help. But on the contrary, I felt elated. Gravid with it, elated and powerful. I was filled to the brim with the sure knowledge that this was our home, our only home, there'd be no other. And it was so precious and vulnerable in the void.

Our world had only the thin, poorly understood membrane of the Shell to shield it from all of Outside and what had we done, in our arrogance and carelessness? We'd gone and pierced it right through.

*I'll protect you*, my swelling heart pledged irrationally at the breathtaking sight. Which was bizarre.

How could one person hope to protect the entire Earth? Surely that was a job for governments, world powers.

*Or Screws*, my mind whispered nastily.

Sure, I'd managed a real bang-up job so far at taking care of Angela, not to mention my own stupid self. But that's how it felt, pathetic or no. In a life entirely lacking in romance, that one moment of beauty smote me. I almost brayed a laugh. I'd finally fallen in love, and it was with the entire world.

It wasn't easy knowledge to swallow, but I now realised that right up until that moment I'd been profoundly vain and foolish. Greedy, self-serving and very, very small, in the way only short-sighted humanity could manage. But now I *had* to be better.

I couldn't believe the Screws worked so hard to keep this view from people! Surely as you frogmarched every human being up here to confront this, one by one, the problems of the world would recede. Hunger, wastefulness, mistrust; they'd all cease being so sodding vital.

Or perhaps the effect would turn out more transitory, like experiencing childbirth. Once the direct stimulus ceased you gradually forgot the agony. You'd have to bring people up here in shifts, forever.

'Over here, Ms Hanberry.'

What, was there *more*?

Cormac had taken a small polished cherry manhole cover off a viewing port at the far end of the boardroom. The cover itself was no bigger than a pizza box, and near bleeding with the vividness of the crimson GATE logo.

I vacillated near the door. That's right, all this and I'd hardly stepped into the room.

Finally I understood why they'd dubbed this place "Threshold." To move to the other end of the room and peek through was to traverse the full gamut of every possible emotion in a few short steps.

To me, the feeling of crossing to Cormac was of plunging straight into that sick, childlike dread of everything you've done wrong. Actions that keep you up at night, rigid with self-loathing. The things you knew you couldn't fix, and the consequences still waiting.

Threshold Station was built *through* the Shell. Mostly within, but her arse dangled Outside. Between two plushly upholstered chairs I could stand and stare straight up and Out through the clear manmade cap. The hole in the Shell. The precision of the wound spoke to me of mathematics and logic. Bare efficiency, and progress at all costs. Especially when paying the price in cheap, replaceable humans.

It was the antithesis of our privileged surrounds, far beyond anything I'd seen practiced on the ground, and merely to gaze *on* it made me afraid, let alone *through*. Although not in any rational way I could articulate. Perhaps my idealistic vow of protection was hopelessly naïve, and already all for nothing.

At first, the only thing to be made out through the viewing port was darkness. The face of thick impenetrable nothing pressed to the gap, glaring in avidly at our brightness and warmth. I didn't want to flinch, but fear twisted me all up inside.

Then I caught the first of them. The tiniest little glimmers of light that I'd seen in the grainy out-of-date video. They appeared like the flash of silvery fish to me, swimming there in the darkness. Curiosity dug in beneath panic's clutching fingers, and sprung them loose.

I found I could breathe again, and treated myself to a series of deep whooshing breaths. I also stank of stressed sweat. Nice one, fatguts; only a couple of hours, and these new clothes would have to be washed already.

Still, I must be made of sterner stuff than I realised. If somebody'd quizzed me on all this before I entered the room, I'd have nodded sagely. Yep.

The inferno of so much emotion boiling together would *absolutely* sear me to a smoking crisp on the spot. I'd never survive it.  And with that established, I would've fled shrieking down the corridor.

*Hey, don't go forgetting monsieur sedative*, my snide internal voice prodded with a stiff finger, keen to deflate all this pride. *Maybe you ought to take time to write those nice drug company folks, and thank them for preventing you disgracing your fancy new knickers.*

My internal monologue was a real dick, but likely no more than I deserved.

'It's …' How could you even say what it all was? On second thought, it was no sodding wonder the Screws kept a tight lid on this.

If the miserable specimens I rubbed shoulders with back home caught wind, there'd be no way they'd continue to drag themselves to their awful, drear jobs each morning. Holiday films and sport spectacles would no longer suffice to distract from the depression and frustration, the endless effort that took you nowhere. *Society*, in short, which heavily depends on compliance with just these things would grind to a halt.

What would we have then? Anarchy? Revolution? Destructive terms so archaic as to make me smile, but the consequences wouldn't be. Thousands would perish without the take-me-for-granted comforts society furbished: electricity, medicine. Clean water and food.

So, bereft, we'd have to set about building an entirely new type of world.

Being a product of my time I couldn't imagine how such a radically new existence might look. I couldn't make myself glance past the destruction should we tear down the life we lived now.

With its sickening that we tolerated because the poison came in such tiny doses, every day, and we never had enough free time to bother about it.

Dr Cormac crossed the room, moving more boldly than I. After all, this was his space.

Did he sit in one of those grand chairs, alone in this crumbling baroque castle, and stare at Outside? What kind of man was he?

He certainly seemed pleased as punch at having a companion to share it with now, if not a contemporary. 'I find that on viewing this, a sip of wine always serves to bring one back down to Earth.'

He gave a grimace. It may have been intended as a smile, meant to be charming. He was even more out of practice than I. 'A neat reminder that alongside all the grandeur, the basics of life must go on.'

'Grandeur,' I murmured. It was a good word. Fancier than what normally crossed my tongue, but no-one could deny the situation called for a vocabulary beyond the day-to-day. In truth, it demanded a far grander person. Somebody outrageous, brimming with confidence and careless bravado. Somebody hallmarked by life for great things. But Angela was dead, and they'd fished me from the heap instead. Everything was wrong.

All I could think to say, was, 'Is anything Michael's told me true?'

'Enough.'

Dr Cormac had his head and shoulders buried in a lacquered cabinet, which appeared to fold down into some kind of kitchenette. A sort of fancy iteration of the adorably small cookspace you get in a bedsit. Bloody ballsack—had Cormac spent his days *living* here? Going about normal activities like picking his teeth and blowing his nose, with that view looming over him?

He fished something rather casually from his pocket and tossed it my way. Something small. That glittered fiercely in its passage through the room against the backdrop of that window.

I snatched after it, fumbled—the notorious bane of any team sport—then had it. Some kind of exquisite faceted crystal. All the prettier for being tiny, about a quarter the width of my pinkie's chipped nail. And a deep rich goldish colour, like poured honey.

The sort of elegant, understated thing you'd see glistening at a beldam's ear, swanning about some gala event, all indulgent strings and candles.

I was charmed. 'What is it?'

Cormac smirked, a more native expression. 'Urine, essentially. Just goes to show, you ought never to put stock in appearance.'

'You tossed me a piss crystal?'

'It's quite sterile. The food synthesizer on board the Capsule spits them out. Ultra-compressed, all the toxins and impurities the machine cannot fabricate anything useful from. Sort of a little diamond. They were everywhere through the recovered piece of the Capsule, like sand, all over the floor.'

A diamond.

'So you see Ms Hanberry, this endeavour we are undertaking is much like archaeology. Mr Formir feeds you his lavish, historical version of events, but we following along have only such small scraps of physical evidence to back it all up. You are welcome to retain that, if you like.'

As bowerbird-enraptured as any woman, despite the gem's dubious origin, I held the piss diamond up to see its crisp facets sparkle. My first diamond. Well, at least I could rest assured it hadn't been dug up by impoverished slave children in a mine somewhere.

In terms of size, it didn't have anything on the whopping engagement ring Michael shackled my sister with. His way was of grandiose gestures, as though they somehow made up the lack of more modest traits, such as honesty or reliability. It did, however, strongly resemble the second ring, which my sister was presented with not five years later.

Angela had been wearing both engagement rings, gaudy and petite, squeezed together on her finger when she died.

Cormac offered me a glass of wine, the sharp peppery scent of which had flooded the room the moment he uncorked the bottle.

I'd never seen such an unashamedly brimming glass. He poured like a venue desperate to get the girls squiffy. You could only tell it was red when the light showed through, igniting tiny crimson gleams in the depths. Otherwise it was as inky dark as the void Outside.

I took an incautious gulp, and nearly spluttered. Either Cormac's tongue had curled up and died, a common occurrence as you age, or he was a man of extreme tastes. Bang on the money about the booze re-centring you, though. A glow lit in my gut and spread outward, sharpening physical awareness right down to my fingers and toes. Suddenly much of my attention was taken up by the foreign sensation of expensive fabrics on skin.

Normally a white drinker, I steeled myself and sipped again. Just like medicine. It's good for you, fatguts, get it in you. You managed to dry swallow those tablets, you can put this down.

'So.' Cormac seated himself, gestured lazily with his glass. 'What a view, huh?'

I started. What, was he *interested* in my opinion all of a sudden? I was rather itchily reminded of how incautious I'd been with this powerful man to date, how unwise. 'I like half of it just fine.'

'I suppose I've no need to inquire as to which half takes Ms Hanberry's fancy. So conforming. So conventional. So *safe*.'

'I'm baffled as to why so many folk got a bug in their shorts over the Capsule in the first place. When you look around, how did the Outermen really help the world at all?'

Cormac's glass was already empty.

And these were big crystal balloons, of the type I'd normally associate with brandy. His tastebuds must be toast. 'Would you enjoy hearing something amusing?'

'Sure.'

What tickled the great Dr Cormac? Skinning kittens?

He certainly looked in the mood for chuckles, with a hint of rosiness to each pallid cheek. Perhaps I'd pegged him all wrong. It was possible Ashley Cormac was no more than your garden variety alcoholic.

A little embarrassed for him I sipped my drink as he talked, so at least he wouldn't have to go it alone.

'This may not shock you, but I was one of those dreadful young lads who *always* found cause to argue with the teacher. Even way back in primary school, they all dreaded me. I saved especial stridency for those exhausted staff who attempted to claim, "Because that's simply the way things are." Or that other rich plum: "It's how it's always been." As though words could be a cork in a mind, to keep everything sealed inside.

'Of course, now I have an appreciation for those poor men and women who were simply struggling to perform their thankless jobs: stuff an exam's worth of knowledge into ungrateful brat heads, so that we could be shunted further up the production line. But it didn't feel like that at the time. It seemed outrageous, and I was on fire with indignation.'

The wine had appeared and vanished from his glass again, like a magic trick. While I was still only halfway through and already struggling. Cormac topped me off anyhow and slid the rest of the bottle into his glass. Charmingly, he had one of those red wine smiley faces going at the corners of his mouth.

'There was this lass who always sat up the rear of the classroom, as though she preferred not to be noticed.'

He sighed heavily, and I stifled a smile behind my hand. Of course there was a girl. There was always a girl with these guys. A dusty memento to be taken down from the shelf and mooned over every now and again.

'I can't even recall her name now. Tiny as a pea, but with this astounding mop of red hair like she'd been raised in the wild by clowns. Skin like ricepaper.

'It was not her way to pipe up in class, and she certainly never did so again, but one day out of the blue up went that tiny paw. She asked our teacher what was Outside the Shell, and there was thunderstruck silence.

'Children are like that. They don't realise when certain taboos have been crossed, or otherwise, they'll often push that barrier to test what will happen. If that was the case, she certainly got what was coming to her.

'Our teacher, pillar of learning who *ought* to have been fostering critical thinking, especially in such a shy moppet who'd shown no previous inclination, actually stood ramrod-straight up the front proud as day, and launched into a brutal harangue on how mankind ought to humbly accept the world as it is. Never seeking to grow, comprehend, or be anything more. "We, as a species, are limited and defined by our reality," or some such flippant rubbish culled straight from the annals of Drive-Thru Digest.

'Ah, even now it makes my blood boil! I could not tolerate it. And the whole while that poor girl, being castigated before the entire class, was shrinking in her seat. Her eyes growing larger as though she wished the ground to swallow her—it was heartbreaking.'

'It obviously left quite the impression.' My own schooldays were a pointless blur. And employers, I'd found, didn't give the faintest toss what your degree was in, only that you had one, as it was a good indicator of tendency to slave thanklessly.

'I'll wager the teacher recalls the incident with crystal clarity to this day, and the rest of the class to boot. I got myself up on the table in front of everyone and told the bully what for. Really shouted him down.'

Yes, I'll bet you were a right little horror to your poor minimum wage teacher. 'Then what happened?'

'Let's say I was incredibly fortunate they'd outlawed caning by then. My parents were called in, and I was hauled before the principal.' Cormac was obviously relishing this. 'So I told *her* what for, as well.

'My mother applauded, and laughed when father tried to hush her.

'The young lady in question avoided me like the plague ever after, of course, as did everybody. I'd established a reputation as liable to do anything, a risk nobody wished to associate with. And as penance I ended up collecting rubbish in the yard for every lunch period, right up until graduation. I still consider it worth every second.'

I started to laugh. I didn't intend to, but once the snorts and giggles began splurting past it became too hard to stop.

'All this ...' I waved a hand at our surroundings—if I didn't get a hold of myself, wine was going to end up all over the boardroom. 'You did all this because somebody once told you *no*?'

'I believe you'll find people are most often simple creatures,' he responded airily. 'Even when achieving something complex, the driving motivation springs from basic personal sources. Can *you* claim grander justification behind the things you've accomplished in your life?'

'I haven't done anything with my life. But not everybody can be *doing*, you know,' I added defensively. 'There's not the space for all of us to be incredible. Most people have to make do with simply *being*.'

Cormac, who'd begun pacing excitedly as we spoke, too wound to remain in his chair, stopped and turned to face me with the view all terrible and glorious behind him. So arresting, he might dissolve away into it.

'And yet, here you stand. In this remarkable place.'

'It shouldn't be me, though, should it? It *ought* to have been Angela. This is just a ... a bad mistake. Fate gone wrong.'

'Fate!' he snorted. 'Poppycock! We construct the future ourselves, moment to moment, without *fate* ever lending a hand.'

'You wouldn't say that if you'd met my sister.' I rolled the bowl of the glass between my hands, to give myself something to look at. 'She was ... better than ordinary folk, you know? Brighter.'

In fairytales there's a beautiful sister and an ugly one. And to the ugly one, valour, as though in compensation for all she's missed. But stories weren't truth: I'd been gifted no special qualities. Angela had them all.

Cormac squinted at me critically, or at least I think he did. There wasn't enough to read in a face like that. 'If that is the manner in which you recall your sibling, then perhaps your presence is a sign that now is your time to become bigger than you've been. A little more like her.'

I spread my hands helplessly. 'Do I really look like I need to be any bigger?'

Dr Cormac spluttered—a lot of his social airs had taken a swan dive with sobriety. He was saved further disgrace by a knock at the door. Although it was more a sort of "ploof" with all that leather padding.

'Yes?'

At the sight of the familiar face that poked into the room I almost shouted with joy. Tall Jake! Not wanting to get him into trouble I forbore rushing to fling big sweaty arms about him, but still fairly trembled in place.

'Ms Catherine's meal is now served in her quarters.' Jake held the door wider for me to step out with him.

'Ah, of course. My apologies, Ms Hanberry. I've been keeping you.'

Dr Cormac waved me on. He was ripe to be burrowing back inside the bar the moment I stepped out, and I wondered how often he managed to restock. It could only be via sneaky midnight missions up the cable, surely they didn't risk those too often? At this rate, Threshold'd be dry as a desert in a handful of days.

I joined Tall Jake. Again, as he shut the door behind us with a soft click, I'd the urge to squeeze him in the sort of hug that would leave him scarred for life.

And I scarcely knew the guy. Wow, no more wine and sedatives for me.

With a jerk of his head toward the boardroom door Jake put a finger to his lips, *silence*, and then a tap at the ear for good measure.

I felt instantly confused. Who was listening, that it mattered what we said? Wasn't that the whole point of Threshold, to be able to blurt whatever you wanted without cross-checking to the $n$th degree?

So we couldn't chat. But still, there was so much comfort to be derived from a familiar set of eyes that looked reasonably pleased to see you. He even gave a conspiratorial wink to lift the heart—can you *believe* these jerks up here?

It seemed Jake was to be a muzzled ally, but in terms of bolstering my bravery not a powerless one. And how had he found himself promoted to dogsbody? That had to sting a fellow whose pay grade encompassed bespoke suits and a rather neat haircut. Such a little land outside time Cormac'd cobbled together up here: a private, aloof castle replete with servants versus the sneering aristocracy.

How peculiar to find myself batting on the highbrow team in that equation. Talk about a fish out of water!

Jake slipped a folded note into my palm. Typed all in full-volume capitals, how I imagined a telegram might look. Of course nobody had actually *sent* a telegram since well before my birth.

It read:

THERE ISN'T ANYTHING OUTSIDE
BAR WHAT WE CARRY THERE OURSELVES.
DO NOT TRUST **ANYONE** ON THRESHOLD.
DON'T LET YOURSELF BELIEVE
THEIR TOXIC FICTIONS.
AND BE CAREFUL.

It was signed,

CHARLES.

# OUTERMEN

## SEVEN

## NOTHING BUT WHAT WE CARRY

JAKE WAS KINDLY escorting me somewhere brand spanking new to visit Michael today, just to keep the freshness in the relationship.

The Outerman's mysterious new quarters had finally been completed, whatever that meant. They'd installed him yesterday to accept crawling supplicants such as me like a lord on his throne.

After all the effort, I hoped Michael's new digs were at least nicer, a tad less traumatic. Having come all this way, so far the last surrounds the poor bastard was ever likely to see had smacked of the brutally clinical. Dark, and sodding depressing.

Dare I hope for a light, airy replica of some seaside villa? Could I believe Michael might also be the sort to while away idle hours dreaming of a searing beach? Of dabbling bare toes in tiny still rock pools, brimming with quivering secret life, that fled as though from a giant?

Pfft, no. *Michael's* dream getaway would be wall to wall with the scantily clad admirers he craved, bubbly girls with no sense. Nothing like my deserted tropical wasteland.

Anyhow, to drop in on Michael now, all I had to manage was a leisurely stroll down what Jake called the long hall. Under my own volition, being of sound mind and body, I was to venture into the perilous rear section of Threshold. Where her ornate ass hung through the Shell into Outside.

It didn't get more unnatural than this.

The long hall was Threshold's "unsafe bit" as Jake fastidiously dubbed it, floating his rather humorous assumption that any of her was safe. Well, whatever he needed to get to sleep at night. And by the sick look on his face he'd be bedding down well up the other end of the station, as far from the long hall as he could get.

The protruding section was plated with heavy shielding like a tortoise, but he insisted you couldn't trust anything back there. Down failed to assert itself with any fidelity. Things could go uncomfortably screwy without notice.

Once, Tall Jake whispered, he got lost.

Which didn't make a lick of sense as the name wasn't clever, it really was just all the one long hall. But he had wandered in increasing dread for hours, searching for anything familiar. With not so much as a peep of anyone else about.

And those were the days when Threshold fairly hummed with activity, spreading the cash around. Four sets of hands for every job. But now this eerie silence, his anxious hearing reporting only a high pitched *pheeeee*. The sickening feeling crept in that he'd been left behind.

The worst was when he emerged back into the busy corridors, sound and bustle returning all at once as though a bubble had popped, hurting his ears. Jake was croaking with sour thirst, famished and shambling in exhaustion. And the clocks, even his wristwatch which he threw away in a rage insisted he'd only been gone a minute or two, tops. Like they were mocking him, making light of how afraid he'd been. A few minutes weren't even enough to have reached the end of the long hall, about faced and strolled back.

Threshold Station made him older, Jake complained, the bitch. A bunch of utterly wretched, lost, wandering hours older than everyone else on Earth, and he never came right. He'd felt out of step with life ever since.

'Is that why you don't like it up here?'

'It'd be neat, wouldn't it? That one experience, spoiling everything. But I've found however you like to simplify it, nobody marches to such cut and dried motivations. We're all just a heaving mess, driven on by the whips of everything that's ever happened. All the things we can't let go of. Being lost in the long hall … it's like it unlocked everything bad in my memories, all at once. I was floundering in it. Drowning.'

So Jake's little tale wasn't much of a motivator. He probably hoped I might barricade myself away in a panic, spare either of us going; and, don't get me wrong, I was sorely tempted.

If I followed Jake's nervous lead and baulked, was Dr Cormac likely to have me dragged kicking and squealing along the carpet, with my nails tearing up long soft runnels? I'd a nasty feeling I already knew the answer. I was going down the long hall, and the level of dignity alone'd be up to me.

It went without saying that my precious sedative stash took a hit, but that wasn't what bestowed the derring-do for me to trail Jake's reluctant steps down the endless hall, as it writhed its way into Threshold's entrails. The pills merely ensured I drifted along the way like a giggling pink cloud, my shoes barely brushing the carpet.

But of course they were actually Dr Cormac's shoes. I had to quit claiming any of this crap as mine: "my" shoes, and "my" room. I wasn't likely to hang onto any of it, step back into my life kitted out like some top shelf dame. In fact, the only thing I genuinely owned up here was what I'd brought. Namely, myself.

In the end what succeeded in getting my big anxious butt rolling down the sinister long hall was the wonderful, wondrous, quite frankly incredible coffee.

Caffeine's absence from my life'd been like a roughly yanked tooth. Front and centre, where everyone can see it disfigure your smile. Can't sink into the numbness of forgetting, 'cause you can't ever stop poking your dumb tongue in the gap. I'd thought I would never get to smell coffee again. I mourned it, and finally lodged helplessly in that resigned stage, that precludes ever moving on because you only remember the good times.

To be inhaling the steam now, I couldn't comprehend how I'd ever become so quietly adjusted to the loss. All those years of misery might have been a bad dream. Its reappearance was an impossibility that severely rocked my ability to process logic.

Just like Michael, but with the feelings in reverse.

Hot coffee delivered right to my bedside with cold breakfast.

Me yanking the sheet to my chin so fast my feet came flying clear of the other end, as some kind of gormless barrier against Tall Jake trundling in with the tray. Man, my toenails could use a trim. Luckily Threshold lay out quality linen, as there was rather a lot of me to shield from Jake's incurious, and frankly probably horrified eyes.

'Go easy on that,' was all I got from him as he exited. As tempting as it was to turn all huffy, assuming it was about me sticking my snout in the food, a lot of crackpots had actually *celebrated* coffee's ban. Cleaner living through torment.

Case and point, he'd delivered a nice, healthy cereal. You could tell by all the grains, and the uniform parchment colour. Here sat congealing gritty evidence that breakfast is in fact the most miserable meal of the day, deserving only to be slept through.

Offsetting it like a mirage was the steaming pot of coffee.

The whole sodding pot! If crying weren't so impossible for me, I might've wept. It was one of those all-steel pots, too stylishly impractical to pick up without searing three degrees clean off your mitts. I had to wrap a pillowcase 'round the handle. I wanted to fling my arms around it and scream, "I missed you!"

A few grim mouthfuls of cold wheat later and I'd drained the entire pot, misery to ecstasy with every chew versus sip. Only bothering with the dainty cup instead of pouring directly down my greedy gullet for nicety's sake, in case Cormac had the pervert brigade monitoring my room. Plenty of ways to embarrass myself as it was, without handing them footage of the hog with her head in the trough.

Of course, it was no easy thing to land back in that saddle. Coffee's bitter embrace held a few quirks fickle memory'd glossed over; no worse than the thorn's role in maintaining healthy respect for the rose.

I hadn't remembered the massive heat flush that makes you want to rip your clothes off—or in my case, sheet. Or the clumsy trembling of an overwrought nervous system: farewell, fine motor control. The alarming heart palpitations that quivered my entire frame. Don't even get me started on the sickly caffeine sweats.

And let's not mention the gastrointestinal flush button, the panicked rush to the bathroom. I hopped in a quick shower after to sluice away the trauma. In living memory I couldn't recall ever feeling scraped so horrifically, sparklingly clean.

Despite all of this, the true wonder of wonders that had remained lost all these years was this springy, newfound sense of *motivation*. Of feeling engaged with reality, wanting to get out there and shake up the world. Small wonder those slippery Screws banned such easy chemical up-and-at-'em. They've kept us crouching in our sealed-up little houses, it's a wonder we've not burrowed neurotically into the ground by now, fleeing the sky. Retreating deeper and deeper, until the Earth boasted a core of ultra-compressed human flesh. One quivering, cowardly organism.

That said, I went and fearfully layered sedative atop it all. You see, this is precisely why I can't have nice things.

At least there wasn't much to the long hall to indicate what lay beyond its fragile skin and start me off on a panic. No windows. Just the hall, looking exactly the same as all those that'd come before. Perhaps with a more mournful air of neglect than usual, which increased further in, but without Jake's dire warning I wouldn't have realised we'd strayed at all.

Dust sheets hung limp over some of the light fittings. Others without globes. I frowned critically at faded, bland paintings peeling out of their frames: they hadn't started out as much, prior to time's creeping fingers wiggling them loose. French provincial rubbish.

Sentimentality of a faux-rustic bent, treasured by retirees who've never had to shovel slop or wring a rooster's scabrous neck in their lives. I hadn't either, of course; growing up in the 'burbs the origin of food was a nasty rumour. I imagine neither activity as a barrel of laughs.

Dr Cormac being his intolerable self had gone and painted a line of heavy red warning across the long hall's carpet, matting the fibres down and declaiming the boundary of one state of existence from the other. Inside to Outside. Sod knows what he used, looked disturbingly like blood. Cheap horrorshow props; couldn't let the investors miss the thrill of their walk on the wild side.

How many of them had lingered uneasily, as I did, on the safe side of the line? Everybody staring shamefacedly at the carpet, hoping for someone else to buck up and make the first move. Perhaps the doctor's shoes had even earned themselves another Roman shower. I hoped he waterproofed them. They looked expensive.

Jake turned and scowled back. Timidity wasn't earning me friends. 'You coming, or what?'

I stumbled in crossing the line, of course. If there's anything straightforward that wants muffing, something nice and simple like walking down a hallway, I'm your girl. Tall Jake caught my arm, graciously saving the further embarrassment of my going sprawling. Again I tingled with that weird hyper-awareness that *someone was touching me*. A unique blend of indecent and intrusive, my instinct on how to respond jerking me every which way.

When we reached Michael's room, which didn't look anything special from the outside, Jake held open the door, sparing my runaway thought train further obsessing. 'We got your pal settled yesterday, so he ought to be up and ready to chat by now.'

I craned my neck cautiously. Only darkness within. Not a whiff of tropical paradise, simulated or otherwise. Typical. I faced Jake and took a deep, patient breath. 'I've said it before, but I'll never get sick of repeating it. Michael Formir's no pal of mine.'

I swung away but before I could advance, a warning pressure on my arm. A gesture I couldn't interpret, being too neurotically occupied by how far his fingers'd sunk into soft meaty flesh, that threatened to envelop them like a hungry amoeba.

'Just … be sure never to forget where you are in there,' Jake whispered hoarsely from behind me. Then he withdrew, and I rubbed my arm.

How in the name of all crap's sake could I forget? I felt like tossing my hands up angrily, for all the good it'd do. I was getting *real* sick of the secretive suit brotherhood, and their well-meaning but pointlessly amorphous warnings. As should be blaringly obvious, I'm no sophisticate. If you want me to understand something, spell it out!

The door clapped shut behind me. Leaving only the slim wedge of light sliding beneath from the hall, and it didn't venture far. And that smell again. Worse, now. The herald of the Outerman's disintegration. I stuffed a hand over my nose, it was old fruit sprawled in decaying puddles on a dank stone floor. Tendrils of grey-fuzzed rot, reaching out stealthily to corrupt what health remained.

I'd formed a habit of getting myself into these situations, hadn't I? Already in a sour mood, I promptly went and bashed my toes on something in the dark. *Careful, you great clot.* Heaved a massive beleaguered sigh.

'Michael?' Would it have killed him to roll out the welcome mat?

An answering sigh came drifting from the darkness. Because *I* was putting *him* through so much. 'Angie's hopeless lump of a sister, again.'

Gee, yep. That was my name alright. He was such a knobshine.

'You still intend t' try keeping her from me, then. Haven't heard enough guts spilled, you want the whole floor slithering.'

I shifted my feet uneasily, the bruised one sobbing. Did the surface feel squishy underfoot? 'You're getting no more than you deserve, Michael.' I couldn't help myself. I'd never been able to, he pushed my buttons so hard.

A grinding chuckle. 'Well Ash's cheap bag of tricks won't fool me anymore. Look around, Angie's sister. I'm home.'

Sure, I could peer about myself to some degree now. Doubtless less than Michael could. And why was he huddling on the floor, all snarled up in rags? Where was his clean white bed?

I gradually made out all I had missed by shuffling so trustingly into the blank dark, and shivers coursed up my spine to rattle my teeth.

The shape of Michael's new room was bizarre, and so claustrophobically poky. Made mine look like the royal suite. Every breath of open space choked with blocky bulkheads and other looming shapes, crammed solid. In their original surrounds they'd no doubt been essential, expensive and mind-bendingly technical. Here, as much had simply been jumbled in as possible, as though none of that mattered anymore. No wonder I'd mashed my poor toes. In hindsight, I was lucky to escape a cracked neck.

I loathed these looming chunks on sight, without needing to know what they were or had been for. They seemed to exude a crawling pestilence of memory. If somebody had disinterred the planks of a plague town, borne it here reverently, to be reassembled bit by painstaking bit, finally whole and bleeding its remembered misery into the dark, I couldn't have hated it more.

'What is all this junk?' My voice quavered.

'I never left the Capsule, you see. I'm home.' Both fond and forlorn, for who'd *want* to belong to a terrible place like this?

I sucked in a careful breath. 'Michael, that is flat-out batshit crazy.'

It sounded dumb. Oh, so *this* was crazy, out of all that's happened? But the Outerman was clearly losing touch with what frail measure of reality he'd possessed. My queasy fear for him, as opposed to the far more rational fear *of* him, sprang gleaming into life.

'Look, you're *not* on the Capsule! Try to remember! You made it—somehow, you came home.' He made a disbelieving sound; something like when you've a bad cold, and vacuum mucus into your airways. I persisted. 'Right now you're here with me, in a room on Threshold. Dr Cormac's fitted it to look like the Capsule 'cause he's some kind of fuckwit.'

Michael wasn't even looking at me. His lumpy, hairless head tilted back against the wall and eyes closed. He spoke into the air. 'I always knew, right here in my heart, Angie'd find some way back t' me. Even all the way Out there. Even *Outside*, you see? Nowhere'd be too far.'

His voice was distant and faded, a reminder of how unlikely I'd be to reach him with simple logic. We were, all of us, too locked up in our heads. Safe behind armour of welded conviction. Any attempt to communicate was merely firing a barrage of our brand in another's direction, hoping for a direct hit, but without receiving anything in return.

Or perhaps the explanation was even more pedestrian. He'd an IV taped to his skinny forearm, the needle looking wider than his bicep and likely including a thick creamy dose of tranquilliser. The tubes were long and coiling enough to reach from the shiny metal stand all the way to the floor. Good time saver, that. I should look into it.

'No … no, I never made it back. You can't taunt me with that. Just beyond that bulkhead there's *nothing*. No world, no Shell, nothing.'

'If you say so, Michael. If that makes you happy.' What harm could cramming a few more lies down his neck do now?

'So tell me, Angie's sister. *When* are we? I lose track all the time Out here—how many of my pathetic little crew are left? All lined up, ducks in a row, waiting t' ask me why I did it.' His voice rose in an aggrieved whine. 'They went and locked me in here, you know. They don't ever intend t' let me out. That's why you've come.'

'Me?'

'I knew Angie wouldn't send me up here only t' leave me like this. If you tell me *when* we are, I'll know what I still have t' do.'

'Paul just came back in from Outside. That's what you were telling me. He was working to get the Capsule more power.'

'He shouldn't have gone Out there at all!'

Michael shook his malformed skull, an anxious trembling and jerking across all his limbs that he couldn't seem to marshal. Nerves cross-wired in all sorts of disobedient ways. 'Nobody should, not ever! What'd he gone and stirred up, by flouncing 'round Out there like he was top shit? What did those things do t' him? And, and worse, what was *Paul* likely t' surrender up t' them, just t' keep his own miserable head on his shoulders?'

Would they finally be handed on a plate what they'd been asking for? Tapping patiently through the hull with their scratchy code, while Michael frantically stopped up his ears, whimpering, reciting songs in the dark, anything to keep them out.

'They knew we were here, now. Fucking Paul, they *knew*. Eventually I had t' warn somebody.'

'I thought you said telling *anyone* was a big no-no.'

He sighed, like my idiocy wearied the world. 'Even though by that stage things were so bad, still I honestly wondered if I might be turning … peculiar. I was all wound int' knots by the things Angie told me, I might be just plain tricking my ears out of dread and all that.

'I sure didn't want t' overstring it and end up nuts. Seen all too clearly where that goes. In my neighbourhood where I grew up, there was this nutty old bugger who claimed t' hear the voices. Started out just some ordinary guy, with a family and all. Ended up shut away all alone in this real rancid old crapshack. He'd really let the homestead go, only a faded tyre swing out back t' show there'd ever been a family. Rope so rotted it wouldn't take *any* kid's weight now, no matter how small. I think the walls were only held up by all the sacks of garbage he collected.

'Thompson, that was his name. Old man Thompson. Couldn't get more ordinary than that. Some mighty big rows with the council over the shit he hoarded; the place ought t' have been bulldozed with him nailed up in it. Big shouting matches out the front 'cause he'd never open the door, Thompson hallooing out the mailslot how he'd sure as shit never chuck out a thing in case "they" got their mitts on it, and nobody could make him. He even used t' sneak about at night and steal other people's trash, like his own wasn't enough. Dad caught him at it, and hurled a slipper at him off the front porch when he claimed t' be doing us a favour. And get this: he ran off with the fucking *slipper*.

'I was so pants-shittingly terrified of running int' him about town during the day. All the kids were, even if the adults thought he was a joke. A bunch of us used t' hang out behind the music shed, pass around a smoke, we were never bothered there 'cause it stank of dried piss. All the best stories were how if Thompson met your eye, even if the old fucker glared out of his shack's streaked windows, then your pecker'd drop right off.

'Lurid stuff, right? We got int' all kinds of detail: all that'd be left would be this awful empty hole in your body. It'd gradually nibble its way int' you bit by bit, while you slept. So slowly you couldn't even be sure it was happening at first. Until there wasn't a single shitting bit of you left, maybe just clothes dropping t' the floor at the breakfast table. Perhaps your Mum and Dad pawing through them, screaming.

'We told each other it was how the sick old bastard sold out kids t' his precious voices, t' keep himself safe. The sort of crap only a kid'd entertain, 'cause it lets him carry on about his knob: along the lines of your own would take all year t' choke down, but Johnny's would be gone in a day.

'*Years* later when I was at uni, one of the kids in my class got the cancer down there. Maybe he didn't shake it off hard enough or something, I dunno. Rationally I *know* that's why he died, the cancer chewed him up, but deep down I got sort of convinced old man Thompson'd got him.

'Sounds fucked, I know. But stuff that really squeezes piss outta you as a kid, it can be real hard t' shed yourself of when everything falls dark. You see, I'd been going around telling the pecker-dropping-off story at parties myself. Give the girls a bit of a squeal, and a shiver t' loosen them up. But then this big jock-style guy cries bullshit, and decides t' go look for himself – something *none* of the kids from my neck of the woods would've been dumb enough t' do, anyone who grew up with the story. He just hated how I'd been slurping up all the attention. And he was a true believer, you could tell, really dug all the ooky-kooky stuff.

'I gave him the address. That's what killed him. And even in front of everyone, I couldn't make myself go with him when the double-dare came through. So there went my limelight: I still pulled a girl, couple of the softer ladies thought it was *more* scary, me refusing t' tag along.

'I got my poon and didn't think any more of it until a week later the same girl phoned up in tears, saying he'd been rushed t' emergency. I didn't even know who "he" was, 'til she spelled it out.

'Bravo and bravado, two bucks snorting and shoving at each other. And then suddenly hospital and death. All over nothing grander than a sniff of college pussy. So, yeah. Even before Angie ordered me t' keep my lips zipped, I'd a fair idea how dangerous spreading stories could be.'

Michael took a long, deep breath. He obviously had things to get out, and had to recall himself to what we were *supposed* to be discussing. 'Well. When it came t' crazy, I'd been one of those dead set against including any fucking headshrinker on the Capsule. Implied we weren't all perfect already, didn't it, which went right against the reams and reams of Ash's press releases.

'*John*, of all the idiots, argued himself blue in the face for one. Claimed it was for everyone's safety, the "whole world," if you can believe that. Finally his whining got Ash's sour old ass in such a pinch, he threatened t' flat-out boot John t' make room, if he wanted one so badly. And John was *considering* it. You could see in his eyes, that's how fucking nuts he was on the topic. Eventually he backed down, though, mumbling t' himself and we all breathed a sigh of relief. But now I found myself in need of a brain check up, so of course the useless psych buggers were nowhere t' be seen.'

'A fair few more of them about than when you left,' I couldn't help interjecting sourly. 'You've a harder time keeping *out* of their sightline.'

'Huh. Well as I said, I had t' warn somebody. Even if they wouldn't listen. I guess I might've been hoping t' just get a nice pat on the head, t' be told it's all my imagination. One of us had t' rein in the nuts before it got out of control.'

Michael's glimmering animal eyes softened a mite, the harsh lines relaxing, and my suspicion tightened like a whip.

'I chose Batheba. It made sense once I'd turned it over in my head: she'd always had this thing for me. Of course, she was no Angie, not by any mile. But if I couldn't find a way t' tell Batheba, chances were nobody'd hear it.'

I tried and failed miserably to conjure a face to go with the name, although the fact of her being female was condemnation enough. No big bucket of surprise there: it'd been ages since the Outermen's big shining smiles flashed up in the news. My brain had blurred the massed lot of them into a series of bright hopeful grins, shoulder to identical shoulder. Fixed expressions, floating above puffy white suits, on a background of stark bridal white.

Clever branding, guys, but a ridiculous shade to attempt any actual work in. To continually appear so crisp the program must have fielded an endless supply of those suits, but what choice did they have? They were the Outermen, and had to live up to it twenty-four-seven. Eternally perfect.

Stupid nostalgic memory. Small wonder that even my old, treasured loathing for Michael was beginning to wane, supplanted by fresh revolted pity for the sunken little homunculus before me now.

'Batheba.' That name again, said with a relish I'd learned to dread of old. Angela had known it, too: the wince, the rapidly shuttered expression. Why hadn't I just gone and punched Michael Formir so hard his head had flown off the moment I met him?

'I reckoned I might be able t' trust her, at least a smidge, with the leverage in place already. And before you bring out that sour cat's piss face, I suppose I genuinely wanted t' protect the others, too. It was rapidly becoming clear I couldn't manage alone. I was so shitting *exhausted*. I had t' sleep, really sleep. And who's t' say that awful whispering things wouldn't just dig their way in through the walls, the minute no-one was watching?

'So I hedged my bets. Decided I'd only tell the lady as much as necessary, and see what happened t' her before I went any further. The corridor was the only place I stood a chance of catching her alone, so I waited there.'


'**Batheba.**'

'Mike!' His name was a frightened snatching-in of breath. While Michael'd tracked Batheba's tottering approach quite well in the gloomy corridor, he had her at a disadvantage. Having quit the flickering lights of the control room Batheba might as well've been blind, with no intimation of him lying in wait.

Michael snorted quietly to himself. "Control room", yeah: a fine fucking joke on the lot of them right there. A room of urgent blinking lies, more like. Packed wall to wall with crimson gleams, telling tall tales of a Capsule that no fucking longer existed.

The precious few green indicators didn't do much for them, either. What if that little jade speck denoting scrubbed-clean air decided to flicker off one day, what then? Hold their breath, one and all, until it was all over? Or up and welcome the corruption of Outside into their cringing lungs, because there wasn't a single shitting thing to be done. Hey, what about the water processing, then? Or the power altogether? Not even two fucking sticks to rub together in the dark.

Nonetheless, Batheba devoted her every spare moment to the control room, and that was a *fuckton* of seconds. Watching tirelessly over ticking instruments that even Sal had abandoned in disgust. Running her slim fingers through her hair, in a meaningless self-comforting reflex.

Once, while Batheba'd been dutifully toting her savings off to the poop chute, Michael had crept into the control room, for a sniff around what had her so pointlessly engaged.

None of the others noticed his absence, a neglect Michael sure wasn't liking the taste of. Day by day, he seemed to be shrinking in the public eye. Becoming insubstantial.

He'd felt something similar at other low points in his life, but it seemed so much worse now. Cruelly exaggerated the further he receded from the fierce blowtorch of Angie's affection. She'd made him feel so enormous, invincible, that he could no longer stagger on without it. He fucking *needed* her. Instead he was Out here.

One of the women on board, and earnest little Batheba was an easy bet, might've soothed him in the balm of her regard for a while. Brought him back toward the real. But really, what was the point? Angie'd changed him, there was no closing his eyes to it. Other women might amuse him for a time, months even, but they were dying embers when he craved the furnace.

Things were getting desperate, there could be no doubt about that.

Creeping about, stained by the ruddy control room light that still got his trained heart pounding (alert! alert!), Michael's exploring fingers had touched a soft, greasy pile of shed hair beside Batheba's chair with a shudder. The strands had been painstakingly gathered together, with the same meticulous care as a still life of flowers.

Perhaps the quiet, nervous woman was attempting to hoard something of herself? No doubt hair'd be expected to ride down the chute too, if he called attention to it. They'd already surrendered their nail clippings. The dust of lost skin, too, and of course tears. Plenty of those. Couldn't squander that priceless salt in private, that'd be *selfish*. And so instead of letting it all go they listlessly consumed each other's sorrows, cycled around the group endlessly.

At least Batheba was a sport about forced time-outs from her chosen nest. Not much point kicking up when Beth already held the monopoly on high drama.

Good old Beth, laying on a sound and light spectacular every time they gritted their teeth and hauled her from the tight confines of the sensor array closet. It was the final entertainment that they all got together for. Fuck knows how she managed entry in the first place: the tiny space was never designed for getting *in* there. Just poke your head through the door and take a reading.

Beth had obviously started out life as one of "those" toddlers, the sort you studiously avoid looking at in public, lest their minder burst into tears. Rolling and squealing shamelessly in the aisles for a candy bar; slowly killing her ashen-faced parents. Beth clearly didn't give a hot shit how ridiculous she looked, just as long as she was getting her way. Made you want to stick her bony posterior across your knee and wallop her. Not the best move with a vicious scrapper likely to sink her choppers into your nutsack from that position.

Quite the different kettle of fish to smiling little Batheba. And Beth was in far too tight with Mr-Shining-Fucking-Armour Paul, not seeming to care the association put her too close to Outside. Outside was a pervasive, spreading blight that tainted everything it touched. Beth, in all her give-no-quarter glory, was the nearest risk of hearing Michael's overtures to Batheba. Her piddly closet of useless instruments was no more than a few unsteady steps from where he stood—none of them were walking so straight these days, their wasted pins bowing slowly under the burden.

Batheba's startled gasp quickly turned outraged; humanity's classic comeback to being scared ... or for anything, for that matter. Might as well wrap the quivering lot of them in cotton wool and pack 'em away, it was the only way they'd stoop to feeling comfortable or safe.

'What are you playing at, lurking out here in the dark?'

Her head was turning, presenting first one ear then the other to the blank space. Trying to triangulate him through habit. She'd have limited success: half Batheba's hearing'd been blown out in the explosion.

'Dark?' Michael coughed a cautious laugh, too aware of the near threat that was Beth. 'I'm not sure you've noticed, it's a bit on the fucking dark side everywhere, we've nothing but dark! Sort of encourages a little healthy skulking, don't you think?'

'Healthy?' Now it was her turn to chuckle darkly. The gust of breath on his face reeked: ha ha, a real shiteating grin. Although of course *that* kettle was too black to call out, they all stank equally. A real stench communism.

'So. You've heard Paul's still agitating t' go back Outside?' Sizing her up.

'Have I ever! I didn't think it was even possible to argue the Captain around on anything, just pisses her off, but he keeps hammering away like it'll make a difference. Well … probably isn't the hammering he'd *like* to be giving her, but …'

'Batheba, Paul *can't* be allowed back Out there!'

Michael wasn't at all willing to revamp the lurid can of worms that'd burst open all over the place once Paul's secret-squirrel crush went public. Like putting your meat to the top dog ever ended in anything but getting your bone bitten off. Still, everybody loves a romance. Even one that's clear idiocy. Paul, Paul, Paul-Paul-Paul, all anyone ever yammered on about. Michael couldn't fathom how they were all missing the *point*. 'Once was bad enough!'

'What's eating you, Mike? Your voice is shaking.'

Fuck you, Batheba, he thought angrily. *Michael* was the wise reader of the small folk, not anyone else. 'Never miss a social cue, do you? Not one. Not anybody's.'

She crossed her arms defensively. 'Might be the only forewarning a girl gets, sometimes.'

Despite the unusual good fortune that nothing unendurable had befallen her yet—well, aside from all this—Batheba couldn't recall a time when she hadn't feared other people. Dreaded them, in fact, with a deep, profound paranoia. She remained locked in permanent terror of what they might do, and scrambled to placate them any way she could.

By careful study she came across as calm, kindly and sensitive. Certainly harmless, staring earnestly up from her waifish frame with those big dark eyes. While all the utter worst of humanity went jangling around the walls of her skull. A leering, capering carousel that never seemed to end. The doom-saying media had never fed such a ripe target. Stuffed unto gluttony, until she locked her doors and nailed shut all the blinds.

And on board the Capsule ... well, Batheba couldn't escape anyone anymore.

Disinterested, Michael tried, stumblingly, to bring his point across. 'And with some things you get no warning at all, am I right? For all your keen vigilance, something always slips through. Batheba ... I'm real worried that it might not be safe Out there.'

'Of course it's not *safe!*' Loud and sardonic, for the slow kids up the back. 'It's not safe in here either, Mike. I dunno if you've noticed, but however long we live not a single one of us is likely to ever luxuriate in safety again!' Itching to peel those illusions off him. Never to know safety, never feel loved. Never again to slide open a window and thrill in goosebumps and gasping to a fresh winter breeze. Or to stand with arms outstretched to drink in the warm comforting light of the Shell.

Never again. Her chest ached merely considering it. Life became unbearable.

Not that Batheba wanted to slash sarcasm at *this* man, of them all, quite the opposite! But she was beginning to feel so close and uncomfortable, crammed in with Michael in the dark corridor.

His assembled needs and wants seemed to press on her with physical weight. What was gathered society, anyhow, but a sanctioned means to demand and take from others?

Ever since her youth Batheba's cotton-candy fantasies of "the one" had been continually uprooted by the reality of being unable to bear people. She eventually settled rather tiredly for guys who were heads-down chasing their own pointless dream. They'd bring their own condoms and be out by morning, the perfect gentlemen. If only Michael weren't the exception!

She'd be so good for Michael. She could tell. He needed somebody. Anyone could see that, just by looking at him, he was one of *those*. Wouldn't thrive too well locked up in himself, tended to stagnate. A man who only truly existed in his reflection off somebody else, and the brighter and more glorified the better.

'Batheba ...' Michael sensed he was losing her to her thoughts. And really, with a straight face, what could he blurt out about what he'd been hearing in the walls? It'd all remained pent inside for too long, gnawing intently at its own limits. Michael was on thin ice, and hysterics kept wanting to crack through the veneer.

This whole approach to Batheba was foolishness incarnate. What, had he thought, he could just blithely chirp, "Oh, just giving you the heads-up that I've been hearing things through the hull. Particularly when it's late, and I'm tired, and so desperately alone. And I'm deathly afraid that all Outside wants t' come crawling into the Capsule t' get me. Because I might be batshit insane and all that."

*Don't tell anyone*, Angie'd warned.

Angie first told him of the voices at a party. One of those glittering spectacles laid on for the Outermen, celebrating humanity's new boldness. She wasn't invited, but what doorman worth his salt would deny entry to Angie?

Beautiful, engaging women were what social occasions revolved around. She probably strode in like she owned the place.

That soiree was the first time they met. Hemmed in by folk carrying on the bland conversations Michael usually dominated, and now desperately wished he was a part of because what this stunning woman was saying made him feel so cold. So out of his element, at a party of all places! The clink of expensive glassware sounding so far away, like he might faint. His nose had been stopped up by the sugary scent of her perfume, up close and personal like a silk cushion over the face.

And there'd been the overwhelming magnetism of her eyes. The command in them. It was awfully cliché, but Michael had felt to be dissolving away. Lost to himself, and whoever he might have been moments before this sparkling creature had tapped his arm and fluted, 'Pardon me, are you an Outerman?'

Caught, Michael was helpless to excuse himself to safer ground. No matter how he longed to. Angie had blithely told him of the voices while standing in the middle of a fucking party. With threads of allure, she'd bound him inescapably to her purpose, and only now was the enormity of her will in doing so beginning to sink in. He'd never measure up to Angie. Failure, failure. Always and forever, stinking failure. Why should he give a shit about even trying?

Michael turned to Batheba, a long way from an elegant soiree here, and settled for, 'We're friends, right?'

Well fuck. She twisted her hands. No rollicking adventure between the sheets ever began that way. 'Sure, Mike. We're friends.' Oh, and by the way, would it bother you if I slide your pants off while we talk?

'And friends keep an eye out for each other, don't they?'

Far beneath the conscious level, where instinct and self-preservation squirmed, Batheba found herself wishing more intensely than ever to step back from the looming man in the dark. Michael seemed to suddenly radiate urgency and need, like a melting live wire. She felt him wanting to suck her substance away for himself until she had nothing left.

She grimly stood her ground, because being seen to retreat was dangerous. It broadcast weakness. A bleeding flank was likely to provoke the human animal to attack. 'Right. Friends *do* watch out for one another, that's the whole point. Mike, is there something in particular that's worrying you? Anything you'd like to talk about?'

'I want you t' eyeball Paul carefully, can you manage that for me? Watch what he does. Monitor for anything that looks *wrong.*'

Now it was Batheba's turn to open up and show him the full force of her misery. Depending on what intimate fracture it pressed upon, their shared fate had afflicted everyone differently. Although for decency's sake she masked it from the others, Batheba had become a still, cold pool of helplessness. Any other emotion dropped into it roused only the briefest disturbance before drowning, and the ripples never so much as touched the sides.

This was Batheba unveiled. She desperately needed Michael to need her. And soon, before despair ate up all that was left. 'Mike, it's only the seven of us now. All those people we once knew, and the weight of their opinions on right and wrong— well, they might as well have never existed. We're all that's left. So what could even be called "normal" behaviour Out here? We can only weigh our actions against ourselves, and there just aren't enough of us for a consensus of decency.'

'Sooo, technically we could do anything. Shouldn't we find that liberating?'

'Liberating? I'm *terrified*. I'm terrified of what we've got locked in here. There are too few of us to do anything but fester, closed up and poisoned, until eventually something horrible breaks through.'

She drew a shuddering breath to continue, but Michael slowly and deliberately lowered his fragrant face to her stinking mouth. The dance of seduction, his tiresome, necessary friend. Batheba hadn't aired her dirty laundry for a simple round of applause, and even Michael recognised that you sometimes had to give a little.

A little fake empathy for her woes. A dash of tenderness and women would topple from their pedestals, because they were lonely, and tired of being strong. They wanted to *believe* so badly.

Except that Beth poked her head into the corridor. Michael jumped back guiltily.

'Surely you two idiots aren't s'posed to be *whispering* out here? Shit, you're both deaf!' Her curly-topped head looked dismembered, floating in blankness with its rough and ready smirk. The tiny dark closet was a mystery behind her. 'Still, you've got one thing right there, love. Far too few of us left on the Capsule. You just hadn't taken the thought far enough.'

Batheba sniffed tearfully, all incredulous on the inside. Had he been about to *kiss* her? 'Aren't things bad enough as it is?'

'Never as bad as you know, lovie.' Beth scuttled her body as near to the doorframe as she dared, refusing to relinquish the closet's safety outright. Her bloodshot eyes darted up and down the corridor nervously, as though she feared some new tactic, even though tea time was hours away. The mob lurking off stage to seize and shuck her from her shell. Not for the first time, Michael thought, *Shit, we're all falling apart.*

'It's not merely behaviour that's consensual,' Beth whispered hoarsely, ready to impart her own big secret.

'You might think it is, but it's not. *Reality* is consensual. Do you see? We're the whole of reality, now. And just like Batheba said, we've got no balance. With so few, what horrors might we wreak on each other, and everything around us?'

'Fuck off, Beth. What about the others back home, huh?'

'We exist, but the world no longer does. Under the circumstances, I'd say that makes them the lucky ones.'

'But we remember them!' Michael protested, sandwiched in and profoundly disturbed by the nuttiness of both women. 'Even with them out of reach, their influence isn't gone.'

Beth laughed hollowly, a witch in her cave, and Batheba shrank against Michael, having made a snap decision on who frightened her more. 'Are you *serious*? Oh, poor Michael. That's just the flavour of crap they use to cap brats' blubbering when the goldfish goes belly up. *It's ok little Bobby, when someone dies they live on in your memories.* Blah-dy blah-blah. Quit acting like some kid. Dead is dead, and once something's gone, it's gone. Irrevocably. And to us, the world is gone.'

'Why are you saying such horrible things?'

Although temporarily on her side, Michael had to admit Batheba whined like an over-taxed child. Her hands were clawed out helplessly, as though to fend off the taller woman.

And Beth, she crouched leering in her doorway, eyes glittering manically. 'Man up, Schultz,' she hissed. 'We've all got no choice but to come to grips with the situation, one way or another. We need to get our shit in order, because … because …' Her hard, unforgiving voice stuttered out.

Always the weak link, at the presentiment of something truly awful Batheba experienced the childish urge to clap her hands over her ears.

'Because?' Michael demanded tersely. Beth had never made any bones about her nil attraction to him; consequently, he'd no time for her histrionics.

'Because of what Paul saw.' Beth seemed to crumple in on herself, the confession finally forced from her. 'Outside. What he saw Outside. But what he told me can't *possibly* be true! That's why I have to stay alert here. I have to listen. If there really is anything moving Out there, I'll hear it.'

Michael's hackles'd well and truly risen; they might as well have punched through the ceiling and escaped. Without thinking, he slipped a protective arm about the little figure that shivered against him, sending dark opportunistic thrills through Batheba's body.

For his part, sometimes horrors were made more bearable by having somebody to look out for. And if all else failed, it paid to have an alternate target to shelter behind. If he played his cards right, given time he could even manoeuvre Batheba to fling herself nobly into harm's way at the critical juncture.

'What did he see? You have t' tell us!'

Beth was shrinking back into her shadowed refuge, folding into the space like impossible origami. A thin, frightened whisper trailed out after her. 'The power hadn't been lost in any fucking explosion. Paul said it looked like something'd ripped long fingers down the hull in trying to hang on. Said the marks felt hot, hot right through his suit. Made him dizzy. Metal'd peeled back fatly like sliced skin. And when he got right in there to make repairs …' she swallowed. 'He said the skin of the hull was packed with bodies.'

'Maybe … maybe other crew, compressed against the hull by the blast …'

'Bullshit. Paul said those bodies were *old*. Mummified old. All jumbled up bones and dried skin, and hollow eye sockets glaring back like they'd never wanted to be exposed, and they hated him for seeing.

'Paul said they were special. Relics. The gathered remains of everyone who's ever been obsessed by Outside and gone mad with it. Those who'd given up everything, they were all there. And they had the wires between their fucking *teeth*!'

'Shit!' Michael almost dropped Batheba, or she him, and they clung together.

'It's impossible, though, impossible. We must be making this happen. It *has* to be us, we're all that exists now. I just have to prove it. I have to keep listening.' Beth vanished into her hole, leaving only the sour scent of her fear behind.

Batheba leaned up to Michael's ear, straining until he bent down to her. He found it a charming gesture, seeing as Angie's approach had always been to grab a fistful of hair and yank him down to her level. Chastisement for daring to be taller in the first place.

'She's as mad as a fucking snake,' Batheba murmured and for a strange moment Michael wasn't sure which woman she referred to, Beth or his fiancée. 'Has to be. Be *careful* around her, Mike.'

With a sympathetic pressure to his hand she moved past, rictus features to hide her thumping heart. He stared after her.

But something was going wrong. Some failure of perspective. As Batheba staggered down the dim corridor she was not shrinking to match; rather, the sides closed in. Closed around until she filled it, wall to wall, impossibly big; tiny Batheba who couldn't touch the low ceiling by jumping was now squeezed like meat down a toothpaste tube. Her skin squeaked along the walls, propelling herself along as though by flippers, until Michael feared it might drive him mad.

With difficulty Batheba wriggled and squirmed around the corner, for all her effort not seeming to realise anything was awry. Her legs kicked helplessly for a bit, drumming on the wall. And then she was gone.

It had been so grotesque that Michael leaned his forehead against the panel next to him, struggling not to vomit. He *can't* have seen that. It wasn't possible. Sleep, sleep was what he needed. All was slipping without rest.

There was a dull thumping within the wall, as of something large clumsily turning over, and he jerked away as though scalded.

The world might as well have never existed? What the fuck where they on?

*Angie* might well have never existed?

'Angie.' For the first time, Michael allowed himself to speak his beloved's name in this horrible place. It wasn't easy to spit out, gagging him like dry powder. Her injunction against loose lips was so strong it'd bled over into all related topics, even her.

But the name evoked her like magic, briskly chasing off his immediate fear. Like getting scrubbed with a rough towel when you come in half-frozen from the deep cold: painful, and good for you at the same time.

It did nothing, however, to dispel his dread of the future. Oh no, there was never peace from *that*, not with Angie. Loving her meant living intimately with dread, on a day-to-day basis. The threat of terrible, incomprehensible events always poised to descend. Loving Angie was like trying to contain a bursting grenade in your hands, frozen in that moment before it all flew apart.

The truth was, Angie moved and dreamed in a far bigger, more arcane world than Michael'd ever wanted to believe in. One that extended far beyond the safety and sanity of the Shell. One far outside his understanding. He'd only dared cross the threshold for her; thrust into it, he had no way to cope. But of course, you felt so *alive* with her. Michael could never conceive of disobeying. All he could manage was to desire and need her, in an endless cycle of thrall.

Beth's cheap little theory had to be pure shit. What did she know? It didn't seem possible reality would allow itself to *exist* without Angie.

And hey, get this, he didn't even have a photo of her to sob pathetically over in his loneliness. She'd tried to give him one, the morning he left—carefully vetted, of course, practically a glamour shot.

Perhaps a newsfeed was to catch glimpse of it taped to his bunk, the awestruck lens slowly zooming in, the audience gaping at this new light in the void.

And what idiocy had he spouted, pressing it back on her? *I'll be home so soon, you won't even have time t' wonder where your pic went*. Some such utterly bullshit bravado. And all the while, icy terror had churned his gut so fiercely that a sprint to the bog may have been in order.

Torn between conflicting impulses, when he got up that morning he'd still believed he might pull out of the program. Brushing his teeth, wiping steam from the mirror with a *squeak*, none of it seemed real. Right up until the moment the Capsule was dangling free on its cable, and everything was far too late. Angie had eaten his brave-face up like cream. *Good lad*. Smiling so broadly at him, all teeth, like she was so proud to see him finally catching on. Which made Michael glow.

He slid down the corridor's curved wall, feeling the relentless rapping in the developing curlicues of his spine. A sob and then another forced their way out from between his clenched teeth. Beth might hear. He didn't give a fuck. He was such a fucking idiot.

I was startled to find Tall Jake sitting on the floor outside Michael's room, waiting. A grown adult plunking themselves on the ground, rather than a chair, always looks peculiar. Smacks a bit of regression. He wasn't reading, or passing the time in any normal way. Just … waiting. Blankly.

With his head tipped off to one side, he almost seemed to be *listening*, a toy with the batteries taken out.

It was sodding eerie.

I approached cautiously. When I tapped his shoulder, I almost expected his gaze to snap up with eyes all-black and fathomless, like in a horror flick. But shaken from that thousand-mile stare it was just Jake, blinking up at me rather sleepily.

Is this how it happened, that time he got lost in here? While he imagined himself wandering, with the thin wire noose of anxiety ever-tightening, was he in fact left sitting blankly, staring and listening to nothing? A touch of epilepsy might explain it.

'You don't have to hang around,' I offered, nonplussed.

Jake climbed to his feet, seeming to shake himself back into brusque normality, for which I was eternally grateful. 'I wanted to be here when you came out. Like I said, you do *not* want to get yourself turned around in the long hall, believe me. I wouldn't wish that on anyone. Haven't been sitting on my tail the entire time, though; I popped in to visit Mandy for an hour or so.'

'Mandy?' Ugly thoughts. Down, girl.

'The woman Mr Formir chomped into when they first brought him up here. She's on a ventilator now; can't hear me, but it feels better knowing someone's sitting with her.'

'But … but he didn't even bite her that hard! What's wrong with her?'

'If anyone knew, they'd be curing her to go home to her kid, instead of just sticking the tubes in. The other two suckers got lucky, assuming it stops at the knuckle. Jammed their fingers in that creep's toxic gob to prise him off, probably saved Mandy's life, and what they got looks like a nasty case of frostbite. Stinks like you wouldn't believe, even through the bandages. Drips on the floor. I can't see those nails ever growing back.'

He sucked his lip, a nervousness he was barely aware of broaching and vanishing. 'So, Ms Catherine, are we back to reality then?'

Jiggling like a toddler, Jake genuinely couldn't wait to burn rubber out of there. Which made me feel far more the jerk over what I was about to ask.

'Uh, in a sec. Tell me, are the recovered bits of the Capsule still aboard Threshold? The stuff that came back with Michael?'

'Sure, that crap's all still here. Although we scavenged most of the useful bits to dress up the Outerman's room.'

My stomach roiled. No wonder stepping into Michael's territory had made me feel weird and sick.

One eyebrow arched theatrically, not a native expression of Jake's. Lips pressed into a thin bloodless line, and suddenly he had Cormac's patented sneer down pat. 'Doctor's orders were to make it look as real as possible. There's no authenticity like authenticity.'

'Could I see it?'

Tall Jake shrugged to hide his disquiet—the whims of women, hey? 'Not a lot of point, 'less you like junk. Nothing left to knock your socks off. And the bits are in the theatre, which is right down the very end of the long hall. About the furthest through Threshold you can traipse without swinging open a door and swimming off through the void. You pull a stunt like *that*, you aren't ever coming back.'

He glanced at Michael's shut door. 'Current examples not withstanding.'

'Please?' How to win him over? I'd never been much of a wheedler, and appealing to Jake's flagging courage'd be too much of a low blow. He'd already proven his chops by waiting for me. 'I really think it might help me get my head around all this.'

He snorted. 'You'd have to be quite the contortionist.'

I obviously wasn't. 'Look, if it can be managed I really want to get all this over with as fast as possible, so I can go home.'

'Wriggle away through Dr Cormac's fingers like a little fishie, huh?'

Not quite how I'd have put it. Jake let out a plosive breath. 'Look … Catherine, I really don't fancy going down there, to be perfectly honest. It's not good for you, the theatre, it's not a good place. Creeps me right the fuck out.'

Man, I was a jerk for pressing this. 'You could just point me down the hall to the door? I'm a big girl. I'll only take a few minutes to nose around.'

'Fine.' In that tone that meant the opposite of fine.

With gritted teeth Jake took my arm and hustled me along. His palm was unpleasantly sweaty; well, I cringed from *every* touch, this time it was with cause. And it only now occurred to my stupid brain that Jake may well have lingered outside Michael's door to avoid a last trip along the long hall all alone. Pinned in here with me by his own fear. I was such a sodding arsehat for putting him through all this.

'Don't know why I came back to this rat-trap in the first place,' he grumbled sourly and I felt, if possible, even worse.

The long hall became even more dilapidated further in. Or Out, depending on how you viewed our progress. Once vivid colours faded. What light fittings remained uncovered had gathered gentle snowdrifts of dust into their glass bowls, sieving them patiently from the dry air.

Even though this was clearly a service or maintenance section, well off the tourist track, I loved that the long hall had still been rather fancy in its day. Rather than a veneer, Threshold Station's old world grandeur went through and through. Although it did make the structure's current neglect more melancholy. Nobody gave two hoots should a utilitarian building tumble into ruin, from ugly to ugly. But it's always sad to see something beautiful gone shabby. The space was meant to be enjoyed, and you could feel the waste.

True to our deal, in fact with a little more fidelity than I'd have preferred, Jake pointed. We both pretended to ignore how his hand trembled.

'You'll find the theatre through that final door, right down the end. Caps off the long hall. Don't open any of the others.'

I guess he really wasn't tagging along. My gut quailed a little, as though forging on was a mistake.

As though we'd protected one another by companionship alone. Of course, this wasn't the time for *me* to wuss out. Eventually I'd have to pick my own way back down the long hall, with its dizzying doors unto doors unto doors.

I glanced back over my shoulder at Jake once, still standing rooted to the spot with his arms crossed. Wearing that judgmental "No good'll come 'a this" scowl that made him appear a sight more elderly and cantankerous.

Be bold, fatguts. Be more like Angela. Push on. Her memory was so strong I both smiled and winced. Which was stupid, and I rattled my head to disperse it. My sister was gone. Dead. And dead people didn't get a say anymore.

As I twisted the door's handle, I almost missed the modest little bronze plaque that said THEATRE, like those found outside doctors' offices. Greened and pitted. I breathed on the surface and tried buffing it up, but only succeeded in making my sleeve dirty. Oh well.

The door opened on vastness.

I'd imagined the innocuous portal Jake had indicated might give onto something cold and functionally industrial, like an aircraft hanger. The plaque alone distinguished it from Threshold's other doors. In truth, the space resembled something even I was familiar with. An especially grand hotel lobby.

I stepped forward into the theatre, where everything was hushed as though it'd been holding its breath all this time, waiting for me.

In the echoing space a series of ensconced lights came on by themselves with a soft "plink!", triggered by my entrance. They slowly warmed and brightened under their furry layer of dust, much as stage lights would at the end of a show.

In this case, to reveal the audience long gone. The cast exposed as merely going through the motions, to an abandoned and heedless house.

Surprisingly, though, I got no sense of chill or mould from the big open space.

What wafted in my face was more like real vanilla, the scent of faint regret. An inevitable decline from fortune. For the first time in Cormac's custody I felt myself to be unmonitored— the lifting of a troubling weight I'd no idea of lugging along. It were as though recording devices couldn't possibly work in the theatre. They were just too modern, too crass. If you wanted to know somebody's mind in a place like this, you asked. Politely. And probably bought them a cup of tea first.

Emerging from the brightening murk, two grand sliding doors dominated the entirety of the far wall. All ornate carved scrollwork around the edge, with the gold leaf flaking off and sifting onto the carpet. What had Jake said? *About the furthest through Threshold you can go without opening a door and swimming off through the void.* I'd little doubt where they led; this, here, was the furthest you can go.

Still I suffered no fear. Only that shadow of vague apprehension you feel on forgetting some critical task, something right at the tip of your sodding tongue. Knowing others were bound to start asking questions about it soon. That couldn't be natural: maybe I couldn't feel suitably scared anymore. I might have expected too much and burned it all out.

Rather surreally plonked down at the centre of such stately environs, the battered scraps of the Capsule were sinking silently beneath their own weight into the plush carpet. Jake hadn't been kidding: it no longer looked like much of anything.

No greater volume of scrap remained than could be accounted for by, say, a wrecked minivan or two.

You could easily envisage the lot of it crumbling away, out back of some junkyard. Hemmed in by mouldering fridges with the doors sprung and leaning against their rusty flanks—no junkman wanted to be responsible for the disappearance of some local kid. But then, wasn't the Capsule the greatest trap of all? How do you make that safe?

My nostrils were stuffed with dust. In the slowly warming illumination I walked all the way around the crumpled heap, with my shoes (*Cormac's* shoes) making faint whuffing sounds in the heavy carpet. My progress stirred slow roiling waves of silt into the air about my knees, a hand cupped over my nose and mouth to filter it out. A curious, investigative circuit that I completed first one way, and then the other.

There were signs of charring in various places. The shadow of a fierce heat long passed. I even fancied I could pick out the shape of a man burned against a long flat panel, his arms flung up in horror, and I shuddered. Even though it was merely my traitorous imagination, weaving images that weren't there. Suffering wasn't hard to imagine; the memory of misery shimmered thick in the air above the Capsule's butchered remains, like rising exhaust.

I was trolling for anything that resembled the marks Paul thought he saw. Any solid piece of evidence you could weigh in your hand, and use to ground Michael's wild tale in reality. But quite frankly, *anything* could be what I sought. The Capsule's remains had been scrunched like a wad of newspaper. Perhaps the damage Paul had reported had even been on some other segment. Something not recovered at all, a piece still flying eternally away through the darkness. Or perhaps it was staring me right in my ignorant chops. Forensics wasn't exactly my field.

I quit my circling. All that money. All that time and money and hope. The lives. And this was what we had to show for it.

It was pretty clear where the last Outerman's broken-spider body, incredibly still breathing, had been prised from the wreckage. Some implement had been used to hack the Capsule open, the way you do a can when you're starving and without the proper tools. Jagged petals bent outward like a flower.

Just beneath, the carpet sparkled like a tiara. Although I knew, I still bent down for a look.

Piss diamonds. The only bit of the Capsule to suit its deluxe new surroundings. I pushed them around in the dust a bit with my finger, but ultimately left them where they lay. I already had one of their brothers glittering fiercely on my bedside table. No call for more Disaster in my life.

I was now crouching right below the hole where they'd taken Michael out. I found the room's soft lighting was designed to foster intimacy, not penetrate the depths of a snarled metal secret, no matter how far I craned. A little whiff of rank smell escaped from in there and brushed by my face. Tired and dry now with the warm bodies gone, but I could well imagine the rancid stench layered around and around the walls of the interior. Just waiting to be activated by a new breath of life.

The dark maw beckoned, but I didn't want its ill luck rubbing off on me. All this time examining, pondering, yet I still hadn't dared touch the Capsule. As an intellectual exercise, could I contort my way in there? Was there any sane chance of doing so without shredding my tender bulk on the deadly metal flakes that curled about, with their shiny stripped-bare edges?

'So this is where I discover you pottering about. Of all places.' Dr Cormac's wry interruption almost had me springing out of my skin like a banana.

I turned to glare. Likely he'd lingered and waited slyly for just the poised moment to make his entrance: my hand outstretched, and mystery thrilling down my spine. All contrived to make us look the right pair of melodramatic twits.

'Go ahead, Ms Hanberry, you can touch the Capsule. It isn't likely to bite.'

So *he* says. I folded my arms. 'So how about we do this thing of yours *without* scrambling Michael's thin brains for the rest of his life?'

Oh. That just popped out. Aghast, I could hardly credit how casually I'd just flipped criticism across the room at such a grim authoritative figure.

This was *exactly* what came of emulating Angela's just-leap-in philosophy, and it was far too late to start back-pedalling now. Anger; sweet, righteous anger was my only way of masking the trembling, burgeoning conviction of comeuppance speeding my way, fast and true.

'For crap's sake Dr Cormac, that poor sod is sitting in his room, *on the floor* I might add, solidly convinced the Capsule never made it back. He's terrified as arse that some kind of … of *things* are set to come munching through the walls any second, and he's going to be slurped up right there in the dark. And …' I was getting louder with bowled-along momentum. Echoing foolishly in the grand space, and not really giving a flip. '… He's so *scared*, so sure, that I was starting to buy into it, too!'

That admission cost me a lot. It felt like trying to explain to your glowering boss your project was late 'cause you'd been waiting up for the Tooth Fairy.

'Good.'

'Good? Really?' If only I had something to throw. I thought of taking off one of my shoes, screaming: *Here, have your stupid shoe back!*

'Absolutely. Your engaging with Mr Formir's paradigm, however unsettling, will certainly encourage him to open up to you.

'However, on the matter of your concern, I wouldn't advise investing too much in things likely to occur for the remainder of Mr Formir's life. I fear that period is likely to reach its conclusion sooner rather than later.'

And then I could go home.

It ought to be an unspeakable thing to wish somebody wiped from existence, merely for the crime of inconveniencing me. But it sprang from the dirtiest, most selfish part of me and I had to own it. Besides, Michael's passing would be no more than correcting a mistake. He was supposed to be dead. That's what everyone thought.

I tried not to sound disgustingly eager. 'How long?'

'Rather problematic to determine. You see, Mr Formir has rallied somewhat since I escorted you both up here, which was of course the intent. I suspected renewed proximity to Outside might well slow the degeneration that afflicts him. Mr Formir also appears to be deploying some force of will. Almost,' Cormac added slyly, 'As though he felt compelled to confess something before the end.'

'So now he *needs* Outside? Needs to be close to it?' Just as we were close to it right now.

I rubbed my eyes tiredly. The silvery dust was getting everywhere. 'Michael's right, in a weird way, isn't he? He never really came home. And now he never will. You bundled him up first, shut him away before he could make it.'

'Whatever you may think of me, I am far from being the author of Mr Formir's woe. I am merely working to save what can be salvaged from a regrettable situation. Mr Formir is locked up within his own head, more resolutely than any restraint I could contrive. While I, I aim to exploit that using his environs, employing suggestion, and any other tool to hand that might nudge his trauma-crippled memory closer to accurate recall.

'Believe me, Ms Hanberry, you could ship Mr Formir back down to Earth, roll him in fresh-cut grass and daisies, and it wouldn't produce an iota of difference.

'He will never leave the Capsule. And it is far beyond the likes of either of us to release him.'

I felt like pointing out tartly there was no need for Cormac to justify himself to *me*.

But I'd accused, hadn't I? He'd a right to respond. Nobody wishes to be considered a dick, not even the dickheads.

'Now, have you contented yourself rummaging about this refuse back here?'

Of a contrary mind, I stepped closer to the Capsule. 'Why?'

'I thought you might fancy sitting down to a proper repast, like civilised equals.'

Equals – did he really think I'd fall for that? Admittedly I *was* dressed the part. Perhaps the great Dr Cormac occasionally found himself all too human, too swayed by the potent mix of appearance and wishful thinking that can override cold hard fact.

When we exited, brushing puffs of dust from our clothes, Tall Jake was still waiting out in the long hall, although he'd ventured no nearer. Standing in an odd slumped posture, with one ear against a wall like a store mannequin tipped sideways. Was he ... *listening* for something?

He stepped hurriedly away from it as we approached, wiping absently at something dark at his ear. Yes, the elegant green wallpaper was blackened there, as though somebody had carelessly leaned a hot lamp too close. It must have rubbed off on him. To see Jake waiting stoically for me as close to the theatre as he could stand, like a loyal dog, put a guilty squirm in my belly. Worsened when Dr Cormac brushed dismissively by.

'I will take Ms Hanberry from here.'

Jake's eyes narrowed. 'Ms Catherine's a grown woman, in case it escaped your attention doctor. I can't imagine she requires "taking" by anyone.'

'Oh, I don't know,' I said lightly, hoping the eternal power of innuendo might defuse the situation.

But Cormac rounded haughtily on Jake like master to cur. He was really getting into this, like he'd regressed in Threshold's ye olde atmosphere. Or perhaps he'd been watching too many historical dramas.

'Don't waste time bandying intent with *me*, especially where Ms Hanberry is concerned! The irony would be insufferable.'

That shut Jake up, or at least stupefied him into silence. Trailing Cormac—a few steps back, just like a good little lady—I tried to project in my glance to Jake all the humiliation and apology the human eye can convey.

Quick to forgive, he gave me back an unmistakable "He is *such* a dick!" face. An exquisite expression on an adult, untarnished since the schoolyard. As I passed he slipped a scrap of paper into my fingers: like guilty kids passing notes right under the headmaster's nose. Jake gave me a last smile, swiping irritably at his ear. Too quick to really see as I passed, but it seemed a trickle of something dark drooled from it, staining his collar.

Jake was obviously the greater rebel. I'd no courage to examine what he'd passed me straight away, not with Cormac so riled up. You could practically see the fur bristle all down the doctor's stiff spine, stamping the floor into submission as he walked.

Seemingly women didn't deserve pockets, as my outfit only incorporated those stupid fake ones. Finally after some dithering, I resorted to tucking Jake's note beneath my bra strap. A real trailer park flourish, that.

Like aristocracy, Dr Cormac and I were to dine in his grand boys club boardroom, at a massive table that must have busted somebody a ripe hernia to carry in. We had big comfy chairs and white linen. And four bottles opened to breathe at the heart of the setting, more than enough to sink me in a coma. Fortunately Cormac'd proven himself gentleman enough to take the brunt of alcoholic peril on himself.

Despite never having done it, this was exactly how I envisaged first dinner with the boyfriend's folks. Every element calculated for comfort, pleasure.

And the players sitting bolt upright, about as relaxed as lightning-struck cats. Just waiting with narrowed eyes to see who'd make the first fuckup and crack the façade.

Pulling myself up to the table, I had to wonder who prepared all this? Was the whole lot engineered by greying, solitary Dr Cormac himself, shuffling behind the scenes and straining grimly with the weighty props?

If not, where did enough funds spring from to pay suits like Tall Jake to play menial? Or all the wine, for that matter; had Cormac been born in a vineyard? He certainly drank like he had.

Soup to start with. Something clear and thin, with crusty bread rolls. I was relieved to confront the familiar: given the setting, I'd dreaded some arcane dining custom such as lobster. Soup was safe, it was hard to go wrong with soup. Just choose the round spoon and stick it in your face-hole. Dr Cormac served us from a tureen, and filled both glasses right up to boot, which I supposed was as the mannered folk did.

So we sat facing one another. Slowly sinking back in our soft chairs, the steam rising and twirling in the air between us. I quite happily had my back to Outside, and so our backdrop from my angle was a view to take the breath away. The warm glow of the Shell as it gradually dimmed toward calm night, and all the safe protected world spread out below.

This was the oldest of social rituals, this sharing of a meal. It was what friends, couples and families did to shore up bonds. Whenever Angela was at her worst, or I was groping about to apologise for some stupidity, I'd visit the market for fresh ingredients and spend hours lovingly baking one of her favourites. And things were always better afterward.

As though he could read my mind as well as peeping creepily through his cameras, Cormac was the first to start. 'Ms Hanberry, you've never mentioned *how* you came to be here, rather than your sibling. Now that we have a little time I wouldn't mind hearing about it.'

Ah. Cunning. Cushion my emotions with good food. By rights I ought to come over too disturbed to eat. When she was wound up Angela forgot meals existed, subsisting instead on air, coffee and nerves. Sadly my indomitable gut didn't operate like some flighty teenager.

I exhaled heavily, sending ripples across the inky surface of the wine. Wine would help. 'Angela was going to be married.'

'So I gathered. Mr Formir is so confident of passing this "test" of ours with flying colours that he's requested a celebrant on standby. Ready for the shining moment they are reunited.'

I bit my lip. That was so sad. 'No, no. She met somebody *else*, after the Capsule was lost.'

Cormac winced. 'Ah.'

'*Michael* sure wasn't worth wasting your life over! Especially not Angela's life, she was destined for big things!' I smiled. Even thinking about my sister made it seem like adventures actually happened. 'If it'd been me, I wouldn't have given him five seconds, but of course Angela had a much bigger heart. She was genuinely devastated for a year or two. It was a bad time; she really needed me to take care of her.

'Then Greg came along, and he was everything Michael wasn't. Seriously, it was like Michael'd only ever existed to provide a counterpoint. Greg helped her out of it, he wanted to see her whole and smiling again so badly. He was wonderful.'

'Blushing like a schoolgirl.' Dr Cormac's lips thinned further, almost a smile. 'I was beginning to form the distinct impression you disliked everyone.'

'Sod it, *I'd* have married Greg given half the chance!'

Sod it. Embarrassed by the outburst, which'd only been half jovial, I took a big old gulp of wine and chased it with soup. 'But you know, Angela deserved him more. She needed someone like Greg so much, after what she'd been through.

'Look at me, talking like I could've had him: what sane man would even notice other women *existed* when around her?'

I sighed. 'I could never understand the way Michael whored himself about, it was crazy. Anyway, Greg was bound to propose sooner or later, lock her in.

'Make her happy forever. He was just the most amazing guy. Me, I wouldn't have even known what to do with it all.'

Dr Cormac listened narrowly, with an uncomfortable intensity that suggested all my petty insecurities and jealousy were hanging out. Well, sod him, too. He's the one who asked.

And while I had quite the radar for risky situations, it'd evolved to deal with the Screws' constant hovering threat. In the face of Dr Cormac's single raised eyebrow I defiantly squelched the blazing mental alarms, thinking Jake had parodied that expression so very well.

'Angela was going to be happy, finally happy, after all Michael stole out of our lives. She was going to be a *bride*. In a big floofy dress, like in a magazine. She ought to have looked ridiculous in that fitting room, perched up on a box, but never Angela. She could wear anything, anytime. Greg was an only child and this was his folks' one chance to lay on a really epic wedding, the whole nine yards. You could tell they'd been planning it for years.'

Cormac was on his second glass already. The man was a powerhouse. 'Ah, I do so enjoy a good wedding. I take it you were to accompany your sister up the aisle as a radiant bridesmaid?'

I barely heard him. He thought he was funny, but he wasn't. 'But you know the bit that kills me, that totally *kills* me?

'With all this going on I was falling over my own feet, and I didn't even know the Screws'd picked her up. I just assumed she was at Greg's place. I had no idea the Screws had Angela until days later when they dropped her on my doorstep.

'Shivering and blank, in one of those flimsy hospital gowns that show everything. What did they do with her *clothes* …'

'Ms Hanberry, pardon the interruption, but the *who* took your sister?'

Now I knew I was walking on the wild side.

'It's a, uh, nickname Angela came up with for Charles' grim lot. Screwed if you do, screwed if you don't. After all, you'd have to be pretty screwed up to screw one, and maybe that's their game all along.'

There was a long, awkward silence which I broke defensively. 'To be fair, we *were* around fifteen at the time. Back then it had us laughing like hyenas.'

'I'm sure it was hilarious.'

'This all sounds so stupid out loud, you know?' He certainly wouldn't be contesting that. 'I … I just haven't spoken openly about Angela, about *anything* in years. I haven't been able to! What kind of world have we made for ourselves, where I can't even talk about my own dead sister?'

'Given our history to date you likely won't credit it as true, but I feel the same way.' Dr Cormac settled himself more comfortably in his chair, staring out the window. The dome of his forehead was so shiny that the Shell's delicate dusk pinks glinted off it. 'I originally conceived Threshold Station as the sort of place where people would venture beyond the hobbles of the social circle. Be entirely themselves, and become impassioned by the types of concepts normally considered impossible.

'Then, later, it became a refuge. How terrible we should find ourselves required to travel so far from home, merely to be ourselves. Become as we *ought* to be.'

Cormac shook himself to return to the moment, a quick shiver like a dog. And the consolation of another great gulp from his bottomless glass. 'So, the "Screws" intervened.'

I could feel terrible pressure building within my skull, grinding in there like torn glass.

Spitting the words out brought no relief. I'd recited this outrage to an empty apartment at different volumes in different voices, even sometimes Angela's, for years without change.

'They took her! Off the street, or from her work. I don't even know how she could have slipped up to draw their attention! I mean, Angela could be reckless, sure, fabulously so. But she balanced it by being so much *better* at keeping things close to her chest ...'

'Than yourself.'

My chin dropped slightly, barely an admission. Cormac leaned across the table to top up my glass. Right to the brim again, you could scarcely move without spilling it. It was an unmistakable offering, of his ilk: here, cope with that emotional backlog the way I do, and you'll be fine. He couldn't understand that a vat of booze wouldn't help me feel any better. It was a noble try, but nothing would.

I picked up my spoon, and then let it clatter back into the bowl. My soup had vanished and I didn't even remember drinking it down, no wonder I was a heffalump. With both sinuses and mouth overwhelmed, furry and musty with red wine, who was to say what the entrée had tasted of?

'Better than me. You could pretty much cover off every aspect of our relationship with that. But honestly, Angela was better than most people. Smarter, bolder, *much* more beautiful. Pretty much how we all ought to be in a perfect world. Nothing scared her. While me, I'm afraid all the time. Even now. This is like a bad dream.'

Now that was a smile, although slight. 'Shall I shake you awake?'

'You know those emote and release places the Screws run? Where they take folk to get their feelings reprogrammed?'

'I'm familiar with the concept, although notably not a single person who's undergone the process has spoken up about what it entailed. By that alone, I have assumed the tours are very much sanitised.'

'They had her in one for *days*, and I didn't even *know*! And then, *then* this fresh-faced kid, so sodding young I could've probably given *birth* to him, dumps Angela back on my doorstep.

'With all the neighbours poking their big beaks into the hall for a tut. And this kid says, "You'll have to watch her." Flippantly, you know? Not even looking up from his sodding clipboard. Not like this is a vital bit of information, and I ought to snatch up a knife and carve it somewhere.'

You could tell Dr Cormac was already coming over a touch bored with my maundering. His attention strayed. Although he was too polite to out with it, he wanted to hurry this through to the end. 'So … they came back and caused her death, somehow?'

*The truth, fatguts. Your precious truth.* But oh, it was so easy to just up and blame the Screws. I already hated them, half the work done already. What they did ended up killing Angela, but I may as well have pushed her myself. Because I didn't believe her. She was always lying.

'No.' The admission hurt, like a cramp tearing me in two. 'The Screws didn't kill Angela, not directly. But they took something from her. Broke something she needed to cope. Whatever she'd been using to come to terms with reality. Angela never said so much as boo to me about it, but now I think she must've been all guilty and poisoned inside about Michael, no matter how calm and perfect her face.

'The Screws went into her mind and cracked it open like an egg. And me, I didn't watch her like they told me to.

'I wasn't even really listening, I was so freaked out when they knocked. Just begging inside for them to go away, so I could slam the door and have a vommie in the bathroom. My guts were climbing up my neck.

'Ushered inside, Angela sat in the lounge room where I plonked her. And that's where she stayed. Just staring at nothing and making this awful dry sobbing now and again. Like she wanted to cry, but her insides had been wrung out of her. The upcoming wedding sort of fell apart, and eventually when she wouldn't go to work or answer Greg's calls I blew up at her, for all the sodding good it did.

'Greg sounded so *upset*. What was I supposed to tell him? And I was so sodding angry—I just wanted Angela back to normal. She scared me. It was like staring into my hopeless future, everyone's future, and I didn't want it. I ran out of compassionate leave, then annual leave. Greg's parents were real shitty by that stage so I was shouldering all the bills, including the dropped wedding stuff. Raging at my sister sparked nothing. I went back to work in a huff.

'That must've been when she called Greg. She phoned him up while I was at work, and nobody was watching her like they should. She went to meet him at a café and talked to him. Angela was always so good at convincing people of terrible, impossible things, you see. At winning them over. I've never met a single person able to resist her. After a while of being worked on, her cause is the only one you see.'

I was trembling, the force of what I held inside shuddering and quaking this poor maltreated frame. At least Cormac no longer looked bored. He listened quietly to the tragedy unfold.

'Once she had him where she wanted him, Angela and Greg went from the café to the local train station. Holding hands, they jumped together in front of the express service as it barrelled through. That's what blew my mind: like she'd sodding *memorised* the schedule.

'How long it'd take to talk poor Greg around, versus when the next train was coming without a chance to stop.

'Bystanders said she was even smiling, you know? It was the sort of stunt she'd pull. S'pose I should count myself lucky she wasn't wearing that ridiculous great floofy bridal gown, too, as the final touch. I got stuck with it. Took me two years to pay off. The designer was ratty with me, too, stayed right on the verge of calling in debt collectors the whole way. What am I even going to do with a wedding dress?'

Saying it was like squirting out poison, without relieving the pressure.

The deformed planks of my life groaned. I was tense as a bowstring in the chair. What sodding good would a big white dress do *me*? I could scarce squeeze a single leg into the tiny thing: a cold fact I well knew because, saddest of the pathetic, I'd gone and tried it on. In the shameful privacy of home, all the blinds drawn. Wanting to see what I'd look like, even if nobody else ever knew it.

'Greg didn't even die right away. He … got caught between the platform and the train. Rescue crews worked to free him for a solid hour, before his heart gave out from the screaming. By then he must've known Angela was gone.'

So here it was. The one unforgivable crime. You're only given one chance to exist. It was a violation so rare, the word "suicide" practically died out between incidents; should its bleak horror erupt into the world, a whole generation often needed things explained. Oh, those poor kids who'd been chattering and waiting to take the train home from school. It'd been a full platform. Angela had needed to shoulder her way to the fore.

I gagged with helpless, agonised pity for childhoods ruined. For all those lives tainted by what my sister had done. Especially Greg's parents.

Instead of a beautiful wedding, what they lavished all that cash on was the burial of a truncated casket that couldn't be opened to say goodbye.

The feeling still often crashed down on me at odd moments, this shuddering echo of calamity that couldn't be taken back. The hideous destruction that was unchangeable and fixed the moment Angela had stood up from the couch in the silence of the apartment, bedsores glowing, her face ghastly, and picked up the phone to call Greg.

Dr Cormac began clearing our bowls, his mouth set in a grim line. If we were normal folk, and my spewing of all this had made anything better, then this would be when he kindly gave me a chance to compose myself.

I couldn't cry, though, and the pause was wasted. I could never cry. The pristine white napkins looked too nice to be blotting up tears, anyhow. They were so simple and pretty, all folded up, like something you'd take home and place on your mantle.

'I genuinely regret hearing of such a terrible ordeal. It's difficult to conceive of anything more negating and senseless than somebody wishing themselves from existence. Willingly giving up any opportunity to ever again influence events, or change minds. But have you considered there may have been deeper mechanisms underlying your sibling's desperate actions that sheer spite?'

I looked up sharply, exposing my raw tearless face. 'If so, I'd love to hear them.'

He set a fresh course down in front of me. Hands a bit thick with wine, so that food slid from one side of the plate to bunch up at the other. Rosemary chops, green beans, mashed potato. Reassuring food. Comfort food. Food to spill your secrets to.

'Mr Formir has stated it himself. Your sister sent him Out there to investigate some kind of voices.'

'Angela didn't hear voices. She had bad dreams. And that's because there's no such thing as *voices*. Just tattered urban legends, and a suggestible bunch of seriously disturbed people.'

'My mother heard the voices.'

Oh boy.

'I am so sorry, Dr Cormac.'

But of course he had a family. Forgetting that was one of my particular failings. Being on your own, it totally slips your mind how everyone else is enmeshed in a support-and-demand network, like a fly struggling in a web.

'No need for apologies. "Seriously disturbed" would have summated my mother's situation fairly accurately, I'd say. Whatever my mother thought she was hearing occurred unmistakably while she was awake.'

We were well into the second bottle already and he twisted the stem thoughtfully, to see crimson gleams dance. Whereas my confession came squeezed out all squeaky with shame, Dr Cormac seemed fine with his. Rather contemplative, in fact.

Perhaps there was something to be said for not keeping it choked up inside.

'The affliction waxed progressively worse as she grew older, or as I did, I suppose. I seem to recall few episodes when I was very young; as a family we managed to carry on more or less normally. But in due course the only way to cope was to have my mother institutionalised, with drugs. The heavy drug therapy Mr Formir is undergoing originally derived from her treatment program. Extracted from the most beautiful crimson flowers. Great beds of them grew around the institute; I used to wade in them as a boy. I was still young enough that the doctors had to explain rather awkwardly why I couldn't live there, all the time, with her. My father was too upset to bear discussing it. Nothing would silence the voices. The very best medicine could achieve was for them not to frighten her so much.

'It was not much of a life, all told. Not a lot of joy. Although to be fair, she always lit up when my father or I would visit, it was like something magical. Enduring the fear, however, day after day, wore her out early. I imagine that toward the end she may almost have been glad to terminate such an existence.

'And yet, in her way, to be tended with such care makes my mother one of the lucky ones. Your sister was incredibly fortunate to only be afflicted by a light touch. Even so, I can hardly begin to imagine what the nightmares must have put her through.'

I caught my breath. Just like that, I was a little kid again. Frozen beneath the covers for an all-night vigil, too scared even to breathe, as I listened to Angela's whimpers and thick-tongued, unintelligible barks in the dark.

I had to stay awake, it was worse not to hear them. People always commented on how I was such a slow, exhausted, clumsy child. They seemed to imagine I couldn't hear, when in fact I heard everything. Always fearful. Black circles beneath my eyes in the few photos that remained.

'It also appears plain that despite your hostility toward him, your sister's regard for Mr Formir must have run deep.'

'Yeah.' The pressure in my skull was almost blinding. I stared out the window where, down below, tiny lights were pattering on in the dusk. All the way down where life was going on. Where I belonged. And where not a single solitary person was thinking of me. 'Sod knows why, though. When they hooked up, I was so sure Angela had a bee in her bonnet over landing a famous boyfriend.'

'You must be finding it somewhat of a relief to know that she wasn't simply using him.'

'No—you know what, it just makes things worse. She cared about him, and still packed him off regardless. Right where he was most terrified of going.'

Dr Cormac tapped his glass. 'Mr Formir *is* a grown adult.'

'Or as close as he could aspire,' I muttered.

'My point is, he could have simply said no.'

'I don't think you're getting this at all.' There was no encompassing what it was like, to have lived with Angela. '*Nobody* said no to her. No matter how weird her demands might get.'

'You never once said no to your sister?'

That was suddenly too much. It all came tumbling out.

'My *whole life* with Angela was a long series of her paranoid rules, her *survival* rules. Don't do this, can't say that.' You mustn't ever, ever cry. Promise me Cathy.

'And all the while she skipped feverishly from one to the next, because sod forbid any rule should ever constrain *her*. Me, I had each and every one of them drummed into me like the last great truth. Angela made it painfully clear that should I fail, we'd *both* end up getting dragged away. I'd have failed her. Eventually I found myself so bound up, I couldn't move without her say-so.'

Now would have been a great time for weak, self-pitying tears. I shuddered with the need, but of course, nothing. Good girl, Cathy. Obedient as always.

'Ms Hanberry, you must be aware that this portrait doesn't fit with the idea of the wonderful paragon sibling.'

'Angela … Angela was …'

The gentle pattering warned me, and I frantically scooped a napkin to my nostrils to trap the blood. My head pounded so horribly I couldn't manage to care anymore about soiling the pristine linen, or who'd clean up the mess. What they might think of me. Oh, to cry, to wail and let it all come gushing out! Release, before I crumpled into a compressed juiceless husk, no bigger than a marble. A curiosity to be set next to the glittering yellow diamond on my bedside table.

'How was she?' Cormac leaned forward in his creaking chair, and of all absurdities those eerie and normally disdainful eyes brimmed with tenderness. A slurred, somewhat drunken compassion, but there all the same. 'The truth, Catherine Hanberry. How was your sister, truly?'

I hung my head. Could I claim to have ever really known my sister? She lied, she lied. She lied to everyone, all the time. 'Angela could be so cruel. She was manipulative, and loved being the centre of everyone's world. Always determined to have her own way. And I always knew it. By the time Michael realised, he was already in the trap.

'I think … I think Michael only cottoned on to the truth about Angela once he was Out there, the only place far enough away to think with a clear head. And he still couldn't do anything about how badly he needed her. I don't suppose poor Greg ever had time to work out what he'd let himself in for. Not truly.' Not until he lay trapped between train and platform, in that hour that went forever, and she hadn't even waited for him.

'It isn't the end of the world, Catherine. People are people. We carry our flaws, all of us, and we do our best. Nobody is required to be perfect. Especially not as perfect as you made your sister out to be.'

My words tasted of choked, metallic blood. 'I never wanted to out and face it, the ways she used people, 'cause I *loved* her. I loved my sister. I loved her so much that I remembered her differently. Once somebody's dead, memories are all they become. I wanted to make Angela a better person. But listening to Michael talk about her, I haven't been able to do anything but have my nose rubbed in it.' I wished so badly to weep.

'I greatly appreciate your honesty in sharing this with me, Ms Hanberry, and with yourself as well. It cannot have been easy. And certainly what you've done is no great crime: *nobody* loves anyone for who they truly are. Nevertheless, I feel honesty is what we must deal in up here, if we are ever to get to the truth.'

Cormac moved to the side cabinet, and busied himself readying some kind of sweets. See? Now that I'd rolled over on request, I got a treat.

Under cover of semi-privacy, cradling my thudding head in my other hand, I relieved the papery scratching beneath my bra strap. I'd entirely forgotten about the note tucked coquettishly there like some IOU, a poor stripper's tip. Following the confrontation in the long hall, I didn't know what I was expecting it to say. Something foolishly romantic. Really went to show, a woman's misguided vanity knew no bounds.

Trying to keep tacky red nose-blood prints to the corners, I squinted to read it.

But it wasn't from Tall Jake at all. The note came from Charlie Screw, who'd printed in heavy bombastic characters:

I CAN GET YOU OUT.
CATHERINE, YOU NEED TO LEAVE

NOW.
BEFORE IT GETS ANY WORSE.

# OUTERMEN

## EIGHT

## A PLAGUE OF IDEAS

MICHAEL LEFT BATHEBA sleeping sweetly, the way they do in old poems.

Swaddled safe in a warm nest of repurposed overalls she'd just "happened" to have on hand.

The scene reminiscent of rutting frantically in the cloakroom of a party, while his lovely fiancée had been enthralling guests in the main room.

Parties were tops for that, the alcohol shaking inhibitions so loose they rattled. Didn't have to turn over too many rocks to find a lady giving that knowing eye while fingering her filigree necklace, fiddling with her hair, perhaps. Some poor bastard tottering free of the smoke and tumult to leave later on'd be in for a nasty wet surprise when he retrieved his coat.

Now that pale, anxious Batheba had finally harried and hounded her way to her heart's content, a faint smile seemed to linger through the drying tears. Though that slumbering brow above was already clenched, in wise apprehension of the future. As though, even in her sleep, she wanted him to feel bad.

*Shit* on that. She'd known full well what she was getting herself into, no sober claim otherwise. *Michael* had only wanted to chat a bit about Angie, like his desires amounted to a bee's dick in this tricksy women's game. He'd carried Angie with him for such a long time, he felt a trembling need to unburden himself. It could hardly be laid at his door how rapidly things'd gotten out of hand.

In fact some four, five profoundly creepy times over the past couple of what passed for nights Out here, Michael'd woken blearily to find Batheba scrunched up nearby like something discarded. She'd been staring at him with grim intensity while he slept, out of it and vulnerable. Might he have even moaned Angie's name in the grip of his fraught dreams, twisting the blade in Batheba's threadbare chest? Served her shitting well right!

To crank up the invasiveness, once or twice she'd even been hanging over him. Succumbing to the urge to tenderly kiss her sweet prince awake.

Flashing his true colours, Michael had shoved her aside with an irritable gesture. It didn't suit to note the humiliation and hurt that blazed across her averted features.

Oh, Batheba comprehended all too well what she was getting into. The cruelty was her belief that she couldn't help herself.

Tucked within the secret carousel of humanity that whirled 'round inside her head, there was a part of Batheba that would never learn, never take heed. It was ravening for love and demanded action, however unwise. Batheba was a woman who had always dreaded the worst. Now, in Michael, it had finally found her.

It'd been the way she picked and ravelled at the topic of precious Paul, and all the things the man couldn't have possibly seen, that finally did Michael in. Following long, hushed pow-wows in the corridor Batheba'd come scampering gleefully back with a whole bushel of *Beth said this*, and *Beth said that*. *Beth said that Paul said*—with his hands over his ears, Michael literally couldn't take it anymore.

Which is why Batheba kept up with such determined neuroticism. Somehow scenting that *this* was the crevice by which she could split his defences in two. Pacing and waving her thin arms excitedly, unwilling to keep her fucking voice down no matter how vehemently he hissed. There might be something Out there! She was gagging to be the first to say it, to spread bad tidings to every man and his dog. Hey, even Michael had to admit it held a horrified fascination.

Until recently, he'd genuinely believed he desired the same. Spill the beans, tell the world! But instead, in a burst of the same craven terror that makes critters cower in the long grass, he'd leaned across and fastened his mouth over Batheba's flapping lips to shut her up, please just shut the fuck up. The fear had been convinced her voice might conjure bad fortune from the very walls.

He'd do *anything* to silence that mosquito-like drone, just long enough to hear himself think.

They rutted on the floor with their clothes unbuttoned to the minimum, neither particularly proud of the odd things the long sojourn was doing to their bodies. The scary thing was, Batheba at least seemed quite genuine about it all. Immune to feeling ridiculous. A couple of times he thought he could feel her quivering lips shaping the words, "I love …" against his bristled neck, his skin hyperalert to such warning signs. Fortunately she'd just enough decency left to recognise the taste of a bad idea.

No matter how often witnessed, Michael never pretended to understand this trait in women. This fever to fling their legs around him and glut themselves on lies. He rolled out the truth and their options, or the honest lack thereof, right up front like a red carpet. Did they think he was *lying*? Or he'd spontaneously change his mind? The pussy wasn't *that* good!

While it never ended happily ever after, at least not so far as he'd seen, still they shuttered their eyes and dove straight in, one after another. Immolating themselves, as though hoping to emerge as something new. Even the pathos wore off after a while. Michael could have left Batheba alone, but he didn't.

He rubbed his aching forehead, looking down at her. He just wanted to think this whole voices thing through, properly, before warning anyone. That's all this sordid liaison was: a snatched chance at some breathing room. It certainly didn't mean he'd stopped loving Angie. Not even rut-crazed Batheba could claim to think so; not when outside of the deed itself, he couldn't stand touch nor sight of her.

To make matters more discomfiting, the distinct mushroomy reek of semen, and let's face it, *lots* of semen, now insinuated its way into the atmosphere's dense fug. Michael'd tried to keep the noise down so the whole shitting Capsule didn't shake with their brutal, combative grunts.

Batheba's anguished sobbing when she thought he'd dropped off was bad enough: theatrically clasping her thin ribs in her arms as though to hold it all together, with her face bowed right down to the floor.

But to anyone with a schnozz on their face there was no whitewashing what they'd been up to. He wondered now why the fuck he'd bothered. Why not cut loose with shrieks of orgasm and despair? Goose these assholes with a little reminder that they weren't dead. Not yet. And certainly not Michael. He had a wedding to get home to!

Batheba shifted at his feet, interrupting his chain of thought which had turned happy for once in fucking forever. He had to resist a powerful urge to give the selfish bitch a punt.

'Don't tell anyone,' she moaned without waking. Angie's admonition springing out of the dark here and now sent a brutal chill down Michael's spine.

'Angie?' he whispered. But it was just Batheba twisting in unhappy dreams.

Michael slid quickly from the room before it could get any worse. No joy in yet another resentful lack of conversation, should Batheba wake. It ate up all his energy merely to ignore the void yawing between them, while she stared with adoring wounded eyes. Enclosed in the Capsule's tiny remains. What a place to try and avoid someone! They were all shut in, and drifting slowly away from one another.

Case and point. Out in the corridor, here came good old John Porliet paddling by. Almost knocked Michael on his ass in the rush. It felt like he hadn't spotted the other man, or his stupid fringe, for nigh on weeks; although in all that time they couldn't have been over a fistful of meters from one another.

Michael caught himself on the wall, then jerked his hand away sharply lest the tapping and scratching start up again. That was the last thing he needed.

In league with Batheba's maddening efforts, the racket made it impossible to concentrate on any fucking thing. 'Woah, where's the fire, Porliet?'

John grunted, turning half aside. Michael Formir hardly warranted a full stop right now. 'Words simply can't express how funny you aren't.'

'Too soon?'

'Get out of the road, idiot! That mad bitch Beth's gone and locked Paul Outside. The Captain's having a conniption!'

Michael experienced the most peculiar tipping sensation. Akin to being swung end over end, before being set gently back on his feet, and all the while both eyes reported he hadn't shifted a millimetre. Even the kids who adored 'coasters would be left hawking back their cookies.

Swooping illusions happened so frequently Out here, when the jury-rigged power blipped and gravity became a happy rumour, that it took a solid think to recognise his overstretched fear trying to snap into shape. That's how out of touch his abused body had drifted: it'd pretty much given up on warning him about anything.

Michael trailed John down the corridor. He couldn't shake the image of himself as a persistent puppy, pestering the heels of the lumbering man. He had to do something drastic about his standing with the crew, before they discounted him entirely. The pack of them were already well on their way to staring vacantly right through Michael to the walls themselves.

But of course, everyone rushed to battle stations for *Paul*. Paul who'd been Out there, and come back (although apparently not for good if he was fucking Outside again!). Paul had become both their lucky charm, and secretly something of a dire albatross they feared to touch—a tricky feat to get around in the confines of the Capsule.

For now, at least, popular favour still fell on the side of "hero" because Paul had stood up to the Captain, positioning himself between her and them.

'Why the fuck would Beth pull something like that? They were supposed t' be in cahoots.'

John shrugged great meaty shoulders. Even under these extremes, with everybody crumbling apart and their limbs coiling up like silly straws, John's body refused to surrender its podge. It liked to be comfortable, and comfortable it would be. The padded weight was the perfect misdirection to the man's over-spinning, ever-agonising mind.

Watching the progress of John's heavy, almost womanly thighs down the corridor reminded Michael of all the rich restaurants he'd never enjoy again. It hurt, a surprising stab of pain, like stepping on a hidden needle. Every time he thought he'd begun to acclimatise, up popped another reminder of all he missed.

John, though, John was loving all this drama. He hated doing nothing, thinking nothing, *being* nothing, which in their present straits took up approximately one hundred percent of the day. 'I'll bet it's Paul who started it, though. Daft bugger reckons we can't hear, but he's been carrying on and on at Beth about Out there. Fucking broken record.'

'Really?' Michael's mouth was so like an old bone, the word caught and ripped his dry lips. Dabbing at them, he couldn't say he fancied the overwrought gleam in John's eye as that heavy pie-dish face swung 'round again. Clearly the fellow's rabid overabundance of imagination had been mouthing away at something. One day soon it was bound to gnaw its way right out of his plus-sized noggin.

'Really real *bullshit*, Michael. You wouldn't credit what fanciful idiocy's been bouncing about in here like some B-grade Chinese whispers. Seems people can't abide the simple, practical idea of an empty void.

'They've got to fill it with something, even the puerile bogeyman. Give purpose to nothing.

'But Paul, now *Paul* will've ducked back Out there to try and prove he ain't crackers. He's all about the proving, our Paul. Out to save what little day we have left. Total timewaster. I tell you, the Captain's really gonna strip the skin off his backside for this one.'

John spat on the floor. It was flagrant wastage, that according to the new law of the land ought to've gone slithering down the chute; and would earn John his own clip 'round the earhole should the Captain spot it. But they were discussing *Paul*. Some token of rebellion had to be laid down. The crew manufactured their own rules.

'Of course, that might be just what he's anglin' for.'

Oh please not this again. Who did Michael have to dip his wick in to get some recognition 'round here! The crew's baffled glee wasn't difficult to understand, though. Who'd ever imagine a masochist whose tenderest dreams involved *the Captain*? And then for that flagellant to be Paul! He looked so *normal*!

No one on the Capsule could depend on their legs too well anymore, but clearly in their stumbling progress they were coming up on the control room. You could tell by the way Captain Orchid's bellowing boomed louder and louder down the corridor. A tone that made you want to pluck your terrified balls from where they'd lodged in your neck and bolt the other way. Michael and John skidded to an ungainly halt in the doorway, tangling each others' efforts to stop.

Steely-eyed Beth was holding the Captain and Sal off the control panel with what looked suspiciously like a home ground shiv. The tines protruding from her fist were a dead giveaway. Now didn't that raise all sorts of tantalising questions about curly-top's private life.

Even from the door, Michael could see that the switch she guarded was still green for safety. Which meant Paul was presumably still twiddling his thumbs in the Capsule's charred guts like a sucker. That, or hammering futilely on the locked airlock door.

'Beth, is that a *fork*?' Michael burst out disbelievingly. 'You couldn't have picked anything else for your craft project? We hardly have enough forks as it is! Well, now I fucking know why, don't I!'

'I like this one,' Beth chuffed defiantly, never once peeling her eyes from the Captain. A wise move, that. Best get your gloves on and handle *that* encounter as you would a very pissed off viper.

'But a knife is *already* a knife!'

'Shut the fuck up about the fork, for fuck's sake, all of you!' the Captain barked.

Of all the inappropriate reactions, John burst out laughing. He couldn't help himself. Really bringing it from the gut, and that was a lot of gut. Hair flopping in his eyes. All people, however staid, have such a moment crouching in ambush along the timeline of their lives. The chance to really lose their shit, in a big way, in front of a whole lot of people. Now it was quiet, introspective John's turn to go cackling into unseemly hysteria while everyone stared.

Michael wished desperately for a camera, he wanted to document every excruciating second. John had always been *the* man in a crisis. Not to seize control, fuck no, but always so unflappable others steadied around him. A nice, low centre of gravity that refused to be shaken, and a mouth that never opened unless the comment had been triple-checked. Or to jam grub in, obviously. The only one who still looked forward to mealtimes.

'Look at the state of you lot!' John wheezed merrily. He was having a grand old time. 'Prancing about. Sharpening *forks* to save you from the big bad Outside. Forks! Why bother? Nobody's going to save us. We're beyond reach, we're all dead! We're dead! The sooner we admit it, the sooner we can decently cease to exist.'

That last was confided with such secretive glee it made his audience's skin fair crawl away. Sometimes a person is awfully quiet. Too quiet.

And when you finally discover what's been bubbling away in them all this time, you want to frantically stuff it back in and slam the lid.

Michael edged away from John as inoffensively as he could. Everybody seemed to be overleaping science and logic to reach these baffling conclusions. Or, more likely, squeezing circumstance to fit the shape of whatever festering, secret belief they'd smuggled aboard. 'What do you mean, we're all dead? Everyone in the world?' It made about as much sense as two plus two equals banana.

John was quite happy to earnestly explain. 'Oh no, the *world* exists, but we don't. We can't, you see, because everyone and everything that matters thinks we're dead. Even my goldfish thinks I've snuffed it!'

The Captain couldn't figure whose direction to glare the hardest in. She was putting out so much hateful venom, her bloodshot orbs might well leap from their sockets and explode. 'You stow that attitude of yours, Porliet. Nobody here is dead, and I'm making fucking sure things stay that way.'

She settled her blazing regard on Beth, as John hadn't yet dared the sheer effrontery of a weapon. 'Starting with little Missy here letting Paul right the fuck back inside, *right now*!'

Sheltering now behind John, who was still bent double wheezing crazy laughter, Michael was white-faced, caught up in his own crisis. One he'd only just been helped to. He could be childishly sluggish that way: when it came to encompassing others' perspectives, or even acknowledging they had them.

Angie didn't know he was still alive! She had to be told! His thoughts raced about in a trapped panic: she'd think he'd *failed* her!

No. No, it's ok, Michael soothed his thundering heart, in a ribcage so light and frail, no more than a paper wasps' nest. Angie would know, somehow. Of course she would. She knew everything, every little inclination that flickered to life within his skull.

Time and again she'd demonstrated her ability to read the book of his thoughts with scornful ease. Encompassing them before he did.

Which meant that sometime soon, Angie would know all about his indiscretion with Batheba—if she didn't already. Little surprise given Michael's scattershot personality. His demand for admiration, and particularly that of women, merely to gain cohesion. He shuddered, clutching his chest to keep the wasps in. Michael could almost feel the waves of his fiancée's fiery displeasure sweeping out to find him here. Battering him to the floor. Doubtless he was to be punished.

His eyes darted this way and that, barely perceiving the drama unfolding in the control room. He had to do something, to make his mistake right in Angie's eyes! And right quick, too. The woman he stood in thrall to was capable of such terrible things.

John, meanwhile, wasn't having any of the Captain's censure. Paul's quiet rebellion had touched them all a tad reckless. Catching his breath; 'As much as I envy your grit in shoving other considerations aside, Captain, with all due respect brute determination can't replace fact. This little team of ours happens to be dead, *dead*, deader than spam. Society, *reality* knows we're dead. Reality, which is entirely cooked up by the great, murmuring, group-mind of humanity. And there's none of *that* Out here, not a sniff. It's all contained back home.'

Beth chimed in with her own brand. 'There's so few of us left, you see; we can distort and abuse reality, any way our minds see fit.'

The Captain massaged her brow. 'Ok you two. Sure. So we find some way of letting home know we're still alive. Let me add that to my list, right behind getting all of us the fuck back there.'

Oblivious to their spat Michael was twisted by fiery torture. He quivered with the consuming dread of a guilty child soon to be caught. There'd be no graciousness from her, not this time.

Angie *had* to be told he was alive, but not before he'd fixed what he'd done with Batheba. He had to fix it!

John wiped tears of mirth from his eyes. He was actually crying with it. 'Go home? Captain, have you even been listening? We can't go home, *we are dead*. Dead, yet we continue. It's unprecedented, utterly unnatural. Say we were to in fact make it home somehow: they'd have to laboriously develop new mental software just to deal with us! Concepts that could become a plague. The utter devaluing of life—we'd be a curse on our own people! Everything would eventually rip itself apart.'

Relinquishing the standoff with Beth, the Captain bulled right up into John's face before his mouth'd even closed on "apart." Shocking in itself; given so little room to manoeuvre, and with bodies waxing increasingly fragile they'd taken to exaggeratedly wide berths. Her face had flushed a dark, angry red. The sort of purplish veiny shade you expect to see right before a heart attack plants its boot in your chest.

Defying physical degradation, she caught him with a left hook so solid John went cross-eyed and sat down hard on the deck. He wasn't fucking well giggling now.

'How's that for fact?' the Captain snarled. 'Feel alive yet? 'Cause I've had it the fuck up to here with you lot and your defeatist theories, your constant whining over how we should sit around on our fat useless backsides.

'Just wait meekly for the end, huh? Well not good enough people. I'm having fucking none of it. *Every* second is precious, *especially* the shithouse ones, and we're going to be ploughing through every last one of them if I have to ram survival down your stupid sheep necks with my fist! You got me?'

'Oh fuck me.' Beth made the initial move toward John but leaped back just as quickly to defend her post. Sal merely continued to look on with crossed arms, broadcasting pained disbelief that they were wasting her time with this shit.

To stay in the good-boy books, it fell to Michael to get down there and try holding John in place long enough to check his skull.

The big man's feet weren't with the program: they skittered and slid dazedly, trying to haul him up on autopilot to face the music. Inadvisable. Once the Captain slaps you down, you stay there. Unless you fancy dancing with her again, and again, and again. She wasn't likely to run out of fists anytime soon.

Even with Michael's firm hand pressing him down, John glared up at Sarah Orchid. 'How the fucking fuck did you end up in charge of anything? 'Cause the only leadership quality I've ever heard fall out of your filth-hole of a mouth is cheap bullying!'

The Captain actually laughed. A clear, high chime of unabashed malice. None of them had heard its like for years; and yet, way down the trail, it was something you never forgot to flinch from. The cruel glee of a child twisting another's plaits. Perhaps for lunch money, merely to throw it in the bushes.

No *normal* person plans to be seen as the bad guy. Thieves are merely taking what's owed them, the benefits life failed to deliver. They deserve it as much as anybody. Racists are just saying what everyone's thinking, right? Every one remains the shining hero within their own head, which is clearly impossible: the world isn't a wonderful giggling playground. Most folk are mediocre, if not downright nasty. Yet on hearing the truth they immediately protest, *But that's not me at all!*

In the Captain's case, John's condemnation cut less than it tickled. Sarah Orchid was a rare bird who'd long ago looked upon what she was with clear eyes, and embraced it. Revelled in it, even.

Eager to discover how far such extremities might take her. It'd been a long, long journey, and she wasn't counting herself out yet.

John stayed on the deck as though glued to it. Right, good. One asshat down, one to go; time to conclude this ridiculous scrap.

The Captain closed on Beth again, feeling Sal's silent support ever-hovering at her shoulder.

She made it to within two quick strides before Beth, who'd been standing seemingly cowed, lashed out with a gibbon's reach. Both of them staggering about weak as kittens, the spectacle was grotesque. Her frighteningly sharp blade kissed the Captain's arm wide open.

Resistance, rebellion. Here was the legacy Paul had sown for the desire of his heart. And perhaps he did so because the Captain clearly had it coming; his humour certainly trended that way. But the others didn't march to the same moral imperative Paul maintained. Their conflicting versions of "right" flailed in all directions. If this was his gift to the crew, *do as you must*, he might've needed to think it through a little better.

Beth's small teeth stretched wide in a feral grin, savouring the flood of rank curses that spewed from the Captain's mouth as though through a sewer grate. Orchid staggered back into Sal's ready arms.

With her own face impassive, Sal was a stone. Just another day on the job, with these lunatic monkeys life had seen fit to foist on her. She shrugged quickly out of her overshirt to sop up the welling blood.

The scent of an artery sliced open came as a thick, rich shout in such close quarters. The fatty lips of the slash gaped wide enough to require pinching together, which made the Captain swear harder. Stitches for sure. Or more likely some heavy strips of gaff, whatever could be improvised. If that constituted a shot across the bow, Beth was a little fucking overeager.

This obviously wasn't the first time 'round the block for the Captain. While Sal fiddled in her arm she set her jaw and rode the crest of sweating nausea grimly, popping out the other side with as hateful a scowl as she'd worn in.

And not so much as a flicker of remorse out of Beth. She stood just as ready to go again.

Not only a woman who'd spent patient, secret hours grinding a nasty weapon long before trouble reared its head, but one who'd obviously dealt violence in the past, without learning a fucking thing from it.

She knew less than your average schoolkid. To be the quickest animal, to lash out first wasn't brains—quite the opposite. It paraded a failed awareness of how quickly events could become terrible. A life leaking away between incredulous clutching fingers. Another irreplaceable spark gone out in the darkness. Here was another profound failure of empathy. In that, Beth was a sister to Michael.

'You won't be trampling your way through here, Captain,' Beth sneered. 'So sorry if up until now you've been allowed to go through life that way. I'm not having that arrogant bullshit from anyone.'

Having clamped the Captain's free hand to the swealed injury, where it closed like a vice, Sal stepped up, all business.

Although notably *not* within Beth's surprising reach. 'Alright Hanrekson, you've made your point. Out with it. What's going on here?'

While Beth fished about for words, Sal tilted her head chidingly. 'You can't leave poor Paul dangling forever, you know. His air'll run out. He went to a lot of effort to prevent our having to breathe any of that shit Out there—don't you think we should return the favour?'

Muddled theories were fine for murky corridors and furtive whispers. But now, in the relative brightness of the control room, everyone was staring at Beth expectantly. She faced off against Sal, as solid and reasonable as the day was long. Somebody who, by the still professionalism of her manner, encouraged you to get your thumb outta your ass and be the same.

Beth weakly thrust her little weapon out as though to fend off their curious eyes. She recognised that she'd not bargained herself into a good position for sanity. She needed to slice through all their disbelief, that was thickening the air before she even started talking.

Send it fluttering to the floor. Nobody could miss the sweat that beaded her brow.

'Paul … it was Paul. Paul told me he saw something …'

'Ought we be listening t' this? Make her put down the fork.'

'Let the woman speak, Michael,' Sal warned without ever unlocking her gaze from Beth. 'When we want your opinion, we'll ask for it.'

That was all the encouragement Beth needed. 'Paul's been carrying on about some *seriously* fucked up shit, ever since he went Out there. Shit I don't like to listen to, but for some reason he's picked me. Lucky fucking me. Creeps around and whispers to me, all the time and I can't shut him up, not ever.

'Just when I reckon I've found somewhere safe to sleep, when I'd *swear* I was alone—as I'm dropping off, that hissing whisper starts up again in the darkness. Only centimetres from my fucking face! Another time it was like his voice, it just sort of oozed out of the solid wall behind my head. Like he was throwing it to freak me out. That must've been it, what he was doing.

'Whispering and whispering. All this crazy shit, like … like his *pecker* was gone, for fuck's sake! Last thing *I* want to hear about. Said there was no point him loving the Captain anymore, it'd all been for nothing. Some kind of invisible shit was eating him in little bites, eating him alive, like those fucked-up bacteria you catch in a hospital. He said it didn't hurt, but he could go and stick his hand right through the hole where his pelvis'd been, front to back, and what would his legs be attached to soon?

'I think he was crying. I felt rain on my face and it was like being home, for a second, before I sat up and screamed at him to piss off. Now, I know we're all scared as ass, but dongs vanishing? That's one seriously fucked up metaphor right there.'

Sal's eyes flickered as Beth's torrent of confession poured out. Brief anxiety, caught up, then discarded as irrelevant. Paul wasn't earning any stars in her book: Sal did not approve of men who harassed women. She usually took it upon herself to do something about it. Something discreet, and thoroughly nasty. 'You said he saw something. What did he see?'

'Formir, bollocks-out naked!' John interjected. 'Enough to send anyone off the deep end.'

Michael pretended to share the thin, tension-relieving chuckles but inwardly he seethed. The butt of *John's* sad-ass jokes, now?

Beth wasn't jollied along. 'It doesn't matter what he saw. I don't believe him. I won't. This shit we're seeing, it's come about 'cause there aren't enough of us, we can't *balance …*'

'Well then, why don't we let Paul tell us himself what he thinks he saw? Then we can make up our own minds.' All reasonableness and clarity. Cutting across the bewildered aggression that was everyone's bullshit reaction to the confronting unknown; case and point of why mankind wouldn't rise any higher.

'No way!' Beth snapped back ferociously, the shiv springing up so fast a spray of red misted Sal's cheek. Sal deigned to wipe it away. 'Don't listen to Paul! If he makes you believe too, it'll end up being real for all of us!'

'Events don't come about by force of belief, Beth. Believe me, I'd've wished my way off to a deserted island a thousand times by now.' *Leaving the rest of you ass-monkeys here to rot.*

The quip wasn't especially funny, not fired out of Sal's impassive expression with its fine mask of red.

The smaller woman still giggled shrilly and wiped the blade on her pants with a quick stropping motion that left streaks of gory warpaint. Her nerves felt stretched tight enough to strum campfire songs.

Sal knew she'd grasped the rhythm of the situation now. She had a handle on Beth's logic, and therefore her sympathies. 'If there aren't enough of us, don't you think we ought to let Paul back inside where it's safe? If what you say is true, then dropping our numbers can only degrade the situation that much faster. Beth, we need each other. We don't have to like it, but we do.'

'It's no good, Sal.' On the verge of tears. 'There aren't enough of us, anyhow.'

'Then let's not make things any worse.'

Beth opened her mouth, then closed it again. Without going so far as to trust any of these bastards, not so far as she could drop-kick 'em, it was awfully difficult to refute Sal. Especially seeing as all the other woman so obviously wanted was for her to settle the fuck down and start acting like an adult.

The way still stood open for her to lunge forward and jam her trusty friend into Sal's eye socket. She hadn't shown her full reach earlier, that artful way of rocking forward on her toes like a dancer. It always paid to hold some in reserve. And Sal would probably stand right there and take it, like the fucking trooper she was.

Finally, knuckles white around her sharp little weapon, Beth stepped aside from the controls.

And that's how it was done. By the proffered hand, instead of the fist.

Fortunately for glorified bullies such as the Captain, Sal's sort rarely coveted leadership. Her passions stayed in reserve for secret wellsprings, of which others knew nothing, and never would. She could endure much with a calm face, for she was never entirely with them.

The masterful demonstration reminded Michael so strongly of Angie that his chest hurt all over again, vibrating, thrumming.

Sorrow and longing became like a pillar of gelid ice, piercing him through. There'd been that same compelling quality, but in Sal it seemed oddly directionless. Submerged for vast stretches, unless she figured on needing it for something.

While Angie had burned, burned all the time; her fuse always lit and ever so fucking short.

That was it, that was the difference! Angie always knew instinctively what she could gain from any situation. Sal just didn't give a flip to go squeezing results outta others, they had little she could want. Even now, it barely seemed to matter to her whether Paul lived, only that the crisis currently bugging her be resolved.

The worst bit was how, done talking Beth down from filleting and dressing the Captain for dinner, Sal simply switched off. That's it, job done. The closing-away of that compelling force of will felt to Michael like light withdrawn. As though, somehow,

Angie's own presence had been lifted from him, and he quailed in its absence. Existence itself was terrible.

With a grunt the Captain shouldered right on by Sal and slapped the console with her elbow, glaring sourly at Beth as though daring her to make a move. Her touch left a bloody red starfish on the board. It was kind of sad seeing her still trying to play top dog, although Beth supposed getting shown up didn't mean you had to loll your tongue out and like it.

The Captain leaned in to the mike, clearing her throat. 'Paul, you can come in now.' Graciously, like she'd orchestrated it all herself. Beth shook her head. For fuck's sake.

All they received was a faint crackle spat back from the speakers. The equipment was becoming worse for wear by the day, and looked it. If Paul were talking, buggered if they could make out the words. But the naughty corner grew dark, as though seen through a haze of smoke.

'Paul? Paul, can you hear me?'

That was a surprising level of concern coming from their noble leader, and Michael glanced across at her sharply. Sudden worry marred Captain Orchid's stern face at whatever her ears had picked out of the garbled mess.

It undermined her authority, Michael didn't like disruption of his nice, neat stereotypes. The Captain *had* to remain a brutal tank, and Sal the bland robot, John a buffoon. If they were human then, well. They were capable of *anything*.

Had Paul's confession been eroding the walls of the Captain's iron-clad heart? Assuming she *had* one. His crush an unlikely offering recalled again and again, almost against her will. Turned over carefully like a foreign treasure. A trinket to only be examined fitfully when there was nobody to level a hilarious finger.

The Captain craned toward Sal. 'Do you hear that? Do you hear him? Is that Paul?'

'Only static, Captain. I don't hear …'

'Paul! Say again, we aren't reading you!'

Still the board showed both airlock doors snugged tight. Paul stayed trapped in that narrow space, a place neither inside nor Out. And whatever the Captain was picking up to put that wild mien over wasn't reaching the others at all.

This was stupid. Paul was probably staring at the airlock door and tapping his busted suit-mike with his nose. Still waiting for his invitation.

Sal stared back at the Captain, and eventually shrugged. *What do you want outta me?* Eloquent with sparse gestures, she even squared her shoulders in the barest approximation of *Sir*.

'Oh, come on then. I'll drag him in myself. That fucker Paul owes me some answers, and I'm right keen to hear his wet explanation for seeing "things" out there. I'm telling you now, it'd better be fucking good.' With that death-grip still clamped to her injured arm, fingers digging in mercilessly.

The whole fucking circus piled down the corridor in her wake, but the Captain ignored them. Paul's infatuation, charming as it was and it'd been a right fucking time since Orchid last felt charmed, ought to make it easier to wring information from his hide.

There it was. The inner airlock door, still firmly shut. Keeping the fire ravaged chaos safely on the other side.

Not quite enough room for them to crowd around, and she threw back a few careless elbows with her good arm. 'Quit jostling, fuckwits, you've all seen Paul's ugly mug before. In case it escaped your bitty attention spans, a stupid knobshine recently sliced my fucking arm right the fuck open.'

'Uh, yeah. Michael, let's step back. I'd say Captain's got first dibs on slapping Paul around for wasting our time.' John's tone may have been jovial, but his dark eyes were fixed uneasily on the sealed portal. Just like that, Michael agreed with a real sour taste in his mouth, a tideline left by drying saliva. He wanted to remove himself far, far away.

The airlock door hissed, Sal dutifully doing the honours as you needed two good arms to operate it. Quite the design flaw, the Captain was now thinking. With a nasty enough injury you'd be unable to get back inside.

She squared to her full intimidating height, always pleased to out-mass the men, as it triggered their insecurities no end. Made a great place to catch hold and swing 'em about. 'Alright Paul you melodramatic fucktard, we're all so breathless to hear …'

The airlock stood empty.

No. Not quite empty enough.

There was a sad little crumple of clothing facing the door, and a helmet tipped off to one side. It looked disturbingly like a severed head, until you peered in and saw that it lay as vacant as the rest of the gear.

Michael shuddered in a haze of overwrought sweat, backing up frantically as the others pressed forward.

For a brief moment he'd seen Paul's shrieking face in that helmet, eyes and mouth bugged so wide it seemed his features would tear away in dripping sections.

The dislocating horror of it took his breath away. And he spotted it not once, but twice.

He'd immediately looked away to the wall, had to. *I didn't see that, I did not see that.* Summoning up a shriek and at the same time telling himself it couldn't possibly be real. When Michael glanced back, Paul's agonised screaming face was still right the fuck there and now gaping directly at him, pleading with him. His balls shrank, and now he lurched forward involuntarily, hands outstretched to help—Paul was a right git, but *nobody* deserved that.

However, the helmet was now clearly empty. Nobody else

staggered back from it in green-faced terror. The vision had obviously been a figment of tight-spun imagination, a cruel trick of reflection. In fact, now the only face Michael could make out in the helmet's shiny smooth planes was his own. White as bone, gaping witlessly, deformed and splayed wide by the visor's curved surface.

Horribly, Paul's abandoned clothes lay crumpled with the inner within the outer, just as he'd been wearing them. Presumably tighty whities and all, although nobody was willing to stick their hands into the creepy as fuck assemblage to verify it. The only bit missing was Paul.

The Captain glowered, toeing distastefully through the heap to satisfy herself Paul definitely wasn't lurking in there somehow. Then she swung to confront Beth, who'd dared to creep to her elbow, shaking her head again and again like a stunned bull trying to figure out which way to charge. Beth looked every bit as sick as Michael felt.

'Did he go back Outside?' the Captain demanded.

'Naked? Are you seriously even suggesting that?'

'An alarm'd be blaring if the outer seal had been cracked since the air purge,' Sal supplied, finally troubled enough to be perturbed. 'We'd have known all about it the second I tried the inner door.'

'That alarm could be cactus, same as everything else on this miserable lump of shit, you lot included. Does Paul reckon this is *funny*?'

'Like I ever want to witness his pasty white buttcheeks plastered over a porthole!' With an aggravated snarl, the Captain booted the helmet.

Surprising everybody, a mass of fine filaments sprang out as it went spinning across the airlock. The Captain leaped back awkwardly as though burned. 'What the fuck's all that?'

Beth knelt and scraped some of it into a soft little drift,

which if anyone had bothered to ask Michael was clearly a shitting poor idea. Rubbing it curiously between her fingertips. Oh, humans just had to dig their grubby paws in to understand, didn't they?

Beth suddenly shook it loose, her eyes bulging. Scrubbing both hands down her thighs to rid herself of the touch. 'It's his fucking hair!'

John made an "upk" sound and turned away, like he'd just belched bile into his mouth.

'Nope. I don't reckon Paul thinks this is funny at all.'

'What did you hear, Captain?' Sal stepped around in front of Orchid, who continued to boggle down at the little drifting piles of hair like a woman slowly losing her mind. 'On the radio. Did you hear Paul?'

'You mean you didn't?'

'I didn't ...' Sal glanced around for confirmation. 'Nobody heard anything.'

'Well I heard him. He answered. All crackly and faint, like he was a long way off, but it was definitely Paul. He said sure, ok, he was coming inside now.'

'Was that all?' Sal was digging like some terrier scenting a rat, and her instincts were rarely wrong.

'Then I thought ... I *thought* I heard him say, *Oh Sarah. You're bleeding.*' With a watery laugh the Captain finally looked up, and although her mouth remained unforgiving tears glimmered in her eyes.

A few drops of her blood pattered unheeded to the floor. 'Paul sounded so fucking sad. He said he was *sorry*. What did he have to be sorry for? Where is he?'

While they spoke, Beth had been slowly reversing herself back into the hallway.

The Captain rounded on her, not so much furious at being made to look vulnerable, but more for the company it was in.

Made it easier for the circling jackals to pick her off. 'Hanrekson! Where do you think you're off to?'

'Out of here, that's for fucking sure.'

'Pick up that hair.'

'You *what*?'

'Pick. Up. That. Hair.'

'I'll be *fucked* if you're sticking *that* down the chute for us to chow down on …'

Michael had heard enough. And witnessed far more than he'd ever wanted to see. He backed quietly down the corridor. Past Johnny-vomit-breath, who was leaning unsteadily against the wall with a hand to his aching brow.

John was trying to figure out if he had a concussion. Of all people, he knew well that hitting about the head was an epically stupid and dangerous thing to do. And usually the first thing combatants forgot. Too many jerks drunk and randy on impossible effects-heavy films, where it was dandy to clock the bad guy because you were always wearing the white hat.

Reality was so much less glamorous. Straight to prison for manslaughter, over a bar fight that seemed so stupid now. Something an immature brat with no control over himself might stir up to feel like a big man. But of course, *actual* men knew restraint, and the importance of the big picture. They knew how to laugh shit off.

Laugh this off: the whole incident was on closed circuit. In fact, fuck, the whole world could watch your idiocy for themselves. They could see how you weren't a man, after all. You'd never be one.

And your snivelling apologies, your thick smothering shame wouldn't mean shit to the bereaved. It was the sort of pickle only being an Outerman could unhook you from.

A fair distance down the corridor, Michael stumbled against the wall, his vision misty.

How could Angie leave him Out here like this? What had he done? Only, Michael knew all too well what he'd done, or rather *who* he'd done. Already he could feel Angie's rage and scorn, deafening within his skull.

*Her? You cheated on me with her? That's the best you could manage, was it?*

Thoughts that continued to thunder and roll as Michael stood looking down at Batheba. Batheba, lying peacefully undisturbed by all the fuss down the other end of the Capsule. So glutted with smug satisfaction she hadn't heard a thing.

Michael stared and stared, until it felt his dry eyes might be scorching their way out of his skull. He wouldn't have been surprised to see the sleeping woman's hair catch alight from the intensity of it. Screaming, the flames rolling out from her head in waves. Burning, burning.

Michael was fraying away. Dissolving. Only ever a patchwork construct of other people's ideas, Angie remained the only one whose vision of him was so profound that he actually came alive. He *needed* her in order to be real. How else would he escape the void?

This was all Batheba's selfish, self-satisfied fault. She brought him to this. Dragged him down. She just had to get what she wanted, stuffing him in between her greedy thighs to munch what little there was left of Michael Formir whole.

She was trying to condemn him to Outside, to save herself.

Before he knew or had planned anything Michael had his hands clamped around the comatose woman's throat. Squeezing and shaking her with all of Angie's white hot rage.

Wanting more than he'd ever wanted anything to wipe her right the fuck out of reality, so their sordid liaison had never happened. Sometimes the violence came on like this, although never so overwhelmingly.

It emerged out of nowhere, a beast with its own ideas on

how to solve things, and all those ideas were red, *red, RED.*

*I can atone, I can!* he shrieked within his head, or perhaps out loud, hoping she could hear. *I love you Angie!*

It was all too clear now that Batheba was a test Angie had set him, she *had* to be. It was just like Angie, flinging temptation in his path so she could sit back with a tight frown to watch the train wreck. Again he felt dumb misery flare in his gut, and it was just like that time she'd caught him pants-down in the cloakroom.

Angie knew his weakness well, his need. Michael's core failings were what'd made him so susceptible to her in the first place. It was his shame that even in the continual bitterness of her disappointment he was unable to stop. He bit his lip and squeezed his fingers together as hard as he could, bloody saliva seeping down his chin. Beneath him Batheba smiled sweetly, tresses shaking all around her eggshell face.

Somebody was barking at his shoulder, 'Michael! Michael!' and 'Oh fuck me!' The crew piling through the doorway behind him. A shrieking, confused beast of many hands dragging him off Batheba.

Where'd the useless shits been when he'd needed dragging off her the first time, before his hips started bucking? John was especially lively for a fellow with a potential head injury, putting his bulk to good use. Not so much the marshmallow academic as Michael had assumed; almost as though he'd been waiting a good long time for this.

Still trying to work out what was going on, Michael was hauled off and slammed unceremoniously into one of the larger storage lockers.

Face-first, so that by the time he got himself turned around they'd slammed and locked the door. The last thing he heard was Beth's breathless summation, 'Well, now we're fucked good and proper.'

Michael really had to agree.

Only now, it came filtering through the hysterical muddle, dredged up from the depths, that Batheba hadn't screamed. Not once, her smile unending. And not because she was so slavishly eager for any touch he deigned to bestow, but because fraught needy Batheba had been bereft of warmth long before Michael laid murderous hands on her.

In the stillness of the storage locker, Michael's own thin smile was sliced to pieces by quills of light from the grille in the ceiling. Perhaps Angie hadn't abandoned him after all.

'But of course, fat fucking chance of bringing the others around t' *that* line of thinking! Oh, sure guys, I *meant* t' kill the shit out of her but somebody beat me t' the punch. Wasn't going t' go down as the most watertight defence in history.

'Nope, it was much easier t' go around believing crazy old Michael killed Batheba and thank goodness we have him locked up, than t' speculate what might've actually done the deed. So, they chose t' overlook a few choice details. Nice, little inconsequential shit, I'm sure. Details that John whispered 't me through the locked door later, begging t' know how I'd done it so he could rest easy. Me, I told him t' spin on it.

'Because sure, I had the ability t' break all Batheba's pretty teeth without leaving so much as a shadow of a bruise on any soft tissue. Course I did. Her gums were perfect, so it sure wasn't any impact injury I've ever heard of.

'The enamel had somehow gotten so webbed with tiny cracks and fractures that it all collapsed int' shards the second they tried t' move her, and came drooling out her mouth.'

Michael took a deep, shuddering breath.

'Angie'll understand. It *has* t' count for something that I was going t' do it. I made a mistake. I did, people fuck up, but I was willing t' set things right.

'Make it all go away again.' Desperate to assert himself as a capable man for all seasons, the self-image he'd always spruiked. But with the curtain yanked back by his actions, Michael was wriggling in the light. So clearly exposed as a miserably insecure, pathetic little worm who'd never grown up. I was inclined toward nasty here, and getting nastier by the moment.

The state of mind I'd woken in didn't help. I was getting really sick of Cormac-induced hangovers. Syrupy red wine layered on coffee on wine, shaken and served in an unhappy pulsating gut that was getting fed whenever. The sediment of both indulgences was building up in my brain; rational thought drowning in settling debris, in the aftermath of eruption.

Becoming well shot of having to listen to Michael whine and grovel, too. All my treasured outrage at the grinding misery he'd inflicted on my sister was returning tenfold, fanned higher every time he spoke of that woman. That Batheba. She revolted me, too, on a whole other level: Michael's contempt for her dripped from every word, yet she'd gone gagging after this bloated sack of pus, anyhow. Case solved. It was probably shame that killed her.

Michael'd failed to surprise, much as he must've done to poor Angela, over and over. 'So you went and cheated on my sister, while back home she was mourning you and falling to bits,' I snapped. 'Oh, good job. Of course you did – it's never *your* fault your pants fell open, oh no. *You gave up on Angela, Michael!*

'Entirely on your own, without anyone's sodding help. A hundred times before you even went Out there, so what's one more, huh?'

Angela had worn both rings as she stepped from the platform, holding Greg's hand. And she'd been smiling.

'What would you know?' Michael sneered. No accusation could assail that ego. 'You *never* knew the true Angie, or loved her. Not like I did.'

The rage that slammed through me was like molten coffee. Enervating, slapping every part of me that dozed into frenetic, trembling life. My sister's wry admonition seemed to linger, *if you've got nothing nice to say …*

Oh, Angela. I've nothing nice to say, alright. Michael didn't deserve that warm blanket of falsehood.

'You gave up on her, and you might as well've killed her yourself! Because she's *dead*, Michael! Angela's dead and you came back for nothing!'

Really, what had I been hoping for? A violent clash of wills? Hysterics? A sudden shriek as his heart burst? Fat chance: nothing ever obediently played out how it seemed in your head. Life insists on shooting off in all sorts of unsatisfying directions. Michael stared blankly at me, and his crumpled features were stone. Anything I threw merely washed off, and I wanted to scream, I needed to hurt him that badly. Just as he'd hurt my sister. And just like she'd then struck at me.

'I *know* that, you dumb bint. And it doesn't make the slightest shit of a difference, not now. Doesn't matter. Angie's still waiting for me.' He actually smiled, a sick twist of lips that looked half-terrified. 'When I finally come t' hear the voices myself, she'll be calling me.'

A vast, disturbed shiver travelled through me, because Michael's words were so abnormal, so plain *wrong*. If I hadn't already witnessed his sordid story, sampled that brief sickening taste of what fear and paranoia had crammed the Capsule, I wouldn't have comprehended him at all.

Even now, I suspected I only pawed feebly at the crumbling edge of it, and that was quite enough.

This then, *this* must be the terrible, warped gift from Outside that the Screws guarded against. Grudgingly, I had to admire them. A thin line of people setting themselves against the darkness, declaring *no further*. They'd taken upon themselves the role that the Shell had performed, before we cut into it. Standing against this sick, wrong obsession.

The desperation and heedless, ravening need that would drive a previously sane mind to conceive of continuance, after the finality of death's hammer came down.

As the astute John Porliet had surmised, if such a disease made it back to Earth it would spread like wildfire. Jumping from person to person as thoughts touched; taking the lost and vulnerable first. Gaining virulence on the bereaved.

The Screws were trying to forestall world wide madness.

I'd never been in such intense danger. I wavered under the sort of clammy chill that heralds a faint. Nobody could find out that I possessed even these shattered, poorly understood fragments of the contamination. I'd never leave Threshold alive. Good ol' Charlie would see to that.

*Work out what they want, as fast as you can*. It was Angela's very first rule, to know your enemy, especially when everyone was against you. If you didn't understand the Screws' desires you stood no chance of faking it or ducking away. So while I stood in the firing line, for the first time I now also had a real chance of squirting through their fingers.

The truth was *my* rule, in the face of Angela's dizzying myriad strictures. One I'd betrayed all too often at the behest of my sister, or Dr Cormac. The Screws, the whole sodding world, that'd clearly rather I be kind instead of true.

The truth was mine, and now I used it to lash out at Michael, because that's the only reason people employ it. To hurt. To flay loose the rich steaming colour of a hated opponent's blood.

'You're dying too, Michael. You haven't got long left.'

He snorted, my best efforts breaking on an unassailable arrogance. 'Paint me another newsflash. I'm just waiting for this shitting test of yours t' be over. I've got *nothing* t' prove, not t' you. Only ever t' Angie. I just want t' see her.'

I wanted to laugh hysterically, or sob. Slowly dying Michael was waiting to see Angela, who was dead. But in the twisted world of Outside never gone. Not so long as this feeble excuse for a man longed for her with all his obsessive might.

The mental gymnastics required to encompass the topsy-turvy concept made my brain pulse, in great flashes of painful light, that drove me to strike back in return. I needed to crush this false belief that'd so sustained Michael. Grind it under my heel.

'What in the name of arse makes you imagine Angela'll see *you*, after what you've done? Oh, I've been telling her *all* about you, Michael.'

He blinked slowly, processing the challenge through his filters. 'I was going t' make it better,' he repeated, stuck on the single track like a dumb automaton. 'I went t' *murder* Batheba, for fuck's sake …'

'But you didn't manage the job, did you? The crew locked you up as a nutcase. Another failure in the life and times of Michael Formir. And it's not merely that. You utterly failed to do what Angela sent you Out there for. *The voices*, Michael—your job. You *failed* her, you found out nothing! What on Earth makes you imagine she'd have anything to do with you now? You've come back to waste her time; you're certainly wasting mine!'

Success, sharp and stinging to the palate, but I was given no time to gloat on it. Michael's frenzied lunge caught me by surprise.

I'd no idea those withered legs still held so much spring. Or perhaps it was hate alone that impelled him across the distance between us. My own hate rose eagerly to meet it.

It was a laughably far from equal match. I was what the peanut gallery generally deemed husky, and Michael's poor withered shape had crumbled an awful way since his strangling assault on Dr Cormac. Although I was knocked back with a shout of surprise, it was like tangling with a kite in a high wind.

I felt more than heard an ominous crunching as I prised Michael's bunched fingers from my neck and flung him down.

I could manage no more, wracked with adrenaline, bent over by a brisk bout of gagging. It was only in part the shock and natural revulsion of having so crippled another's body. Those fingers had felt so *wrong* that my own had instinctively crushed them in a panic to get them off me. Hollow little bird-corpse digits, scarecrow fingers, jutting against the sky above a bone-dry field of ergot, just waiting for the flame. I'd been sure that with the twisting and snapping, foul dry feathers and time-blanched stuffing were about to come pouring out of his wrists to drift about our feet.

Clutching both paws to his buckled chest Michael rocked on the floor where I'd flung him, moaning. And now the truth came to me so clearly it was like a searing brand placed across my eyes. This moment it seemed I'd longed for all my days, it was a sordid thing, with no vengeance to be found. No satisfaction, because nothing I did could change a sodding thing. Not ever.

This was something to only ever be ashamed of. All the rank ugliness and resentment I'd treasured within for so long, finally sprayed across reality, so that everybody could see the ichor of my foul heart.

I ought to drag Michael to the boardroom for the whole world to witness. Slam his pitiful, broken body up against the glass and shriek, *You see what I did? This is what I am!* If I could stand to touch him.

Instead, being a great fat coward, I ran from the room to find help.

I couldn't stand to linger uselessly, watching the suits splint and bandage Michael's crushed hands. Just as they couldn't resist the occasional accusatory glares, at causing them more work. What sort of awful person would do this? Thank sod I'd not run into Jake.

How could I tolerate Michael's cries and broken sobbing, the only comprehensible words of which were *Angie* and *please*, knowing I'd caused it? The racket was pathetic, but wasn't I doubly so? What sort of awful person?

I ought to have been able to let it go, the long nurtured poison. Released in a wash of pity the first time I laid eyes on the broken remnant of the Outerman. I should have seen how his ordeal had inflicted quite enough already, without needing my cruel unforgiving thoughts to hurry the process. As it turned out, I was far more like Angela than even I'd imagined.

There was only one place where I couldn't feel accusing eyes, everybody knowing what I now knew. So I hid out in the theatre's vaulted emptiness, huddled in the shadow of the Capsule's crumpled remains. Wrung too tight to breathe by grief, yet still I couldn't cry. Hard, cold bitch. Not even a drop, to squeeze out some of the terrible pressure that was crushing me.

Piss diamonds lay scattered, glistening and beautiful about my feet in the dust. I stared at them blankly. The theatre was the final place to be alone. Filled with slowly drifting motes. The shadows ruched up beyond brief pools of light with the silence. Sure, I was hiding, from everything in life that must be endured.

In fact, I'd come here with a confused idea of clambering into the Capsule's embrace. That was where shame went, to seal itself away from the world. But even now, I was too terrified of being swallowed up inside.

There'd been nothing left but a helmet full of hair. Her shattered teeth, drooling to the floor. I was scared that if I gave myself up entirely, I wouldn't ever get to climb out again.

So as a compromise, I gritted my teeth and slid my arm inside. The Capsule's impenetrable darkness sliced the limb off cleanly. If another hand had grasped mine there in the dark, there was a good chance I'd die of fright.

Sitting there, staring at the glistening floor, my pulse hammered so loud I feared I might be having a heart attack. It drowned out even my shallow gasping breath, the roaring in my ears.

'Angela?'

My voice was a strengthless squeak. I couldn't look.

'Angela, are you there? It's Cathy.'

I both longed and dreaded to hear my sister respond. It would be the end of me. I waited, but I waited for nothing. Not a peep, bar my own thin hitched breathing. My hand hung in nothingness, and nothing clasped it. Still I kept it suspended there, stiff with fear and trembling already, as penance.

I sat, and I remembered Angela.

But not the sharp side of her I'd confessed to Cormac, spat out with the wine as though bitter and choking me. Those were the memories I found easier to recall because they dovetailed so well with the blame, the unvoiced cry I'd spun my existence around. *How could you give up, and just leave me behind?*

It was an accusation that'd muddied with my hatred toward Michael, two streams running together in the dirt. Until together they achieved a rancid power that blew through me. A dead flood, withering all else that might grow.

No. I sat quietly, took the time, and finally remembered the sister I'd loved. Once upon a time it'd been Angela and I against the world. We'd looked out for each other as best we could, although clearly neither of us were perfect.

Maybe it was an idealised state that couldn't last, not against a world that wanted in. But there'd been moments and flashes when we were so happy, it was like a dream.

Clowning around a supermarket on pay day, while other shoppers glared balefully: *What've they got to be so joyous about?* The hilarity of busting Angela trying to sneak the last of the midnight icecream—she'd been eating it in the shower, of all places.

And when I raked back the curtain and yelled "Gotcha!" she laughed so hard it came bursting out her nose in twin jets.

Night after night, Angela's nightmares had woken me. But then my terrified sobbing always woke *her*.

My sister Angela, who crawled across to my bed and chafed my icy hands. Wrapped her fear around my own. She'd dry my snotty tears with anything that came to hand, even her own long shining hair, which tickled dreadfully. Laughter finally cracking through to break the backs of both our fears.

My sister. Who put her face close to mine and whispered, 'Don't cry, Cathy. Don't you ever cry. I'll never let them get you.'

I sat in the dust and remembered, and shuddered with the impotent need to weep for my lost sister, who I hadn't been enough to save. For myself, as well. For being abandoned in a world where not one person cared for me. For all the love I had withering inside, with no-one to lavish it on. Angela was gone, and she was never coming back.

When I withdrew my aching hand from the Capsule, something gleaming came with it. One long strawberry blond hair was tangled about my cold stiff fingers.

I do find it hard to get with the program come the crack of dawn. And in this case, so far as my throbbing head could tell, the floodlights clicked on right in the stark middle of the sodding night.

Blinded, I thrashed about stupidly as though to claw the onslaught from my eyes. The light was drilling a hole straight through me to China.

Gradually the room swung into bewildered focus, and I found that in that brief time Dr Cormac had flickered like a figment of my imagination, from the light switch to looming right beside the bed. Staring intently down at me with bloodshot eyes like a surprise guest stalker.

Luckily I was too fuddled to respond coherently, with what ought to have been an instant leap of terror. Also awfully fortunate that following the incident with Jake and the breakfast, I'd taken to sleeping as tightly buttoned as a virgin bride. It certainly didn't feel good having my nose rubbed in Cormac's ability to just waltz in anytime. No lock on the door. Apparently no consideration for privacy, either. I truly had nothing to call my own up here.

Oh, except myself. Whoop di-doo.

Oh look, he'd brought the bottle.

'I *do* recall you, Ms Hanberry.'

'I should hope so,' I grumped, rubbing my eyes, unsure what tack to take. 'There aren't that many of us up here.'

There went the eyebrow again. 'From prior to the Accident. It took some racking of the brain, but we *have* been acquainted previously. Your sibling used to bring you to functions, if memory serves.'

Of course she did. Everything in my life came via Angela. 'She'd drag me along kicking and screaming, more like. I didn't fit in at those fancy dos. I'd catch famous people glancing over when they thought I wasn't looking, wondering why I was there. Nobody ever looked at *Angela* like that.'

'I recall the dynamic between you was quite fascinating to observe. As though you literally required your sister's approval in order to laugh, act happy, to so much as secure a drink from a passing tray.' Cormac over-enunciated every word in that special way the late night drinkies bring on.

His thoughts had obviously achieved a state similar to some complex and perfect tower of cards. Just a few more sips should serve to push it over entirely.

A lot seemed to want winning free of his mouth before then. And if he were unlucky, the same would hold for after, too. 'So, please enlighten me. What do you do, Ms Hanberry, now that she cannot give it anymore?'

'What do I do?' I echoed, stalling for time. I cautiously levered myself upright in bed, wishing vainly for quicker wits along with a host of other traits unlikely to materialise at this late date. This conversation had no indications of which topics were unsafe, until I blundered into them. 'Well I'm not sure you noticed, but I was asleep just then. Doing pretty well at it, as a matter of fact.'

He snorted softly through his nostrils. Apparently enough wine would erode the old world charm right away. So, Dr Cormac wanted a grown up's answer, then. I shrugged. 'I don't know I especially do anything. Angela was the one for all the excitement and drama, even if she had to go mixing it herself. Me, I just … get through the day, I guess. Go to work. That kind of stuff.'

Cormac plonked himself heavily on the bed, as though forced to earth by my admission. I shuddered away in my skin without moving. Was I to have no personal space?

Sure thing, Cathy. Up here you can have alllll the things you own.

Dr Cormac perched twin glasses on the veneer bedside table

next to my fiercely glittering little diamond. Filling them, and slopping a share on the floor for good measure. He peered down owlishly for a moment before shrugging. Oh well. It was his carpet. 'Don't you feel yourself obliged to accomplish more?' *Or anything?* 'Your sister is gone. Her rules: poof! Gone. Quite frankly, you could do as you please.'

I'd been eyeing the wineglass unhappily, and took the tiniest sip to be polite. My gut instantly reported back, there was nothing in the world it wanted less. 'Once they're laid down, I'm not sure the rules can ever entirely be gone. Not really. They just sort of become your way of life.'

His shoulders slumped further, like I'd really administered a blow. What was going on in that narrow, balding head of his? What depressing personal truth had I just affirmed?

Could Cormac have come skulking in here looking for a little comfort, some reassurance? Wow, sorry buddy. Are you ever barking up the wrong tree. 'Dr Cormac, I can't help feeling that's not what you came busting in here to hear.'

No more classy-guy; he stiffly drained his entire glass in one go. From that sort of behaviour it was a quick stumble to slugging directly from the bottle and I held my breath, waiting for the mental cards to collapse into ruin. Amazingly, perhaps from long practice he managed to steady himself. And still the impulse to chat overrode his need to safely drown such words, at the silty dark bottom of a river of wine.

He fixed his eerie hazel eyes on me. How I hated that colour.

'I wished so often that my unfortunate mother had passed much sooner than she did.'

'That's a terrible thing to say!' I blurted before my brain could engage. Mental gearstick stuck and mouth revving.

Of course wishing somebody dead was an awful secret, an abomination no decent person would admit to. In verbalising it, letting it out into the world Dr Cormac displayed remarkable fortitude, and what did fatguts here come back with? Something he sodding well already knew, right down to the bone.

'Isn't it,' he agreed heavily. 'And a profoundly selfish assumption, that mine is the greater right to happiness in my life than my mother to hers at all.

'Not made a whit better that, on her good days, she'd have wholeheartedly concurred. The effects of her "voices" were horribly disruptive to my youth, my ability to form simple companionable bonds with others. At least they appear simple to one observing from outside.

'Any child less grounded would have found himself broken by the experience. In our little trio, I was cast as her confidante. Far more than my father, who for all his love flatly refused to sit by the hour listening to her paranoid whispering.

'Yet even as a child, and the only one who'd hear, I could never quite bring myself to believe her.'

He twisted his glass morosely to watch the burned looking sediment swirl. 'I'm quite sure she was aware of it. Going crazy with torment did not make my mother stupid, whatever the other consequences.'

'So you didn't just want to weasel some kind of cause for the … the *Accident* out of Michael, did you? You were after something more.'

Thin lips twisted sourly. 'Mr Formir's testimony on either front has proved frustratingly inconclusive. I personally ventured a great deal to prise the Outerman open. I've drawn the ire of Charles and his ilk, your "Screws." I am beginning to fear there may be no answers to be had at all.'

'Well, sure, Michael says he heard a few scratchings here and there. He thought he saw something weird. But he's also a certifiable fruitcake.'

Cormac looked, if possible, even more melancholy. His face dragged in the wine puddle on the floor.

'And your sister's dreams? Are they not worthy of more credence?'

'As I'm sure you've gathered, Angela lied *all the time*. If she'd been a country, it'd be the national pastime. I wouldn't put it past her to have straight-out fantasised the whole thing to come off as more dramatic. Probably lifted it from some trashy magazine at the checkout.'

Didn't it sound neat like that. So rational. I didn't wish to go feeding Dr Cormac anything to latch on to, anything to do with the voices. If that required a big fat lie, so be it.

He must've smelled dishonesty on the breeze. 'Did *you* ever dream?'

'Not about mysterious creepy voices, that's for sodding sure!'

'Ah, but you did dream about something.'

'I have … I used to have this one reoccurring dream when I was little. But it's something just … stupid.'

The corners of Cormac's shadowed eyes crinkled up. 'Do tell? Threshold is a place for letting truth out, after all. Even should it sound unlikely.'

Fine. 'I used to dream about being a chicken.'

Saying it fast didn't make it sound any better. But the mournful truth was, I missed the richness of those dreams. Night after night I'd been a baby chick, all curled up in its shell. Warm, with a red beating light all my own. Perfect. These were the known limits of my world, and everything I could ever want had been provided.

Angela used to shock me from the comfort of those happy dreams with her wailing. Shrieking at unknown voices to leave her alone. Stop saying that, she didn't want to hear it.

'I warned you it was stupid. Huh. I haven't dreamed it since Angela died—I hadn't even thought of it, until you brought it up just then.'

'You were certainly on the money, that *is* odd.' He sighed.

'But, I fear, not relevant. As incomprehensible as anything, I suppose. Given your affinity, do you consume chicken?'

'I think it's fairly obvious there's little I won't eat, given the chance.' But that got him scrutinising me through the bedclothes as though invited to be a perv, and my vulnerability loomed large in my mind. Nervously, I tried to flip him onto a new topic.

'Dr Cormac, have you been putting yourself through all this because you feel bad about your mother? I mean, it can't have been all terrible; don't you remember anything *nice* about growing up?' One rock, set stubbornly in the course of the flood that swept us all along.

'Memory!' Cormac flapped a hand: *bah!* 'Recollection is chronically unreliable; hardly an anchor to cling to. I concede that perhaps tonight I find myself leaning toward the worst life's had to offer, by dint of morose inclination.'

Mm, *and tipsy*, I almost added. Self-awareness didn't seem to incline the doctor to dispel his gloom and go sprinting joyously for green fields.

'So you chase about after that elusive something better than memory, then. Something real. Evidence you could fling like a brick. But even you have to see that Michael's tall tale's about as reliable as *he* is. All he's accomplishing in the retelling is what he excels at: ruining lives. I don't get how having him back has done you a jot of good, Dr Cormac, there's just no proof to be found. Of *any* of it. And with no more Capsule programs there'll never be proof.'

Cormac bridled as well as he was able; ruined, drunk and terminally melancholy. 'That won't suffice. Not for me.'

'Well it's all you've got. Besides, not even a mountain of fact trucked right to your door was going to make your mind up about your mum. That's not how belief works.'

Now Dr Cormac hung his head in his hands. He was

probably deeply regretting starting this fiasco of a conversation in the first place.

'I'd really like to go home, Dr Cormac. There isn't any point keeping me here any longer.'

The doctor's eyes glittered calculatedly through the cage of his long bony fingers. For all their physical difference, Dr Cormac suddenly exuded so much of Michael's slyness that my momentum blew away like steam. All I had left was dread.

'I can't allow that, I'm afraid. Not yet.'

'But I'm useless here! What more could you possibly want from me?'

His response was grotesque. Already too close for comfort, Dr Cormac twisted from his looming position and clumsily tried to kiss me. I couldn't help twisting aside, desperate for air. His mouth was a shiraz graveyard.

'What are you doing?'

'You're an intelligent woman. What do you suppose?'

My brain supposed with uncharacteristic swiftness. I was sequestered away on his station, unable to leave. In a room I couldn't lock. A room he could come barging into any time he fancied, like the lord of the manor exercising his rights. A scenario straight out of a fifty cent romance, and I was getting to experience firsthand just how unsexy and frightening it was.

Dr Cormac had managed to worm most of himself onto the bed. The man could move fast when he was of a mind to, with a hectic insectile speed. His head darted forward, our teeth clacking together as he tried to kiss me again, testosterone insisting that the maiden doth protest too much. One pale hand clamped onto a breast, like he was trying to force open a door handle.

I grabbed it in both of mine so he couldn't feel my terrified heart. 'Please, just cut it out.'

'Why?'

A thousand reasons! 'Dr Cormac, when grownups want to bump uglies they don't have to crawl inside a bottle to manage it.' This freedom to say-as-you-think was heady stuff. Enough to get drunk on, and wouldn't we then make a lovely pair. It encouraged me to be reckless, and no doubt humiliate myself profoundly. Oh well. I was no stranger to that.

Logic was failing Cormac's poor soaked brain. His cool rationality buckling like a sponge, so you could practically see the grog run out.

'Ah, I see. It's that *Jake* you're hoping to buddy up with instead.' Well of course. The only way a fellow's ego could brook refusal was to imagine you turned toward another. Not at all because I was sodding tired myself, worn down and grieved. I mean, sod forbid the prospect of a drunken grapple, with all finesse bludgeoned away by drink, should send my libido to an early grave. And Cormac had woken me up. Of all crimes, disturbing my precious sleep was the worst.

So what if I *did* fancy Jake a little? I wasn't hurting anyone, and a big fat nothing threatened to come of it anyhow.

Just look at Cormac, he had to be blind raving drunk before he'd even consider storming my gates, and me one of about four women up here! But my self-censure barely had time to run up to full charge. Cormac continued, a familiar sneering tone that hearkened all the way back to the day we met.

'You *have* cottoned on to what he is, haven't you? No? Oh dear.' Certainly knew how to play a crowd. 'Your "Screws" worked so mightily to sell us on Charles being their man, I never imagined anyone might have actually bought it.'

My stomach clenched. I *was* a moron! The revelation stung; I felt awfully betrayed, but had trouble pinpointing exactly why. Surely it weren't as though Tall Jake had *actually* been my friend. It shouldn't come as a shock to find he'd merely been doing his job, in looking out for me, in thinking about me.

Trailing me up here to help. Had I really thought he'd done that? *Followed* me?

And never mind Dr-Bloody-Cormac, who claimed Threshold as his last great bastion of truth. *He* could have warned me at any time. Only bothering now because he felt stung, and instinctively wanted to slap back.

While I hung about agonising, I'd been facing a man of action. Cormac's suit pants were around his bony ankles already, and spattered with wine besides.

They ought to be shaken and hung neatly over a chairback to await drycleaning. *Cormac* ought to be shaken and hung neatly over a chairback. At least until his senses re-emerged.

But who would have thought it; turned out wine was my secret ally. By the time he managed the tip of the condom his sodden penis had thrown in the towel altogether. Baffled, he knelt there on the bed holding it in his hand. Looking exhausted and utterly hopeless, like he might cry.

The great Dr Ashley Cormac. A sloppy drunk. I might've guessed.

At that moment I felt cruelly divided into two women. While one was very sorry for this much-reduced figure, cut down at the knees to the level of human, the other impatiently wished he'd get his shit together. Demanded, in a tone very much like Angela's, to know when he planned to quit staring, forlorn as a dumped puppy, as though I should be the one to save him. I just couldn't react normally to others' emotions anymore, not after such gruelling constant overexposure to them. No more than I could unblock my own feelings.

It was an impatient way of going through life, that was for sodding sure. Always waiting for everybody to hurry up and get it over with. Still, no sense in inflicting my shortcomings on others. I could logic my way through the gestures of kindness, even with its natural flow blocked.

I threw back one side of the doona and Dr Ashley Cormac crawled in gratefully. With his expensive clothes, death breath and all. He settled the weight of all his sorrow and mortal uncertainty on the mattress next to me with a deep sigh. I could practically hear the clatter as the house of cards finally blew over. There'd be no more thinking tonight.

'Warm,' he mumbled contentedly, already succumbing as alcohol pressed down. Then he was out.

Wonder of wonders, I managed to doze a bit, too. *That's* how much I loved sleep. Loved it despite the light rather wastefully left burning, so reminiscent of that first excruciating night I'd spent lodged at the GATE Corporation's hospitality. Napped even through Dr Cormac's whining snore, the wine's histamines having packed his sinuses like cotton candy. *And* the limp heavy arm he'd flung across me, like he owned the bed.

Idiot, Cathy. He *did* own the bed.

When I started back awake, through gummy eyes it took me a bit to figure out what the sod was going on. I'd seen Angela hunched over a cup of tea to grind through the same process the morning after a big party.

Stringing it all together like a necklace adorned with bright flashes of humiliation. Did that really happen? Oh no. And then I said *what*? The type of relentless recall you can't expunge, and just know you'll never live down. The urge to pull the doona over my head and disappear was overwhelming.

All items within my limited field of vision seemed hyperreal, one extra dimension over our boring ordinary, and loaded with dire import. Swimming in its little pool of wine, the diamond glowed with the richness of spilt blood.

Right. Come on you useless lump. It's already more early morning than night, can't lie here forever. Count of three.

One!

Twooooo …

Wincing at each groan of the mattress, I slid myself gradually from the bed to land with an undignified thump on the floor. Almost took the entire sheet along for the ride and blew the whole operation. The funny thing was, I needn't have bothered. A stampede of rampaging elephants wouldn't have broken through Cormac's snores, let alone the solitary elephant trying to escape.

I scuttled to the wardrobe and shucked into fresh clothes rapidly, lest my guest open bleary eyes and catch me exposed in all my awful glory. Blouse inside-out? Sod it. I wasn't going for aesthetics. I just didn't want to tackle what I had to face next in my sleeping gear, which reeked of Cormac's frenetic sweat. You could bottle the stuff and sell it at a cellar door.

Courtesy of the bathroom tap I left a big glass of water beside the bed, because I wasn't a total jerk. Recent events had left me sympathetic to the wretchedness of a hangover. Even a bucket might have been a nice idea, but scaring up janitorial supplies was beyond my current scope. I quietly let myself out.

Threshold's corridors looked more abandoned than ever by night.

Under the lime glow of stand-by lighting, and with the Station's scant occupants tucked safely in bed. It was creepy. The same form as what went by day, but lacking the substance. To keep my bravery up I reminded myself that the only things up here were ourselves. Our weak, fallible selves, and all we dragged along with us.

It took quite a bit of poking around those parts of Threshold I thought I knew, now unfamiliar and eerie in the wee hours of the morning, before I finally located Tall Jake. Or Traitor Jake, as he ought to be dubbed now Jake the Screw. He was holed up in the boardroom. Taking advantage of Dr Cormac's conspicuous absence to settle himself in like he owned the place. Seated casually at the grand window, one leg crossed over the other and staring across steepled fingers.

Only not toward home, which was where my longing eyes were immediately dragged, so powerfully I actually staggered a couple of steps under the pull. No, Snake Jake gazed vacantly into the vast, empty depths of Outside. At my entrance he swiped absently at a thin runnel of drool that'd escaped his mouth, largely beyond his awareness.

Automatic motions from a brain that didn't wish the right hand to know what the left was up to. Who knew how long he'd been stationed there?

Turning, Jake could read every ripple of my expression the moment I set hesitant foot through the door. Of course he could, he was a Screw. Unscrewing folk was his bread and butter, so he could stand by and watch all the little pieces fall out. Perhaps it was just my wishful thinking that saw a brief dismay flit across his familiar features.

He rose to meet me, all matter-of-fact, no longer the Jake I knew. Playtime was over. 'I'm sorry to have deceived you in this manner, Catherine. But bravo for seeing your way to the truth.

'I'm awfully proud to have been here to witness your undertaking such a difficult journey, the bravery it took. You see, truth does little for most people, it brings them no comfort. A curse they would quite happily do without.'

Taking both my hands in his—which I allowed numbly—Jake beamed down at me, so sincerely his whole face glowed. Perhaps he meant it. Who could tell with Screws? They thought they were out saving the world; and for all I sodding well knew, they might be.

Me, I'd walked straight into the monster's clutches. Now to see if I'd survive his embrace.

'Ah. I can see that you're stilted around me now. People always get so terribly *nervous*. I assure you, there's nothing to be feared. Same old Jake. It was only to protect you that I never unveiled the full story. Let me merely say now that we were watching Michael *through* you. Monitoring how he touched other people. Specifically, ordinary people like yourself.

'You see, Catherine, we wished to prevent the Outerman inadvertently bringing something back with him. Something from Outside, something terrible. A contaminant that might spread. Yes, we let you step into harm's way, on behalf of mankind, but I was sure you'd be up to the task the moment I laid eyes on you.

'And you were never too far from our regard, Catherine, even in your utmost extremity. Nobody ever is. Take comfort from that.'

Was the numpty genuinely blind to the threat underlying his words? Or could he be enjoying a chuckle at my expense, even now? I'd not opened my trembling mouth for so much as a peep while he rambled on, saying terrifying things in his friendly, familiar way.

Now he turned us both to catch the light, so he could bare the secrets of my face in the lovely dawn just beginning to break across the Shell. The monster's claws quivered, set to rend.

Had my old bud Tall Jake a weapon hidden about his person, to strike me down swiftly? Or was it only my mind he needed to scoop out and leave quivering on the floor?

But I was prepared. Truth was my shield, beautiful and clear. Let him stare through me end to end. My voice emerged squeakier than usual, but the words stood firm. 'I think Michael coming home was a mistake never meant to happen. A surviving Outerman hasn't changed a thing for anyone, not even Dr Cormac. It hasn't solved anything. The world has already moved on.'

Jake's relief was palpable. *Despite* his moments-ago assertion I had it in me to climb every mountain. 'Catherine, I think you're going to be fine.'

And what if I wasn't? What if I'd answered with cloudiness, deceit, or even just broken his grip and run?

The warm morning light shone full on my face, but across Jake's shoulder all I could see was Outside and its beckoning darkness. It seemed to open up. To spread until it swallowed everything and I could see no more.

Jake twisted curiously to see what I was staring at. 'Ah. Terrible to look into, isn't it? Both fascinates and repels the eye. Fact is, Catherine, humanity's incurably terrified of Outside. With mighty good reason. The fear is woven into our psyche. Removal of it now would destroy us. Those few who seek it are aberrations; to be *eliminated*, they should never have been lauded for it!'

Well sure, *now*, I beamed resentfully at the back of his head. But only because you lot made it that way. By the time he swung back, my face was all innocence and light.

'Jake?' I asked plaintively, squeezing his fingers with all my scraped-together shreds of feminine charm. 'I'm more than ready for you to get me the fuck out of here.'

# OUTERMEN

## NINE

## THEIR CODDLED PEACE

MINE WAS A SODDING narrow window of opportunity now. And without even a sip of beloved caffeine to grease my resolve. Still, I intended to make the worst of it.

All this time while I'd been drifting idly with the flow the jerks surrounding me had been bouncing desperately off the walls, acting wisely or otherwise along paths of their own choosing. I could hardly manage worse.

And I found myself goaded, some, with gritted teeth into reluctant action. Screw-bloody-Jake's last condescending titbit for me had been, 'Now you be sure to stay tucked in here where it's safe.'

I sarcastically added my own "little lady."

'And try to stay off Dr Cormac's radar. Given the deluge of booze he's been putting away it oughtn't be too much of an ask. I've had such a time keeping the liquor cabinet stocked, I'm getting scared to poke my head in to see what damage he's done. I've never seen the like.'

'You've been *keeping* him toasted?' Given Cormac's rapid disintegration it seemed a cruel thing to do. And a bafflingly counter-intuitive move, coming from a Screw.

'I'd count myself guilty of enabling at worst. It's not like anyone went sluicing the stuff down his gullet for him. And he's Ashley Cormac. Never even questioned where it came from. Just raised the glass as his pompous due.'

'But still, you didn't expect him to resist.'

'All in the name of loosening the doctor's … let's call it "single mindedness." It was imperative to clip Dr Cormac's wings somehow. Don't forget, that drunken fool's will once warped the entire world. Can you imagine what he might have achieved here, given his full faculties, fixated to the exclusion of all else? And at what cost, even to himself, let alone the rest of us. I can't even picture it, and I'm rather keen to keep things that way. I just need you to sit tight while I make some arrangements.'

With a fraternal peck on the forehead, no less, which almost earned him a spray of disgusted bile. The kiss galled fiercely. No longer any doubt, the slinking git knew full well I'd fancied him.

But only a little, I comforted myself. Not enough to have appeared *totally* foolish.

Even that didn't console much, as the Screw had likely cultivated my affections deliberately. Working diligently to squeeze the best from me that he could. When it came to bravery and do-gooding, a rosy outlook could nicely backfill what inclination lacked. Well I'd woken to his little game now. *Spit* on his pity-peck!

Oblivious to the resentful storm I had brewing, Jake concluded with a comforting pat to my arm. 'I'll have you safe home before you know it, Catherine. Finally all this dangerous nonsense will be over.'

Over for *me*, perhaps. But I wasn't so naïve as to imagine the Screws'd wave the other players free of this nightmare quite so fortuitously. I could do nothing for Dr Cormac. And following his efforts tonight, I wasn't really inclined to try. But I might be able to help the other one.

Once Snakey Jake had trotted his self-importance from sight, I gritted my cringing fortitude and counted backward from ten. Jittering nervously, in case the slippery sod decided to double back to assure himself I was being a good girl. Just because it was so excruciating, my teeth grinding about my jaw like pebbles, I forced myself through another ten to be safe. And while I stood about counting, the day lights clicked on. Simmering green to a gradually warming butter-coloured glow in an instant.

I went to get Michael.

Perhaps things deserved to run their native course, but I *couldn't* accept Jake scooping him up. For that to be all he had left over the final long days of his life, to endure being mercilessly picked and prodded to bits. That left only one other exit from Threshold's aging, tarnished splendour. Something the Outerman couldn't accomplish alone.

In a way, from what narrative I'd picked out of the threads of Michael's insanity, what I intended would be the culmination of all he longed so desperately for.

In a way.

All this darting, daring action was relatively new to me. I'd ventured halfway down the twisting guts of the long hall before I wondered, with a burst of dismay, how I was even going to move Michael. Once the problem occurred, I trundled to an uncertain halt.

Well he sure couldn't spring up and skip the distance on his withered little legs. Being a sturdy lass, I could probably heft his diminished doll-like form. But I didn't fancy touching him for a bare second longer than I had to. In fact my hair crawled hideously at the very idea, all over my body which was a novel sensation.

Instinctively terrified that Michael harboured something transmissible. Special delivery from Outside to me. Which he did, funnily enough. Just that the danger was all to my mind, rather than the more bountiful flesh.

I knew I'd be no good at this! Stymied so early in my quest I stood and pondered rather vacantly for a while, with my head tilted to one side. But that was far too creepily similar to Traitor Jake's tales of coming adrift back here. So I shook myself into motion. Any direction was better than none with the clock running out. Let's try prying into a few of these officious looking doors I had no business opening.

Meeting room, typing pool, conference room. Cormac's grand venture must have supported a massive administrative staff in the day. All familiar as dirt to the everyday life I'd been pulled from, only looking even more sadly unused than the rest of Threshold.

I wondered where he'd found enough professionals willing to venture up here. And where had they ended up? Had they landed other jobs following the Disaster? Or found themselves tarred by association, fated to swell the ranks of the homeless and mentally ill? It was a brotherhood who'd share their pathological hatred of Outside with open arms.

Each of these rooms gave the impression that all those people had simply stood with one mind and marched out.

On one desk I found a coffee mug and an old orange, that'd been left to mummify together, so long ago that even the opportunistic mould had collapsed into dust. The cup really dated it. The little still life genuinely was a relic from another time.

Well of course, I reminded myself. The Disaster, it all went down before the insanity that was the Screws' assault on coffee. It was hard to remember things hadn't been like this forever.

Aha! After dismally poking around only the third room jammed too full of them to move, I detangled and wheeled out an office chair. The banging and clatter of freeing it from its fellows rang out awkwardly in the dead silent air, making me wince, but the long hall stood deserted. Nobody in their right mind wanted to be up this end of Threshold. My find was sturdy for its kind. Even had arms, a slight step up from the economy model, the sort of luxury staff fight over. So far as improvisations went it got a gold star.

While I was checking the chair over, and savouring my uncharacteristic cleverness, a few of the hallway lights began flickering and jittering. Even the ghastly stark spotlights of emergency globes, which ought to be on a separate circuit, joined in the dance.

I peered up at them, bewildered. They'd never done that before. Was something wrong with Threshold? A quick glance around confirmed I'd wandered far from the beaten track. Should the aged structure decide to peel away from the Shell, I hadn't the foggiest where to go or what to do. I'd be fucked.

Then every scrap of illumination directly above my head blinked out. Nowhere else up and down the long hall. In both directions the lights continued to quiver anxiously in place. Just here. Just me in my little puddle of dark. Clutching my purloined chair and wondering fearfully.

Fizzing. There came an ominous fizzing sound.

Like angry snakes dissolving, thrashing about in a puddle of themselves. The bulb above my head filled up and spilled over. Specks of creamy foam drizzled down onto the carpet all around me.

Now, I'll be the first to admit that household fixtures aren't my specialty. I think they're filled with argon or something. But moisture plus electricity equals bad, that was a slogan everyone could get behind.

As though to illustrate my point the hot filament popped with a miniscule "crack!" enough in the silent hall to make me shriek, just a tiny bit. The mystery foam was whispering as it ate down through the carpet, and I indulged in a humorous little arm-slapping dance, terrified it might be on me. The sibilance intensified. Snakes screaming.

I started walking again. Much faster, to get out from under the phenomenon, my faithful chair rattling over little lumps in the carpet. We had a long way to go, the chair and I. And quite the burden to carry between. Huffing a little as I padded along, I patted it reassuringly.

'Don't worry. It'll be ok.'

Sometimes when you're colon-clenchingly scared, it's better having somebody else to worry about. Even if that somebody's a chair.


The door to Michael's room was cracked ajar. Another uneasy aberration I'd not seen before. All Threshold's portals ought to stay snugged tight. Sealed, unless you wanted something from them. Neglected and festering away in darkness, not leaking their secrets all over the place.

'Michael?' I poked the wheely-chair cautiously inside.

Reluctant to venture any of my own bits without assurance of not getting them bitten off. Sorry, but there was only one of me, and whole rooms full of chairs where this one came from.

Lying in the lance of illumination from the door, Michael's foetid little nest of blankets and rags was cracked open like an egg. The Outerman's wizened form had abandoned it. By shoving the door wider to let more light storm in I found him, curled by the far wall like a drift of brown leaves. As far from the long hall's intrusion as he could drag himself.

I could see he'd managed to tow his IV clattering along for a goodly part of the journey, before the tall silver pole finally tipped over. Then he'd gone and ripped the needle from his arm. Probably in a fit of temper, and likely using his teeth, as thanks to me his fingers were out of action. Using those same bright square teeth to then chomp into the clear bag and suck it dry of whatever it held.

In the shadowy nook, the white medicinal bandages and splints of Michael's poor hands stood out shockingly. Once again I squirmed from heartfelt shame. If I'd seen him flinch from my voice it might have been the end of the mission.

It would be deeply facetious to claim that in attacking Michael I'd injured myself just as badly. Didn't, after all, see *me* fumbling about with both wrists locked in plaster. But what'd been fractured within me wasn't anything you could splint. I'd murdered that ridiculous, noble sense of myself as the "good guy" that we're all born with. I wasn't good; I could see now that I'd never been. And I'd never be so blissfully righteous again.

When Michael raised his rumpled little face I breathed a sigh. He was indeed afraid, but it didn't seem to be of me. Rather, trapped in his persecution fantasy Michael feared what I might bring.

He held up both broken hands imploringly, shoulders jittering beneath the weight of the casts, as evidence of what a good lad he'd been. How much he'd endured. And gamely, he tried to smile. 'Is it now? I passed? Am I going t' see Angie?'

I wished for no more than the floor to open up and swallow me.

'You passed,' I answered as gently as I was able. 'Of course you did.' Looking down I noticed my hands were white-knuckled on the back of the chair. Abusing innocent furniture, too. I forced myself to let go.

Rather than the expected triumph, grief caved the crumpled man's features in. 'You said she was dead.'

What a time for sanity to rear its ugly head! I thought so fast it felt like my brains were on fire. I wasn't here to uphold the truth. For once, I intended to be kind instead, albeit a twisted breed of kindness. 'That was part of the test, Michael. And you passed, you passed the final test. You kept believing in her. So now I'm getting you out of here. I'm taking you to Angela.'

For all my sincerity he gave back a thick, dark chuckle, like oil on the lungs. The shadow of sanity passed so briefly over, and then far away, it seemed. 'You can't go letting me *out*. The crew locked me up, you fucking dolt. Ironic, as behind a locked door *I* was the one who was safe. For a time.'

'You don't have to tell me any more about the Capsule!' I overrode impatiently, casting nervous glances out into the long hall. 'No more stories, you've already passed with flying colours. We just need to get out of here.'

Like I'd have any luck short circuiting the motor for his flapping narcissist mouth. Michael was all set to spew up whatever he wanted off his chest, irrespective of willingness to listen. Grinding more and still more of our dwindling time away. As an audience, all I wanted to do was scoop him into a chair and rush him out of there.

'I'd been on my own, staring at the walls for such a fucking long time before Sal unlocked the door and came rushing in. I'd never seen her like that before: like a tiger had her tail. Normally nary a hair out of place was Sal, even while we were all dragging ourselves along the deck, too rickety t' stand.

'She wouldn't arch a toity nostril at a fart. Yet here she was, slamming the door frantically behind her, locking the two of us in. And I could hear something slamming around out there.'

'**WHAT'S GOING ON?**' Michael asked dully. The eternal question Out here that barely raised a laugh anymore. As though Sal were likely to answer.

He remained duly seated so she wouldn't suspect he was about to try something which he bloody well wouldn't, not again. Once, during the infrequent little meal time pow-wows when he got visitors, Michael'd gotten somewhat fired up protesting what was slopped on his plate.

While Jeshu'd been an ass, and an obvious dick when it came to electrical safety, he hadn't deserved to be mulched into an entrée. Just what the fuck did Orchid intend to do for dessert? Slice off their limbs one at a time, feed them back to them as they lay swaddled on the floor?

He'd stood up, all the better to gesticulate with. And the Captain had slapped him so hard his head rang. Thousands of generations of testosterone-fuelled aggression ignited in Michael's blood, clamouring for dominance. But lucky for him, quick impulse came shackled to a more recent intellectual capacity.

Submitting to a mere slap sure beat the alternative; his brains were spinning. The Captain betrayed no hint that her hand hurt, although force like that ought to have cracked the wrist. Fair sex or no, the Captain was a woman for a man's world. She'd pulled herself up tooth and nail, and was more than capable of putting him on his ass and seeing he fucking well stayed there.

Looming over him, she was waiting for him to make his move. He could see it in her eye.

With such hospitality it'd been a long while between visits.

Even with Sal's dramatic entrance Michael had been languishing so long he found it difficult to rouse. He'd been in the process of settling down gradually into a quiet heap. Was this what had happened to Paul? He just waited too long?

Sal set her ear to the panel briefly, and then her back against it with a dry laugh. 'The Captain's guarding the door.' Was she talking to herself? 'Of course she is. Nothing could make *her* release her stranglehold on life. You could set your watch by it.'

'Where are the others, then?' Michael asked, becoming mildly interested in spite of himself. Abnormal behaviour out of straight-stick Sal was quite the novelty.

'The others? They seem to be just … carrying on. It's the only option they've got, after all.'

'How do you figure?'

'If any of them decide they don't wish to keep going, that it's all too much, then tough grating shit, 'cause the Captain'll force them on regardless. You should see her; she fully intends on keeping all humanity from the void by sheer willpower alone. She'd quite happily excise the whole world's free will and autonomy to save us from ourselves.'

'Fuck the Captain's glowing biography, Sal. What is she, your girlfriend now? How about telling me what's going on?'

She hardly appeared to register his frustrated ranting. But then, nobody seemed to listen to anybody anymore. And Michael had double-discredited himself with attempted murder.

'Do you want to know what the Captain's ultimate fantasy would be?'

'I'd quite frankly rather poke my eardrums out with hot forks. Oh, wait, if *somebody* hadn't been going around turning them int' fucking knives, that is.'

'You were right on the money with that little tiff you threw over the chow. First smart thing I've heard you spit out.'

Officially it was "the chow." Nobody else went so far as Michael, calling their lost crewmates by name as the mess was ladled onto the plate. They wouldn't have kept it down.

Sal might have been equally amazed or disgusted by his resilience. 'The Captain'd have us all with our arms and legs removed, just like you said. Stuffed into padded cocoons and fed our own ground up redundancies, while goggles ply us with jolly pictures and music. And there she'd sit herself, nice and calm, in a chair facing the door. Cradling a shotgun, probably. Poised to defend our coddled peace against all comers.'

Michael shrugged painfully. What did she expect? 'It's exactly that shit they drum int' brats at school, isn't it. "Every moment must be seized, there's fuck-all after." Don't tell me you escaped having t' recite it at morning assembly, same as the rest of us. Obviously the drivel lodged in thicker skulls a tad more firmly. So look, I appreciate the social call, but is there any topic on your agenda that *doesn't* feature our illustrious leader? Want t' tell me about anyone else at all?'

Sal shuddered, although it was never cold Out here. Her body was reacting to dread. Michael was already sorry he'd asked, realising too late she'd been clinging to the idea of the Captain like a woman drowning. 'Sure, I checked on everyone. Doing the rounds in case Paul tries to get back in. Bastard's got to eat sometime.'

Michael didn't bother commenting on how unlikely Paul's reappearance would be. Neither of them wanted their fur rubbed the wrong way, they were already tense and discomforted enough.

'I was following *orders*, which the rest of you slack assholes seem to feel too good for. I checked on the Captain last.'

Oh goody. The Captain again.

'She was fast asleep in the naughty corner. I snuck in close enough to check she was breathing, and found the air was all hot around her.

'*Just* around her—I jumped back and it was gone. This horrible unclean burning, like … like you're swimming, and suddenly you're floundering through a patch were somebody's pissed raw acid in the pool. Thrashing in acid.

'I backed right the fuck off, slapping at my arms and legs. That's when I realised there were words on the smooth metal wall above her sleeping head, and they'd sure as fuck not been there before. The Captain slumbering on with a little smile, like she had things under control, and no fucking clue.'

'What did it say?'

'I didn't want to get close enough to be sure, but the writing looked scorched on. Scorched *in*, scorched into the wall. It said **"Sarah, you're bleeding."**'

Now Michael shivered. He didn't like this one bit. There'd always been this assumption about the Capsule that when serious trouble finally stopped slinking the sidelines and came at them, there would stand the Captain. An immovable shield with a snarl on her mug. Nobody fucked with Captain Orchid.

'Was she?'

'Do I look like a fucking idiot to you? I didn't hang about to check her over! I came straight here to lock myself in with you. Fuck knows what I've got sprouting in me from stepping into that corner the first time around. Flakes of crispy burned shit all over the floor and drifting in the air. I'm going to toss these clothes out the airlock.'

'But then … how do you know the Captain's guarding the door?'

Sal looked puzzled. 'What the fuck are you on about, Michael? Where else would she be?'

Both parties flinched back as what sounded like a low groan threaded beneath the door. It was an unintentional sound, the sort of grunt people tend to expel under heavy exertion. Air forced from the lungs. Was that the Captain?

It sounded for all the world as though she were laying full length out there, with her face pressed to the crack under the door. But why would she be doing that? Did she want to be let in?

'Uh, did any of the others see it? Don't you think we should call them in here too?' Bodies, lots of warm living bodies were what he craved. Camaraderie, so they could laugh about the absurd flights of morbid fantasy. How scared they'd been.

Sal fidgeted, worried and upset. 'I don't think so, they're both … uh, *busy*. Beth was right fucking serious about not picking up the hair that sprayed out of that helmet. *Paul's* hair. She' gone and cut all her own hair off and hidden it in the walls. When I poked my head in she was clipping John's hair, too, without waking him. Even kneeling on his chest. I tell you, that guy's one bastard of a heavy sleeper. He didn't so much as twitch, just snored away like a walrus.

'I didn't make a squeak in the dark, but Beth knew I was there right away. Slippery bitch. Her head flipped up and she grinned right at me like she was so pleased. Put a playful finger to her lips. *Shh.* You know, John's going to be royally pissed when he wakes up; he loved that fringe. Gave him something to hide behind while he was thinking.'

She hesitated.

*Please don't tell me*, Michael pleaded silently. *Swallow it down. I don't need t' hear any more of this shit.*

'It was hard to be sure without proper light. Fuck, it's impossible to see anything clearly in here. But Beth was crouching over John like a goblin, the scissors going *snip snip*. And she didn't have any eyes.'

*Oh fuck no.* 'What?'

'I mean, she didn't have any fucking eyes! Beth's sockets looked like they were stuffed with fucking hair! It didn't look like her own, either.

'Nobody on board has long red-blond hair like that, fuck knows where she got it from. All the little strands poking out trembled as she smiled at me, and glints ran to their ends like fire. There was hair between her teeth, too, great clots of it. Like she'd been chewing the stuff outta a clogged drain. Michael, I'm sure this sounds monumentally redundant, but something horrible is happening to everybody.'

'You don't say. What's going on with you, then? You seem fine.'

One hand drifted unconsciously to her chest as though it pained her, but Sal stared down her nose at him with icy distain. 'That is absolutely none of your fucking business. What is it about all you fuckwits, you think you can just prod someone and see their life story tumble out. When you're all too busy tooting away on your own sad horns to hear it, anyhow. No single thing worth listening to has ever been waved around like a flag.' Her eyes narrowed distrustfully. 'More to the point, what I don't understand is why nothing's happened to you yet. The worst you've faced is being locked in a big cosy storage cube.'

Only a year or so back, Michael's confident bluster would've been, "Because I'm better, that's why". But he knew with a surge of warm certainty he spoke the truth when what came from his mouth was, 'I'm being looked out for. Protected.'

'Protected? Really?' Nobody had told Sal sarcasm was the lowest form of humour. 'Care to share your little secret?'

Michael Formir was never one for keeping things to himself. 'I'm *meant* t' go home, is all. I don't know how, but I'm meant t' be with my girl. Seriously. It's like it can't possibly happen any other way, because that's what *she* decided.' He linked his hands to hide their trembling. 'She's reaching out t' me. All the way Out here. Her hand is over me, no matter what I do.'

'That sounds like straight to DVD bullshit, you know, but you're clearly eating it up. We gotta be talking about a real peach of a lady, here.' It would have to be a special kind of woman to put up with this muppet.

Now the tremor in his hands was so pronounced Sal couldn't miss it, except out of politeness. 'You don't know the half of it. You wouldn't ever want t' cross her.'

'Well seeing as your lah di dah doesn't know me from squat, and I can hardly phone down and ask her to extend the favour, then I figure the best place for me must be to hole up in here with you. Where it's *safe*.'

'I can't see that working out so good for either of us, Sal. She's never been keen on me hanging around other women.'

'Can't imagine why. And it doesn't fucking matter any, because I'm staying right here. The bitch can deal with it.'

'I'm *serious*; I'm warning you she …'

Another low moan from without interrupted their anxious banter. Even as Michael boggled, too nauseated and fascinated to move, an ooze of flesh began to force its way under the door and into the room. There wasn't clearance for any human appendage to squeeze passage, not even a child's fingernail. Nonetheless here it came.

Flesh, bulging and bone-white. Striated from the exertion, with deep purpled stretchmarks that slashed across it like lightening bolts. In it came.

That was when the screaming and pounding began at the door. Fists battering the panel, without regard to harm. It sounded like Beth and John, pleading in high hysterical tones to be let in. At least until the voices spiralled up into squeals, squeals like swine being tortured, like swine being forced beneath the door. An animal trapped in an escalator might sound like that as it was sucked under.

Long past running, Sal and Michael frantically dragged themselves away across the room until the far wall halted them, which wasn't any-fucking-where near far away enough.

Sal reached across and grabbed Michael's arm, gasping as the none too solid door began to shudder in its frame. Her fingers dug into bone. Their crewmates were frenzied out there. Lock or no lock they were taking the place apart, and their voices rose together in a high mad wailing. A tide of pale blubbery flesh, divorced of any humanity, advanced along the floor.

'You know, if there's anything your sweetheart intends to do!' Sal shouted, shaking him like a rat. 'I'd say now's the fucking time! Otherwise the very last thing I'm doing is taking you with me, Formir!'

The whole room shuddered, flesh slopping from left to right across the floor. And then exploded as the Capsule's noble remnants that'd survived this far finally broke apart under some catastrophic impact. Spilling a spray of tiny diamonds from its ruptured guts, spinning and glittering in the void.

Rather than being flung clear, the metalwork clenched around Michael like a jealous fist. Sal was smashed brutally into the floor plates as the ceiling descended, burst like a balloon, and then she was just gone. Only her fingers remained. No longer connected to any hand, but clamped so tight onto the promised safety of Michael's arm that they could not let go.

'What do you mean, there was an impact?' I shook Michael gently. 'There's nothing Out there!'

Michael grinned and I recoiled, seeing that a number of his perfect white teeth had dropped out in the telling. Irrationally I cast about as though they lurked somewhere in the gloom, waiting to bite me, to burrow in.

The places they had sat in his gumline were now deep dark holes, that gaped wetly and seemed to tunnel right up into his sinuses. And the stench, the *stench* that gusted out. No longer apples, but entirely slime and rot.

'Are you still too thick t' get it? *We hit the Shell.* We'd finally, finally come home.'

I crouched to lift him up. 'In the chair with you, Michael. Coming home was merely the start. It's time to join Angela.'

Stupid, I ought to have figured there'd be no slinking about the master's house. Threshold was too loyal a lady. Dr Cormac managed to intercept us in the long hall, looking like every miserable hangover since the dawn of viticulture. He was doing well to be on his feet at all, and my heart went out to his rumpled disarray, in all the ways I'd failed up until now.

'Ms Hanberry.' He winced. The lights were stabbing directly into his brain. I expected to see him stagger but Dr Cormac's spine was infused by his rigid will, a sight better than steel by far. Just look at how calmly divorced from embarrassment he was. While I stood scarlet-cheeked and could scarcely look him in the face. 'I'm quite confident that what the *fuck* you think you're up to is about to become evident, any second now.'

Seated stiffly in the chair in front of me, Michael's lumpy head craned from side to side like he grooved to hidden music. Really, he was straining to catch our drift. Before taking him from his room I'd needed to double up my stockings as a blindfold against the hall's light, regretting instantly how ludicrous he looked with them wrapped around his head. I comforted myself that the many indignities inflicted on Michael Formir were almost done.

Also, it was a great day for make-do.

I stared down at my shoes, but my answer was impressively resolute. Almost as though I felt it. 'There's going to be another Accident is all. Only this is one the world will never hear of.

More luck to them.'

It was no trick of the light; Cormac's bloodshot eyes grew saddened. All the pricey couture and high hopes he'd lavished trying to polish me up to his level. And surprise, surprise, I'd let him down after all.

'You're set to savour your long-awaited revenge, then?'

I shook my head urgently, daring to glance up. 'I know it looks that way, like I'd always imagined, but it's the exact opposite. I think … I think this way I'm actually helping him. It's his only way out.'

'We could still beat them, your Screws. We might unearth fresh evidence, something tying them to the Accident …'

'But the question is moot!' I pointed down through the floor, to Earth. 'Nobody's running around down there asking if it was sabotage. Humanity will never venture Outside the Shell again; wherever that drive sprang from, it's *gone*. For better or worse, this is all we're going to be. The entirety of our future will now unroll right where we were born.'

The despair on Cormac's haggard features verified it, although he did well to whip up a rallying serve of indignation. 'And what of those responsible for the Accident? Should they get to stroll away from all they've done? What end could possibly justify these means?'

'Well they got what they wanted, whether it was by Accident, Disaster, or whatever. *They've won*, Dr Cormac. And I'm sorry but it's just no good struggling to undo the past. The past and its mistakes are dead. Unreachable. *This* is our world now, and we have to manage as best we can.'

'And thus, you throw in the towel.' Wistfully, like I'd ever been ra-ra for the cause in the first place. 'Ms Hanberry, don't you ever miss the way things were?'

How could I not? But I answered honestly, rather than kindly. 'It'd be like missing being a child, wouldn't it. I'm all grown up now; enough to recognise the simple truths. I can only do what I think's best.'

I sighed, and finally met his disquieting eyes head-on. Their inflamed nature only emphasised the green shadows, making them glow in his sallow face. 'My life is small and ordinary for a reason.'

For a moment it looked like he would shove me aside, regardless. Take custody of the chair himself. At which point I could genuinely claim I'd tried, and wash my hands of the whole mess. But the good doctor stepped back. He was genuinely staggering now; what propped him didn't seem to want to serve duty much longer. He had to lean heavily on a wall. At the same time the lights began flickering again, as though Threshold were restive beneath her master's touch.

Michael couldn't *see* Dr Cormac humbly give way before us, of course. But his hearing had remained impeccable even as the rest of his sensorium collapsed in, feeding him nonsense and fears. 'Well, isn't this the shock. A bit of bloody altruism from the big man himself, Ash Cormac.'

Cormac's thin lips whitened and unconsciously one hand went to his rumpled collar, where the bruises Michael had bestowed once bloomed. Ancient history now, and the Outerman hardly any physical antagonist anymore. But sullen memory refused to lie quiet.

He also clearly didn't fancy Michael's casual familiarity. In fact so far as I could tell Cormac didn't like anything, really. Oh, except wine. Everybody treasures at least one thing close to their heart. 'I'd hardly lift a digit for *your* benefit, and I ought to have known better than to anticipate the least whiff of gratitude. I do this for her.'

I shrank under the pointing finger, but Michael didn't need such guilty cues to seize on. His mind licked along the gutter, and expected no better from anyone else. 'Oho! *Now* the sick truth comes out! Been putting the great white noodle t' the dowdy sister, have ya Ash? It must just kill you that I got the hot one.'

We were certainly trending to extremes. Cormac had hit as disgusted, and me as humiliated as we could get. One more push and we'd fly apart.

'Wait, wait!' Michael flapped his bowed arms as I tried to hurry him past. Such was his determination that if I hadn't stopped he'd have toppled from the chair, and who knew what a fall like that might do? I pictured him shattered across the floor like a china cup. And it wasn't a great stretch of imagination to see Cormac's backhand putting him there.

Shadows flared and swooped around us, crawled up the walls. Far from merely flickering, the light above us was now jittering in a frenzy. I dearly wanted out from under it, but this was a clash of the big dicks' club. I seemed to be the only one afraid that standing here was like crouching in the bullseye of a target.

Squinting against the flare, I could see all the other lights down the long hall behaving themselves nicely. Pretending at normality. Oh, all except for that dark puddle way down where I'd stood previously—that'd never come back. Discreetly hiding where the carpet was eaten away to bare-bones floor.

Michael hissed up at Dr Cormac, pawing at him. The Outerman's voice was giving out like so much else. 'Lean down here, you spindly git. You want your shitting answers, don't you?'

Cormac's crimson basset hound eyes met mine and I shook my head frantically. *Don't!* There was no way this could be a good idea. That seemed to decide the doctor, and who could blame him? It wasn't like my exulted opinion had carried the day up to this point.

Cormac condescended to lean down to Michael's seated position, although still wreathed in scorn. And the moment he did so, the frenetic light above us blinked out entirely.

In the dark, blindfolded, Michael was whispering harshly in Dr Cormac's ear.

And I quivered right beside them in lily-livered fear, having quailed this way when abandoned by the light before, but only now recognising the source. What I felt was the rise of Michael's warped efficacy. He became, in a sense, *powerful* in the dark. Even as it burned the brittle remainder of his life away. The Outerman stoked the last rag-ends of himself now to pass some dreadful knowledge to Cormac. Something from Outside. It'd be nothing that would do the doctor any good.

The gifts lurking within Michael, freed by the darkness, weren't meant for our mundane world. Our everyday egos, trudging away on our treadmills. I hoped very much that whatever granted Cormac his immunity from the Screws would hold out. The moment they suspected what Michael's whisper was seeding, they'd go slicing through his brain. And no measure of influence would save Ashley Cormac.

I managed to catch none of it, which was exactly the portion I longed for. In fact, my own fraught panting stopped up my ears with a roar, exposing my panic to all around me. As his face bent close beside me in the shadows, I was forming the sudden impression that Cormac had no face. Just a featureless, listening blank of skin like an eardrum, Michael's hiss impacting it. Something I only glimpsed for a moment, which was fortunate in preventing my scream.

Then Cormac staggered back, out of our sinister little pool of darkness, back into the glaring light. His eyes were huge. Dark, injured holes in his face—yes, he had a face. I was obviously wound too tightly.

All the man's sneering self-assurance had been blown away. Curiously, with that cleared off it was a face I could have genuinely liked. Intelligent. Sensitive.

'What did you say?' I whispered to Michael. Despite not wanting a bar of it, my rebellious fat gob charged ahead.

Michael chuckled thinly, and didn't bother to whisper. 'Something precious. Everything he wanted. Every bit as he fucking deserved.'

'What?' Didn't anybody speak "normal" around here?

Although huffing from his exertion, Michael managed to look both guilty and pleased. 'I went and placed Outside in Ash's dear old noggin. Now he can carry a taste of his precious program with him always. *That's* something t' drink up t', all right!'

Without another word to either of us, Cormac turned and staggered off down the long hall. He was having a hard time of it; ricocheting off one wall, then the other, and kept one hand clamped to his skull as though it pained him. As if he could feel it cracking wide open. Only an optimist could hope it had to do with his hangover.

I wanted to go after him. I had terrible visions of what an alcoholic might do, determined to drown himself and what he now harboured. But we were running out of time. *Jake* wouldn't be standing about like this, waffling. He had drive, influence. Me, I'd only a single office chair to my name. I needed to get things rolling.

'You could've left him alone,' I murmured resentfully. 'He was going to let us go.'

The theatre door banged open, rudely disrupting the stillness. We rattled and bumped our way inside in a gentle rain of dust, where the Capsule's venerable remains were vanishing beneath a grey shroud. It was like Threshold had begun absorbing the poor relic into herself. I thought the wreck at least deserved a velvet rope. Perhaps a little plaque, declaiming the brief age of heroes over. Only it was absolute that nobody'd ever come to see it.

The chair's castors made a silky, gritty sound grinding through the dust, like we trundled over fine snow.

The theatre's rich golden dimness was forgiving enough to remove Michael's blindfold. At the sight of the Capsule he looked doubtful for the first time on our little jaunt.

'But … but I'm *in* there. Aren't I?'

What on earth could I say to that? 'It's not anything anymore, Michael. That's why it's here. Just a memory folk are trying to forget.'

'It can't possibly have been so *small*. Shit—it looks pathetic.'

Abandoning him, I crossed the theatre and went to the huge looming doors. Doors that were almost incomprehensibly big. That stretched up and up toward a theoretical ceiling too high to see. So grand. And weirdly they also seemed old, my bones called them ancient, and flinched from them. It was an antiquity only my intellect acknowledged they couldn't possibly possess. I stood before them diminished. They emphasised my smallness, but I was used to that.

Like a tired, overwhelmed child I set my forehead against their panels and listened with all my might.

But of course, nothing called back. What had I been expecting?

I turned back to Michael. Only to find he'd wriggled down from the chair and dragged himself all the way over to the Capsule, leaving a slug-like trail in the dust. Like puzzle pieces that need to be twisted and snapped together, he was in the process of folding himself back into that tiny, familiar space.

A spasm of fear touched my heart. 'Michael! Not that way! You have to come here, over here. Angela's waiting for you.'

He froze, staring back at me. A clam half out of its shell.

'Honest. She's just past these doors. All you have to do is open them and step out.' Or wheel out. Or drag yourself. Whatever.

I puzzled a bit at how he'd manage the doors with his broken hands, then wrote it off as a foolish concern. Michael Formir had already done the impossible. He'd traversed Outside, and come all the way back for my sister.

If he had to hammer his way through the barrier on bleeding stumps, he would. Besides, for a portal that big there had to be a sodding button somewhere.

Something I was hardly about to bestir myself finding out. This was it. My part done. I'd delivered Michael, and hopefully by the time those doors opened I'd be as far away down the long hall as I could get. Back to brave the humiliation of Jake's disapproving eye, to start my own journey home.

The opposing forces of Michael's mind: that was, the splintered mess that'd so grotesquely immortalised one woman, sending Angela's memory skidding free of the ultimate finality of death; versus the arguably sane fellow he'd been before my sister burst onto the scene, seemed to grind together in their awful polarisation. So horribly that he cradled his malformed head between his forearms with a whimper of pain.

Perfect, invincible Michael had been intolerable, demanding a good slap. But *vulnerable* Michael was worse, a thousand times worse, as even in suffering he retained every inclination toward showmanship. Michael Formir's broken figure would never crawl beneath the porch to expire in quiet dignity. He had to spill his guts with a pewter knife atop a mountain, to the roar of bloodthirsty crowds.

Michael slowly slithered back out of the Capsule. He approached by pulling himself along army-style, with both elbows. And he goggled fearfully, *fearfully* up at the doors behind me as I strode past. Surprisingly, he seemed hesitant.

'Catherine! Hold up a second.'

Wow, he *must* have been feeling low. In living memory, it was the first time Michael had used my name. I hadn't even been certain he knew it.

'Angela really is something, you know.'

I reluctantly halted my retreat and turned, as unwilling as ever to venture close and touch him. 'I know that, Michael.'

'If you want t' make anything of yourself one day, you ought t' try being more like her.'

I actually laughed. 'I could strain at it 'til I'm blue in the face, but I doubt I'll ever be much like Angela. Not likely to make anything of myself, either. It happens.'

'I suppose.' He seemed keen to stall my departure, rather than genuinely engaged in conversation. His nervous gaze flickering again and again to the waiting doors. 'Ash craved his own special piece of Outside, some marvellous secret. Shall I whisper you something, too? One before I go, how about it? Perhaps something from Angie.' He seemed to instinctively sense he wouldn't be traipsing home from this one. But was that his rational, or raving nutter side speaking?

Now I did pat his brittle shoulder, fighting to suppress a wince. It seemed the humane thing to do. 'That's ok. If it's from my sister, I'm pretty sure I already know.'

He mewled piteously, and closed his eyes. 'I didn't let Angie down, then?'

I could well imagine how my sister had received disappointment. Swallowing a great surge of pity, I gestured toward the grand doors as I turned away. 'I know you won't, Michael.'

I certainly didn't linger to see him off. This was no sodding train station. Besides, his pathological need for admirers was part and parcel of what ended him up here in the first place, a monster I wasn't inclined to feed.

I fled the prospect of direct exposure to Outside and slammed the theatre door behind me. It made a satisfying, solid clunk and I thought again how all doors on Threshold ought to remain shut. But in the muddied depths of the theatre it was the biggest door, the grandest, that was about to slide ponderously open on its silent oiled runners. Hopefully for the last time.

Jake was furious, of course.

For all I went back and waited meekly in the boardroom he must have encountered Cormac somewhere and sussed the lowdown because he strode in, seized my arm like a hostile takeover, and frogmarched me out. Nobody's who's been cooking up a storm loves chomping into a fait accompli sandwich. Served him sodding well right.

Genetics sure have dealt ladyfolk a bum hand, when we can be swung about by those *supposed* to be our complementing gender. Even the mildest of fellows seem to feel perfectly justified laying hands on the goods once their dander's up.

As Jake roughly bundled me along to the gondola and I took my last farewell look at Threshold's melancholy halls, I wistfully wished I'd been born with a touch more Sarah Orchid. A brash, violent woman, aiming to not only keep pace with men but annihilate them. She'd have broken Jake's grip, sent him ass over teakettle and then swaggered haughtily under her own steam.

Now here was a surprise. Charlie seated comfortably in the gondola, awaiting me, smiling his welcome. His little lapdog Jake hopped in as well, setting the carriage swinging sickeningly with his brusque, angry movement. He was sure to clap the door pointedly shut with rather more force than necessary.

With a lurch that made me scrabble at the wall and then drop into a seat, away we went. All cosy with our knees almost touching. I craned my neck to keep as much of Threshold Station in view as I could, knowing I'd never return, and wanting to commit this last sight to memory.

Too often you miss the opportunity to say goodbye. Stupidly busy, your mind somewhere else, only realising once you've left that it's final. Threshold was like a child of another age, neglected and forgotten, eagerly offering up something precious she'd found. Her marvels smeared thickly in dust and still proffered hopefully, forever, to no-one.

Wrapped up in myself, I belatedly realised Jake had his face mashed against the glass, too. Striving for his own final glimpse. With my eyes on him he turned away at last and pinned me in my seat with his glare. Intimidation was something he'd been unable to swing before, but of course I hadn't been leery of him back then. Merely dreadfully embarrassed over what I'd done to his car. Now of course, I'd give my leg for the chance to spray it around all over again.

'I still cannot believe I went back up there. Following *you.*' There was more than a hint of this having been all my fault. Grotesquely, as though Jake were trying to pretend to be just two people chatting, that nothing had clarified between us. While Charlie smiled beatifically for the moment and left him to it.

'Threshold's a terrible place. I hated her quite adequately the first time around.' He actually *brooded* for a bit, as though I ought to give a single flying fuck how he felt. 'Took forever to get her out of my dreams, you know. I guess I can only hope it won't be like that again. Not sure I could stand it.'

Idiot. *I'd* no intention of dreaming about any of this, or brooding over it. More than enough things in an ordinary life to spoil your day. I was saving all *my* imagination for warm visions of beaches I'd never see.

Besides, we weren't "buds," not by a long shot. Until I came under actual interrogation, I didn't owe Jake so much as the time of day.

We descended through cloud, and a brief squall of rain rattled the glass. Although the air vents clicked on with an officious hiss it grew noticeably colder, and the windows fogged up. I squeezed my hands between my thighs. Fancy clothes weren't made for real weather. Thankfully, I had a lot of thigh.

Jake kept on, endlessly patient like his kind. Unless I flung myself out into the wind, and it was beginning to look tempting, I wasn't escaping this conversation. You can't ever not fear the Screws. Even after they unthread your head and take the top off, I'd imagine.

'Yes, an oppressive, terrible place. I'm not at all surprised to find it's somewhere "accidents" happen.'

I glared, finally pricked into responding. 'Accidents happen *everywhere*. And they'll continue to do so, I'd imagine, at least until the day we turn out perfect. And that's a sodding long way off for most!'

That really seemed to tickle the mutton out of Charlie. 'Humans don't have to be *perfect*,' he chuckled. 'Not by a long shot. They don't even have to be better, Catherine. They just need to be themselves.'

Perhaps things would go smoother if I smiled back, but I'd gladly cut off my own face to spare Jake the satisfaction. I was brutally exhausted, and already plummeting into the scratchy irritation of caffeine withdrawal. The residue of my emotions were little better than a thin paste scraped around the sides.

We sat a long time in silence, and the only thing I could feel for sure were the sluggish depths of my former existence, reaching up to claim me. My face must have been dragging on the floor.

As the gondola bumped back down to the ground, Charlie finally burst out with, 'Good gracious, nobody's *angry* with you, Catherine. Well, Jake here's rather peeved you set his plans awry, but the outcome's just as efficacious and you performed precisely as I'd hoped. You were entirely yourself, and shouldn't have to be anything more.'

I stared out of the moisture-streaked window at the parking lot, where chill wind hissed across the tarmac. Their car, the very same car, stood waiting. Oh, I hope they hosed it out!

Charlie leaned forward. 'I would be wishing you all the best, but I'm proud to say you're quite the level-headed woman. Hardly need luck from the likes of me. Take care, Catherine, for we'll cast an eye on you now and again. Now, where is that umbrella? From the looks of things out there, we'll need it to have you into the car safely.'

Jake handed me my battered handbag—now where had that been? It looked so sadly shabby against the fabric of my clothes, even with the blouse carelessly inside-out, that I felt sorry for it. That handbag had served me faithfully. The two Screws bundled me out of the gondola, and into their shiny silver abduction express.

My return to the front stoop of my building went as unremarked as my departure had been. I refused to dignify Jake with a final glance as the car pulled away, although Charlie insisted on shaking my hand. I took small satisfaction in slamming the front door behind me. Even though by then they'd already driven off.

My mailbox was overflowing. Bills and advertising junk had been crammed in with a determined hand, until they formed a compacted mass I was too tired to prise apart with my nails. Finally I abandoned it. Would all my life be like this?

My key worked, so at least it appeared I hadn't been evicted yet. Perhaps somebody had recounted my sordid whisking away to the landlord, and they'd elected a judicious period of wait-and-see as the lesser peril. Anything beat becoming involved.

When I pushed open the door to my apartment I expected a flood of memories. After all, this had been Angela's home too, which was why I'd never wanted to leave. Instead I was assaulted by a terrible stench, so intense it was like being physically shoved.

I reeled helplessly, thinking something must have gone seriously wrong, trying to remember what I'd left sitting in the garbage. Having the misfortune of being plugged directly into my nostrils, my numbed lobes finally caught up.

Ricardo.

Angela's fucking cat had been my responsibility. I was supposed to look after him. Look after a sodding cat, I mean, how difficult was that, really?

It would've taken so little for me to mention it, to ask somebody to pop in, but I hadn't spared a single thought. Too selfishly caught up in what I was doing to care.

Ricardo hadn't been a *total* idiot: he'd spread the contents of the bin far and wide, wolfing every scrap that seemed remotely edible. Some of which would have made him sick, no doubt. The mess was like his final "fuck you." But he'd no thumbs to turn a faucet. Collapsed in the hallway at last, where he lay panting and staring at the door. Probably calling out piteously while the neighbours stopped their ears.

Michael. Ricardo. With nobody left to hate, now how was I supposed to feel?

An unfamiliar sensation crackled like cellophane in my chest. No—not unfamiliar, merely absent a long time. Something I'd not felt since I was a small child. A hot lump rolled up my throat in waves, but for once it had nothing to do with chucking my guts.

Suddenly I was on my knees beside the pathetic clot of fur that'd sunk into the thin carpet. Weeping for Ricardo's lonely end, and my own role as the cause of it. Weeping with painful anguish, like bringing up bile. I covered my face at the uncomprehending desperation the poor stupid beast must have felt. Wondering why I wasn't taking care of him anymore, servicing his demands, when I'd always been there.

I cried so hard because the truth was, I'd never been a good person. Never cared about anyone more than myself. Not a sodding thing.

All the lifelong tricks I'd used to mask the truth and get through the day had been ground wafer thin by the assault of Threshold, Michael, Dr Cormac, all of it. Bang, bang, bang, one after the other, without relief. Now the frail remains were swept away by the violence of tears. All the weeping owed by my adult life, come home to roost.

Sunk prostrate into the carpet beside Ricardo's remains I was turning myself inside-out with anguish.

I was no more lovely than him: all the rottenness on the outside of me now, exposed shrieking and bleeding to the air. Held up for the world. My voice rasped away in my chest to hoarse, airless barks and still it felt like I'd never, ever be able to stop.

# OUTERMEN

## TEN

### ONE FOND MEMORY

THE MYSTERY PARCEL was just weighty enough to feel valuable. And so the postman kindly lugged it upstairs and knocked on my door, rather than leaving it perched atop the mailboxes to get nicked.

I was pretty sure the blue-rinse duchess down the hall made nibbling and prying into other people's affairs her civic duty. Like we couldn't all see the mounds of ripped open envelopes that went out with her trash.

Opening the door rather awkwardly, I tried to offer a tip but the postie smiled and waved me off. All part of the job, innit? He collected my signature, tipped his hat, a gesture I'd only seen in spaghetti westerns before, and trundled off bashfully. Just part of me job, innit. I'd say his good deed for the day was done, but he struck me as a fellow who dispensed them hand over fist.

I carried my new parcel through to the kitchen. Even now, I still checked every few steps for Ricardo lying in wait to send me sprawling. Even though the days of black-hearted cat espionage were long gone, and this an entirely new apartment … well, new to me, anyway. My new digs were so piddly I had trouble trying to stuff my *own* memories in between the chipped walls, let alone getting residual feline creeping in too.

It felt funny, thinking how not so long ago the loss of a bond I couldn't afford, coupled with hunting somewhere new to live and a fresh job to boot, would've seemed insurmountable. Silly fatguts. I'd really had no idea, had I?

My world wasn't any less dangerous. But now I'd weathered having to reconstruct my shattered coping strategies, brick by brick from the ground up. And this time around I could pick and choose to my heart's content from my sister's crazy and rigid rules, rather than taking them all on board. Those that'd kept me alive, and those that kept me constrained. I boldly discarded anything I didn't need, although still muttering *sorry Angela* during those early days. And I wrote whole new prescriptives to fill the gaps.

The reality of the parcel turned out a sight smaller than it'd first appeared. The contents looked bulkier because they were wrapped neatly, first in rough brown paper like what butchers use.

Then in a layer of old newsprint; *Disaster Strikes the Capsule!* I read as I set it aside. More crinkly brown paper, then stretchy clingfilm like a packed lunch, and a final skin of the yellowed ancient news for good measure; *Outermen Lost!*

I began to suspect an elaborate prank, although I couldn't imagine who'd sent it. I'd continue unwrapping, layer by layer, until surprise! The big fat nothing in the middle. Witty and annoying, like some kind of metaphor. The process put me in mind of Threshold. Her long dusty halls, settling slowly into final abandonment. Only, standing in my poky kitchenette with the quiet afternoon glow streaming in, Threshold Station seemed a very long way away.

It was only once I breached the clingfilm that I got my true inkling of what the little gift might be. The change in the room's air tipped me off, becoming indefinably warmer and richer than it was. The apartment's simple colours radiated mysteriously, more vibrant with promise. Suddenly I was tearing rabidly at the parcel's vestments, until I finally held the little paper sack of contraband in my incredulous hand.

My mind got to racing. I'd have to devise some brewing apparatus, but no worries there: the eager addict's desperation will always win through. And I ought to seal the windows before the neighbours got wind. Depending on inclination they'd either be turning me in, or hammering down the door.

It was quite the risky little indulgence I held. Apparently, in somebody's eyes I'd earned it. For now, I just closed my eyes, and let the luxurious aroma of ground coffee bloom blissfully through my scuffed but bright little apartment.

## Also by BP Gregory

## Novels

Flora & Jim
The Town
Something for Everything (Automatons book two)
Automatons (Automatons book one)
Outermen

## Novella

Only Skin

## Short Story Collections

Vu Ja De – Collected Short Stories Volume Three
Orotund – Collected Short Stories Volume Two
Cacophony – Collected Short Stories Volume One

KATE KNOWS
WHAT SHE
SAW

The
T**O**WN

BP GREGORY

**KATE KNOWS WHAT SHE SAW**: a burned out ruin. But the evidence is gone, and nobody else believes the town was ever there.

She knows the town exists. Determined to prove it at any cost, in poking around the outback Kate risks exposing herself and her friends to the slew of horrible urban legends, reticent locals, and too many people who vanished over the years with nowhere to go.

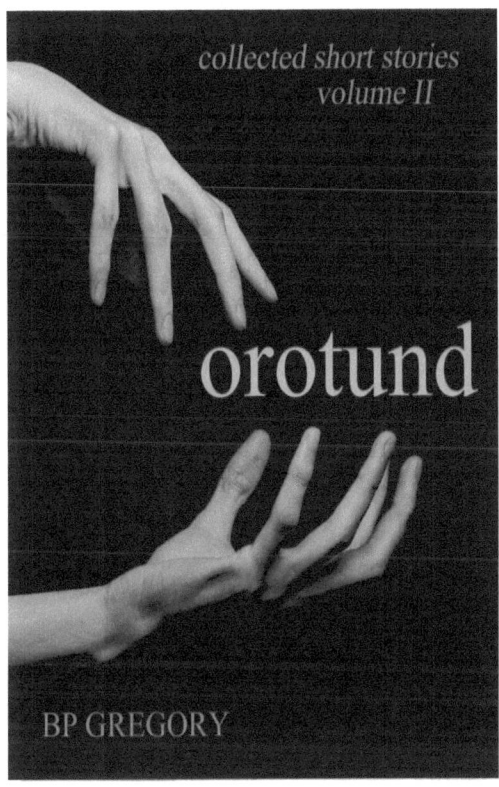

**A PAROLED MONSTER**, a prostitute and a policeman all see a little girl lost, but this isn't the start of a joke. An isolated, frail old man trapped in his apartment; what possible threat could he pose to the sociopaths next door?

Take time for a stroll down humanity's eerie back alleys and enjoy BP Gregory's newest short science fiction, urban fantasy and horror stories neatly packaged together in Orotund: Collected Short Stories Volume Two.

Author and avid reader BP Gregory brings monsters, machines and roaming cities, insanity, betrayal and lust! With such tales you shouldn't always feel comfortable or safe.

For sneak peeks, more stories, reviews and recommendations as she ploughs through her to-read pile visit bpgregory.com.